Copyright © 2023 by Luca Evola
All rights reserved. Except as permitted under the U.S. Copyright Act of 1976, no part of this publication may be reproduced, distributed, or trans- mitted in any form or by any means, or stored in a database or retrieval system, without the prior written permission from the author.

This story is inspired by the life and imagination of author Luca Evola. To protect the identities of actual people, all names and titles bearing relationship to the author have been altered. Characters and entities may be depicted compositely.

Evola, Luca, 1988–
Arabala : a novel / by Luca Evola. – 1st ed.

Summary: A daring Middle Eastern girl explores a rebellious love with a beautiful American boy in British Columbia, their illicit relationship ending in a tragic accident that is eerily foretold.

ISBN 979-8-218-21294-0

Vipera Aspis Sculpture by Jared Balibrea
(7thGolem)
Interior design by Luca Evola
Cover design by Luca Evola

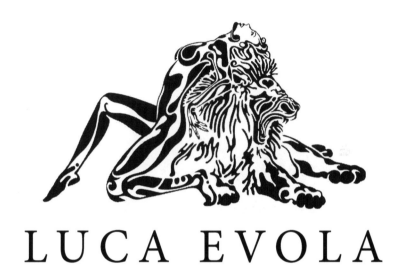

CONTENTS

1 UNEXPECTED
2 DESERT FLOWER
3 UNDYING THIRST
4 LUSCIOUS ALLURE
5 DARK PRINCESS
6 TENDER LOVE
7 BODY AND COLOR
8 LATE OCTOBER
9 A CRY FOR HOME
10 SUSPICION
11 HASSAN
12 THE DRIFT
13 INTIMIDATION
14 THE DREAD
15 BREAKUP CALL

16	HOPE FOR A LAST
17	A LONG KISS GOODBYE
18	BLACK BIRD
19	MORIBUND
20	THE WANDERER
21	THE MISSING RING
22	CHRISTMAS DAY
23	THE MORNING
24	RUN AWAY WITH ME
25	BLACK LOVE
26	INTO THE TREES
27	THE SUN WHO KISSED THE MOON

ARABATA

UNEXPECTED

CHAPTER ONE

Driving through the wet mountains it feels as beautiful as it is haunting. The mist and clouds catching at the tops of the trees casts a magical effect on the heart and eyes as thousand-year-old cedars tower above the road. Moss and lichens saturate the forest floor beneath the droopy limbed hemlocks. Through a mountainous Arcadia where glaucous clouds hide the tops of enormous Douglas firs. Pretty familiar with much of the North American West from my past camping trips I still have never lived this far away from home. But still I am pleased to be leaving as I head north to go and live with my uncle in Vancouver's Historic Shaughnessy, British Columbia.

Mostly heritage homes the coastal boundary was named after Thomas Shaughnessy who was the former president of the Canadian Pacific Railway. Notoriously posh the Shaughnessy neighborhood offers a taste of historic elegance with lush garden views and immense grounds. With almost an old-growth forest feel every street directs the eyes with wide verdant boulevards and winding crescents. And half of the old world estates were built before or during World War II, and all just a stone throw away from everything that is worth exploring. Sidewalks are lined with thulian pink redbud trees and towering maples. No doubt the most beautiful place that you can land after crossing the peace arch at the boarder.

Having secured my study permit with some impressive strings pulled thanks to my uncle Louis my move to Canada has been something that I have been trusting to happen for months. Still mostly unhappy that I am abandoning my mom to fend for herself, I am facing the hard truth that I cannot stay in Seattle. Leaving home I think about how difficult it would be for me to find a place if my uncle had not urged me to take the guesthouse behind his property. This change happening for both our best interests since he also pays me to take care of his online store. Some know-hows that I took advantage of back in high school just so that I could buy myself more trail running gear. And all of it having led to this moment that is now allowing me to sever ties with my drunken and unstable stepdad.

With it not being too long a drive and taking in all of the change that is happening I in no time at all find myself at the edge of Shaughnessy along Forty-first Avenue.

My uncle Louis's home stands more modest compared to the other homes in the neighborhood. His stone grey shutters framing the pearl-tumbled brick. The streets lined with peeling river birch and nuttall oaks that stand in front of the classic architecture. Vancouver being one of the few cities that offers a La Grande Jatte appeal with brick terracotta and sinopia streets winding through the romantic parks that blanket the floor of a towering infrastructure. Downtown is only thirteen minutes. And the mountains are only forty-five minutes from the house.

"Hey Lucius!" Louis calls my name, walking up to my car with his hoodie on over his thick head of hair. Seeing my uncle Louis smile in anticipation of my arrival makes me feel welcome. And then I recall him trying to get me to move to Shaughnessy ever since I began working with him now more than a year ago.

Before I can even climb out of the car Louis moseys over with his black curly ponytail and his bushy beard as dark as a crow's nest. His South Beach tan a stark contrast to my more pale Cascadian complexion. His deep peace-and-love voice rendering him to be only a mellow softhearted man.

"Hey," I reply to Louis, feeling my legs stretch as I reach up to hug my lonely uncle.

"You made it here safe. I've got dinner on the table—get in here," he tells me, smiling and giving me a single pat on the back.

"Are you happy to be moved out of your mom's house?" Louis then asks, not acknowledging my stepdad, Damien.

"I am. I'm just tired from the drive," I remind him.

Everything then looks the same as I enter through the front door. Same as the time that my mom brought me to stay for the summer a few years ago.

CHAPTER ONE

The forged iron chandelier hanging in the foyer. The beautifully arched windows, coffered ceilings, and the exposed brick all giving his home its unique warmth. The entry distinguished by its large oak doors that are even heavy to push shut.

"*The Alphabet Versus the Goddess* by Leonard Shlain. I ordered you a copy before you got here," he says, grabbing the book off the wooden console table just inside the door. "Verifiable right-brain dynamics that venerate the Goddess and that will awaken the sacred feminine in us all. Historically mind-blowing."

"Thank you. . . . It sounds really good," I tell Louis.

Immediately after devouring some homemade bruschetta with salmon and of course listening to Louis talk about his eCommerce site he then hands me a key to the guesthouse and gives me my space. Having come only with enough boxes to stuff the backseat and trunk of my car I then hurry and help with the dishes before getting settled.

Walking around the back of the house the dark canyon-like archways buckle under the drab molding and moth-eaten brick that leads to my new sanctuary. A warm brick holds together the entire structure with unique layers adding historic character to its concealed location. The moon light illuminates the large window panes and mosaics that line the doorway glass. Being only familiar with the bare canvas of washed apartment walls it's nice seeing the ornamental detail and features about the living space.

Standing inside the guesthouse living room that hasn't had its windows opened in years I visualize on the blank canvas against the wall my summer travel pictures from Oregon to California to Utah. My eyes study the texturally rich allure complementing the warm wooden accents that illume a faint glow. Apart from some dusting I think to myself that the place is perfect. The large windows accessing the outside light are all built into the back upper level where a smokey boho-meets-cottage bedroom sits. The plush bed linens are kept just a few feet away from a cozy book nook that looks outside. The brick walls, wood floors, and tall ceilings all creating an abundance of space. Thinking that all it needs now is just my string lights that I have boxed—and then my CD player.

Seven-forty a.m. I grab my phone to stop the alarm from going off, my hair strewn over my face and blocking the domineering light that shuttles in from the window sill. Watching the visible dust float by me under a blinding sun beam I remember that today is my first day of class with Mr. Petrov who teaches core English.

Quickly I stand up to throw on my black jogger pants and my grey t-shirt. Dragging myself out of the house with nothing but my ID and keys I remember that my small notebook bag is on the front seat, having spoken to a Mrs. Etienne just yesterday about coming in to see her for my student door key.

Placing my hands on top of the steering wheel in my black '91 luxury sedan, I twist the rearview mirror before backing out of the driveway. Gradually turning out of the neighborhood I feel like a young prince sitting in his sage leather chariot turning the block like a yacht over still water.

Just a few streets west towards a seaside campus I park behind the student services building peeling the windows away from the frame of my car for a better look. The main building built in 1925 in Collegiate Gothic style sits like a fortified castle boasting stunning views of the Burrard Inlet. Admiring the beauty of this place that is surrounded by majestic waters and mountains it then dawns on me that my two best friends are both back in Seattle.

Resting my eyes for one more minute my moment of peace is then sideswiped by a group of obnoxious punks hurtling passed my window.

Standing up out of the car feels a little overwhelming. Feeling like I didn't really want to leave Seattle. But again reminding myself how it was more like I needed to.

Squeezing passed the double doors and migrating towards the central office I in no real hurry begin my search for Mrs. Etienne. Always a little bit nervous walking inside of a new building a tight feeling in my stomach starts up. The smell of floor cleaner and the voices echoing off the walls aid the astringent torment beneath my skin. Most of the first year students are all plugged into a device that does not seem to further anymore their displayed level of intelligence. Space cadets and wood pushers fumble over their headphones and belongings as snippy "Veronicas" viciously gossip about nothing. Twisting and weaving between the other students through the main entrance hall I begin to suspect that this college is no different from the one that I just transferred from in Seattle. All except for its stunning outdoor location.

Stepping into the central office I begin to look for someone who might know how to find the admissions counselor who has my door key. Waiting behind a messy line of people to ask the secretary at the desk I instead choose to slip out as quickly as I can to avoid being caught in the sneezing coughing

CHAPTER ONE

crowd.

"Excuse me," I speak up, grabbing another student's attention. "Could you please tell me where I might find Mrs. Etienne?"

"Sure," she says, pointing her finger. "It's down the hall. Make a right when you see the art on the wall and then make a left. And it will be on the very end near the back double doors."

"Thank you," I tell her, quickly continuing down the hall after noticing her tired eyes turning to look me over a second time.

Finding Mrs. Etienne's office I notice that the blinds on the windows and doors are closed. It being strange how quiet it is on this side of the building and how dark the hallway is due to the poor lighting above. "Surely someone must be inside?" I then wonder. Reaching for the doorknob after seeing that the light is on the door then squeaks as I try slowly cracking it open.

"Come in!" Someone says from inside of the office directly across from the waiting lounge. Stepping inside the lounge below a vaulted ceiling with the exposed wood above I then notice the large bookshelves with printed pamphlets for high school seniors who are thinking about their promising future.

Continuing into Mrs. Etienne's office and caught off guard, time then stands still in one swelling moment as my curiosity draws me to be ever so still in thought. The indistinct sound that she makes stops my heart leaving these eyes that hold her climbing up in desperation to remember where I am. She is the first ever to seduce me, like a warm powerful melody, and with an absolute fascination. Conservatively sitting down behind the door reading I make note of the incredible lines that veer beyond the vantage of what beauty I can absorb. As if having stumbled upon an undiscovered passage at the center of nature's secret that has led me to wonder. A woman if whose flaws were to unveil would only make her even more distinctly unique with beauty. Her ivory-colored complexion bears the brilliance of champagne balanced by a hint of ochre. Ringlets of black thread and pearl also lay gracefully alongside her charming features. Her lips look as if they speak of love often but only to herself. Her style and elegance and posture display the pure determination that she has made clear in her mind. The slight indent on the bridge of her adorable nose complements her slender face and endearing qualities. Her elegance alone surpasses any expression that I have ever before encountered. There she sits in long black dress pants with the perfect crease down the front. Her small feet showing through her black sandal-like heels that wrap around her thin ankles. Her pants waistline reaching up passed her hips secured by a leather belt and designer buckle. She wearing her grey-collared dress shirt tucked in, allowing only me to make note of those lines that press firmly and loosely against her body.

    Trying to pretend that she has not gathered my attention I attempt to turn my head without saying anything to her. Not even a smile. But in that same moment that she raises her head to look at me I can do nothing but stare right back. Seeing that she is used to the ridiculous lust of delusional roosters who can hardly love themselves—let alone know how to love a woman with absolute and unconditional favor. Watching her look up at me she questions the beauty that most men believe her to possess with an almost displeased notion of herself. Her eyes seem to almost deepen with a sorrow that only I feel impelled to acknowledge. It is her second take of me that gives her away and it is her argument of self that moves me with a determination to reveal within her all that causes me to marvel. I feel anxious to know her and anxious to explain to this beauteous creature why there is no need to question. For the first time in my life I feel the strongest desire in my heart to give this one woman the one true peace that I have only now found. Silly I know. Only in the eyes of such grace whose heart longs for those answers do I now feel relinquished to impart. Her haunting eyes seem to climb inside of my body where my soul can rest no more. It is her faint smile that lifts me up and tears me down. It is this feeling that I now consider to be that great mystery—even that mystery worth knowing and loving for as long as my body gives me breath.

    "What can I do for you, Sir?" Mrs. Etienne asks. Easing my way into Mrs. Etienne's office after passing the young woman whose attention has been drawn back towards her book I then casually sit. Gathering what I can about Mrs. Etienne and the many home comforts that clutter her desk she then is gracious enough to welcome me. From the photos I can tell that Mrs. Evelyn Etienne is married with two boys. She is a thicker woman—"healthy" some might say. Black short straight hair with plenty of undiscovered personality. And perhaps the kind of person who might display a short fuse simply to retain a good feel in her role as admissions counselor.

    "What can I do for you?" She again asks.

    All I can think about is the young woman sitting outside in the lobby behind me. Feeling as though I am wide awake in a dream I find myself still thinking about her like I just realized what love is. Still swimming in those eyes of hers and searching for a way to legitimately revisit this tiny space—uncomfortable as it may be.

CHAPTER ONE

"I spoke with you yesterday about coming by to get my student door key," I tell Mrs. Etienne, feeling a little disoriented.

"And tell me your name again?"

"Lucius Korbin. . . . I transferred from Seattle."

"Do you have your driver's license?"

"Yes ma'am," I reply, handing Mrs. Etienne my ID.

"Thank you," she says, snipping it from my hand like a duck diving for a pinch of bread.

I try letting myself like Mrs. Etienne, only I could see her latent snarl surface the moment that I stepped foot inside her door. Sitting transfixed by how fast she works her keyboard she even manages to look at me from out of the corner of her eye while she is typing. My key then pops out of the machine beside her desk.

"Here is your key," she says, handing it to me.

"Thank you," I tell her, not really sure about what to do next.

Stepping outside of the office and into the lobby where the girl is seated I see her sitting perfectly still as if she has not a care in the world. Passing by her again she looks up at me securing an attentive but cautious smile that nearly stops my heart from beating. She is glowing with the kind of beauty that only heaven could permit as if perhaps vulnerable for the way that I feel. And never would I have expected her to say anything to me—except she did.

"Hey," she says, looking up at me with a smile that hides behind her dedication to remain focused to her book. My heart sinks down into my stomach.

"Hey," I reply back.

Looking at her and reaching for the door to leave I know that nothing in this world can comparably hold my attention. Closing the door carefully from the other side I stop to try and understand what I am feeling. And I feel ridiculous. Perfectly aware that there is no such thing as love when you first meet someone. And yet her gaze alone is a reflection of the splendor that has inspired the greatest painters and poets of all time, whose visions have been engraved into the stars. Even if she had not uttered a single word. She is intelligent, loving, and creatively put together. "And when she speaks . . ."

"Surely her acknowledging me was a mistake," I tell myself.

Stepping outside the south entrance doors and taking a seat on the staircase everything that I fear the most begins to claw at my emotions. Thinking about all of the failed relationships in my family who seem to have been cursed. Even having come to believe that love is just some foolish desire or human weakness fated only to fail miserably. Swallowing to accept that only some are destined to taste how sweet and wonderful love truly is. Hoping to never see Damien when I glimpse into the mirror I still fear on the other hand that I may destroy her. Still seeing that face and those eyes that remain indissoluble in my mind. Punishing myself with whatever false hopes there are in feeling something for someone else the most cursed part of me wants to forget that I even saw her. But still it is only the tiniest discouragement battling this forceful plunge to see her again.

Sitting on the steps outside the voices of swarming students walking the East Mall becomes more faint as the swaying trees above protect me from the blazing sun. Sitting now for almost thirty minutes I still am absolutely certain of one thing. I do want to see her again.

Standing up and walking back inside the south entrance I stand a moment examining the door to Mrs. Etienne's office. Walking over to the trash bin I then toss my new key inside of it. Carefully I then poke my head back inside the door to see if she is still sitting there with her book. . . . "She doesn't look like someone who'd be in trouble her first day of class," I then think to myself.

The door then creaks. Looking up at me she then pretends not to notice.

"Can I help you?" Mrs. Etienne again asks me. I again step inside the rest of the way.

"I actually need another key if you don't mind," I speak up, glancing down at the same girl who now sits there pretending to ignore me.

"What happened to the one that I just gave you?"

"I think it got away from me when I was helping someone to pick up their papers off the floor."

"You've got some nerve boy," She lightly puffs, not wanting to believe me.

"Yes—but you are looking lovely this morning. How can I not look for an excuse to be here instead?" I reply.

Mrs. Etienne expresses little as she tries to conceal her faint smile and doesn't say anything after that. Pretending to admire the things on the wall she again hands me another key.

"Take that sweet talk of yours and go on. And don't come back here asking me for another key," she humorously warns. "Are you going to be alright finding your next class?"

"I'll try my best," I tell her.

Mrs. Etienne then intervenes, asking her assistant to escort me to my class after calling her by name. Only there was no response.

CHAPTER ONE

"Go on," Mrs. Etienne tells me.

Standing up and giving the counselor a somewhat nervous smile I then place my key in my pocket before turning around to step into the lobby. I then see the same girl who said hey to me putting her things down on her seat so that she can stand up.

"Thank you," I tell her.

She then gives a faint smile. Only she says nothing to me. I then open the door to walk with her outside.

"I'm sorry about that."

"For what?" she asks.

"I didn't mean for her to distract you from what you were doing."

"It's okay. I show all of the new students around anyways," she shyly smiles.

"I'm Lucius," I tell her, thoroughly delighted.

"Mahru," she replies, with a sort of timid amusement.

"Mahru is a lovely name." I look at her again. Her smile and charm compare to none. And though she seems pleased to walk with me it is not something that she cares to express. Like me I see that she chooses to be reserved as she observes.

Making our way down an empty hall she stops walking and looks at me. I also stop—unaware that my eyes have become so fixated on her.

"Is there something on my face?" She asks.

"Yes. . . ."

"Are you serious?" she again asks, terrified as she grabs my arm.

"Only as serious as to how remarkably breathtaking you are." She then lets go of me. She then turns to keep walking, smiling only a little. Cool and casual I take pleasure in the after-glow of her gentle grip as I follow close behind.

"So there's nothing on my face?"

"Nothing that you thought was there—no." She remains quiet. "So what does your name mean?"

She smiles. "It means the face of the moon. . . . And what about your name? What does Lucius mean?" Moving through a small crowd of students I step in front of her to open the door to go outside.

"It means the morning light I think."

"Lucius. . . . Lucian, Lucifer. . . . Like that?" She turns and smiles.

"Yes," I tell her, watching her toy with my heart in her hands.

"What's the matter? Does the cat have your tongue?" She asks, mischievously.

"Yes...."

Mahru stops smiling. An unpleasant concern now sweeps over her face. "That is the nicest thing that anyone has ever told me.... But you should be more careful."

"How come?"

"Because my brother, Malik, also goes to this school. And he wouldn't like the way you're looking at me."

"Do you mind the way that I look at you?" She looks away and smiles but hesitates to respond.

"Your class is right here," she says, trying not to make eye contact with me.

Standing in front of the building that leads to my English lecture I reach for the door. Turning to look at her she stands there anxiously uncertain. Her eyes capture me and hold on to me for only a moment.

"Thank you, Mahru.... Maybe I'll see you again."

She then smiles at me and walks away as if to say that my idea is a bad idea.

Sitting in my English class as Mr. Petrov pauses his lecture I express my heartfelt adoration by sketching Mahru's portrait onto a sheet of paper. I am not yet sure of her nationality. Only aware of her adorable accent that makes her English ring perfect in my ears. Her stride reminds me of the ocean that shuffles back and forth in a harmless élan of waltz. And her furtive vibe is completely her own, she reminding me of no one.

Drawing with pencil her beautiful features from her face down to her waist I try to act like I am still taking notes. An uncompromisingly figurative composition ensnares me with a beauty and process of making her appear lifelike. Depth merges from one side to the other in harmony with the arranged space dictated. Seeing her is that escape door to that realm that my heart does possess.

The dark auburn sitting next to me is listening to the sound of nothing as the rest of the class takes notes from the board. Occasionally she leans over to peek to see how my sketch is coming along. And she watches as if waiting to speak to me.

"I like your drawing," she whispers.

I smile only to acknowledge her.

"My name is Mandy."

"I'm Lucius," I tell her.

"Who is your drawing of?"

CHAPTER ONE

"Hey!" Mr. Petrov forewarns, glaring at Mandy.

Slouching back into her seat the sun sizzles behind the closed blinds that glow a flavescent cornsilk. The hum from the large window fan drowns out the conversation between the two professors standing in the doorway. And as an orange glow brightens up the room from a summer's sun the green from a maple tree is visible just beyond the curtains.

Finishing my drawing as my burly professor finishes conversing in the hall I then quietly stand up to excuse myself.

Quickly walking outside across East Mall back to Mrs. Etienne's office I try and hurry to catch her before she leaves.

Peeking inside the office door in search of Mahru I then see that she is not there. With the intention of giving her my drawing I was hopeful that it might be a way for us to restart our conversation. But something tells me that talking to her is going to be difficult.

Returning back to my class I slide my drawing back into my notebook that I brought with me. Trying now to focus on what is being lectured I patiently wait for my class to end.

Keeping an eye out for Mahru the entire afternoon I never saw her again. After my last class let out I in no hurry walked along East Mall to the parking lot hoping to catch her. Wondering if she lives on campus or if she drives herself home. And wondering why she told me to be more careful.

Maneuvering into the driver seat of my car I check my phone to see if Louis ever texted me anything work related. "Please upload new merchandise and change prices and descriptions." Easy-peasy.

Arriving home I receive another text in the driveway. "In town for a meeting. I'll be back before seven. —Louis."

Throwing my school bag on the kitchen counter inside the guesthouse my phone then starts to ring.

"Hey honey! How was class today? Are you all settled in?" my mother, Liliana, asks.

"Yeah I'm all settled in. Everything is good."

"Oh, I'm glad to hear. And is Louis doing okay?" she then asks, always pushing small talk like she is afraid to ask me anything real. And all to avoid me asking her about Damien and if she is happy.

"Louis is good. Everything is good. . . . School is uhh . . . it's just school.

Same here as it is there in Seattle. Except it's beautiful up here."

"Yeah, I bet. I am so proud of you honey. And I miss you already."

"I miss you too," I tell my mom, tired and wanting to relax. "I gotta get some work done though. Let me call you later," I assure my mom, trying not to seem too frustrated.

"Okay—I love you."

"I love you too. Bye," I tell her, troubled in my heart because my mom does not even try escaping from such an abysmal disease. Having grown tired of seeing her being mistreated. And home is still a somber place for me. She could never stop Damien from striking me or shoving my face to the wall. And I cannot stand to hear him verbally assault my mother. He is a certified asshole. The kind of coward who will beat on an eleven-year-old boy just to make himself feel like a man. I think about my mom whose sadness has become a slow and poisonous form of suicide. My face buckles in a useless attempt to retain my silent tears. I try to accept that my mother may never be happy. With tears down my face I tell myself that I will become the man I am my own way. More than what I would have ever become under the demented ways of that disputatious beast.

Hearing Louis pull into his garage after unpacking everything and wrapping up about an hour of work I notice that I am beginning to feel tired. With my thoughts shifting towards the girl that I met today I carefully cut some paper from the top of my dresser. Fashioning a neatly folded substrate I feel promptly inspired to write before taking a bath. Not caring how ridiculous it sounds or if it offends her, I only desperately want to express something real— my eager aim towards this stranger no matter the warning or consequence.

Folding my letter to her and leaving it on my dresser I finally decide that it is time for me to go to bed. My anxious heart calms feeling my entire body relax into the cool summer sheets. The sounds of crickets fiddle a tune as a sun-set tree breeze hums a gentle whisper outside my window. There being nothing left to fill my thoughts except for the girl that I saw today as I feel only a gentle peace.

DESERT FLOWER

CHAPTER TWO

My morning alarm sends me thrashing to turn it off the next day. Stumbling over to my half empty closet I look to find something to wear. Brushing my teeth I then put an apple in one pocket and put my written note to Mahru in the other. Quickly grabbing what else I need I then lock up and back carefully out of the driveway.

Parking my German sedan and watching all of the students on campus I can feel my heart pounding. Rejection, nervousness, my childhood feelings of inadequacy because of Damien all eating at my nerves. But I know now that there is nothing to worry about at home and that there is nothing standing in the way of me and what I want anymore. Pushing one of my long ringlets back up into my deep golden nest of curly hair I step out of my car.

Walking inside the student services building I walk straight to Mrs. Etienne's office. Looking through the small holes that dot the blinds I try to see if Mahru is inside. Noticing that she is there I look for another way in. Refusing to use the same door I decide to use the door adjacent to Mrs. Etienne's office to avoid being given any grief. Quietly slipping down a dark hall through the other door I pass two empty rooms with no lights on. Turning the corner to look into the waiting room I see Mahru sitting on the sofa. But I also see another office with its door open. Seeing the light on and hearing a stack of papers shuffling against the desk I know that someone is sitting inside facing the door. Hoping not to be seen as I walk across moving in front of the door a woman's voice asks, "Can I help you?"

I turn to see a woman in her early thirties seated at her desk in a suit dress. Her long brown hair is pulled back into a bun with a dark package of all attitude that appears bewitching against her underlying calm. I look at the plaque on the wall which reads "Mrs. Johnson". Looking to my right I then see Mahru notice me in the small hall space across from where she is seated.

Casually entering Mrs. Johnson's office I make myself comfortable in her guest chair. "I believe you can," I reply, to Mrs. Johnson, thinking it better to be honest about why I am here. Placing my letter to Mahru on top of her desk I begin to explain.

"The young lady sitting down right outside this office is someone who I am quite fond of, Mrs. Johnson. And I intend to give this to her. Perhaps you can read it and tell me what you think?"

Mrs. Johnson displays a curious smile before picking up and reading very carefully my letter.

"Do you think she'll like it?"

"I think she'll love it," she kindly acknowledges, her seeming almost taken aback with admiration. "Go ahead and give it to her," she smiles, handing my letter back to me.

"Thank you, Mrs. Johnson," I complement. Catching the counselor's smile before leaving her office I quietly wave goodbye to her.

Stepping passed Mrs. Etienne's office I quietly sit down beside Mahru. Her modest smile reveals her amusement from watching me try to avoid the admissions counselor.

"Hello again," I tell her, watching her squirm slightly in her seat with a sort of discomfort.

"Hey," she replies. "What are you doing here?"

"I want to give you this," I tell Mahru, handing her my letter like a little boy coming to the wishing well. "I wrote it last night."

She takes the letter from me with a concerning look on her face as to what it might contain. I patiently watch her take her time reading it. And I watch her heart sink down into her chest as all sorts of questions surface behind her blush.

Her eyes heal as does her smile and she knows not. And she only knows the voice in her head, not the voice in her heart. Only there is more magic, more passion, zest, and feeling, hidden down deep within her that has yet to breathe out of that mysterious place that is her heart—seemingly an

CHAPTER TWO

abyss of unheard of power treasured and held tightly by the darkest parts of her. Only if a kiss filled with fire could spark light into that dark world. Only if something marvelous were kind enough to wake her from her sleep so that she may share her magic, her kiss, and her love. A love that has never burned like the searing sun over fevered white sand. A love that has never burned like the deep fiery veins that flow underneath the earth. A kiss that has never felt so warm. Magic that bestows an otherwise incomprehensible art to every atom and form of energy that observes from every corner of the cosmos. Observing with delight to create something that much more beautiful as if it were somehow possible to mirror or mimic a love that seems only fitting for gods.

"Did you write this?"

"For you, yeah."

She tries to cover her faint smile and admiration.

". . . I'm speechless. No one has ever written me like this before." She glances at me as if she has become a little confused and a little more in love. Almost pressing her fingertips against her temples as if troubled she then looks at me with astonishment.

"You make me feel incredibly special," she says, her eyes climbing up to her forehead as if to also infer some sort of dispassion.

"I would never want to make you feel anything different," I assure her. ". . . Let me come back and see you again?"

"Okay," she smiles, she seeming to ask herself if it really is okay.

Pressed for time I leave as quickly as I came, disappearing into the darkened hall across from the office lounge.

Quietly entering my class, I somehow avoid Mr. Petrov's scoff about being late. Of course this only works when he is talking and facing the dry erase board.

Sitting and thinking about her I hear him going on and on about Shakespeare's Antony and Cleopatra. Bored with Shakespeare's archaic writing style I still can't deny how everyone's death manages to hold my attention. And what better way to die than for love? And what better way to tell a story of love's passion and rage? "What a strange way to die," I then think to myself.

Seeing her eyes the way they watch me in my mind I can't help but notice there is something different about her. She is the name to the face that never escapes my thoughts. And everyday I am more curious to know her. Her delightful smile and charm gives life to everything in bloom . . . to everything that burns a vibrant color . . . all life carrying a wish to be noticed by her eyes that have the power to uplift, to grant transcendence into that higher realm and bestow love that remains eternal in the wheel of existence. Her eyes are magic. And not because she wants them to be. But because they are as they are . . . always. And her eyes reflect her kind soul, her strengths, her love. And she is by design immortal, eternal, life-giving, and forever. Doomed to a material existence on a throne of beauty she searches to find her meaning to existence . . . the sacred fuel that keeps her fire alive in this life before she carries on to the next. Always carrying on—dancing through what we call time—taking with her that star-like glow that mirrors the heavens above. A reminder of that which was from the very beginning . . . and all seen inside of her eyes. A lasting eternity. Those shining jewels that give compliment to every surrounding feature. Her voice as smooth and as gentle as the wind. Her thoughts as easy as the passing clouds that mesmerize the heart and mind. Her warmth—a summer's evening. Delight in her is to hope that she may cast her eyes upon your soul where for every pain there is a cure.

"Lucius! . . . Are you following along?" Mr. Patrov asks.

"I am . . . I was just momentarily distracted by the similarities between Antony and Cleopatra, and Romeo and Juliet."

Mr. Patrov glares at me smoothing his rich ash and fossil streaked hair with his hand before touching his grey stubble. He then continues lecturing.

By eleven a.m. I felt lunch had already taken forever. And of course since I had a certain someone on my mind I began making my way to the admissions counselor's office. My only hope was not to annoy her or to get her into any trouble.

Coming around the corner from enrollment services I see who I think is Mahru entering the south admissions office, only she is wearing a loose iron and charcoal scarf draped over her head.

"I'm still thinking about that letter you wrote me this morning," Mahru says, as I come quietly into the office to sit down beside her. I look at her waiting for her to tell me more. ". . . Are you that kind and marvelous thing that's going to wake me from my sleep?"

"Only if you let me."

She looks down smiling and biting her lip.

CHAPTER TWO

". . . I almost didn't recognize you with your scarf on."

"My dad wants me to wear it. It's part of my culture. But in here I take it off."

"So where are you from?"

"My family and I moved here from a small village in Egypt. We were picked in a lottery to come to America when I was eleven years old. It took me only a year to know the English language. I started school here my last year of junior high."

"Wow, Egypt! How did you learn the language so quickly?"

"I had to. And hearing it everyday helped me to learn faster than my parents."

"What are your parents like?"

"Well my dad has a lot of influence and still plays a large role in our village back home. He is also a professor of Classical Arabic and Islamic studies here with the Faculty of Arts. Islamic history and Islamic theology and philosophy. But he works in the Buchanan block D building further north on campus. My mom runs a clothing boutique. She wanted to live here because of how green it is. And my dad was kind enough to grant her wish. But the thing about living here is that my family disapproves of the culture—especially when it comes to being married and all of the divorce. It isn't like that where I come from."

"Would you disapprove of me?"

"No. . . . I don't disapprove of you," She replies, smiling as she looks down at the book sitting in her lap. "What are your parents like?" she then asks, intently listening.

Feeling shamefaced to know that my story will not comfort her any I stay temperate enough to share some truth. "Well I never had a dad until I turned eleven. He is not a kind man. But I love my mom. And she loves me very much. And because Damien and I don't get along, I'm living with my uncle Louis," I reply, looking at Mahru to see if she still feels that I'm worth conversing with.

"I can tell your mother loves you and that you are your mother's son," she warmly expresses.

Looking at her I am left wondering what she sees in me. My golden locks and bold features that are all infused with kindness and a gentle heart? Perhaps my perfect smile. Something that I am often told. Maybe everything that comes to mind as it clearly is for me whenever I stop and look at her.

The office door then opens and we immediately turn our attention to who is entering the room. "Hey . . ." Mahru says, acknowledging a girl student who seems surprised to see us both sitting side by side.

"Can I see the keys? I left my other notebook in the backseat," she says, nervously smiling with curious eyes. Attractive and with an acute sense of awareness her loosely voluted black ringlets hang down the side of her ears and jaw line.

"Yeah," Mahru says, reaching for a set of keys in her pants pocket. "Madge, this is Lucius. Lucius, this is my twin sister, Madge."

"Hello," I gesture kindly, dismissing her nervous shakiness for shyness. She glances at Mahru again and then back at me.

"Hey," she says, smiling at me with genuine enchantment as if to already know who I am.

"I'll be right back," Madge says, quickly retreating with Mahru's car keys.

"Your twin?"

"Yeah. Her and I are close. And I already told you that my brother Malik also goes to school here. But you must know that he can never see us sitting together because he might tell my dad."

"And that would be bad?" I ask, trying to ease my feelings of being dispirited and disheartened.

"My dad would be angry with me. And I don't want to upset him. So you can't let anyone see you talking to me outside of this room. . . . Are you sure you still want to come and see me?" she asks, fearing my brief silence to be a semblance of having lost hope and courage.

"Of course I do," I smile, seeing her smile back at me as her anxiousness dissolves. Confused by her dire imperative for secrecy, I still encourage, ". . . Come swimming with me Saturday. It's a really short hike. There is a waterfall."

". . . Is it okay if my sister comes?" she asks me nervously, not wanting to say no and further risk weakening my attempt to befriend her.

"Yeah, bring whoever you want to come with you."

"You know my dad would kill me if he found out," she utters with grave concern, her sad eyes smiling back at me. She then wears a look on her face like she absolutely refuses to tell her parents, afraid of being locked up in the house, or even worse, seriously punished.

"You don't have to tell him," I tell her, wondering if she is changing her mind. She then tears some paper from her notebook and begins writing.

CHAPTER TWO

"Here is my number. But don't ever call me. I will call you. And you can text me," she says, her eyes and voice affirming to me her concerns that have become more pronounced.

"Okay," I tell her, realizing that there are many things that I don't yet know about her.

"You are sending me your number?" she asks, as I press send. Her phone immediately receives my text.

"Now you have my number. And you can call me whenever you want. . . . I'm very much enjoying getting to know you."

"I'm enjoying getting to know you too," she says, this time not sounding so afraid.

Her sister Madge then opens the office door to return her keys. Seeing the time I then stand up to head to my next class.

"Bye Mahru," I tell her, she nodding at me with a smile. "It was nice meeting you," I kindly tell Madge, she acknowledging me just the same.

Shutting the door to the counselor's office I then wonder if she will actually call me. Already so in love with her I think about her smiling back at me. And she is so different and so carefully contumacious. And I do not even understand her. And I have never met anyone like her.

Seated in my environmental engineering class I tear another sheet of paper from my notebook. Carefully tearing the edges I can already visualize what I want it to read. And I know that I have just enough time to give it to her before she leaves the student services building.

> *Blessed with a desert flower my heart no longer dry*
> *to love her is to live and to lose her is to die*
> *bathe me in the Nile and renew my blood as yours*
> *my golden heaven in the clouds radiant forevermore*
> *risen from the water where my life will now begin*
> *inscripted in your heart made a part of yours within*
> *frail as an infant I wrap you in my love*
> *tight as if a boa there to feast inside your hug*
> *gazing in your eyes I realize how I am found*
> *blessed to hold you having both my sight and having sound*
> *ask me if I love you and I'll tell you with my kiss*

*passing you the love that I once held when you I missed
eyes shut tight injecting the most powerful of drug
the only drug that God comply—my Egyptian love*

UNDYING THIRST

CHAPTER THREE

With the greatest anticipation you can imagine my first thoughts once I awoke Saturday morning. The sun is shining as the warmth of summer still lingers in the air. And I am madly in love with a desert girl who has bedeviled and bewitched me the moment I laid eyes on her. Forbidden to speak to me she is already an experience that is strangely daunting and exhilarating.

"She will find an excuse not to come," I tell myself.

After brushing my teeth I stash some grapes and cantaloupe slices into a tea tin. Stuffing a sheepskin throw and wool blanket into my dry sack I also stuff my light goose down bag and foam pad. My swim wear is just my black microfiber underwear underneath my split-leg running shorts. Pulling my long curls back into a bun my phone then begins to ring.

"Hey—Good morning! Where are you?" she asks, parked in front of my uncle's house.

"I'm coming out now. Keep coming back," I tell her, closing the door behind me and pointing for her to park to the side.

Embracing her as she stands out of her 1985 turquoise defender I feel an electrifying pulse of warmth and magic. Taking in the beauty of this morning that mirrors the splendors of heaven I stand all amazed at her dazzling smile. I catch her smile again as she turns back to look at me. And she conveys to me with her eyes how deeply rooted her feelings are. "Hey. . . . Was it easy to find? And where's your sister?"

"She's helping my mom today. I told her it was cool. And it was no trouble finding where you live," she says, having no other distractions seeming to weigh in on her mind, only being here now purely in this moment.

"Good," I smile, looking at her.

"What?" she asks, blushing from me being quietly possessed and so fixated, she growing more uneasy by the second.

"I just uh . . . I love looking at you. And I'm so glad that you came."

"Me too," she says, taping the toe of her foot and blushing as she looks away. "So are you ready to go?"

"Yeah—just let me grab my bag," I tell her, walking back to lock my front door and to throw my dry sack around my shoulder. Clicking my car remote I throw my stuff into the backseat as Mahru fastens her belt on the passenger side.

"Your uncle's house is nice," she says, backing out of the driveway.

"I think so," I reply, being agreeable.

"Hey—turn right. Right here. I want to show you where I live too. It's not far. And no one is at the house right now so it's okay if we drive by it," she says, watching me as if I were as beautiful as the morning. "Okay now turn here."

"There it is," she says, pointing.

Slowing the car down I see the stone work and iron gate. Two verdigris figures guard the entrance. The winding cobblestone and ornamental hedges lead to the twelve-foot Honduran mahogany doors that seem impenetrable.

"The house once belonged to a Spanish developer who moved to New Zealand. He kept the French chateau look but altered the interior to more of a modern Moroccan feel."

"It's beautiful. . . . Do you want a house like that for yourself?" I then have to ask, wondering if I should turn the car around if she says yes. And then could I?

"I do not need a house that big. My dad can only afford it because of the land he inherited from his father. My dad owned so much land in Egypt. All we have there now is just our house."

I scrunch my eyebrows feeling discouraged as if my pride wasn't already weakened by seeing her parent's house—furthermore wondering if it is normal to hide the guy or girl that you're going swimming with. "Well you know I could never live in a house like that."

"It is a lot of work to clean it," she says.

"I like to have fun. I love being outside. I'd be trapped working for the rest of my life living in a house like that."

CHAPTER THREE

"Well I like that you love being outside. I like being outside too," she smiles. "All I want is a warm hobbit hole . . . a lover . . . and these mountains."

"A hobbit hole? Like in that movie?"

"Yeah," I smile, watching her smile back.

Getting closer to our destination I watch her look out of her passenger window admiring the view that leads into the mountains. Keeping my eyes on the road, she watches me, smiling at me with a growing comfort that never seems to change. She then reaches for my hand that rests over the center console. Moving my fingers further apart with hers I can tell that she adores my smile. And she sees that she is a part of this dream that has suddenly become real to her. Watching Mahru rest her head against the headrest I grasp how gentle the soul can be and how the simple pleasures in life can fructify this binding joy.

As a cream pearl light shines down through the fog we tunnel through an old bridge to our destination. Into the mountains to where the road is small enough to be consumed by the lush greenery that bends over into its path.

"Is this it?" she asks, curious as to why we are parked in an unused parking deck by an old lumber mill.

"We're here."

"There is a waterfall here?" she then asks, with disbelief.

"You'd never think so, right . . . ?" Hiding my keys under the vehicle I then look to see if anyone might be watching. Grabbing my black sac from the backseat I nudge my head in the direction we're going.

Walking away from the parking deck parallel to the mill the soft dirt quiets our footsteps. Not even the devil could be drawn out from the standing fire hazard built along the abandoned sidewalk. The broken windows and rusted stairwells lean out over the undisclosed trail in a silence that echoes beneath a murky virescent blue. Mahru follows closely passed the thick brush that leads to where a footpath continues into the forest. Carefully she follows me, climbing over the large fallen trees that consume the old path that once was. Passed the pink whirling butterfly plants and fiery begonias. The sounds of chattering squirrels and chirping birds are soon overwhelmed by the powerful falls that are now only two hundred feet away.

Approaching closer to the falls the sun reappears warming the water and the rocks. Picking a few salal berries growing nearby I hand some to her. Coming closer to the waterfall I reach for Mahru to follow me closer to the water's edge. The water further down becomes something like a transparent Caribbean blue as the sun soothes both its shallow and deep pools. Mallards and Canvasbacks propel themselves across the aisling waters. Reminded of my love for what I see and how it continues like the ripples in the water I gaze into all that is dark and mysterious. Frogs and turtles pace through the brisk and shaded waters. The gentle tree breeze tells the stories of the ages. Light dances above the liquid shapes as forest fairies skim this paradisiacal oasis.

Standing with Mahru on a large slab along the calmer water I sit my sac down. Taking my pants and my shirt off I look to see if Mahru likes what she sees. And then I see that it must be true—what the other girls say about my legs, stomach, and everything else.

"Damn," she says, looking me up and down.

"What?"

"You. Everything. Your butt. You're so beautiful," she tells me.

Setting my clothes down on a nearby rock I carefully step closer to Mahru. I watch to see if she will step back. But she remains unmoved as she keeps her eyes focused on mine.

"You think so?" I then ask, listening to more than just what she says.

Watching her I realize that she has the complete inability to keep still of what is stirring inside of her. Be it though the complete lady that she is or intends for me to perceive her as she painstakingly finds it in herself to remain as visibly undisturbed as possible. Already invading her thoughts rousing pheromones secrete from my neck and all over. Still inching closer and scanning every curve of her face for what art calls the golden mean.

"Yes," she says, her eyes wide and reaching for me to hold her closely as I reach out to touch her.

". . . You are absolutely beautiful," I tell her, long at the mercy of those feelings that have now taken a hold of me. Every expression from her body language and eye contact manifests her feeling love for me. And in her eyes she is surely aware of my undying thirst for her.

With my face gently touching hers I feel my heart melt as she grabs a hold of me. Brushing my thumbs passed the edges of her forehead my fingers then twirl her hair. I don't want to think about how. I just want what I am feeling to belong to me. And despite her being afraid I still want more than anything to nurture those feelings that I know are there. And more than anything I know that I will always want her and I will always need her.

With the sun on my neck I draw my lips just passed hers—gently planting my love against her smooth face. Letting her know with my touch that I will wait for her out of respect and most importantly out of love. I then feel her

CHAPTER THREE

heart sink deep into the unknown where only there she becomes fully aware. As my lips begin to pull away she draws herself closer to me, allowing me to seal another kiss firmly against her forehead.

"One more kiss," she says, reaching to finger my lips with both her hands. She then carefully inches closer to me as if she is about to be kissed for the first time. A heart propelling uprush of seismic energy fills my body and soul with a radiance that burns before our lips even begin to touch. As my lips fall upon hers I am welcomed by all that her heart covets. Only in her kiss do I receive the one answer to all that matters. Only here am I offered a way to live when I would have rather died. In the hold of her lips am I found secure from the rest of the world. Still tasting her lips and watching as this Virgo naiad seeks this Aquarius.

Watching Mahru peacefully come down from where she has ascended I am taken by the energy disseminating from around her body exuding excitement. And taken I am by her touch and that look that remains constant in her eyes.

Knowing what lies on the other side of the river I walk over to the water's edge. Looking back at her to make sure that she is following me I wait for her to catch up. Looking up at the draping branches swaying overhead, I next glance down at the water, fixated by the liquid shapes that merge into one another, it being so mouth watering that I have to leap in. Splash! Like lips to an ice cold glass I swim to the crystal bottom. Not wanting to scare Mahru I then push myself back to the surface inside of this blissful awakening that speaks to my inner thrill and sense of peace.

"Oh my God that looks so cold! I don't know if I can do it!"

"C'mon! There is something that I want to show you!" I tell Mahru, throwing my sac around my shoulder. "I have blankets and food over here so that you can get warm!"

Pushing myself further out into the water I turn around to see if she is coming. And then before I even have a moment to doubt her she loosens her long sleeve shirt over her head and pulls down her black skin-tight jeans. Putting the temperature of the water from my mind I keep looking at the most beautiful creature that I have ever seen. Her fair skin tempers with the colors of olive and sand as she sports a solid black bikini. And her crow curly hair reflects a raw umber that turns underneath the light. With the allure that she does possess, and being a gentle soul, she moves like a goddess along the wet stone. My eyes cling to her in a subtle trance examining the lines of her body. Every dip and every curve moving in front of the soft sky behind her as flickering blues and greens peak through the canopy above.

"You want me to get wet?" she playfully asks, her black curling hair hiding away hints of reflective shades that rotate beneath the soft light. I motion for her to get in with my hands.

Pretending to be a little afraid at first she slowly edges herself into the water while holding on to my hand. Realizing that it is more difficult easing into it, she lets go of my hand, gliding all of the way down into the cold water.

Reappearing at the surface she takes a deep breath, her body trembling as she wraps her arms and legs around me. "Hhaaahh! Oh my God!" she shouts, with a refreshing cry, pulling her hair back with the biggest smile. "Oh my God, it's cold!"

"Yeah it is," I tell her, feeling her legs and body wrap tightly around my waist, feeling this most exquisite creature awakening something ancient in me. She then steals one more kiss from my lips before asking me with her eyes if we are going to get out of the water. "Come follow me," I tell Mahru, swimming through the veins of the earth like a slow moving ship cutting through the sea.

Swimming alongside of her through the dark water we find our feet again on the layered slabs where the mist from the soughing falls masks us both in the gentle rapture of our being in each other's arms. She follows me to where the white of the falls finds familiar water catching its roaring pour.

"It's beautiful . . ." she says, telling me in my ear, smiling at me as she warms herself against me. Pushing her hair away from her face she moves closer to embrace me with that one sure kiss that holds me so still, her soft skin warming every inch of me as her heart beats close to mine.

"Come, we're almost there," I tell her, turning back and looking into her eyes as I see her look back into mine.

Carefully guiding her up along the seam of the waterfall there is still a safe enough distance between the wet rocks and the dry ones. To her surprise I lead her passed the hanging clematis vines and into a cavernous gap tucked away behind the thundering falls. Holding Mahru close to me we both inch into the crevice. Following her from behind I make sure that her step is careful as she continues to make her way into the cavity behind the falls.

Sheltered from inside of the falling water where a shadowy enclosure echoes an eternal rain, we quickly become surrounded by all that is soothing and utterly serene. With every step that she inches closer towards me her feverish body emanates so powerfully and intense. Feeling dreadfully responsible for

CHAPTER THREE

unavoidably keeping her inside of this torment that she thinks to control I reach for her waist gently pressing my thumbs. Sighing immediate relief inside of these arms her lips drag across mine so slowly that I anticipate a standstill from top to bottom, deceiving me, meticulously intriguing my senses with her extraordinary touch and kiss.

Intending for us to stay and to eat I stop to unfold two warm blankets. Laying them over top of a foam pad and my goose down bag she carefully ties her wet hair up into a bun. Leaving the food tins at the edge of the soft warm arrangement on the ground I then remove my black underwear without warning her. Catching her by surprise I watch her stare as the taste for sex moves into her mouth and ignites this spell. Reminding herself that nobody has to know she thinks about how long she has waited to feel what she feels now. Telling me so much by how she holds onto me with her stares. And I see her already thinking about it as I urge her to warm herself between me and the fibers that will allow no warmth to escape through.

As the water roars above our heads she removes each piece of clothing with her arms pressed against her breasts. So naked and so beautiful she crawls into the blankets and into my embrace. Naked and warm between the wool and the down layers I gaze into the windows of her soul, she being anxious to share with me this experience and pleasure of being together. Her eyes tell me that there is no place she would rather be than right here with me. Feeling our incredible warmth converge into one another she gives in to her want and need to love, her shivers beginning to dissipate between the coverings and her love for me as I persist to embrace her with a most tranquil and decided kiss sure to be remembered for as long as there is time.

Rubbing her face onto my stomach she slides down my body desperate to smell me. Bound by the sudden rush of emotion that reverberates through me and as I remain intent on awakening her I push my fingertips upward over her neck as if pushing a coin from the edge of heaven—waiting to catch where it falls as if I were in all places at once.

With my golden curls falling over her black shining hair I breathe in deep her gostoza aroma. Gently attacking her pressure points I leave her completely vulnerable to my wanting her, she seducing me with her gentle rhythm that seems to make me forget as a medley of magical sensations spins me in circles.

Carefully placing me inside of her she allows me passage to where our souls unite and where they thirst to construct a deeper meaning for one another. She feels my swollen pyaar gently pressing her body into the quiet concave of this energetic sphere. And she hastens my love as I reveal to her my gentle ways that excite and nourish her every capacity in all mind and body. Taking to her exaggerated lines that press firmly against me with a wet friction that builds between the cold and the heat. Tasting and smelling her body that warms my heart to its core. Allowing my mind to speak through my gaze as I look into her rich brunneous eyes where hints of sable shimmer across the reflection that mirrors her heart.

Completely vulnerable to my wanting her I hold Mahru in my arms wishing for her happiness and for her a life with me. She still looking into these eyes with a joy that no earthly being can honestly describe as I look right back into hers. Assuring her of how much I truly love her.

Seeking me out again her lips form a precious mold over top of mine. She reaching deep down into my place of content to reconfirm with me that she too knows who I am and why I reached out to her. Looking into her eyes and touching her face with my lips I see how beautiful and mysterious her love is.

Lying peacefully in my keeper's arms, my heart is secured by the still reverence of having become the keeper of her. Her gentle body close to me sets me free and bestows a peace that is like heroine moving through my blood. The way that leaves float like clouds down a gentle stream. Like water, the most powerful and life-giving, blood fills my Vesuvius vein and pleasures the inside of her. Giving and taking in the same way that the earth breathes and lives forever. Her playful bite increases my affectionate appetite. Her curves and softness are to me a star-gazing wonder that holds my attention with an utter fascination. She is a woman. Loving and eternal. Loving her wild like a thundering storm that yields soft warm rain to ease my pain. Her warm body and loving touch feeding me as her kisses receive me. My touch traveling her shores like the sea that beats at her heart's core.

"Love me for a thousand years and then find a way to come and stay with me for one more day," I tell her, as she smiles back at me.

Gently my hands move across her back the way that a swan drifts above still water. Cherishing the feeling of her being so close to me I feel her kiss and her nose press firmly against my neck, feeling her hands moving down my backside and her gentle grip where I am most vulnerable. Sliding my hands down her body the way that water pulls back from the edge of the seashore my touch revisits her smooth surface. Her perfect form gifted by the mother of all that is. Metaphysically transmuted by the memory of her love that will now live inside of me forever.

CHAPTER THREE

Feeling Mahru using all of me as a vessel to cure her own weakness she reconstructs her strength from inside of that delicate place within her heart. Holding her warm naked body so wet, I gradually apply my lips to her most tender outlets, admitting her entire body to fusillade with excitement and pleasure. With my lips I fill the gaping holes that cry out inside of her as I become even more beautiful to her. Penetrating the many layers of her consciousness as my hands slip down her arcuate back our bodies build upon an afterquaking that intensifies with each turn of the limbs. Feeling her ability to feel close and connected our bodies move together in one fluid formation. She again finding my lips as the two of us lie comforted in each other's arms behind the greatest force on earth.

Sprawled out over the flat wet stone that supports our growing urge to love and be loved we lie hidden from the rest of the world at the center of the earth. Two hearts becoming one as the beauty of our love emerges from all that was once mysterious. Giving her what was thought only to exist in her dreams as the susurrous roar above our heads silences our endless cry for love.

LUSCIOUS ALLURE

CHAPTER FOUR

Holding her in my arms and looking up at the water pouring over the edge of an enormous rock I feel such a serene and perfect peace. And the joy in my heart that she gives is so powerful that it even scares me. But I put it from my mind because she is mine right now. And right now I know is all that matters.

Rubbing the tips of my fingers down her back she tries to pull me closer as she nuzzles her face into my chest. Never have I drawn or seen with my eyes anything so beautiful. Nor is she something that I could have ever imagined. And how she ended up lying next to me I cannot even comprehend. All I know is that I am not ready for this day to end.

"What are you thinking?" she then asks, resting her chin on my chest as she turns her head from watching the roaring falls.

"I was thinking maybe you can come back with me to my place. Maybe you could let me make you something to eat."

"Like what?"

"Salmon and asparagus, maybe?"

"I love both of those things."

"C'mon, let's go," I smile, standing up to put my shorts back on as she lays there admiring my body to the deafening sound of water falling.

Wondering how long she is going to stay at my place I catch her smiling at me as she slides back into her wet bikini. I wonder if she is just having a good time with me. And I wonder if she is just using me as a way to rebel against

CHAPTER FOUR

her parents and her traditions. But whenever I look into those eyes of hers nothing seems to matter and all over again I am at a loss for words. And her wild stares tell me everything that I want or need to know.

Swimming back to the other side of a sun-illumined pool I am ensnared by the mere sight of her as she naturally swims closer towards me. Her smooth face so adored and loved by the gods. Again realizing that I am nothing but passionate about this creature who does mirror the splendor of all that is treasured by our Great Mother and creator. Above every living thing I keep staring at her most beautiful creation. And it does not matter what she wears or what she says when she speaks. And I think about how most women will spend time caring about the way that they look when really there is no need. Because when a man truly loves a woman he does not care for those things that she will try to hide her face with. And her sense of pride is just as beautiful as she is. Wondering perhaps if I might evoke in her this hidden strength. But I do not think so. And her little mistakes only render her to be still perfect in my mind. Her eyes alone could soften the heart of the coldest creature walking the earth and even destroy them. Her beauty is this and even more than what I could have ever previously imagined.

Watching her climb back into my car her whole world is taken by a calm that does give heed to her every impulse. And so she lures me from inside my passenger door. Leaning against the seat of my car I steal another kiss from her all-telling lips. She pulls my face closer to kiss her mouth and her neck as the sensational vibrations emitting from her do cause me to feel that I might evaporate into nothing. Forcing myself to close her door I climb in after walking around from the other side.

Pulling out onto the road of a wanderlust landscape we leave through the Pinecone Burke Provincial Park. Through the alpine mountain range and past the cascading falls we head home with a slow burning anticipation for what the rest of the afternoon will bring.

After about twenty minutes of driving and talking high school sweethearts, I notice it then becomes quiet. Expressing what she first thought of me the first time that she laid eyes on me, I then notice a concerning thought weighing behind Mahru's eyes. It is a concerning thought that she even tries to hide from me when I look at her.

"What?" I then ask.

"You know in Egypt where I'm from men can have as many wives as they want. And for many married Muslims the first time that they meet is on their wedding night. Extreme devout groups are always persecuting anyone who they believe are lesser than they are. . . . You know that my parents would never allow me to date or marry anyone outside of their arrangement. And my family is still very much firm in our traditions."

Wondering why she is telling me this and feeling her concern weighing on me I then counter her fear by responding with "Well, what I feel for you could never be subject to any law, tradition or custom." Noticing my feelings being a little bit hurt I wonder if Mahru can also see.

"Did you know that before the Quran all literature in the Arabic world was comprised of romantic poems and adventure?" she then smiles.

I shake my head "no," watching her look at me.

"The commonly accepted interpretation of the Quran says that a Muslim man can marry a non-Muslim woman, but that a Muslim woman cannot marry a non-Muslim man. And good girls from good families are not supposed to talk to boys."

"Well I'm glad that you are talking to me," I reply, worried that her feeling nervous will change her mind about me.

"It's embarrassing just to think that we're not even supposed to be speaking to each other right now. I think it's ridiculous."

"Me too," I tell her, believing that she still wants to see me.

Holding her hand and pulling into my driveway I bunch her fingers together like a bundle of lily stems before pressing her sweet-smelling fingertips to my lips. Taking my hand she then calms her growing anxiousness by pressing my fingers to hers.

"Can you kiss me again?" she then asks, with an ardent glow about her kind face.

Happily I reach for her lips, tasting the sweet nectar from her mouth and spirit. Mahru kisses me gently, knowing from the moment that we first kissed that I could never get enough of her love. She nudges for me to kiss her sweet lips again.

Getting out of the car to walk around for Mahru she is already beating me to the door with a look that is kindly telling me to hurry. Turning my key into the door I catch her squeezing her waist with still a burning desire.

"Your place is nice," she says, loosening her hair as she follows me inside.

"It's more than I need for just myself."

"It's warm and cozy," she softly reiterates, her eyes wandering down her legs and back towards me.

CHAPTER FOUR

Carefully I replace her wet towel with a blanket as she stands by the large window that overlooks the flower bed above the brick walkway outside.

"If you want to have a look around I'm gonna make that salmon," I tell her, turning to walk behind the kitchen counter.

She grabs my hand and gently pulls me back towards her. Looking at me she shakes her head no with her eyes fixed to mine.

"Not now," she says, inching closer to me with a kiss that welds to me in the bonding of beauty that seems almost imaginary. Her kiss takes everything from me, giving back only what she would have me keep as I reach for my breath. Carefully she kisses me longing for our love to be made. Caressing her underneath her neck and face I give my soul's kiss to the side of her face, kissing her again above the eyes, sliding down the bridge of her nose as I find her lips once more.

"You taste heavenly," I tell the girl that I have so strongly sought out, she smiling before again finding my lips.

"That is because I just finished the cantaloupe that you had in the car."

"No—it's not that. . . . It's just you. And you are just as heavenly to look at." Looking into Mahru's eyes she looks back up at me as if admiring the most grand view from the highest cloud.

Stepping out of her shoes she twirls around pulling me by my fingers. Pressing me to follow her upstairs she quietly tiptoes on the wood floor.

Reaching my bedroom she draws near to me. Her warmth converges into my energetic radius as the feeling of her moves across the hair on my neck like the silk of grass whispering in the wind. A smile arises from the edge of her lips. She then focuses on the wall behind me.

"Is that me? . . . Did you do this?" she asks, drawn and fixated to my drawing of her that hangs near the entrance of the room.

"I tried to give it to you after class. But since I don't have any pictures of you I thought I'd keep it."

"Or maybe I can give you a picture of me for it?" she then suggests, absolutely astonished. "A picture for your drawing of me?"

"Maybe," I tell her.

"Okay then. It's a deal," she amiably dictates, smiling with her secret love for me that maybe is not so secret anymore.

"Okay," I express with a smile, pulling her closer to me.

Wrapping her arms around me she wants me to hold her tight and close, wanting me to never let go. For a split second I feel her think about where she is as I watch her ask herself if she should be here or if she should go home. But in that same split second she is completely swept by something more powerful and more demanding of her natural desire and thirst.

Bound by the slow swaying of affection, we stand in the way of each other, proposing that one sure kiss that has only freed us from this unusual and tortuous frustration. Placing my face against hers I release this agony that has built up inside me from not knowing if I can have her. Feeling her wanting me in that way. Wanting me the way that she has never wanted anyone before.

Smiling that beautiful smile she reaches with another kiss that breaks me. With wet secretions priming our love lust her eyes call for me to fill her body up with love. Guiding her by the hand I move with her to the other end of the room where my bed is placed away from the light that shines in. Neatly placing herself down where I lay my head at night she sprawls herself out with a yearning stretch. Motioning for me to come and be with her I climb into my bed and lie next to her, holding her the way that she has always longed to be held, her beautiful hands moving gracefully across my neck and chest as she reaches for both with her lips.

Absorbed into this feeling that never left me my heart becomes increasingly unsteady like a Miura behind the sweltering gates of a charged arena. Her fingers like whirling pools of river water swirl down my arms and chest as I now belong to the purlieus of her love's imagination. And the way that she looks at me sends the clearest signal of her need for my intimacy that she longs to feel from me. I feel myself melting from the inside out with this appetent yearning to love her. And pressing my lips to her chest our hearts engage in this extraordinary magic that descends upon us both.

Never before have I felt such serene indulgence as this. Her kiss like honey to lick and suck feeling the warmth of her skin touching mine. Stroking my hair down passed my face and again back behind me she illustrates her intensions with me. Her eyes like a crescent moon that carries the deepest love. Her rich edges define her face making my body numb. She looking up at me as if she is lying underneath the stars as I lie next to her.

Tucking herself underneath me with both her arms wrapped tightly around me, my heart softens as she gently places her face underneath mine—feeling her lips press firmly against my neck. Adjusting her nose and face against me she tugs my shirt. Knowing that I am only here to surrender every part of me she moves her hands down my waist lifting my shirt. Leaning in to kiss her gently once more I discover again her adorable smile as she lays her head back down next to mine, she kindling the flame inside of me that speaks to her, my heart yearning for her as I do know without a doubt that her love is everything to me.

Holding her in my eyes her hands push upward again gathering the material from my shirt until it reaches over my head. Unhooking the top button from her denim shorts I stare deep into the lambent ecru of her eyes as hints of russet and jade glimmer across them both. Watching her hands touch me her lips move down my torso. Carefully removing each layer that is slowly loosened we quickly find each other completely unguarded and in tender redress of this culturally taboo setting, our arms wrapped tightly around one another with every piece of clothing thrown onto the floor.

Lifting her high into the sky with my slithering tongue between her thighs she feels the sweetest tension liquefy her entire body. Her slender arms and hands glide and slide naturally in such a graceful performance that her movement does seduce every part of me. Feeling her warm bare skin so close to me I hold her inside of my gentle embrace. I marvel every elegant strand from her karakul-like ringlets that fall down beside her face and shoulders. Like Cleopatra the splendor of her darling features give charm to that undulating delirium that she induces. Tasting herself on my fingers and mouth her kiss and her lips follow my every decisive movement. The edges of my fingertips move down the muscles of her back the way that a drop of rain travels the wet colocasia and homalomena. Every smooth stone that dreams by that peaceful stream is shaped and likened to her smooth body that moves like the water. Feeling her fingers and her lips nuzzled into my neck she grants me sweet refuge. Never in all my life having ever wanted something so badly the way that I want her.

Pushing apart and together with my tongue the soft wet lips of her pink flowering petals a quivering call for moisture gathers in that secret place. Her single touch then sends shock waves down my entire vessel sending our bodies into a confluence of luscious allure. Kissing her with her eyes securely closed I hold her like she is my life making love to her soul. The deep brown embers glowing from inside the richness of her eyes reveal to me just how irresistible I have become to her. Watching her reach out to kiss me the stars from heaven thrust themselves to the earth in a glittery glow encircling these two hearts in a bird-like formation that delivers our love from this cultural hindrance. The curves of her lips gyrate duly over mine for a duration of fitting ecstasy that adduces her unyielding conviction in me evermore. Fermented in the pulp of her demulcent lips our kisses contort within this impassioned expressiveness that defines the candor of our love. Tasting the serum secreting from her chamomile kiss I am enchanted by the closeness of her. Her fine glacé lips bear the splendid petimezi of all hidden vineyards. Her touch is as still as a mist that warms a cool forest as she feels for my naked body from head to toe.

Now fitting all of me inside to reach and to touch that interstellar world withinside her I also feel her lips and hips sliding and grinding. So wet bearing down and lifting herself so carefully as she feels in length every unit of measurement. Climbing me and growing me as an incapacitating force kicks and swims through the veins of my love. Kneading her warm skin I take notice of what God has clearly given us. She always rescuing me with her smile as she touches me with her gilded fingertips.

Whetted by that sultriest desire effusivating from her eyes I find myself athirst as glacier light reflects from the vibrant glow of her mysterious gaze. Here in my arms she is warmed by that translucence peering through the forest canopy. Here every kiss becomes translated into creation. Her spirit is transfigured traveling to the ends of the earth where the course leaves of green pastures move through her fingers.

Crawling down the face of her luring body she hastens this pulsing quaking love lodged deep passed her dewy folds. With the calm handling of my brush-like stroke I caress her beauteous body from below the hips and forward drawing a deep subcutaneous rote that results in excitement. Her astired and tortuous figure harmonizes with my body igniting this love-starved theia mania as she consumes me inside of her fire. Stranded to her beautiful island the movement of her body gives me cue by her curvaceousness and tour de force of flamenco. Trembling with an evocative craze that is utterly overpowering I reach out to subdue her in an emollient moistening of quiescent arousal. Our bodies move across one another the way that smoke rings dance and turn shapes across the space that they know to be there. In the way that Mother Nature gives birth to the spiraling twists of color that mark a beast or rouses a flower to glow our love does imitate.

Steeped in the replete libido of her lady-like mien she reaches for me, giving me soft praise beneath this masterful and spastic amour, she hastening me as we meld into a lulling mélange of impassioned movement. The eurythmic motion of her strumming legs cling to my body like the sheltering wings of an egret. Her rapt sleeves hold me with a reveling affection as she feels an ecstatic and renewed sense of wonder.

Squeezing my sarpa with its bine-like nerves bulging between the contours of her lush thighs our rotating parts sluice inside of my devouring her. Exploring and tasting that tremendously satisfying sempiternal world an intercrural quaking sets fire to her measureless pleasure. In the incalculable kinetic junction of an organic orgasm that smells of heroin and tastes of muscatel our pendulous hearts plunge into a restive swelling. Flooding her Nile with the thick throat of my swollen ling we simultaneously erupt above the zenith of all life energy. Spoondrifting from her frothy shell-pink lips her body and mind like ocean mist is absorbed into the atmós—the heavens. All pressure releases her spasming impetus as she squeezes my blood-filled hyphal flesh of the gods— she feeling a separation of spirit from body.

Pulling all of the way out the curving slippage of her dynamic vehemence hums over me in a refreshing fixation that imbues this inseparable bond of the eternities. Polishing her thighs with our warm dripping secretions we experience a spiritual alchemical metamorphosis as we bathe in the pure essence of ecstasy. Traveling with my fingers the length of this mythical creature she consumes from my other hand every morsel of my love.

Under the influence of such an entrancing climax I am reminded of the inundated calm before the storm as I find my mind to see through those same eyes that I have before. No desert autumn colors on the horizon more vivid than the tone of her warm ivory flesh. Her legs and back shifting in my sheets like the serpent-like swivels curving down the spine of the mountain.

Gently her purling hips begin weaving in and out, oscillating against me in a balmy nubile urge of effervesce and obsession. Again I occlude her recumbent orifice with the soft clasp of my wet lips, satiating my guest with an all-stimulating and interplanetary escape. In a largo samba-like motion I simultaneously absorb and alleviate the tension lingering beneath her plum fuselage as an overflowing ovulation of seismic and fulminating convulsage travels through the apex of her feminous core. Carefully I follow the crevice between her legs like the gentle waters that flow through the shaded gorge. Watching her levitate into a liberating reflex of celestial zest her panting grip again begins to measure the odometer of our obsession.

Gradually relishing in her scent absorbed into my flesh I lie beneath her seductive spell feeling an utter peace. Light and fuzzy like the dandelion seeds that float the breeze on a warm summer day, floating in and out of body like the wind. Finding myself rejuvenated in her by returning what she has clearly given me. Her human kindness and love my water and air.

Rustling from the ode of her seducing nature does her soft soothing approach captivate my fascination. In our mingling coalescence we do heed the mollifying remediation of our sexual right and commitment that remains unremitting. Feeling these hands, arms, and legs twirling with one another we quietly hold each other still. Even finding myself quietly possessed and wondering how I could ever convince her to love me forever.

The coral bell colors in the sky now all bleed in from the light that enters my bedroom window. With every movement and every kiss so does every possibility sway the heart. She fills all of the emptiness inside of me with her love. And feeling so much love from her only impels my need to give more to be greater. Casting my eyes upon this woman who does give herself to me is still the most exhilarating of all that is entirely dear to me. She is the mast holding the sails to my soul. She is that divine poultice that cures my open heart.

Watching her lying so still in my arms I endearingly acknowledge the irrefutable truth that she completes me. Her slim deerlike physique clings to me nestled inside of my embrace, her lovely hair still strewn down her face and onto mine and as soft as the flower that she does move across my face and neck. A vinal shine turns over shades of cerulean and jasper from her expressive lips revealing a jewel-like surface beneath a light that remains colorfast in a kiss composed of infinite grace. Absorbed into this state of rest she still makes me the absolute center of attention, dovetailing in an erotic entwinement that impels me to knead her coiling flex. Her resplendent fullness macerated into my bosom grants me a restful anodyne enabling the allay of my inner soul. My touch gently hydrofoils over her jawline and jugular, sending her body into a medley of resonating intensity, watching and feeling my kiss impregnate her inner soul and heart with a limn love of the mind's eye.

Touching her soft skin she nurtures me and ameliorates me entirely as if she has been celestially fashioned in the art of sensory catharsism. Carefully and meticulously I make a memento from the palatable nectar of her lithe rotund lips. Her perfect lips weaken me with a most beautiful omniscience. Mending the seems of her love with mine I climb the nape of her neck and in my crusade to the tops of her branches I am still the sepal of her enchanting and sovereign beauty. Knowing that she is there for me excites me to grow and to lift her up. And in this I am made better. And only here do I notice that I am alive—knowing that only here can I be allowed to appreciate and understand fully.

In her eyes I find a glimmer of immense joy giving radiance to that smile that I so adore. Reaching for me she gives me the kind of kiss that says to

CHAPTER FOUR

me so many words. Aware of my love for her she feels inside of my arms me holding her close. Her soft savory kisses are to me god's love made manifest. Her paralyzing touch is where I sleep peacefully in the unfurling of a surreal surrender. Feeling her stroking the length of me we lie quietly tucked away into this cushy crevice where we find all that is familiar to our hearts, where two souls become fused into one, two souls being closer to heaven than any one man who has experienced for himself that one place where God himself would rather be.

All of my body and mind now drift in and out of this serene hypnosis, hypersensitively tactile to the slightest movements, drifting into a melodious slumber where deer leap through the falling mists of cascading falls in the foreground of my imagination. The allure of cassia, jasmine, and rich petrichor renders me a comely elixir for me to surrender to. Holding Mahru in my arms I see my place in the great universe. Lost in the silent unspeakable memory of her my slightest movements convey to her my deepest affections.

In the quiet gaze of my introspection my whole being surrenders to an amorous succession of internal and incandescent substance. She is my syzygiacle empyreaness. Thinking if only I could look at her in the same way that I look at the moon—never looking at her anymore differently than what I know her to be. Wanting to believe that she will always keep the rest of me safe. Loving her because she loves me back, even when my love is all that I have to give. Knowing that I could lie looking into her eyes and kissing her delicate lips for an eternity and never care for anyplace else. And like all men I am flawed but made whole in her arms.

Holding her I see that the words expressed in her eyes are what I must learn to hear. Here and now understanding that she could never be flawed. And with each second that passes I find myself wanting more and more this solemn responsibility to nurture and strengthen this precious creature. And allowing her to find rest in me is something that I cannot deprive her of. After all, I know what she is going through. And I know her to be still a prisoner in her own heart. And so it is here and now in my weakness and strength that I commit myself as her safe asylum.

Still in each other's arms neither of us are very opt for the use of words, as both of us know that there are only so many things that can be said. This veracious and solicitous gaze that Mahru gives to me coruscates round the ocular corona of her delicate and divine features of which she does commend to me within her voluptuous embrace. The creamy eglantine, sanguine, and fuchsia of her vivifying kiss enfolds a sedative ellipse over mine that turns me into vapor. More to me than any other part of her that is absolutely diamond it is her ardent and decided kiss that is most dear to me. The dangling kinks in her hair slide gently down the sides of my face, she avidly making me the counterpoint to her sensual exigency. With each kiss she disarms me and heals me of my heartsick love. With each kiss I am where the veil between here and heaven has broken.

Mystified beneath this circumambient spell that whispers to me in the soft company of an endless love I find myself inextricably converged into the serenade of our indissoluble state of awareness. Indulging myself in the unparalleled taste of her formfitting kiss I am rendered weak in the arms of her distinguished beauty. Here I am also made strong in my heart as I find myself taken by all that she does give. She is to me all that has ever been of any worth as I do value her delightful spirit, valuing the way that she looks at me as she does with a void that I long to fill. Knowing now that I will never be content until my heart is met with her flesh. Here with Mahru I am only what I am and loved dearly for every bit of it, she still reaching for me and comforted with all that we do give to one another.

"Whenever you kiss me I feel like all of those things that you say to me in your poems," she tells me with a smile.

"I will forever wonder how you exceed my every description of you," I softly reply, she responding to me by the way that she pulls me tighter.

"At night I will dream of this day and hope someday that my every wish to always be with you will come true."

"I hope that your wish will come true," Mahru smiles. Returning a smile I gently run the back of my hand down her warm body. "But you'll have to make love to me whenever I demand it," she then adds, playfully.

I try to retain consciousness, feeling it almost slip from me while listening to the very sound of her voice.

"Okay," I comply, attentively, searching again for her lips.

Gently slipping into a decelerated cessation against the galvanizing elevation of her kiss an ethereal and indubitable cognizance instills in me a descried enamor.

Drawing the back of my hands curatively down her neckline I begin to unravel her denuded and portrait-worthy physique. My hands conduce a ketch that sails passed her midriff to where my hands become my lips, reinvested as a gentlemen between her tailbone and flowering sanctum. Wetting the corollas of her pink flowering lips I try my best to make her feel completely and utterly alive. Here is where her fingers run through my hair as if I am all that she has left inside of this great universe. Her svelte hands gracefully slope down my triceps in a tremulous urge, she desperately receiving my refined companionship that she has craved for too long.

Saturated in this oleaginous substance our culminating love abides, raveling in the tender mercies of an analgesic daydream. The respiration of her full sigh does reflect to me her wonderment, furthermore devoted to this refulgent cohesiveness that bonds the tenacious soul. And I declare that my love is no temptress, she being in need of all that I have to give. Still this lingering thought of why she remains prisoner does trouble me. And so I make it clear to her that I will do anything it takes to free her of that which does dissociate her love for me.

Resting gently between my arms she is now afraid that she must leave. Feeling her kiss my eyes and face she then finds my lips again. Holding onto her I return a kiss so close to her lips before pulling her closer to me as if it were possible to be even closer. Here in my arms is where I will picture her when she is not here. Here and now still holding onto the only thing that has ever been this dear to me.

"I never imagined my existence could be so perfect as this," I tell Mahru.

"I never thought that I would ever fall in love," she replies.

Again her kiss keeps me still as she then touches my smile. She reaches up and brushes my hair slowly as she draws her hands down the sides of my face. Kissing her fingers and hands I try to keep them in front of me. Smiling with her eyes closed Mahru touches my lips with her hands.

"What's this?" I then ask, touching the gold ring wrapped tightly around her finger.

"It was my mother's ring. She wanted me to have it for good luck. The ring also belonged to my grandmother who was very beautiful. My mother once told me the story of how my grandmother married for love, which is uncommon in Egypt. Ever since she told me that story I wanted this ring, and to find love for myself. And now I have," Mahru smiles.

Pressing my lips and running her fingers across them gently she looks at my mouth the same way that she had earlier today, looking at me the way that she did the first time that she kissed me. Gently prying them apart she now runs her fingertips across the bottom of my lip with a curious childlike fixation.

Again I realize that she is as needful for me as I am of her. Touching her warm stomach I pull her left leg in crossed with mine. Closing my lips around the ring of her tiny finger I taste her and love her. Piece by piece she lets me taste each and every part of her, smiling at me with a wonder that again grows into a series of sweltering exchanges. She is the one woman who literally takes my breath away. And yet I realize that she is as trapped in my love as I am in hers. Wondering how those beautiful stars in the sky brought us together. Wide-eyed and wondering with all that there is to wonder.

Embracing me as I indulge myself in her, she too indulges herself in me, curling up into my arms. She now makes the kind of noise that might easily secure a carnivore to its prey. Wishfully leaning into me with her lips that become free for me to cradle I catch her lips with my entirety. Watching her beautiful face adore me she discovers even her very soul that is no more just a whisper beyond her quietest thoughts. I feel her cling to me the way that one clings to a raft when out to sea. I lie confused, yet in every moment so satisfied. Inseparably smitten we have become here marinating within each other's grasp. She becomes free of those questions that have all been answered with a single kiss. Still tasting heaven so near to my lips holding her here in my bed.

Carefully moving below her neck I kiss her below the clavicle and chest. Advancing below her breasts with a limber crawl I give my attention to her abdomen and waist, slowly and methodically embedding my lips into her smooth body. Feeling her body react in a sensitive manner that does war with an imploring force, her hands encourage me to continue. She lies restlessly over the tops of my shoulders as my hands grip a hold of her thighs and waist. Drawing me back into her bosom from the motion of her hips and hands she carefully directs me towards her lips once more, guiding me by the frame of my lower jaw with both her arms gently reaching.

"Kiss me more," she spells a mellifluous utterance.

Lying down with her and kissing her lips softly I give my whole heart to her, sharing with her the last of this enchanted evening that is now coming to an end. In the far reaches of my mind I dread that something will try and keep me from her. Not knowing when I will see her again I put my fear from me to instead cherish every moment with her, already in my heart aching and longing to hold her again.

Glancing at the time on my phone I am torn with every second becoming more precious to me. Never before have I ever encountered anything so rare and beautiful in all my life. She being so close to me and yet so very far away.

Looking up at me she feels my concern as I lie gently caressing her. She sees it in my face that I care deeply about her and that I am wondering about what will happen to us. Reaching for me she embraces me even more as if to tell me that she will never let me go.

"Come back to me," I plead.

"I will. I promise," Mahru assures me, even though she knows that it will be difficult. "I have to go now," she reminds me, holding onto me tightly as if to capture the memory of how it feels feeling me hold her so close. Killing me to hear her say those words my face displays to her the better part of me that is grateful that she has come.

"I wish that I didn't have to go."

"Then don't. Stay here," I tell her.

She kisses me again. "Don't worry—I'll come back."

Nodding my head and my eyes I try to comfort her with my smile, brushing her hair and kissing her sweet mouth.

Holding onto Mahru for as long as I can she then begins to get dressed. Watching her at the edge of the bed I reach down to pick up my clothes from the floor.

"I love you, Mahru. And I need you like I need each breath," I tell her, moving her hair out of the way as she pulls her pants up passed her thighs.

Catching her beautiful smile she looks up at me with those eyes. Trying to dismiss the pain of seeing her go I too say to her, "Kiss me once more," catching her as she falls into my arms. She then kisses me to where the sounds of our lips do excite my mind. Holding Mahru in my arms I rest my face against hers, afraid in my heart of this fear that lives inside of her.

"I will be back soon. I don't want you to worry," she tries to reassure me, still hesitant about having to leave.

"Okay. . . . C'mon. I'll walk you outside."

Feeling Mahru watching me I stop her at the entryway to my bedroom. "But don't forget this," I tell her, handing her my drawing off the wall to take home.

"Are you sure? I can have it?" Mahru asks.

"Yeah, you can have it. But now you owe me a picture."

"Okay," she smiles.

Letting me hold her one last time before I escort her outside, I then walk with her to her truck. Opening her door for her to climb in I then reach to kiss her lips once more.

Watching her back out and pull away her soul-stirring eyes say goodnight to me one last time from her driver side window. And then right then I realize that I am more in love than I am even able to fathom.

Standing in the driveway after she disappears around the corner I wonder when I will see her again. "We didn't even eat. But our hearts did feast all the day long," I think to myself.

Standing under the warm hue of dusk for only a moment I then go back inside to lie down in my bed.

Rubbing myself into the sheets to smell her I realize how deeply changed I am and how fabulous I feel. I think about how making love is like the wind slipping through the blades of grass that move over the mountain and down into the valley until it reaches the sea. It is both birth and breath. And for the first time in my life something excites me. And that something is already far beyond precious to me. But what I am most afraid of in the deepest recesses of my mind is that my love belongs to a frightened girl who fears a hidden consequence.

DARK PRINCESS

CHAPTER FIVE

Come Sunday, I never heard from Mahru, until the end of the day. And when she finally called me it was only for a few minutes on the phone. All that she told me was that she needed to play it cool since her parents were home. And I agreed. If that's what you feel that you need to do. And then she told me that she told her parents that she spent the day with Zuzana, from school, who needed help writing an essay. Then she told them that afterward they went to the mall. But who would tell their mom and dad what really happened no matter who your parents are?

After speaking on the phone with Mahru, I thought less about how strange it is that her dad can never have a conversation with me. And I shrugged it off so long as she promises to see me and promises to keep talking to me. Any intuitive feeling or concern that I get I toss in the back of my mind. And sometimes I even naively wonder if her dad would actually like me.

Thinking about Mahru's soft eyes and gentle smile causes me to tremble every time that I picture her face. Her face is what calms me. It is her face that gives me comfort in the midst of those impermanent tasks that challenge me each day. The mere sight of her excites my efforts as she is to me the most and the highest. And then I think about what her body does to my body. And the more that I think about her do I find myself wanting more.

As Monday finally permits me to again visit with Mahru in the office, I quietly enter, finding a glow about her face that expresses her deepest joy. Only Mrs.

Etienne realizes that she now has two helpers instead of one.

Being witness to my unyielding determination to see Mahru, Mrs. Etienne stops punishing herself with the inevitable, and instead puts me to work stapling papers for all of the new students.

"I knew you'd be back. You can help Mahru staple that stack over there," the counselor tells me, before sitting back down at her desk.

"You know my dad saw the drawing that you did for me . . ." My heart almost stops, surprised, but happy to hear that it seemed to be a nonconfrontational and casual thing.

"And what did he say?" I then ask, seeing that it hadn't yet turned into something bad.

"He said that he used to do that for the girls too. Then my dad warned me. I told him that it was just done by someone at school as an assignment. Then he told me that I should hang it up in the house and so I did . . ."

"What do you mean when you say that he warned you?"

"He just warned me—and told me to be careful is all," she replies.

Watching Mahru I can tell that there was more to that conversation between her and her father. But I instead pretend not to notice since she does not want to tell me.

"Well I'm glad you hung it up so that you can see it," I tell Mahru, she being both silently thrilled and nervous about me sitting next to her.

"I am too," she says, her eyes now desperately wanting me to see the person that she hides so well.

She then doesn't say anything as she somewhat smiles and sorts through her papers. But watching her and feeling her dancing aura move all around me I can feel her wanting to touch me and wanting to connect with me.

Watching her blush and watching her trying not to smile, something then comes to mind to propose. Hoping that she will agree to let me paint her I then ask, "I wonder if you will help me with something that I want to do?"

"What is it?"

"I want to paint you. I would like to paint a portrait of you."

Smiling as she keeps separating a stack of welcome packets, she feels the depths of her anxious rage, still flattered and worried. "You can paint too?"

"I can. With oil."

"I don't know," she smiles, nervous, but still wanting to say yes.

"You seemed to like my pencil drawing. Just leave it to me."

"Who is the painting for?

CHAPTER FIVE

"Maybe for you. Maybe just for me. Since you took my other picture."

"Oh yeah! I almost forgot. Here. . . . You can have these," she then says, handing me a few recent pictures of her. I take a moment to look them over and then smile, happy that she remembered.

"Thank you. I really like these. . . . I'd still like to paint you though."

"What do you need me to do?"

"Just let me take a picture of you. Then I can prep the canvas. Whenever you can come—just come. If you want to help me."

"I want to help you. I just have to be careful since my dad watches me so closely. The other day he warned me again about being out alone and again asked me if I had any guy friends."

"What did you tell him?" I ask, curiously.

"About what?"

"About you having any guy friends."

"I told him no."

"If you told him that you are with someone what will he do?"

"I don't know. But I know that he will get really upset."

"More upset than me if I found out that you and I can't be together?"

Seeing her try to conceal the faintest expression of discontent I quickly turn her to me and comfort her with my gentle kiss.

"I think about you all of the time. Everyday I wake up wishing that you were lying next to me, just so that I can watch you exist in a place where you are loved. And I long for your warmth. And I want to watch you brush your teeth before bed and see you get dressed in the morning. And more than just a phone call away," I then wholeheartedly tell her.

"I want the same things that you do. But we just barely met," she tells me, touching my hand on the sofa in front of the bookshelf. "You don't understand what it's like growing up in my home. You don't understand how my family thinks and what our traditions are like. I want to be with you too. . . . I guess I'm just afraid."

"I don't understand why you would be afraid," I then gently tell her.

"I just know that my dad would never forgive me. And he might even do something terrible if I were to tell him that I am in love with you."

"What if you had to choose?"

"What do you mean?" she then pretends to not understand.

"You know what I mean. . . . If you had to choose between being with me, or letting your parents dictate your future, who would you choose?"

47

"I don't want to choose. And even if I did my father would probably kill us both."

Listening to how afraid Mahru really is gives me a clearer understanding of what her and I are dealing with. A little startled by what she said I decide to lighten up our conversation a bit.

"Well then let him kill me. Because I would die for you," I then quickly tell her, reaching for her smooth precious lips that carefully open up to me as soon as I reach for them.

"If you keep talking to me like that I might have to come and see you right after school," she says to me with a smile.

"I'll see you after school then," I tell her, doubtful, hearing her voice become calm and tender from the glow of our kiss.

"I can't actually come."

"Why not?"

"My dad will be home," she says, seeing the disappointment surface on my face. Religion then finds its way into our conversation after a strange and awkward silence is pushed between us.

"So you know that I am Muslim, right? What about you? Are you a part of any religion or house of worship?"

"No. . . . Well I grew up Orthodox Christian. And then my grandma has some Cherokee blood. But very little. Enough that my mom kept Native American art and things of antiquity scattered around the house growing up. And what we had lying around the house eventually lead me to be curious of other beliefs and ways of thinking."

"Like what?"

"Like Buddhism, Epicurism, Dao De Jing. . . . Even Islam."

"And what do you know about Islam?"

"I know Muhammad was illiterate and the Quran compiled 20 years after he died. I know Allat, the Arabian moon goddess, has been worshipped for far longer than Allah. The Islamic star and crescent is feminine. And more than 100 years after Muhammad's death women were denied an education after men and women had read side by side in the days of Muhammad. After the Quran was written women were segregated from men by a screen and relegated to the back of the mosque. Later, women were only allowed to pray when the men were not present. Some even prevented women from entering mosques altogether. In the days of Muhammad, men and women prayed together in mosques. And men come out of women do they not? Just like everything comes out of the earth."

"I can see that. Just like it doesn't say in the Qur'an that a woman cannot go out of her house or go shopping. And I don't believe the Qur'an itself mandates that women wear hijab or whatever. In my country the men are always telling the women how to live and how to dress."

"Religion also comes from the word "religare," a Latin verb that means to bind down, hold back by tying, or to thwart from forward progress."

"Where did you learn all this?" she asks disconcertingly.

"My uncle taught history and Latin here at the university. Not anymore though. He gives me books. He says I can't know where I'm going if I don't know where I've been."

"Your uncle Louis? Who you live with now?"

"Yeah. . . . And this past year I have just wanted to be myself. And I feel like reading helps me. I want to be an independent thinker and to one day be more environmentally proactive. My focus and study here is natural stability. And if it means getting rid of, making unfashionable, or antiquated, traditions, laws, governing bodies, or whatever, and picking apart the fundamental flaws that perpetuate our destructive behaviors and beliefs, then for the betterment of preserving the natural world . . . I just think religion divides and creates angry people. And I think all holy books have holes in them. I would rather people share, love, and heal this one earth that we have to be stewards of. Changing the negative impact that humans have on the planet is more important to me. And I believe that a lot of people pretend to care. And I also believe that we are here to live. Not to kill each other in the name of a holy book or for political struggle. People should feel connected to each other, with love, tolerance, respect, and understanding. Breathe, love, sing, dance and live. . . . I love loving you. I love exercise and getting oxygen to my brain. I love to move my body, perfecting my physical strength, mental, and spiritual body. I love natural sounds like rain, oceans, and streams. And I love feeling free. And I like you. . . . That's my religion," I smile.

"I like that you like me. . . . I've never met anyone like you before."

"I've never met anyone like you."

"I know it's a silly question . . . but why do you care so much about the environment?"

"I care about this one earth home and planet that we have to live on, because if likened to how we use our own body, environment is irrefutably the difference between, say, cancer and optimal health. And which is a better way to live? I mean you have Fukushima and needlessly killing the whales who feed the phytoplankton that give the earth more oxygen than the rainforests. Rainforests that they are cutting down everyday. I believe that the earth cannot sustain where we are heading."

"Do you think there is a God?" Mahru then asks.

"I think time and space infinite is contained in a spec of dust on the wing of a butterfly. And like the Vedas say, if there is a god, he would be like you or me and not know that he or she is god. God to me is energy. Electricity and magnetism. Sexual, like nature. Alúna."

Liking what I said and loving the way that I say it Mahru leans in closer for a kiss. But as the office door handle turns she withdraws to a solitary posture pretending to be focused on something else.

To our relief, Madge, then walks in smiling at us both as if we are all old friends. Perceptive, hushed, and subtle Madge watches me with absolute intrigue. Just as kind and beautiful, they are both the same height with the same hair, same eyes, but no identical resemblance between the two of them. And different from the rest of her family, Madge, is the only one even kind to the idea of her sister being fond of me. She can also never seem to stop watching me with curious eyes. Seeing them together I wonder if it will ever be possible to one day call them my family. And more and more I wonder how the future will unfold as I imagine all that is perfectly absurd.

"You know Lucius is a very good writer," Mahru tells Madge.

"Yeah, I know. . . . Why don't you write something right now? Just so that we can see you do it. Here. . . . Take this pencil," Madge then says, as if to prove that I can do it.

"Okay," I tell Madge, looking at Mahru's beautiful face before focusing.

Mahru tries to tell me that I do not have to do it before she is interrupted by her sister.

Moving the pencil across the paper, I am fascinated by the two of them. They are both radiant. Mahru, most of all. And there is no argument about me being unquestionably handsome as they quietly talk to each other, both watching me.

Mahru seems only positively satisfied as she sits close to me. Her heart rages as I can still feel her watching me. As my adrenalin and focus peeks the words all fall into my lap. "Every quirk, nervousness, and expression bestows a fondness. . . ."

Handing my notebook to Mahru, she asks, "You're already done? Has it

CHAPTER FIVE

even been five minutes?"

I look at her as if to have lost all track of time.

"Hurry! Read it to me!" Madge tells Mahru.

> *Dark Princess of the mother with eyes that can cast a spell*
> *making me believe that I have been lifted from hell*
> *more stunning than Nefertiti*
> *you must see her to believe me*
> *I conjure my inner genie*
> *and ask for her love to free me*
> *as radiant as the sun her physique that of a goddess*
> *every quirk, nervousness, and expression bestows a fondness*
> *luminous eyes that harbor a caring spirit*
> *more breathtaking than sun rays caressing the waves of a haunting*
> *image*

At first there is a silence as Madge smiles at Mahru. Sucking her cheek Mahru then puckers her lips with a grin as she stares right at me. Sitting back slouched into the brown Chesterfield sofa she then smiles that beautiful smile.

"You're really good," Madge tells me, her eyes wide and direct, smiling, and now backing away to give her sister some space. "Mahru, I'll see you later."

"Okay, bye."

"Thank you," I tell Madge.

Mahru reaches over and places her hand inside of mine. Carefully, I lift her hands, unfolding her fingers to where they touch my face and lips before gently placing them back down at my side.

"I agree with my sister. You are really good with words. And when you are in bed with me . . . ."

Nodding my head I confide, "I am wild about you?"

"I know," Mahru tells me softly.

Later wrapping up in Mrs. Graham's Earth and Ocean Sciences class, I surprisingly catch Mahru standing right outside the doorway in the hall. Her black curls are partly veiled by her watercolor scarf with birds and botanicals forming a painterly tableau. Remembering Mahru telling me that she does not wish to be seen with me I hang back.

Waiting inside for everyone to leave the room I put my notes in my drawstring bag as Mahru carefully walks closer towards me. Without breaking eye contact she then presses herself inside of my gentle grip feeling my hands.

Looking up at me with those eyes I feel myself trembling from the thrill of her standing so close.

"Thank you for being my friend," she tells me, leaning inward to softly kiss my lips.

"Thank you for being mine," I smile back.

"You have the most beautiful smile," she then tells me, before casually walking back to the doorway entrance, her eyes turning to catch me once more as she disappears around the corner.

Feeling like the downy parachutes from a dandelion catching in the wind, I slide my bag around my shoulders, desperately wanting to believe that she might someday put her faith in me and still be close to her family. From star dust created beyond the stellar vaults of heaven, her character is subtle and beauty exquisite. I can still see her French elbow-sleeves and scoop neck with the Renaissance autumn leaves, berries, and birds on black. Dazzled by her Asian floral pants with the gold patinaed blossoms all of the way down to her black ankle strap sandals. From the first day that we met I have prepared myself to be patient and to wait for her for as long as it takes.

After school I decided to pick up some new art supplies to resuscitate this old hobby of mine. And being a curious dilettante I know will inspire in me other things when I am not working for Louis. And I know that if anyone saw my other work that they would know that managing websites could never be exactly exciting work for someone like me.

Later, after catching up with an entire line of web merchandise, and watching the evening sun settle, I realize that I do not want to trouble Mahru too much incase her dad is home. And so I refrain from texting her. But eventually as the sun begins to set I become more anxious, especially as the sky becomes black.

Waiting for midnight to creep closer I finally decide to text Mahru, hoping that her dad is already in bed.

Hey! Will I be seeing you again soon? Are you going to call me tonight? I would love to hear from you. Always I think of awakening your innate spiritual nature, immersed in both attraction and pleasure, loving you as would fawn and fairy. I am eager to enchant you and to take you to heights unbeknownst to you. To sail amongst the stars free until life permits us to again experience such tender moments as this. To grant you what every man should know that a woman needs. And what you want. Just between us. To gorge ourselves of that spiritual sexual food that we crave and until we can again quench this wild thirst. Are you afraid to enjoy me the way that I already enjoy you? Anyways goodnight. Sorry it's late.

"How about Thursday?" she quickly texts back. My phone then begins ringing.

"Hey. . . . What about Thursday," she asks.

"I am yours—you do not have to ask. Do with me as you please. I am here waiting for you. And I will wait for you for as long as it takes."

"Would you wait an entire millennium?" she relievedly asks.

"I would wait an entire millennium if it meant being with you."

"Yeah but we'd both be dead by then. What do you say to that?"

"It doesn't matter—I would still wait," I tell her.

"Well, lucky for you I don't intend to make you wait that long. All that I think about all of the time is seeing you again too. And anyways how can I say no to you when you send me text messages like that?"

"Sneak out of your house tonight and come and see me," I tell Mahru, in love with her absolutely adorable accent.

"I can't do that," she continues to be playful.

"Well then, whenever you can. I just wish that I was holding you in my arms right now. All that I want in this life is you. You could come live here with me and we will never leave our bed."

"I want to hold you in my arms too."

"Then come and see me tomorrow."

"Thursday. I'll come at five. Okay?"

"Okay," I tell her.

Mahru stays up with me, listening to the sweet sound of my voice as she keeps her eyes closed. And imagining what it must feel like waking up in my arms she gradually grows more tired. Imagining as she travels from one fantasy to another. Replying with only sweet simple words between full single sentences.

Candidly and poetically I describe my undying love and what it was like the first time that I saw her look at me. Doing most of the talking, Mahru can only come to mutter a few words at a time, aware that she is almost asleep.

Softly singing *Place To Be* and *Man In A Shed*, Mahru falls asleep with her phone still lying next to her face. Placing my phone on speaker I listen for a moment to the soft sound of her breathing in dreams.

Whispering to her goodnight and ending our call I am comforted by this peace that she gives me. It is a comfort in knowing that she has given her heart to me even when she could very well be torn from me. Knowing that she is always thinking of me as I think of her.

Gazing at the moon before shutting my eyes, I pray that our love will never be burned down by any who do not wish to understand its endless meaning. And I pray and wish that our great love with time will prove its worth to all who do shun its integrity. Sincerely asking that our love be forever displayed across the shining halls of heaven where the light of love between these two hearts can be given safe haven.

TENDER LOVE

CHAPTER SIX

Two moons and five phone calls later Mahru manages to sneak out of the house after her father leaves for work.

After school I patiently wait for Mahru at the guest house. Too excited to read or work on anything else I sit by the window.

Wondering if Mahru will actually come I get up to prepare a bowl of sweet cherries with some cantaloupe. Wiping the stems and the rinds off of my cutting board my phone then rings.

"Hey—what's up?" Mahru asks, trying to control the happiness that consumes her whenever she speaks to me.

"Hey! Just waiting for you," I tell her, delighted.

"I'm walking up to your door right now," she then says, me hearing her car door shut over the phone as I then peek outside my window.

"K. . . ."

Opening my door I see her almost at my doorstep with a brown paper bag in her arms. Smiling at me in her black hand-washed bateau neck and petite white leggings I invite her inside.

"Hey," she says, gently putting her arm around me and sharing with me that smile that is drawn from her whenever I am near.

Gently kissing her, I take the bag and set it on the counter. Lifting her up inside of my arms she is aglow with the kind of joy that she so effortlessly gives me.

"I want you to try this Egyptian food that I brought," she then insists, sitting next to me while I lay on the sofa. Agreeing to a taste, she then carefully covers a slice of her Egyptian bread with halva, a sesame spread marbled with little pieces of pistachio.

Eager to see my reaction she feeds it to me. Tasting its soft nutty flavor with surprise, I mutter "Mmmmm."

"It's good right?"

Mahru moves it closer to my mouth again. I take a second bite before she takes the third.

"It's good . . ." I confirm, nodding my head while chewing. "How long do you think you can stay?" I then ask, consuming the rest of it from her hand.

"Only for a few hours," she says, leaning into me and seizing that one kiss that she dreams of.

Taking the plate and placing it on the coffee table, she then asks, "Is there maybe someone else that you love other than me?" circumspectly pretending to be the victim of her circumstance as she taunts a serious question with her illumined gaze. "I mean, are you sure that you don't want someone else?"

"No, I don't want someone else," I tell Mahru, looking into her eyes to tell her that she is all that I love.

"Is there anything else you want to ask me?" I then ask, carefully brushing her hair away from her face.

"No," she answers, pulling my face closer to hers.

"I've missed you," she then says, grinning her beautiful smile.

"I miss you every second that you are not with me."

"Well I'm here now," she says softly.

Sitting on top of me she presses her sweltering body into mine, displaying her affections with her body and mouth. Holding her closer to me she brushes my face with her hands before offering her precious lips. Stroking my neck and chest her arms reach over top of my head as she quivers with rapture and the breaking of bodily tension.

Pressing my lips to hers I carefully pull her shirt over her head and loosen her lace push-up bra as she squirms for me with anticipation. Working my shirt loose she unties my white linen shorts freeing my pressure-building bulge underneath.

Quickly finding her way into my bed every part of me belongs to her as I become fascinated by her all over again. Drawing her legs behind me I heal her heart. The curves of her body move in ways that challenge and excite me. Her

CHAPTER SIX

hips move up and down as if her slender figure is sliding over a uneven terrain.

Watching her desperate and itching to feel me reach the middle of her, she grabs ahold of me, pulling and tugging with her desire for me to awaken her spirit.

Pressing up against her in a raging fire that barley reaches her lips I take her to the farthest isles of the sea and to all the ends of the earth with each motion and placement of applying myself to her. She gives herself to me here in this moment where heaven reveals itself. And heaven exists only within her as she fuels its ability to reach out and touch me, safe inside of her everlasting love.

Holding her close I see that her love is what holds me still—caring not for the potential fact that my heart might crumble before tomorrow. I cover up this feeling that I have of losing her even though I want to believe that I know her all too well. This lingering pain I try to conceal when she sees it torturing me. And as strong as our love is I know I can be nowhere but with her here and now.

Every part of her trembles and shakes as I taste her lower body. Gently rocking my lips back and forth from below her waist towards her neck I stop at everything that there is for me to take notice of as if time is meaningless. Time with her being all that is precious relishing each and every destination on her womanly map in the same way that the bee is attracted to each flower. The very touch of her body exists as the center to my own existence. Worshiping her I fuel her as she does the same to me. Our hands and arms move creating a slow dance that is prurient inside of this serene bliss. I count each breath as if each breath were a person of understanding and reasoning. She is my sun that rises and sets. She is the spiritual mortar that seals my gaping wounds.

Drawing four fingers up the sides of her stomach my hands create an invisible wave that sounds beneath her skin. Molding her torso every which way as if it were clay for me to experiment I study the lines of her iridescent form flowing in a rhythmic beauty that fascinates me into this fixation. My finger circles around the rim of her belly button as if to enjoy the sounds that might come from a crystal glass. Her every touch absorbs my ability to discern thought as I become rested in this feeling of absolute ecstasy. Even life without her I know would indefinitely destroy me—having solemnly delivered my spirit to this angel that slips down from heaven just to be with me.

Holding Mahru in my arms makes me feel young and makes me feel old. And here there seems to be no question as to how strong our love is and always will be. Reaching for her face both my hands caress her above the eyes before drawing a single finger down the side of her face in close examination of her perfect beauty. She takes each breath in congruence to my every touch. Holding her close to me I follow the main artery reaching up into her brain cavity, ever so gently grabbing a hold of her shape with each amalgamating crimp of my lip's kiss. Her honeyed lips overlap in a mesmerizing sequence of twists and turns defining all of what nature is within this gravitating romance. Beautifully naked in a sciatic squirm of innate belonging her igneous hourglass-like figure curls up against mine in an aqueous and liquescent manner.

Tightly entwined in the salacious magnitude of this yearning bachata her second nature becomes aware of herself in me and I in her. Unashamed she woos me with her altruism and childlike glow. Gliding over the emollient ewer of her extricating kiss our hearts conjoin in this luminescent rectitude of irrepressible euphoria. Sketching down her solar plexus by my touch abreast we bask in the bounteous espy of everlasting jubilance. When we kiss it's as if we are dancing in the serene existence of Mother Nature's melody. Her slender arms and hands revolve around my face and shoulders with an enchanting gentleness like gracious fireflies gleaming against the starry dusk of a fervid fantasia.

The restlessness of our ravenous appetence distends into a fascination of poised determination. My lips again sift down the caramel facet of her goddess-like fortune. In a fervently dexterous and sinuous groom of pulsating fusion my hands corrugate down and up her soft round buttocks utterly satisfying my lady's love. Down the fibonaccious curves of her gluteus derrière my lingam inches deep inside of her, she carefully swallowing me whole with that warm slippery opening between her thighs. Curling my nerves with her suctioning rhythm and flow I watch myself reappear and disappear inside of her. Launching between the strait of her isthmus towards the Sierra Nevada I cause the ravine of her chasm to quake like the flitting of a cello. The sensation of her medicinally efficacious touch clutches me with a servile verve of wondrous amour. Flowing passed the brim of our firmamental love she now abides with me in the au jus loosening of her fluid fusillade.

Various textures surface from the body after an intense and hypnotic rubato that has left us cradled here together in this sensual wonderland. We are as the sizzling sun and its evanescent vapor that has found itself small and susceptible underneath the frondescence of a dripping rain.

Taking a deep breath her small fingers reach out and strum down the virile colonnade of my detailed abdomen. The gradual and immeasurable placement of our love thoroughly nourishes our unalterable existence—freeing our spirits from this destructive mentality of mortality.

Fastened to her bosom while advancing over her creamy quadriceps we pivot in an andante rendition of equilibrial alignment. Having her beside me to feed upon my presence fortifies me, lifting me to that highest altitude where she continues to take haven in me with all of her mind, body, and soul.

Traveling up the collum of her deified individuality, I inquire for myself this intimate and evident expression that exceeds in those eyes a pronounced crooning of pianissimo. Gracefully I draw my attention down the formation of her elegant thighs imbedding the anesthesias of pressure to revive her from this worn state of survival, survival being the distance and deterioration between the soul and its counterpart. Because when my hands touch her body I know that I am responsible for alleviating the effects of this distance that suffers the heart. And I am responsible because I am in love with her. And to this responsibility I know that I will never be a stranger, solemnly declaring myself as the one part of her that will never weaken. She is the bird compass to my dry lips and pathless journey. And I am all that she has here and now, to whom her spirit will regenerate by the nurturing of our tender love. And calling her my dear or my darling will never satisfy the meaning or depth of our emotion. It is simply in the way that I look at her that overwhelmingly redefines all meaning or expression. Her unbroken smile is to me all evidence of this mesmerizing language that is roused by the red tantric skill and by all extrasensory perception. And equally sensual to what is sexual, all of her mind, body, and soul is to me the one thing that I truly find inescapably and indescribably exquisite. Every inch of her inside and out so mysterious. Like the burning sun that you can rarely see in that smoke-filled sky. Like the beauty of an endless desert.

Taking from the palette of my pellucid imagination I now make physical that breathtaking summit that lies beyond what most are capable of reaching. Consummated by the feverish sensuality of our love her stellular features emanate from the synergy of our biding ananda, feeling all that is visceral whispering to me and here where there is no greater power. And I surrender myself to her here in this place where god does reveal herself and where love can love truly. Our love existing alongside the upholdment of an evolving energy that abstains from becoming dim—even under this trying and cautionary circumstance. Her tantalizing indulgence through ebb and tide enthralls my curiosity, even as she holds me so quiet and still. Undressed and undone we are unnamed in the scheme of all that men work for, hidden away here in this place where we belong to god instead of men.

Rested alongside of her hindmost and elegant torso her lush curly head lies carefully against my arm as her lovely curls partially cover her gorgeous smile. And I watch her stare back into my soul as her long black hair reaches out across my shoulders and face.

Floating down the vale of my lover's sylphscape I advance her with the ruminating suction of my lips as if I were au courant in the art of human cartography. Her fingers slide through my golden locks with that same deliverance that comes from navigating the back of a wild horse—again to the place of her unrest.

Like the sherpa who climbs to the very top to experience that wonderment of escape her love speaks to me with that calm gentle whisper. Here the color of her skin stands vibrant against those dark curls that fall over her immaculate figure.

Gathering her against the fulcrum of our love I introduce every part of me to her again. She stops to adore my lips before I seal my kiss to her stomach. And she surrenders all of herself to me.

Combing her fingers through me as I complement her body, she seduces me, rubbing her soft warm yoni with more saliva, again achieving Shangri-la as my tongue skates inside the opening of her vesica pisces, releasing her divine nectar.

As the sky slowly begins to darken its shade of color the night continues to stay alive with all of the many colors living and breathing underneath it—and all beneath the warmth of a gentle darkness.

As our time together comes closer to an end Mahru playfully exhibits an Egyptian dance that requires an artful and fluid motion of the hips, arms, and wrists, as she moves over top of me. Taking considerable pride in conveying to me the movements that she has acquired as a practitioner of dance she gestures her arms and hands alongside of her body and face. Watching her being abundantly full of this immense energy brings me to gaze at all that she does carry inside of her heart. From her smiling laughs to the plentiful kisses that sustain her unabated love—her ahava. And never have I witnessed anything so lovely and divine as Mahru. And almost dissociated from the rest of the world whenever she is with me.

"I've never seen anything more enchanting," I proclaim, as Mahru crashes back into me—blushing because I have given her complement.

CHAPTER SIX

Feeling her warmth so close to me I still cannot help thinking about how strange it is that she will not permit me to meet her family. And I think about the potential danger and risk with all that is not allowed.

Watching her become aware of the time I encounter a slight discomfort that I can almost see in her eyes, and what she knows too but hides, seeing in those jewels of hers only the fear of what her father will do if he ever finds out. Still she finds a way to taste my lips and comes right back to me, here and now burying myself into her body and chest, like taking shelter in the hollow of a tree that rescues me from the storm.

Catching sight of the clock once more Mahru regretfully withdraws from me her warm embrace as she turns to sit up. Knowing that her mom and dad will be home soon Mahru insists that it is now time for her to leave, it already being clear to me that her simply speaking to me in public is enough to get her scolded or lectured. Sensing so strong her fear over what she knows is punishable I find that my only reason for wanting her to go is so that she does not get into trouble. Sensing a stiff consequence hiding behind her darkling eyes I see that she could very well be left defenseless should her dad discover where she was. Still her meeting here with me in my bed our love does prevail. And we remind each other that we are still human and that the heart is far more powerful than some vappous law or religious precept.

"It's okay—I'll be right here waiting for you to call me," I tell Mahru.

"I love you," she then tells me, her words being sound to my ears like the scent of sweet nectar to the first flying creature introduced to spring.

"I love you too."

Kissing me again Mahru tells me that she has to leave. "I have to," she says, unbearably. "I don't want my parents wondering where I am."

Feeling a slight disappointment in my heart I try not to look at her with what I am thinking, but instead I get up to try and help her get dressed.

"I will come back."

"I know," I tell her.

Escorting Mahru to her truck she still clings to me with an unyielding fixation. Kissing her goodbye even feels effortless as hard as it is for me to see her go.

Opening her truck door for her to be seated inside I then lean in with the door still propped open.

"I forgot to take your picture today."

"I think that I can come over tomorrow," she immediately smiles, almost forgetting that she is supposed to be nervous as she prepares to head home.

"You are the greatest most beautiful thing that has ever happened to me," I then tell Mahru, continuing to wonder what it is that makes her still so mysterious, and curious as to why she is not much for words, even though a part of me seems to already know why.

Kissing Mahru on her head she then starts up her car.

"I have to go now," she kindly whispers, pushing one of my golden curls away from my face.

"I know. . . ."

Being kind to her wish I again kiss the grenadine from her petaled lips as she receives my love with absolutely all that is left of her.

"I'm sorry," she says.

"It's okay. . . . Just come back to me."

"I will," Mahru smiles.

Standing up to close her truck door she rolls down the window for me to again lean inside. Kissing my lips goodbye she carefully then backs out of the driveway.

Watching Mahru drive away happy still does not ease my concern as I continue to worry about her. And I let her go with a smile and without barraging her with the burdensome reminder of her circumstance. And knowing that I can never *make* any decisions for her, I also still can't help but wonder if it is even possible to be brought into her family's respects. Feeling this constant tension like I could lose her at any turn I even feel now my heart punching through my chest for fear of letting her drive away. Pacing because of how all of this seems so silly to me really—this difficulty that we face. But still it is obvious to me that whatever she is dealing with at home is very real. Only hoping and wishing that it will not be too long before she decides what she wants. And from what I think that I understand I even wonder if a sort of rescue is what she needs.

Stepping back inside of my quaint guesthouse and noticing many of my windows cracked, I naturally then seek to escape the slight chill lingering in the night air. Feeling more responsible for her than I have ever felt before I can only seem to fear now what will happen to us. But at the same time I am still filled with this unimaginable joy that comes from me loving her.

Before I can climb back into my cozy bed to rest, Mahru calls me, conversing with her sweet convictions as she reassures me of her most sincere love, speaking softly to me like she does when she is lying next to me.

"Sorry about that. I didn't mean to keep you waiting."

"No—it's okay. Can you stay on the phone long?"

"No. I can't. My mother is asking me to help her to get some things ready for her friend's reception. Then I have to go and pick up my brother who stayed over at his friend's house last night."

"But maybe we can talk later."

"I'd like that. Maybe after I help my mom."

"Okay. Just be careful out there driving while it's wet."

"I will. I gotta go. I'll talk to you soon, okay."

"Okay," I tell Mahru, trying not to press her with my feelings of wanting her so badly.

"Bye," she says, her voice quietly slipping away from my ears.

After she hangs up I sit and stare out of my window, hoping to catch light of something that I hadn't before, sitting and wondering how we will break this cultural binding that lays hammer and nail to this wall that keeps us apart.

Lost in a forest of thoughts I then quickly find myself asleep in bed with all of the lights still on. Even with the ceiling bulbs shining through the blood of my eyelids all I can see is black as the night willow again hangs her head. And I sleep wondering when I will see her again, and wondering how much of her voice I will get to hear before the weekend is over.

BODY AND COLOR
CHAPTER SEVEN

As the satiable sway of summer begins to tuck itself into hiding I wake up and look out of my east-facing window. Noticing a blinding light hitting the tops of the trees all things beautiful then appear to me and my mind sees her. I then anticipate the moment when she will again be in my arms and under this spell that I cast for only her.

Clasping the short hairs on my face I turn to my CD player on my bookshelf to play something. *Thinking Of A Place* by The War On Drugs plays as I stand up to grab a t-shirt from inside of my master dresser. Readying myself for another day of mostly morning classes her face and her voice is still all that I can see and hear.

Two classes and an ear-full of constant lecturing later and it finally becomes time to take a break before sitting in on my Earth and Ocean Sciences class.

Moving up Main Mall and east on Memorial Road I try to keep an eye out for Mahru's brother, Malik, having only seen his handsome picture once before on her phone—and on my laptop when she pulled up his profile on the roster for the UBC soccer team.

Wondering if I am feeling a little bit paranoid I advance closer to the student services building where she is usually inside helping students or completing class assignments.

Opening the south office door I find Mahru sitting quietly inside.

"Hey," she says, softly, with a sweet longing for me in her voice.

CHAPTER SEVEN

"This morning I was reading some of your poems that you gave me. They're all so beautiful. I wish that I could give you something special like that," she says, me catching the raw emotion that almost tries to slip from her voice, feeling my heart bend just a little to the very sound of her.

"You give me everything just letting me listen to you—just hearing you speak to me. And every time that you look at me with those eyes I wonder how I'll ever be able to repay you. You have no idea what you mean to me," I return, unfeigned in speech.

"I want to kiss you and rub my face all over your naked body."

"Come over then after you get out of class," I tell Mahru, sitting beside her on the sofa as I twist one of my golden curls from my head.

"I can follow you home after I finish up at the Food, Nutrition and Health Building, 2205 East Mall. I should be ready to leave at about two-thirty."

"And then I can kiss you and rub my face all over your naked body."

"How can I resist you when you are so beautiful to me?" she blushes, gently touching the tips of my fingers as she becomes inwardly tormented that she can never say no to me.

"Am I always beautiful to you?"

"Yes. . . . Always," Mahru smiles, feeling all kinds of thoughts arouse in her mind. "So you can't wait to see me naked again, huh?" she continues, more than confident behind that magnificent grin.

"Seeing you naked is all I ever care to think about," I smile.

"Oh yeah?" she says, looking a little nervous, her eyes still filled with a love that trembles with affection.

"I just realized too that I don't have to be home until later tonight. I will be all yours. At least for a little while."

"So do you want to follow me out from the parking lot?"

"Yes, I do," she says.

Leaving the Earth Sciences Building a few minutes early, and only one block from where she is, I tell myself that I am going to get to my car first. Only I am surprised to already see Mahru standing outside of her old safari truck, smiling and leaning against her tailgate that stands a faded sea tortoise color in her white jeans with her legs crossed.

Quickly pushing through the lot and tapping the horn Mahru pulls out behind me. Watching her in my rearview we then manage to squeeze out of the parking lot before the other hurried students block the exit.

Moving down the road I continue to watch Mahru in my mirrors. The thrill of her love follows close behind, and how much in love she is I can tell by her smile when she stops at the light right behind me.

Pulling up through my driveway to park behind the main house Mahru then gets out.

Smelling the scented evergreens and the late blooms behind her truck I study her radiant glow as she steps closer to me. Feeling me kiss her lips so delicately as she reaches under my shirt to touch my bare skin she then follows me into the guesthouse.

Removing her light tan cardigan inside Mahru then helps herself to the grapes and cherries prepared on the counter. Lifting her up off the ground and into my arms I then carefully place Mahru onto the sofa. Kissing her as she feels her fingers move through my hair I feel my entire body levitate. Tasting her mouth once more I then hop up from the sofa to grab a handful of juicy grapes that enter my mouth all at once.

"Hey! Where are you going?" she exclaims.

And then just as quickly as I leave the room, I return, adjusting the settings on my Canon Mark III.

"I don't want to forget this," I tell Mahru, showing her the camera in my hand.

"What do you want me to do?"

"Let me take your shoes off. The quicker I can get your picture the more time we can have together."

Following me while eating her grapes, I remove her fawn-colored long sleeve and white bootcut jeans to attach something more lengthy to her elegant form.

Reaching behind Mahru to undo her lace camisole I kiss her before removing her under garment. She assists me in putting her hair up to help balance her many ravishing features. Playfully talking with her mouth full I assemble her to be my pastiche from what few classic materials that complement her dishabilled figure. Not frontally naked the long piece of dark fabric that falls down to the floor is fixed to her. Adjusting the lines in the fabric she then leans in for me to kiss her succulent lips.

"Will you take your clothes off now?" Mahru asks.

Giving a slightly diverting look I then remove my shirt from over my head, tossing it aside. "How's that?" I smile back.

"Much better. Now I am ready for my close up," She says, twisting in her

CHAPTER SEVEN

seat with a primed appetite that has nothing to do with her stomach.

"One more thing," I announce softly, bending myself near to her. Reaching for her lips ever so gently I ease her silent rage. It is a kiss that ignites with a passion orbiting around her rich demeanor. With my love I express a kiss that arranges her charming configuration, lifting her to that place beyond the meandering falls where she feels touched by all that she does know and love. "Now you're ready . . ." I tell her.

Mahru then adjusts her female shape to perfection after I take the time to show her what I am looking for. Directing her to emphasize placement and contour of her lines and limbs I watch with wonder as she handles each rearrangement with a natural knowing. She is rich with the kind of character and emotion that I could not have drawn from anyone else.

Seeing her face separate onto a screen an unsettling notion then whispers that what I hold in my hands may one day be all that I have left of her. Capturing her beautiful smile I begin to dread. And for a moment I dread that one day she may disappear.

Masking my uncomfortable intuition by changing my gear, I then switch to the Kodak Medalist that Louis loaned me. Determined to achieve the magical aftereffect of antiquity I then capture something that appears left from a time warp.

I then notice that everything about her can sometimes seem so unreal to me—both of us being a part of this tender bond and cultural complexity. I then think to myself that such love and such beauty should be named if not forever recognized as it is done here and now. And just like that something distinctly unique then appears, she giving evidence to the magnificence of majesty as if she were the daughter of Pharaoh himself.

"Okay, that's it! These look really good."

"Okay—good! Because I'm ready to let my hair down and take you upstairs," she then says, stepping down from the chair.

"C'mon," I tell Mahru, kissing her before taking down the ornamentation from her hair and upper body.

Seeing that she is a little bit cold I reach for a throw blanket to wrap around her. Setting both cameras on the table Mahru then follows me upstairs.

Walking passed my new paint table Mahru then becomes curious of the many little things spread across my shelving.

"So this is your paint?"

"Yeah. Sorry about the mess. I'm using the oil—not the acrylic. Do you want to try it?"

"No. I would just mess it up."

Taking a small piece of canvas and placing it in front of her I squeeze some fresh paint onto a clean palette. Stirring the paint a little I then place a Filbert brush inside of her hand before helping her to dip the tip into a circle of paint.

"The secret is to remain perfectly still," I tell Mahru, guiding her wet brush down the canvas before kissing her on her temple.

Dipping her finger into a dab of blue paint she then slowly draws a line down from my sternum. Making a mess of me her smile then lifts me to that place that I travel to when I am with her.

"What do you think?"

"It's beautiful," she tells me, watching to see if I will forgive her for getting me dirty.

Her throw then slips down beneath her ankles as she daringly reaches her hands inside of a storage tray that is filled with several different colors. Rubbing its substance between her fingers she then drags her colorful hands down from my shoulders to the rim of my drawstring. Gazing at me she then carefully unties my shorts with her hands covered in a triad of color.

Pulling her close by her hips I wait for Mahru to direct her eyes towards mine. Leaning into her beautifully naked body I kiss her succulent lips as she throws her legs around me, guiding me down to the wooden floor that is covered with a large sheet of canvas. Her lips cling to mine the way that a caterpillar clings to a limb, attaching her mouth to mine as she smears the paint from my body to hers.

"Wait. . . . More," she says, begging me to fill her in against the primed weaves of canvas that become filled with more color from our every movement.

Drawing my fingers down the lower portion of her neck and passed her stomach I kiss her once more. Guiding her hands down my chest with our fingers partly intertwined I drag them all of the way down in an oily residue that slides like a buttery spread. Her eyes then soften as her lips become that place where my heart can escape.

Bumping the standing table with my heel the paint tray falls to the floor as little spatters of paint graze our legs and feet. She finds refuge inside of my kiss as our bodies find one another. Naked and covered in color we move across the floor over a large sheet of canvas that captures every stir and motion. As paint and sweat smear into the fabric the memory of a free and spontaneous

CHAPTER SEVEN

creation begins as we surrender ourselves inside of a breathtaking kiss that warms me. Smudged into a colorful resin our love blossoms. Time is still and there is nothing that can take the place of this bond and this passion that continues to become more with each kiss.

Taken by the instinctive beauty of solicitude we both lead one another in poetic faith. Inside the splendor of each breath and each kiss we make all that there is to make. And our gentle love only intensifies with each passing hour.

"What a mess you are," Mahru finally tells me, lying over top of me as she smears the paint on my chest.

"I know," I tell her softly, pressing the oil between my thumbs and her hips as I gaze into that sky that is seen in the glimmer of her eyes.

"This paint is going to come off, right?" she then asks, catching her breath.

"It'll be a little difficult—but yeah."

"Well then . . . let's see if it will come off," she urges me.

"K," I mutter, closing my eyes and stealing a kiss from her as she basks beneath me in shades of blue and purple. I then seal her heart to mine with one more kiss. And then another, and another, and another, until I am sure that she is fully satisfied from the overwhelming exhilaration of our endless love.

Carefully helping Mahru to her feet she then points to the fabric on the floor that is marked with our print of affection. Leaning forward with her toes she then reaches up to kiss me. And with my lips I hand to her my heart along with every other part of me. Watching us run down the inside of her leg her lips are what persuade me the way the cool wind twirls and dances with the colors of fall. Her smile establishes a kindness in me. And she is the only one who I truly do love dearly with all of my heart.

"I wish that daylight didn't have to come between us."

"I love you," I then almost whisper, drawing strength from that feeling that I feel whenever she is near. "And I will always love you."

Drawing near to me as perhaps the most peaceful woman in existence I can still tell that she is afraid of loosening her arms of me. Entrenched in the irreversible bond of our kiss I then calm her precious spirit.

Wiping her tears away from her smile, I then pick Mahru up and carry her around the hall and into my white clawfoot tub. Carefully setting Mahru down inside I then grab several cotton rags from the bedroom. Filling the tub I then begin using almost as many rags as I have to remove as much paint from her body as I can.

"I'm sorry for making a mess," she says, looking at me with hopes that I will forgive her, forcing me to respond with only that which reveals to her just how darling she is to me.

Climbing into the tub Mahru then carefully helps remove the paint from my shoulders and arms, she creating the kind of memory that she will never forget as she wrings out her rags and washes me down.

Using only water the paint successfully loosens from her body and mine. The colors slip through my hands and fingers as I move across the canvas of her slender physique. Vibrant colors become more grey as they blend together, sliding off of her and into the drain. Gripping at her body has never felt so natural, almost sculptural like, gliding across the smoothness of the human medium that captivates me. Being attentive to every square inch of one another allows us to not suffer being unnoticed. And never have I seen another human being so relaxed and comfortable. Washing her entire body she too takes the initiative of making sure that I am washed clean as she feels for me and any dirty thing left clinging to me. My hands slip passed the ridges of her rib the way that moisture catches between the shapes that mark a turtles back. Her eyes watch me the way that nature studies her curious guest who seeks for himself the origin of his creation.

Asking Mahru if she is ready for me to shampoo her head, I then carefully lean her head back. Bathing her in my arms she then finds herself someplace else as she seemingly drifts in and out of consciousness. My hands gently rock between her curls as I work loose any paint that might have found its way into her thick head of hair. She arches her back, twisting her fingers inside of her hands that have become wrapped around me from behind. Sliding her hands down my thighs I rinse her wet hair with a warm pitcher of water.

Turning the water knobs off I then reach for a towel to dry her face and hair before I dry my own. Feeling confident that Mahru is ready for change, I then decide to ask something that I have never asked before.

"Marry me," I then almost whisper, pulling her towel tighter around her shoulders and legs as she sits in front of me in the tub. Noticing a moment of dead silence the mood suddenly changes.

Flattered and nervous, Mahru leans slightly forward as if to contemplate this dubious contingency. Carefully turning her face to me I then kiss her softly, she returning her love to me deep inside of a kiss that declares to me her unyielding obsession.

"I want you. And I want you to be happy," I tell Mahru.

She then smiles at me before almost nervously and defensively hesitating.

CHAPTER SEVEN

"You know that I want to marry you more than anything in the whole world," she says, looking at me with eyes that tell me that I still do not understand.

"Then come and live with me?"

"No—you still do not understand. I need you to understand that I *want* to marry you. But . . ." she tries to explain, holding on to this unsettling and unavoidable reality that is crushing her heart.

"But what?" I ask, almost hesitant as I wrap my arms around her before gently pressing my lips into her head.

"It's because of my parents, Lucius. More precisely my dad. And he still acts like we are in Egypt. And in Egypt, it is okay for a man to beat or whip his daughter, or rape and even murder his own wife. Once a man in our village killed his wife for sleeping with another man. The police held him for only two hours. Then they released him even though his prints were on the knife and her blood all over his hands and clothes. Women are even thrown into jail for being victims of rape. A woman who has been raped can also be killed by someone in her own family, just so her family's honor can be protected. This kind of thing happens all of the time in Egypt. In some places if a woman does not cover her face she can even be killed and nobody will say anything. And you can't keep expecting me to tell you again and again," she says, now letting the tears that she has been holding back spill from her eyes down her cheeks.

Turning Mahru around she lets me cradle her in my arms.

"Hey—everything is okay. . . . I'm sorry."

"Don't apologize for something that I did," she then tells me, with tears in her eyes. "This is all my fault—all of this. I distinctly warned you and told you about my family when we first met."

"You're right. You did tell me. And I didn't listen to you. But I am happy that I didn't listen. And forgive me for not knowing what to do or what to say. Just know that I love you. Just know that. . . . Okay," I tell Mahru, still holding on to her with my hidden agony as a tear then escapes me. "I will always love you, Mahru," I then say softly. "Near to you and far."

Pressing her face into mine her emotions turn inside of her as she squeezes my wrists. She makes no time for tears knowing that we can cry for as long as we want whenever we are away from each other.

Tending to her inner wounds I calm Mahru with a kiss that holds her so still. But lost in both fear and love the soul still feels disheartened.

Readily our insatiable romance builds momentum as I move her to my warm bed where a part of me wonders how I might conceal her wings to keep her from ascending into the stars. And I wonder how to disguise this angel to be seen rather as an earthly being and to keep her from being called away. And her smile still says all that she could ever say. And she has me in that way and I have her to thank because of it. And I am home in her love. And there is no place for me but in her arms.

An utter peace then consumes me from the feeling of her body resting gently between my legs, she stretching across my body and clinging to me with every fiber of her love. And it is here where the skies part and reveal all of eternity, making love the way that love was meant to be made.

Pushing her skinny fingers across my hands Mahru then looks over at the clock.

"Is it time?" I then ask, moving her hair from her eyes.

"No—it's not time. Don't worry. . . . Just hold me."

She once again becomes so still in thought as I twist her black curls between my fingers.

"I have been in love with every part of you since the first time that I laid eyes on you. Isn't that worth searching for—even if it takes lifetimes?" I then ask Mahru.

You are perfect," she nearly whispers, with soft eyes, gently touching my face. "That is what you are."

Kissing Mahru, she then kisses me back.

"Do you still want me?"

"Yes. I still want you," she returns, torn by me even asking the question.

"Okay," I whisper, sealing my lips to hers as she pulls my body closer.

"Do you still want to run away with me?" she then asks.

"Yes—I still want to run away with you. We can leave now if you like."

"You would do that for me?" she then nervously asks, hiding something else behind her smile.

"I would," I tell her.

Mahru then looks down. Trying to make it so that I can't see it she then almost seems hurt and confused about something that I have no possible way of interpreting. Shaking it from her she then smiles at me as if her wall of worry is impenetrable to prying eyes. Mahru then leans closer, reaching for my lips graciously and without pause.

Moving her fingers up my stomach she then turns me on like a switch as the energy from her touch moves through my whole body. Kissing my stomach while suspended her lips carry the kind of power that resides in mysterious medicines. Her mouth moves across my body as she pinches the backs of my thighs. With her careful lips she caresses me at the waist and moistens my aching tumescence. My composure breaks inside of her firm and gentle grip as I fall into her with all of my fears, frustrations, and love combined. Twisting withinside of her genial allure the thought of all foreign hostility fades.

Lying on her back her body perks up at me like the white lotus that reaches for the sun's love. My lips run over her silk skin like water drifting downstream. Gently coming into her with all of my love her kisses are filled with an incredible ability to give as her body merges into mine. The sound of relief escaping her lips commends my escape transcending me into the pureness of love's unseen realm. Feeling her take absolute pleasure in me my love consumes every part of her. Absorbed in and out of this wild spasm that takes control of me her urges then become steady. Her smile and her touch alone could render me completely defeated. Obsessed with the sheer taste of her I know that my appetite will never cease.

Taking a deep breath Mahru squeezes my arms tighter around her body before drawing her slender arms up around my face and neck, brushing me with her soft hands. Mahru turns to kiss me fervently and strategically as if to try and win my heart yet again. Feeling life enter me erodes all turmoil and confusion. And it is clear to me that heaven exists and only in her. The smell of her body and breath and the way that she looks at me seems all a dream. But I am wide awake in this dream and more in love than I am even able to fathom. And I feel appreciative, feeling so strong the need to protect her and everything that she is to me. If only she could cleave to me outside of these walls the way that she does when we are alone. Feeling that this love in my heart for her is immense and that there is no question in me whether or not it is real. Especially when the thought of her consumes me throughout every minute of the day.

Stroking her back from underneath the covers as she rests against me I take my turn watching the clock. And touching her body I lie inside of a calm that has never felt so still.

Another hour then feels like only minutes as I sadly realize that it is now time for her to leave.

"Hey. . . . It's time."

"Noooo," she mutters softly, rubbing her face into my chest.

Rolling onto my back Mahru then crawls on top of me one last time. Pressing her forehead into my chest she gently pulls my hair with disappointment and desperation. And making less eye contact with me the more quiet she becomes.

Sliding my clothes on I then watch her, wondering if having asked her to marry me makes her more wary of me. And as she puts her clothes back on I am desperate inside of myself to know what she is really feeling.

"Thank you," Mahru tells me, as I then help slide her arms into her cardigan sweater.

Slowly moving downstairs to open the front door I then quietly walk with Mahru to her truck as she feels for my gentle kiss to cherish. The sweetest look reveals in her eyes as she looks back at me. And then all of the sudden I see in her eyes a love that disguises her disturbance and discouragement.

The sound of her engine turning over is met with one more kiss before she then backs out of my driveway. And then the second that she is out of my sight I feel a painful aching in my heart.

Standing at the end of my driveway I question if this inner anguish is a reflection of what is true. Putting from me this slow and miserable death that seems so certain I then wonder when I will see her again. Still a part of me questions if I should have even met her. Something that I hate to think. Because imagining her gone I cannot even bear to comprehend.

Going back inside I immediately begin to backup my digital photographs of Mahru to my external hard drive. Afraid of potentially losing them I also know that the sooner they are printed the sooner that I can begin painting. And I know too that if I stay busy that I will not have time to think of this thing that troubles me. This thing that tears at the flesh of my heart in the black of night. This veiled devotion that is slave to some duress of tradition. This unnatural thing that suffers my heart from an unfamiliar and foreign land.

LATE OCTOBER
CHAPTER EIGHT

Four weeks later I begin to notice the many jack-o-lanterns on the doorsteps on my street. Warm leaves smother the wet black roads and perfectly hedged sidewalks. Pumpkin and baked apple permeate the crisp clean air. And Halloween is now only two weeks away.

The guesthouse has become the one place, aside from the admissions office, where Mahru can see me in secret. But only when her parents are not home. The in-between days that we spend apart are mostly filled with the passion of my written substance. And secret late night conversations over the phone create a longing to remain closer than ever before.

For the past few weeks now Mahru has fallen asleep almost every night to the sound of my voice. We try to keep each other awake from both sides of the phone. But of course the body eventually gives into sleep. And each day I know that the sun will again rise into the sky. And each night I think of her in my dreams. Each night recognizing that I usually sleep pretty well when the last thing that I hear is her sweet utterance.

Whether on campus or in town there is no place I can go where Mahru does not dwell on my mind. Simply knowing her is as if to at any moment look off into some distant sea that speaks to my soul's mind. The very thought of her slow-dancing voice curves down my spine with a sweet addiction for all that her love does embody. And Mahru knows me to be a simple man. And she knows that I can give her nothing except what I feel for her. Still she adores me and answers me with only a fondness.

Twice a week Mahru works with her mother, Ianna, who owns an upscale clothier boutique. On those two days Mahru helps with the inventory and marks price tags when she is not processing payments at the counter. The shop sits over in Fairview on Fourth Avenue and Maple Street. It is the building with the Haussmann-style stone and the large arch display windows in front. Just a ten-minute walk from Kitsilano Beach where you can see the mountains towering high above West End and downtown. The shop is full of high-end modest clothing just for women. But Mahru tells me that it is sometimes difficult working with her mom who can be almost snide to the point of embarrassment. Every time that the sun bathers peek in her shop sporting spaghetti strap tops and sexy denim shorts, her mom averts her gaze, expressing mild contempt with the customers. But Mahru tells me too that deep down her mom is sweeter than she lets on. Personally though I do not think that anyone should be pressured about how to dress. People are naturally sexual and even beautiful. And who can blame them for wanting to stay cool when the temperature in the summer is stifling?

A few times Mahru has poked and teased me about the guys who hit on her at school and at work. Kindly I remind her that they have absolutely every reason to try and talk to her. Besides how can they not marvel in the presence of all that is absolutely lovely and rare? Playfully demonstrating her cleverness and confidence Mahru tells me that I have a way with words. Still she tries to win me over even though she already holds the key to my heart. She adores me the way that I adore her. And she playfully accuses me of having many girlfriends—forcing me to provide her with a counter response that affirms otherwise. Everything that escapes her tongue challenges me. Her personality is filled with an unforthcoming zest that guards her loving sentiment. And most of the time she seems to know exactly what she wants. And her eyes will at times give her away. And in her eyes I can see that she has been waiting for me to find her. And the closer that I am to her the closer I feel to home. I only hope that she will one day take possession of what she desires most. If I am in fact what she desires.

Yesterday morning after discovering Mahru and Madge in the office lounge, Mahru later explained to me why Madge was wearing a uniform waistcoat and dress pants. Most weekends Madge helps Air Canada passengers as a wheelchair service agent at the airport. She works there four days a week before class when she is not helping her mom run the store. Mahru tells

CHAPTER EIGHT

me that Madge enjoys it. And from the looks I get from Madge at school I am pretty sure that she knows that her sister and I are having sex.

Everyday at school Mahru still focuses on getting the best grades so that she can potentially find herself in a solid career in her field of nutrition. Where I want to be five years from now is something that I am now contemplating myself which seems all so new and strange. But what I find even more strange is how we both seem to talk about everything except us. Everything we say to each other seems only meant for what is happening now. Never any mention or hopes of what might come later. Every time ignoring this nauseous intuition and gut fear that worries that there can be no future for us.

On and outside of campus I can never really seem to carry an interest in making any other friends. None except for Mahru. All conversation seems dull with my class and peers. And of course I am not permitted to speak about us to anyone. I can never show anyone even a picture of the woman who I am in love with. My beautiful Egyptian flower who I love to taste, smell, and feel in my arms.

When I am alone at home or out for a run or a walk I visualize those things that I believe will make me happy. And when I do I see only her. She is the sun peeking through the blinds at ninety degrees voicing cool air as a tease to come and wake me. My thoughts are of her the very moment my eyes awake to that light of morning. I think of her every minute of each day. And it eases my soul to know that my heart is with her even though I cannot hold her to me before she falls asleep. Still my dreams are besieged by the inevitable threat of what is at hand. And I think about the kind of family that Mahru comes from and how respectable her family is compared to mine. And it bothers me sometimes how different we are. And it bothers me only because it seems to be the one thing keeping her from embracing what she truly feels. But perhaps she feels truly indebted to her family in ways that I could never understand. And I wonder if her family could ever permit us to marry. If she will ever be free. But unfortunately I can only bring myself to fear the worst. And my only hope is to again be near to her before the weight of time suffers me anymore. And the more love we make the more I fool myself into believing that she is mine.

A CRY FOR HOME

CHAPTER NINE

The silent crunch of fall leaves grind underneath her tires as Mahru pulls into my driveway. Fiery reflections melt down the front of her windshield as she turns to park on the moss-cracked cement.

Watching her smile before her door opens I look up and get that feeling that I get and on such a clear day. The rudeneja of autumn is likened to that tender warmth that adorns her. And I keep buried the excitement that I feel as a part of my cool posturing act. Pretty sure that the look in my eyes can withhold no pretense.

As Mahru anxiously draws herself closer to me I instill that kiss that I can never stop longing to give. Tasting her lips never ceases to amaze me. And her loving lautitious lips are what make me forget this strange world that we live in.

Smiling back at Mahru my uncle then steps outside his backdoor in his short shorts and Birkenstocks with a garbage bag around his shoulder. Dark and muscly in his white v-neck Louis looks like he is tossing a napkin into the garbage.

Startled by the unexpected company Louis apologizes for having his earbuds in and approaches Mahru to be introduced. Stroking his beard with one hand he extends the other.

"It's finally a pleasure to meet you. I can now see why Lucius here is smitten by the mere sight of you," Louis says warmly, being nothing but kind to

CHAPTER NINE

this illusive lover who has captured my heart.

"Thank you. It's a pleasure meeting you," Mahru kindly acknowledges, taken by his warm candor.

"Mahru, my uncle Louis. My mom's brother," I introduce, watching her feel pleased and light by the warm welcome.

"A pleasure," he says again, extraordinarily in awe over her ability to brighten his entire morning.

"Mahru is going to hang out here with me for a little while before she goes to work. I can update those t-shirt ads after lunch if that's okay."

"Yeah that is fine. Thank you for doing that," giving me a fist bump instead of hugging me.

"Thank you," I tell Louis, seeing his smile appreciate the work that I do for him.

"Mahru. It was very nice meeting you. You're always welcome here. I'll catch you guys later," Louis says, making his way back to the main house.

Mahru lifts her hand to gesture goodbye as I feel myself being even more in love from the way in which she so gracefully exhibits herself.

"Your uncle is really nice."

"Yeah, he is a peaceful Buddha," I tell Mahru, grabbing her by the waist and meeting her with a kiss as we mosey into the guesthouse.

Shutting the door behind me as I remove my sandals I catch her biting lip with that beautiful smile. Kicking her shoes off she then warms my heart with another kiss.

"It is so nice being able to meet your family without being scolded or warned about spending time together. Being lectured about honor and sex."

"Because God is going to judge you right? And then hellfire and eternal torment," I retort, both of us moving onto the large leather sofa in front of the open window.

"Right. . . . You know before we moved here my dad told me that I would meet a lot of boys who will want to fall in love with me and marry me. And he told me to remember my education is the most important thing and that my family's honor is in my hands. But I think that it is even more ridiculous how so many women use sex, shame, and guilt all in the same sentence. What so female bodies are here to give pleasure as opposed to receiving it?" she says, disquieted, wrapping herself in my arms as she buries her face into me.

"It is your body and it is your life. You should be free to be who you are. And who you are is also your body. Free to feel the sun on your skin. Free to love who you choose to love. Free to choose what makes you happy."

"Muslim women should allow pleasure into our skin. The fluctuations and harmonies of our physical bodies do not bar us entry to spirituality and faith, but only remind us of our relationship with the divine," she freely argues, squeezing her arms down around me.

"*You are* divine. So loving, so intelligent. Absolutely divine," I smile, with a tender heart. "And I agree. We have all been intellectually, sexually, and spiritually repressed," I add, twirling her hair around my finger.

"People shouldn't ask if you feel guilty or if you prayed after you tell them that you had sex. I could never feel ashamed for having sex with you," she adds, gently pulling down on my shirt.

"Nor am I ashamed. And what we have is much more than just sex—to me. I am in love with every part of you. The goddess in you. Your very soul," I tell Mahru, touching my forehead to hers.

"I never imagined a man so in tune. So aware and awake. So beautiful," she happily expresses, stroking my face with her finger before tasting my kiss.

Feeling the nerves in my face quake and tremble my whole nervous system is alerted as if shy to the earth's most powerful substance. And only from a single kiss. Charmed I am by this single glowing flare of fire that is drawn to me. And witness to her warm touch and glowing smile that reveals all that is possible.

"A love that seems only fitting for gods," she reminds me.

"Speaking of gods and goddesses, I just finished a book," I smile. "It reveals goddess worship as the oldest standard for every culture on every continent going way back. Creation coming from women. Childbirth, fertility, the late harvest. The apples plump and the gardens overflowing, celebrating the harvest from the feminine womb of the earth. Showing all religions are pagan in origin with respect to the earth, The Great Mother. Most male deities originally being female deities. How a few men in Egypt sought power and decided you could only worship one god, in him, a man god. And killing anyone who refused. Even Muhammad said Allah is supreme and solitary and to dissolve goddesses or be condemned to hell. And so it makes you wonder what influenced Muhammad as an orphan boy when his merchant uncle traded with all those Christians and Jews. Promising life after death if you believe in him instead of her."

"I would love to read it."

"Here. You can have it," I tell Mahru, handing it to her. "This is why men

CHAPTER NINE

burn books and threaten you with hellfire. Because they don't want you to know that you are god. You and me."

With a freeing affirmation of thought she studies me with awe and eager to know more.

"And you can't stop people from having sex. You can't forbid nature to do what it's designed to do. It is in our nature to be beautiful. To express our bodies and to worship them," I clearly and unpretentiously profess.

"Can I worship you right now?"

"Can I worship you?" I playfully ask, she suddenly trying to escape my wet tongue that slides up her neck towards her ear.

"Aaaahh! Hahaa!" she laughs.

Hearing her adorable laugh I stop to express my love so gently. Reaching for me her smooth hands move across my back and neck. Indulging myself in her senses I carefully listen to her powerful heart beating. Holding on to the one person that I am closest to our innocence finds the kind of love that allows us both to feel safe and at home. And whenever she is near I am only hers and nothing more.

Moved by a creative whim I begin wording impromptu . . . "Gently wording things that you love to hear. Careful kisses from my lips to your body. If making love were on a scale it would read severe. All we do is stay at home for the party."

"Did you just make that up?" she asks with disbelief.

"I did," I proudly admit, surprising even myself.

"Maybe you can be a singer and write your own music."

"Music is dead. I wouldn't make any money," I sheepishly deviate.

"Come on. Sing me something else. Something as sexy as you are."

"Now I can't. I'm nervous."

"Come on. . . . . Sing to me."

". . . . . Your kisses hold my lips like I hold your hips. . . . Going through you slow like a bag of chips. . . . Over dips . . . giving lolly licks anywhere you pick."

"You are amazing," Mahru tells me, the satiny ammil of her lustrous gaze burning as my hand spills passed her warm Venusian alter.

With a lubricious body so full and curvaceous she oozes with a back-arching appetite for sex in the loveliest way. Quickly kissing me she stands up and pulls me to follow her into my bedroom.

"My pussy has been jumping so hard just thinking about you," she tells me with her avid lust, she pulling me closer to my bed. Wanting me like the rain wants to fall I hear the roar of her growing silence.

Focusing her eyes on me her hands feel for the bottom of her shirt. A lip-tease distracts her getting off on me watching her. Revealing her bare-skinned callipygous figure she is as free as a bird with her love for the sky. And she without sky lie hopeless and die—begging me with those sthenic eyes to revive her.

Quickly finding her way into my bed her clothes come off faster than I can lose my shirt. A tingling in the energy field forces me spellbound and by the shape of her dancing through space like a brazen flame as she moves around my bed. Her piquant figure pulses with a heart-pounding salacity. Goatish and flirtatious her body reveals an array of premeditated fantasy.

With our eyes and bodies guided by a language far older than words her heart peeks through the keyhole of her desire. Letting the soft animal of her body love what it loves I guide her hand to touch what she craves. Squeezing her buttermilk lady-lumps her protruding tips are hardened with hunger. Wanting my hands, arms, and lips like the ocean craves the shore I travel her Gobi dunes and supple thighs. Having a body covered with secrets wishing to be discovered she bites my neck and digs her fingertips into my back.

Feeling her sexual energy that fuels our natural biology I awaken her stylish and instinctual beauty. Raising her Kundalini the Ida and Pingala fuse together with a self-loving goddess energy that unfolds into a beautiful awakening. Slow surfing the length of her body with a serpentine moonglade I feel her heart overflowing with rage. Prowling the sizzling Sahara of her warm naked skin I breathe and taste her fleshy silken leas. My curls taste her body the way that a hummingbird flutters the face of a desert candle. Feeling her face pressed against the warmth of my swollen jewels she twirls her tongue outside my anus. Tasting the soft wet crown of my bulbous erection she pushes my cock deeper into her throat with a lepid moan.

Catching the auroral lūcidus of those eternal gems her leafless libidinous body opens up to me with her legs moving further apart. Lathing her wet throbbing mussel back and forth my tongue travels from her clitoris to her anus.

Stimulating her erogenous roused yoni pot I feel the magnetic pull of her lunar swell.

Torn between waiting to come and feeling herself almost climax she arches her bare back to stop and grab the back of my head. With a raised rathe lip

CHAPTER NINE

and a panting of breath she nods for me to be inside of her.

Like the sweet surrender of pine sap oozing from its crevice I taste the oil-bearing perianth amidst her ornamental magina. Quenching my thirst from her supernal ram, her holy grail, an emerging pressure sweetens as my buoyant limb dives deep inside of her urogenital triangle. Pulling the back of my hair her vaginal muscles tighten around my engorged stipe and golden cap. Every cell in her body feels numb and alive from the stirring sensation of my vein-pulsing knob pushing deeper.

Feeling high tide I pinch my fuse to avoid detonating as she carefully follows my slowing rhythm. Taking the time to feel myself inside of her she can hardly restrain herself from such a satisfying high.

Skydiving into a shaking fainting fit she reaches a toe-curling apogee as she thrusts herself against my firm ample body. Weightless she feels an unfettered and primifluous le petite mort as I cream all inside of her. A gushing transcendental sensation nourishes. Wading through her indulgence her elevated affection wraps my chiseled body with a shared embrace, my love like a sylvan serpent around her cream Khongor body.

The light hitting her displays a multitudinous array of colors, her body as mesmerizing as a birch covered stream with opalescent light illuminating its forest depths. Creating an energetic flow inside of her soft curved body our muscles and nerves harden like the mellisonant strings that echo an Angolan lambada. Following the abdominal line of her torso that leads to her flume gorge I notice her to be the most beautiful living thing to exist on the face of the earth.

Begging me to stay between her legs and to give her a refill my hard expanding nerve penetrates her shakti kona and ascends her inner chakras from her supreme sacral source to her luminescent crown. The color of her sun-sleepy peaks press firmly to my flesh in my quest to the center of her chalice. With a feeling as deep as the ocean and an ecstasy as high as the 36 constellations I push and pull the waves of her moon in the sweet waters of pleasure. Blooming in the shadows of darkness I taste the sweet salt of her body as she squeezes my bed sheets.

Noticing four hours of our crazed addiction to each other having slipped from our hands we are still in love with each second that escapes us.

Turning to pull me closer she longs for me as if her body and soul have been dormant for nearly a century. And so I continue to give her the most of my love as light and dark shadows caress the image of her naked luminescence.

Played by her playful charm and adoring wit I am carefree and blissful as we lie inside of each other's grasp. Letting go of all misfortunes that stand in the way of our expressly forbidden love I foolishly hope that what we have will never end.

Looking up at me as if she is not compromised by what her family dictates her smile stops the world from spinning. Warm as the sun she comforts my restlessness. Over and under inside of this place we call ours, never calm and yet so still.

"I love you," I tell her, pushing my fingers along her jewel-toned body.

"I love you too. Maybe I can come over tomorrow," she then says, feeling down my entire body with her soft smooth hands.

"Okay," I relievedly express, hoping.

"You are so beautiful," Mahru tells me.

"Tell me more about that book you gave me. About the goddess," she then says, wanting to hear me speak, having told me before that my voice is soothing to her ears.

"You know Michelangelo?"

"Yes."

"Inside Michelangelo's Creation Of Adam, God's left arm encircles a beautiful female figure, Sophia, located at the center of the brain. The snake in the garden of Eden is Sophia, consort of God, the Holy Spirit, dove of Aphrodite, goddess of divine wisdom, teaching us all that to love is to be divine. The Romans hid this from christianity. In gnostic gospels she is called the mother of the universe and mother of the creator God or Yahweh. Her full name is Hagia Sophia, meaning holy female wisdom. Communicating with Sophia is communicating with your soul, the highest aspect of yourself. She is the Kundalini snake. Your Muslim Kaaba also represents the creative earth mother. Kaaba means cube or square. A square is a rudimentary prison or matrix—the material plane. Priests who attended the shrine at Kaaba were known as sons of the old woman. The Islamic flag has a goddess moon. The black stone in the corner of the Ka'bah is shaped like a vagina. And the mihrab is the vagina shaped prayer niche in a mosque. Like all religions Islam arose to replace a Pagan ruling system that later grew decadent under the imposition of patriarchy. A ruling class that produced deep divisions and stresses in society."

"That's very interesting. I know too that Al-Bukhārī's written Hadith contains contradicting statements about Muhammad's egalitarian attitude to-

CHAPTER NINE

wards women. One Hadith saying that women are the supreme calamity. But Aisha, the most influential wife after Khadījah, quoted Muhammad as saying that the three most precious things in this world are women, fragment odors, and prayers," Mahru tells me.

"Al-Bukhārī also had letters burned that Muhammad wrote to his wife. It is crazy how things become so far thrown from their original meaning. And how time and words confuse people," I tell Mahru, skimming the back of my fingers down her tempean physique.

"Well I'm not confused about you," she says, her sparkling eyes being forward with absolute adoration.

"You don't know how happy you make me," I communicate, waiting for her to tell me it's time and hoping she might think up some excuse that will let her stay a while longer.

"You have no idea how happy you make me," she says, feeling my body with her soft slender fingers.

Like fall leaves gently finding their way into every corner and crevice, my lips find her, my body moving in ways that causes her entire body to curl up around me with a yearning. Sliding all of the way down her warm flesh, I cure her aching heart, creating with my hands and lips this pain-free image that is mirrored back to me—she healing me by allowing me to give of my all-gentle and loving touch.

"I think that it is time for you to go home now," she says, playfully pretending the situation in reverse.

"Do you mean that it's time for you to go home?"

"No. It's time for you to go home," she quietly reiterates, gently pressing her fist into my chest and for a moment allowing me to see the misery that is filling in behind her watery eyes.

"But I am home," I remind Mahru, looking at her in such a way that allows her to know that I mean I am home whenever I am with her. Watching her battle something fierce inside of her she places both her hands on my face and kisses me one last time before getting up to put her clothes back on. Confused I grab her hand to get her to look at me.

"I know you're putting yourself through a lot just to be here. Just know that I'll do anything for you. And you can always tell me anything," I calmly convey with a desperate aching inside of me to understand what she is feeling.

"When I call you later we can talk more. I just gotta go," she says wistfully, with regret, hurrying to get her leggings pulled up and shoes back on.

Walking Mahru to the door in my sandals and shorts I kiss her goodbye with my soul-touching lips that act like a painkiller to all the noise in her head. Wrapping her thin thistle scarf around her head the light in her eyes comes back and brightens her entire face.

"I'm so sorry for getting like that in front of you. It's just you know that I'm not supposed to be here and it's hard because I know what it does to you," she explains, looking at me as if I'm going to want to stop seeing her.

"I'm always going to love you. And I'm here for you," I assure Mahru, catching her smile and wondering if what I said comforts her any.

Opening the front door I watch her leave when I know that she doesn't want to. And it is strange to me seeing her leave to go home when really her home is here with me. Throwing a sweater on over my head I walk with Mahru outside.

"Thank you for inviting me over," she says, grabbing my hand as she tries to console me about her leaving.

"I'd force you to stay if I knew how to."

"I know. I'm sorry that I can't stay," she emphatically replies, muzzling the truth when it comes to expressing what she really wants—which is to stay.

Climbing inside of her sea-green Land Rover I claim from her once more an all-consuming kiss that reaches her soul before it touches her lips.

"I'll call you later today after I help my mom with her store," she tells me, rolling her window down as I carefully shut her door. Smiling back at Mahru I step away from her car. "Wait," she says, reaching for me to come closer as she leans out of her driver side window.

Taking my hands out of my pockets to rest my arm on her car she kisses me once more. Moving her hands down her legs with an anxiousness that moves her to feel her black curly hair she then smiles back at me.

Turning her large off-road vehicle around Mahru waves to me. Hoping to catch sight of her binding eyes once more she glances at me from her rearview.

Feeling the weight of this risk that she is taking as the sound of her truck fades into the distance I then grasp that she is gone again. And the part of it that hurts is me being the odious anathema of an intolerant tribal mind. Dads, moms, brothers, sisters that I know I would happily adopt as my own flesh and blood. Asking myself why love has become so difficult for me to understand. Asking why my feelings are being crushed and at the same time overpowered by this incredible love that comes to my door. She hoping that I will be just as in love with her as I was the day before.

SUSPICION

CHAPTER TEN

Passing the Sunday matinée after an early hike I make my way to the Indigo on Granville for something handmade and elegant to write on. The nearby avenue stands adorned with extravagant displays for Misch and Patagonia. Dazzling prints parade exciting tastes and smells suffusing from the open-door cafes. Friends and lovers are chatting over coffee. And beautifully lit fountains ensphere drops of water propelling themselves into spiraling organic gems.

Thumbing through the aged paper inside of the store my mind stresses more over Mahru feeling upset. Pushing it from my mind I try letting it turn into more of a distant haze for me. Still this disastrous oddment over my heart and mind poses an important question. But never anything clear enough for me to confront. Each day I just keep trying to maintain the image of strength and love alongside our differences. In a society where we are expected to always be right and never wrong as we venture away from the nest of grade school and now our post-secondary education. Confused by a culture that imposes its rules or rule—as does every culture. But naturally I feel love has no such boundaries. Yet everyday I am thrown by this abstract ideology that besets our unlawful but sacred advantage. And I worry about her every time that she messages me through text. But I am here because I am in love with her. And I know that she loves me too.

Paying and leaving the store I contemplate her safety in sneaking off to see me. Just yesterday it scared me seeing Mahru so upset. And I know that my frustration exists because I am afraid of losing her. Feeling my heart shackled to the wall of my love's looming and menacing demise I conclude that her dad must be a real monster. And meeting her mom and dad is already an obvious no. Still she is more to me than life itself. And feeling this still endless resonance of hope that permeates inside of my heart how can I deny this gentle voice that comes looking for me? How can I deny the love sweltering withinside the safety of my breast? Knowing this thing called love that allows me to believe in only that which truly matters. And longing to be touched by the only one whose love can cure me.

Leaving my purchase on the passenger seat of my car I then merge easily from curbside parking.

Passing Park Square on Forty-first Avenue I curiously glance behind the neatly trimmed boxwoods and emerald green thujas that lengthen as privacy screens. And the temperature gauge in my rearview reads a rare sixty degrees this sunny October twenty-fifth.

Pulling into Louis's driveway around behind his house I am quickly enveloped by the red emperor maples and lily magnolias that are sheltered by the taller evergreens further back. But surrounded even by such beauty under my skin arcs this piercing need for her. Pushing my car into park my peace then immediately leaves me.

Stepping inside of my front door I quickly then throw together some tomatoes, avocados, chopped lettuce, and olives while waiting for my computer to start up. Wanting to hurry getting all of my work done for Louis I begin to wolf down my salad. Not foreseeing enough time to mix any paint and work on Mahru's portrait, I then shrug off the satiating thought, especially after such a tiring hike that has taken up most of my day.

Plopping down on the sofa with a spork in my mouth I decide to start updating Louis's website. The trickiest part of it is ensuring the quality of the images made available to me and then using a little Photoshop. Then copy and paste some trendy T-shirts and slab pottery. Upload to a shared folder and *done*.

Feeling a little tired I then shut my laptop and set it inside the pine coffee table in front of the sofa. Sitting up and tugging my Dolman sleeves I then take off my knitted pullover sweater. Pulling down on the shaggy blanket behind me I then decide to curl around the Mudcloth pillows that suffocate the cloud leather daybed.

CHAPTER TEN

Finding fair comfort in feeling the soft Mali cotton against my skin the smell of leather and wood help remedy my rigidity. And then suddenly my taut tiresome mind dozes off with my last thoughts being of Mahru.

Listening to a soft crescive chime between the dream world I then sit up and see on my phone that I've just missed her call. Looking down to see the time I also realize that I have been asleep for almost two hours. Immediately I then pick up my phone to try and call Mahru right back. But it keeps ringing and ringing.

"Hey," she finally answers. "I tried calling you a few minutes ago."

"I was asleep for a couple of hours. That's why I missed your call."

"That's okay," she says, as I lie back down with my eyes closed.

"So talk to me." I mutter, still tired.

"I just wanted to see how you were is all," she says.

"I'm okay. I've just been waiting to hear from you."

"You sound a little upset."

"I'm not upset," I calmly continue, wondering if Mahru is putting out to me something that she herself feels—an underlying matter that we have avoided talking about all this time, especially when she knows exactly what I want to talk about and how it makes me feel. "I just wish that I could know what you are really thinking sometimes. I want our lives to make sense. Because I want you. Not having to wonder when you're not here how long we are going to last. And if I am going to wake up one day and discover that I can never see you again."

"Don't think like that. I wish too that things could be more simple, Lucius."

"What were you gonna talk to me about?"

"I don't know if I want to tell you. Because I don't want you to worry."

"Can you just tell me? I care about what is on your mind," I wholeheartedly plead.

"I mean . . . the thing I was gonna tell you is that my mom and dad are having a man visit us. He is flying in from Cairo next week. My dad says that he would be a good husband for me. Everyone keeps asking me when I'm going to get married now that school is ending for me. When I expressed that I wanted to pursue a career my dad ignored me and said that he's too worried about me getting involved with a boy. And he tells me that me getting married is what's best for me. And he tells me that I'm lucky we're not in Egypt still or he would have married me off at fourteen," she frustratingly details, me feeling again this torment that has wracked the depths of my soul for the past month and a half.

Crushed by the thought of her being intimidated and browbeaten into another man's arms I quietly ask, "Are you going to let your dad push you into this?" almost grimacing with tears as I mull over the partial mind of her dad forcing her from me.

"It's just a visit, Lucius. I don't have to be interested. Nothing will even happen for several months."

"Let me meet your dad. I will talk to him. I will convert to Islam. Let me just—"

"My dad is not someone to be reasoned with, Lucius. He will not listen to you. And even worse you can put me in danger. You know the severity of this."

"When are you gonna tell me that I can't see you anymore?" I then ask, my silent tears spilling from the bowls of my eyes.

"I'm not. But you are making me feel terrible now. I just wanted to tell you what's going on. And now I don't even think I should've done that," she says, credulously dismissing the recognized gravity of the matter.

"I don't want you to feel terrible. I just don't want to lose you. Not when you could just come live here with me. . . . I love you," I tirelessly express.

For a moment I hear no response and then wonder if she is crying or has hung up. The thought then crosses my mind that she doesn't have the guts to break up with me.

"You know that I love you," she desperately conveys as she again becomes silent.

Listening to Mahru her voice sounds a little less resolute than it did yesterday afternoon when she left my driveway.

"Please understand that—" She then stops talking, startled by the sound of a downstairs door. "I can't talk right now. I have to go—okay," she says, regretting the sudden urgency to hang up the phone as she pulses with fear, she hearing her father starting to casually walk up the stairs to her bedroom.

"Okay," I tell her, immediately gathering what is happening as I also hear a dreadful urgency in her voice.

"My dad is coming," she whispers.

Listening to the silence of her hanging up I suddenly feel my heart dissolving into a rich corrosive acid that slowly begins to eat the rest of me.

"How can her father not even look at me in the eyes? How can her family not even want to understand this great joy that we have in each other? How

CHAPTER TEN

can her parents love her and not want to understand the way that she feels? How will they ever understand anything worth understanding if they refuse to listen to their own daughter? Would he really hurt her if he knew?" So many questions. Heartbroken from being kept in the dark about *the one thing* that matters most to me. "How ever did I end up loving a girl that I could never have?" I then ask myself, feeling alone on my path towards aggravation and frustration, spinning around this carousel as I try to see our future when I close my eyes.

All that I feel now is this overwhelming shadow of endless agony that suffers my heart, it leaving me for dead on the very floor of this place where life was thought to have given me a new kind of happiness.

Hearing my phone I look down at my caller ID. Seeing her name I remain leery of the fact that her dad was just present. Putting the phone to my ear I wait for her to speak first. But I hear nothing. Only a silence with the earmarks of a deadly saunter through a trapping thicket. Still I continue to listen until the line is gone from the other end.

Thinking it again to be strange I close my phone. It could be her dad trying to find out who she is talking to. Afraid of what will happen to her I stop myself from calling her back. And it eats at me that I can do nothing. Like a stupid boy sullen and under the thumb. Powerless and ignorant. Destitute amid the blazing sun on this waterless island in my heart and mind.

Twenty minutes later Mahru calls me back.

"Hey," she says, crushed as she tries to conceal the betrayed and confused emotion pounding inside of her—her unbroken solidity still followed by reserve.

"Are you okay?" I ask, with an uneasiness about my breath.

"Yeah. I'm okay. My dad just was coming up here to talk to me. I'm sorry I had to hang up like that," she says, still alarmed.

"You called a little while ago. But you didn't say anything."

"That was my dad. He was checking to see who I've been talking to. . . . Did you say anything when he called?"

"No—I put the phone to my ear and waited for you to say something. And then the phone just hung up."

"Okay—good," she says, taking a deep breath, me listening to her nerves faintly rattle her voice. "That was *way* too close," as if to have just escaped a horrific and hellish end of life.

"Before I called the last time I was downstairs with my mom and dad trying to convince them that their suspicions are all for nothing. Malik led them to believe that I've been spending an unusual amount of time from home aside from going to work. Not because my brother thinks anything. It was just an accident."

"So you're okay?" I ask, not knowing what to think of the drama that is unfolding at her house.

"Yeah. Everything is okay. I am just worried about you. And don't worry about what I said. I don't have to get married if I don't want to. And I've been thinking about what you said—about coming to live with you," she says, tasting in her mouth the lie of her hiding the truth of her father's abhorrent will to force her hand and what will happen should she choose to stay living with her parents.

"Okay. . . ." I mutter, careful to be convinced.

"Just forget that I said anything—please. I'm sorry."

"I just want to feel your warmth in my arms. You are in my bones and deep inside of my heart," I tell her, unforeseeably shaken by the suffocating emotions that have pressed me this waking hour.

"I wish that I could come and see you right now," she sniffles, bleary-eyed from all of the pressure that is weighing in on her at home.

"Do you think you can come over tomorrow after school?" I half-heartedly urge, hearing her smile as I gather her relaxed to the sound of my voice.

"I'll have to get back to you about that. My parents are starting to watch me more closely. And I'm afraid of what will happen if I let my dad think that I'm running off to see you."

"He is your dad. I can only hope that he is invested in what makes you happy," I retort, upset that she is afraid of letting me talk to him.

"He is. He is invested. He just only understands his world view and because of the way that him and my mom were married." She then doesn't say anything. "You don't need to worry about that—and you know how I feel about you—so. . . ." she argues, catching the conflicting truth of her statement.

"I'm just troubled. All I ever do is think about us and what I could do to make it easier for you to just come and live with me. I am making twenty-eight hundred dollars a month part-time with Louis. The guest house is free right now. I just want to be with you," I frustratingly assert. "I don't want to be constantly reminded of our differences. I just want you."

"Do you want me to come and see you soon?"

CHAPTER TEN

"I always want you to see me."

"Okay—how about I come and see you Tuesday? And I will see you tomorrow at school. It'll be okay," she tells me, trying to eliminate my sense of overwhelming concern. "Look, I can't really talk right now. I have to go. My parents are downstairs arguing and I don't want them to wonder why I'm up here so long in my room."

"Okay. . . . Are you gonna be alright?"

"I'll be okay," she whispers. "I have to go now."

"Okay. I'll talk to you tomorrow."

"Bye," she says.

Closing my eyes I try not to cry as the phone hangs up, and I think about how dumb it is that I don't know what to do. "Anything is better than being frightened by this manipulative thing that segregates us both," I tell myself. Knowing that her cultural differences weigh heavy on us both I can't help but feel alarmed to the fact that I might lose her. "Why won't she run away with me? Why do I find myself frightened and so in love at the same time?" It is painful enough just seeing her leave when clearly she wants to stay. Troubling thoughts of her father's warnings and mild suspicions now forcing her to tread carefully. And now tied up in all kinds of spousal pairing that her family is organizing between here and her little town back home.

Moving onto the linen chair that faces the window I worry that her father might try to push her into marriage while this man is visiting. And I worry because I know very little about what it will be like for her if she does not choose. Sliding my hands down the nail head trim onto the floor to see the moon from the window I think about the way the bed was when I last saw her lying in it. I think about how I might prove myself worthy to her father should he and I ever have the pleasure of meeting. Perhaps he will see that I truly do love his daughter and that I always will. "Isn't that all that matters?" I then ask myself.

Sitting in front of my living room chair, I wonder if her dad is even capable of involving himself in an act of violence against me, or even his own daughter. And I remember all of the stories that she told me not so long ago. The exact words from her lips concerning this despotic and repressive part of her existence. Me having thought about it much over the last few weeks. Even nervous at the thought of her telling her dad about us by herself. Even though naturally it should be exactly what I want. I only question why she has been so afraid. And I ask myself these things because I have seen the fear in her eyes. Even leaping from the gentle sound of her voice. And so now I try to convince myself that it is all or nothing, she being the living center to my entire existence.

The thought of losing her again then strikes me with a bitter pain. And I cry quietly like a cold naked child. Tired from standing in the midst of this virulent war that seeps into my path like a rankling fog. All radiance and beauty plagued by this insipid ignorance.

HASSAN

CHAPTER ELEVEN

Slouched into my chair in Mrs. Graham's Earth and Ocean Sciences lecture a muzzy numbing sensation comes over me as Mahru lingers in the forefront of my mind. The want to participate escapes me as I wonder what I am even doing here. And then it comes crawling up behind my shoulders to the front of my head. Pulling off my knitted mock neck sweater I let it fall down over the back of my chair as I feel it getting too hot. I then think it unjust and cruel me hearing in her voice this desperation and being worn down by it. Still she pressures me into believing that there is nothing I can do. Persistent on being vague and seeming to discount this threat to us. Then I recall her trying to rid of me the first time that we met. But how can I feel wrong for wanting to love her? Like my idea of the simple joys in life I somehow thought that love could exist in the same way. That it would be more like what I had pictured in my mind. But as an enormous uncertainty pries its way into my way of reason I am confused as to what part of her will acknowledge what she herself must do.

Watching my lecture end I then get up and head to my car to swap my books.

Contemplating her wanting to see me in view of what might be dangerous I still gather the courage anyway and mosey to the admissions office by the back entrance.

Stepping inside the door I then see that she isn't there.

"She just took some paperwork to the main office for me. She'll be right back," Mrs. Etienne informs, neatly sitting at her desk in the backroom.

"Thank you," I acknowledge, having a seat on the brown sofa where Mahru usually sits.

The door then opens and Mahru greets me with a smile. Only it is a smile quickly ruined by a vapid downward spiral. And for a split second she seems to tell me something most despairing with her eyes. Unnerved by the subtle threats made towards her and having foreseen what would happen to us she resumes her calm and insouciant stance. Something I might have missed if I wasn't watching her so closely.

Still not knowing how to make it all okay with me, she glances over, deep down wanting to remain true to her feelings for me.

"Hey," I communicate, sitting casually as I look over at her. Noticing her brief unease I smile indifferent to question this havering when in the lovely reverence of her presence.

"Hey," she says back, wearing a crinkled pashmina scarf, not knowing if she can handle arguing about what is happening at home.

"So what happened last night?"

"Just more of the same. You must not wait any longer to get married. Honor your family. You are already now twenty-one years old," she mocks, describing her parents berating offensive.

"So who is this guy that your dad is inviting?"

"His name is Hassan. And he is actually a distant cousin of mine," she says with embarrassment, before again becoming quiet. "When I was a little girl I maybe only remember seeing him three times. I do not even know him. It all seems so weird."

"Your cousin?"

"Yeah. The last time that I saw him I think that I was seven or eight years old. Long before we moved here. The only thing that I know about him is that he is an accountant and that he had his jaw broken a few years ago when he was at school."

"What, so he is in college?"

"Actually he graduated college a couple of years ago. He is almost seven years older than me. And that is all I know. My dad is the one arranging it of course. I don't see why he can't just let me get married like my grandma did . . . when I'm ready. And with someone that I choose," she says, looking at me and feeling worried that I'm going to stop talking to her.

"Yeah," I mutter, looking back at her wondering why we are even having this conversation. I watch her become more nervous as she looks away.

"Madge tells me that I should just run away if I do not want to go through with it. But she also tells me that I will never be able to see my family again. Her, my mom, and my brother," she says, gravitating towards her dad's decision instead of her own as a tear crawls out from her eye.

Looking at her I don't say anything only out of consideration for not wanting to pull her away from her mom, brother, and sister.

Looking away and trying not to cry at the thought of not seeing her anymore Mahru then grabs my hand. Bending my lip and turning my head so that a tear falls without her seeing it I then look down at her hands. Sitting up I quickly glance over at her and then back down at her hand inside of mine.

"I know you can't stay long if you wanted to come by tomorrow. And I know that you are busy this week," I tell her, trying to pull myself back together as I smile at her.

"I actually promised Zuzana that we would watch a movie tomorrow and do some homework together. And you know with my parents keeping a closer eye on me now, it's probably not a good idea."

"Yeah—you're right. . . . So what movie are you guys gonna watch?" I then ask, discretely wiping my wet eye.

"It's called *Capernaum*. It is a Lebanese film directed by Nadine Labaki. I love all of her movies. But this one is about a little boy living in the slums of Beirut. My dad will not let me watch it at home—so."

"So you've seen it?"

"I have seen it before. But my friend hasn't," Mahru smiles.

"I will have to check it out."

Looking at Mahru and sensing optimism in her voice I then try shrugging off the hurt emotions that are maybe visible on my face.

"Maybe I can come by in a week or so after they leave."

"I would like that," I tell Mahru, she moving one of my curls to the side of my face. Feeling her inner elbow leveraging against my waist she twists her fingers behind me. "Are you okay?" I then ask, waiting to make eye contact with her as she lifts her head from my shoulder.

"I'm okay," she tells me.

The urge to kiss as we usually do then doesn't come. But instead only a slight peck on the cheek as a strange and unnatural disparity becomes wedged between us. Without even trying it then feels like I am beginning to push her away. As if my hands are tied. And I see myself making the mistake of saying nothing when I just want to say everything. But I don't. As she carefully pulls closer to me for one more attempt I pretend to be ignorant as I feel my heart still being crushed. And I want to cry but I hold myself together. But a tear then exposes my bluff and I am left only able to express the truth that is overturning from my eyes and face. Looking at Mahru I then succinctly remind and enlighten.

"I want you in my arms like roots consume rain. To warm my body beside yours like bathing in the sun. To hear the rhythm of your heart in my waking ears. Dancing in spirit around the edges of your body. Wanting your love that burns like fire when you kiss me—anywhere and everywhere. You loving every part of me—loving every part of you," I steadily voice, wrinkling my lip as my eyes then wander the room. My eyes then glance at her again before looking away.

"Lucius. . . . All of this will be over soon, I promise. I love you so much. I will come and see you after they leave—okay?" she immediately replies, alarmed by my growing unease.

The office door then opens as an unsuspecting student walks passed us to visit Mrs. Etienne. Having turned our attention away from each other, Mahru scoots back closer to me, pulling her scarf down from around her shoulders. Moving my face closer to her she wipes away my tear with her hand. Looking at my lips and eyes she looks to see if it is okay to kiss me. Not caring if the admissions counselor is listening or if someone else comes through that door, Mahru pulls me closer, reaching for my lips that cannot hide needing her kiss. Quietly tasting her lips in front of an open door that carries the faint sounds of an urban oldies station I feel from her the kind of kiss that melts me every time that she comes to see me. High from her kiss and yet ravaged by this news that shakes me with dismay. Holding her face and pressing my face against hers, she closes her eyes, her hands gently grabbing my thick head of hair before touching my face.

Quickly wiping my face before someone else sees I inch back a bit and move my hair out of the way of my eyes. Taking a deep breath I then sit back against the brown tufted leather cushion. Glancing at the clock Mahru then reaches for my hand.

"I love you," I tell Mahru.

"I love you too," she tells me with a smile, desperately trying not to cry.

"I'm gonna get back to my class," I tell her, quietly taking another deep

CHAPTER ELEVEN

breath.

"Okay," she says, still worrying about what I am thinking.

"I would do anything for you."

"I know," she again smiles, offering me a sense of comfort in the way that she looks at me.

Leaving through the front office door I accept that whatever happens next is all up to her. Believing that she still wants me and cares about me I mosey back to my class pushing back any unfavorable obscurities that pervade my sense of peace. And I want her to be free of this. Because I care about her. Hoping that this man, Hassan, leaves and never looks back. Questioning if it is even possible for any man to turn away after seeing her. Eyes that impose an overpowering sensation and a curiosity. A face forever unforgettable. And me still feeling deep down that things will only worsen from here.

Finding an empty seat before my lecture in Groundwater Contamination begins my pocket then vibrates. Quickly glancing down at my phone I read Louis's text.

"Lucius! I'm preparing an early dinner before I catch my 6:00 p.m. flight. Hope you'll be here :)."

Totally having forgot about Louis and him leaving I start to text him back before Mr. Wong walks back in.

"I will see you soon. I get out at 3:10."

Pulling my car into the driveway and arriving home I try to shake the suspense of this dream state that clouds my mind. Climbing out of the car disappointed and with my hands in my pockets I walk to the backdoor of the main house which is usually unlocked.

Moving through the garage doors and into the house I see Louis in the kitchen pulling a sizzling iron off the stovetop. Seeing him excited to leave for a few days I begin searching for the kind of time that might take my mind off of Mahru and her unwanted guest.

"Hey brotha! Get in here and fix yourself something to eat. I made plenty," he says, pointing to the Asian wraps and the vegetable lo mein that he made himself.

"Thank you," I tell Louis, pretending to be cheery.

"Take this one," he kindly urges, handing me a full plate as I question my appetite.

"This looks delicious," I complement, afraid that chatting with Louis will open up a serious word about the reality of my relationship with Mahru.

"How is school going?"

"It's going just fine. I'm passing everything," I report, my eyebrows raised, which usually means that I'm not telling the whole truth.

"What about Mahru? How is she doing?" Louis probes, paying closer attention to my delayed answer.

Feeling the pressure of not being able to fool my uncle I begin picking apart the grim truth as I emotionally ready myself for what I know Louis may say. Pausing to answer and appearing to be recovering from a punch in the stomach I decide to try starting from the beginning.

"Well—she is a beautiful girl from a good respectable family. Only she says her dad would kill us both if he knew about me and her. I am unworthy of his daughter because I am not Arab or Muslim. And I've never seen someone so afraid of their own dad. Except maybe me when I was twelve. But this seems like other level shit."

"Lucius—I'm sorry. . . . Are you both still talking?" he then asks, motioning for me to follow him to the dining table.

"I talked to Mahru today. But I feel like she is starting to distance herself from me. Maybe I'm distancing myself too. This guy named Hassan is flying in from Cairo—her cousin. Maybe right about now or very soon. Her dad wants her to marry him since she is finishing school in December. I offered for her to come and live with me. But she is afraid. And what worries me is feeling like we don't stand a chance. She loves me. But she is afraid of something. And I still don't get it and I feel like it's all my fault. I'm the one who kept on when she told me to walk. I've been in love with her since the first time I laid eyes on her." I stop to try and gather myself, hoping to perhaps receive something that will cure me of this apparent torture that is beginning to drive me mad.

"Lucius—I'm sorry this is happening to you. But it is happening to her too. Be strong for her. And I hope that she listens to you. You know I got your back no matter what. How quickly is her dad trying to push this marriage?"

"She says nothing would happen for months. And she has thought about coming to live here. I just know that she loves her family too. And I feel like I am pulling her away from them."

"But you see there is time. Wait to see what happens. I know how you feel. If you love her don't give up on her. Be there for her when she needs you. It is not easy for her either. She could be protecting you. You don't know her dad."

"I know," I mutter in agreement.

CHAPTER ELEVEN

"You wonder how people can still be hellbent on Jesus and Muhammad. Especially when people like Iamblichus have said that the Chaldeans had 490,000 to 730,000 years of astronomical observation inscribed into baked bricks. Christianity and public schools still having reservations about the earth being 10,000 years old. Nobody really knows what is going on. And ultimately those things have no weight over matters of the heart."

"I can see everything happening to her. She doesn't want to be manipulated. Emotionally. Intellectually. None of it."

"It wasn't that long ago that women were given the right to vote. People claiming authority mortified that you and me would claim authenticity on our own minds. But that's the way it's always been. I am a priest. I am going to sell you on the idea that you are not good enough. So this is what you have to do."

"Intense emotional fear," I mutter, only hearing the chaos in my head.

"Sophocles said that nothing vast enters the life of mortals without a curse. And truth and happiness are blurred between what is written and real experience."

"Maybe time will sort it all out by itself."

"Everyone you see is tired behind the wheel. They are here for only a short time. And then you die. Never knowing who you are or where you come from. She loves you. But young people especially in her position are almost always making decisions based on fear. Just remember that you are not here in this life on this planet to tread lightly. No Sir. Mark Twain reminds us to break the rules. Kiss slowly and love truly. And never regret anything that makes you smile."

"Yeah but what would you do if you were me?" I then ask, wanting the simple answer instead of the philosophical one.

"Feel the fear and do it anyway," he says, squinting his eyes at me with his raspy voice.

"Yeah. . . . Okay," I nod, holding my head up as my eyes gather water.

"You don't know what will happen. Just be there for her."

"Okay," I mutter to myself.

"Whatever happens I want you to call me," Louis then says, as he gets up from his chair to put his plate into the dishwasher. "My Uber car is almost here. You've got a key to get in if you need to. Eat whatever you want in the fridge. I don't want any of it to go to waste. I'll be back Monday."

"Thank you for everything," I tell Louis, hugging him goodbye before he throws his black midsize travel bag around his shoulder.

"You're my nephew. I'll look out for you. . . . . . . Alright I'm ready."

Walking outside with Louis as his Uber driver pulls up I stop in the middle of his brick walkway and look towards the road. Catching sight of each street lamp that shines against the warm red and purple hue of night I wonder if such a thing could still be beautiful to me if I were to lose her.

"How can I not be afraid?" I then ask myself, waving bye to Louis as he climbs into his driver's black Ford.

Hearing the car pull away I then step inside of my front door and walk upstairs to lie down.

Taking all of my clothes off I then feel my chest expand and contract from the torment of this grueling agony that suffers my heart. I cling to my bed linens the way that a water droplet clings to the dead stem of winter.

Crawling under the covers I turn myself behind the sheets looking for her scent that reminds me of her kiss and every time that we have been together. Staring and facing the ceiling my tears escape my eyes. And as I finally fall asleep the veins behind my eyes yank the light switch to my brain as the darkest and loneliest feeling consumes me.

THE DRIFT

CHAPTER TWELVE

Slipping down the hall and into the admissions office I find Mahru sitting in her black turtleneck and her elegant tribal leggings. Wearing a fall Rajana paisley scarf she appears not as pleased to see me as she vaguely acknowledges my entering the room.

Crossing her legs in her wood-trimmed combat boots Mahru turns her head slightly. Sitting down beside her I notice that her feelings have been hurt. Behind her eyes she seems almost vacant as I press her to utter some brewing and looming thoughts.

Gathering that some serious words have been tossed around at home Mahru carefully continues anyway with casual conversation. Distancing herself with talk of what her parents expect of her I recognize that she is trying to tell me something. But the two of us are only lost between her not wanting to tell me and me not wanting to listen. The heavy burden of her family pressuring her to marry again becomes a stir. And all I keep fearfully anticipating is her pushing me away. But still she throws her eyes in my direction with an aliferous affection.

". . . So have they flown in yet?" I decide to ask, she teetering an unnerving position as I soothe her with my gentle eyes and flawsome composure.

"They arrived last night actually. My dad is having them in our home until Friday. Every evening they will be having dinner with us as soon as my dad gets home from work. And my mom wants me to come straight home so that she can make sure that I look nice."

"Your natural beauty is flawless. What does she want you to wear—make-up?"

"I guess she's just being my mom. I definitely think they are both making it more complicated than it needs to be. Maybe tonight I'll get to listen to my conservative parents discuss whether or not sitting side by side is halal. Or idolize my virginity in front of everyone like I am some sort of prized cow."

"What is that—halal?"

"It is just a word that we use to say what is acceptable or permissible."

"That's very interesting. Hell and hallelujah also come from the Hebrew word Halal or Helel? Halal also means Lucifer, the light bringer, the sun. Also ruler of the material plane or hell."

"I've never heard that."

"Halal is an Egyptian god or Jupiter. And Hallelujah means the shining light of Jupiter. The Hebrew word translated as Lucifer is Heylel or Star of the Morning. Our cerebral fluid is called "christos" in greek. It's called the christ. Jacob climbs the ladder or spine and calls the place "pineal." The pineal gland. Cut your brain in half and you see the Eye of Ra around the pineal gland. Your third eye. Paul calls it the christ within. And 666 does not mean the devil. Adding the 36 constellations of the zodiac equals 666. It is the time that it takes our solar system to cover once on its orbit the path around the great sun. 6 x 6 x 6 equals 216. The twelve zodiac signs = 2,160 years. The earth's rotation which lasts for 2,160 years is an astrological age. The average rate of precession is 66.66 years per degree. The earth orbits around the sun at 66,600 mph. We are carbon based lifeforms. Carbon is six on the periodic table. Almost every atom in the body has six protons, six neutrons, and six electrons. The 666 Gyan Mudra in Sanskrit means knowledge. It means three, six, and nine or mind, body, and soul. Six is sex. Nine is the cycle of completion or nine months that it takes to make a baby. Religious stuff is really just about the earth and our physiology. My uncle is always talking about it. Even the numeric value for The Name Of Allah is 66 in Abjad numerals," I tell her, with a henotic gaze about my face.

"I am not kidding—how do you know all of this?"

"My uncle. He is also like a teacher of the different mystery traditions. And so as a teacher he puts things in simplistic form to create a sort of lens for anyone to see what is hidden. The things that are clearly there but that most people overlook."

CHAPTER TWELVE

"In Islam you never encounter any doubt. Everyone around you believes in the oneness of God. That God is the creator of all things. Shahada is the first act of worship saying that there is no deity except God and that Muhammad is his messenger."

"God is definitely the creator of all things. But I also think that if all of the religions are calling each other liars then you have to go back and study the origins of these stories and symbols. Because it is also completely asinine that people hate and kill each other when in essence they all worship the same god. All of the stories are the same. Everyone's holy books are nearly identical. People are just too ignorant and refuse to see it."

"Well—and Islam prohibits Muslims from killing, oppressing and abusing others and mistreating your relatives. But obviously we see this happening everyday. Not to mention Islam when it spread a murderous campaign of conquest and conversion just like the Christian crusades. Captives offered decapitation or conversion. People have killed more in the name of God than anything else. And they want to tell me what I should do with my body? That I can't have sex? That I can't love someone who is not Muslim? If we are all loved by the same god and belong to the same god then how does that make any sense?"

"Well why do we have to force our ideas onto other people? Especially when people are going to prove you wrong one hundred years from now. Terence McKenna is a guy that I like. He says we have been slave too long to ideology transmitted hierarchically. He says to trust your intuition. He says that authority is a lie and an abomination. That it isn't real. And that what is real is this experience and this moment. Not god. And he says that we should be free to change our minds. And I agree with him."

"I want to be free to make my own choices and form my own opinions. And I want to be free to love you. Not because someone else says that I should. Or for fear of punishment or judgement. And people angry at me and each other for what? For nothing."

"Yeah," I quietly voice in agreement, torn by the conflict seething from her heart and mind.

"And it is crazy how Muslim men and women are supposed to avoid any interaction that might lead to sexual or romantic activity prior to marriage. What if you find out that you don't like the guy in bed? Or what if he is mean to you? With my family there is no such thing as dating or relationships. It does not exist. But outside is another story. Your friends go out to the movies and hold hands. Even men from honor communities seek sex with western women while they sternly police the conduct of their own daughters and sisters. Tightly controlling the sexuality of women while a double standard of conduct is invariably found with the men. It being acceptable for him to have sex outside of marriage but not her. Patriarchy is not just prudish. It is also hypocritical. Being told to lower our eyes when we come across the opposite sex. They raise us to not even know how to talk to the opposite sex. But they want us to quickly get married? Traditional marriage half of the time does not even make a woman happy. In fact it averages the same as finding someone in a casual relationship. And I've met several girls who have married young and then the husband abuses them. And then their parents will tell them to just deal with it. Because it is better to avoid the shame of being divorced. Imagine how many women are trapped in unhappy relationships because they are afraid to disappoint their family."

"Contemporaries of Confucius wanted their women to be modest. But instead of a burka or hijab it was a grotesque amount of face paint. And their feet were tied so that they couldn't walk. And it breaks the arch in your foot. The pain is unbearable. And all to impress a potential husband. A practice that resulted in being deformed. And women were beaten if they refused. The Chinese accepted the subservience of women to men as natural and proper. And the foot binding didn't stop until the government prohibited the practice in like the 1940s. It took twenty-five hundred years to admit that it was a stupid thing to do. And one of the sayings in that time was that a woman with no talent is one who has merit. And then they only wanted boys so then the baby girls were treated badly. And also in the Arabic world women didn't wear hijab for more than two hundred and fifty years until after Muhammad died. Only then did know-it-all men make it a custom to veil their women. A practice that diminishes a woman's power because you are covering your face. And powerful men love to show us how much power they have—don't they?"

"Yeah. My dad."

"Yeah—mine too," I tell Mahru.

The two of us are then silent.

"If you were to tell a congregation of Muslims that you were leaving Islam I know some people would be traumatized. Some of them would be crying. Many ex-Muslims don't contact their family at all for fear of physical abuse or retribution. Their family shuns them. For some Muslims leaving the faith is a religious crime. They can even be sentenced to death. And I recently read

CHAPTER TWELVE

about a man who had a gun put to his head after leaving Islam. Another man also fled his family out of fear for his own safety. And after that his family hired a private investigator to find him. A young girl that I used to know I remember her parents wouldn't let her study. But we should be free to live with it if we choose or live without it if we choose."

"Well how can two billion people all be the same? And then the guy who compiled the Quran pieces it together twenty-five years after Muhammad died. Also the words of an illiterate man. And that doesn't raise any questions?"

"So many times I think that I do not believe like my parents do."

"I think that all holy books have holes in them. Truth, freedom, and love are the only things in this life that I think are worth living for."

Mahru smiles at me for the first time all morning. But remembering who she is having dinner with this evening her smile disappears. Looking down at her hands and turning her grandmothers ring around her finger she grows more anxious.

"Are you okay?"

"Yeah I'm fine. I was just thinking about this dinner tonite. And trying to wrap my head around these people claiming to know the word of god. But you know what I don't think that they know. Because in most of them you don't see love in their eyes and in their heart. Only fear."

"I think you should question everything. Especially what they want you to believe."

"I am amazed at how much you know," she then smiles.

"I just know a little. My uncle is a great teacher. And in recent I've had many a reason to do my own investigating."

"For me."

"Yeah. . . . For you. . . . And you know what else?"

"What?"

"I don't think you are a Muslim. Your religion is forced and inherited. I just think that you should break free and be who you are and do what you want to do."

A moment of relief is expressed on her hopeful face before the automatic response to her daunting world weighs in on her with a brooding fixation. Turning her head she looks down and pushes her fingers through her hair as if overwhelmed. Wanting to tell me something she then instead stops herself and leads the conversation someplace else.

"I just have to get through these next few days. You probably won't hear from me just because I need to be careful. I can come and see you after all of this is over," she tells me, touching my hand and removing it as another student passes through the waiting lounge to enter the admissions office.

"Okay," I tell her, brushing aside my suspicions and sensitivities. Afraid of getting hurt I withstand the pounding emotion of me wanting to tell her that I love her. Unutterable doubt then surges through my head.

Taking my hands and placing hers inside of mine Mahru then tries to break the troubled look on my face. I smile at her even though I am still torn about her having to do this. She wipes a tear that tries to escape my eye. And then I feel chiming against my bones the dread of the clock ticking.

Pulling my brown heathered v-neck Mahru reaches to kiss me as I gaze into the eximious miyabi of her aesthetic splendor. Kissing her loving lips what becomes most important to her is needing my forgiveness. Almost as if to say that her love being kept from me is all her fault. But before her lips are freed from mine I make it known that she has never wronged me. And with my lips I share with her that she is clearly all that I adore.

"You should go now. You're going to be late," she tells me, holding face perfectly as she refrains from crying.

Getting up from the seat next to her I take a lengthy glance at her to make sure that she is going to be okay. Seeing her curl her fingers with a hand-gesture goodbye I then proceed to walk outside.

Stepping outside the door with her out of view a tidal wave of wariness comes crashing down onto me. And I feel an unspeakable sadness. And I know in my heart that I want nothing more but to love Mahru and her family. It only hurts me knowing that I would be seen as nothing more than a connate stereotype drawn from an entire civilization. Khalil knowing that I am wrong for her without ever having met me. Whose daughter I do love. Never having been given the opportunity to prove myself worthy of her. Unresponsive because of this apparent and foretold abandonment as I still find in my heart this willingness to give to her my love every time that I see her. Because I love her. And because I am even moved by the mere awareness of her presence.

INTIMIDATION
CHAPTER THIRTEEN

My lunch-break visit with Mahru was the same the next day, apart from her adding in the awkward bit about dinner the night before. Wearisome and suffocating were her exact words, describing everyone else as enjoying themselves and as they paid no mind to how she really felt. Sitting quietly most of the evening and everyone expecting her to just go along with it. And being afraid the whole time of making her dad angry with her. She feeling pressured to conform or else suffer the condemnation of some moral facade. And then a lascivious Hassan being delusional with his cognitive bias and fugacious charm. Sensing no obvious indicators despite her unmistakable unease. Having an incapacity to observe all while spewing his superficial knowledge. Oblivious and bovine. Him sharing no concern or mindfulness as to how she feels about him. Believing himself to be the main event as their parents sat watching them from a distance. And Hassan even had the nerve to ask Mahru on their first date if she is ready to marry him.

Returning home after school my whole world appeared very different as I felt my state of confusion worsening. Loathing my neighbors and this negative perception of my nationality. Wanting to sympathize with Khalil and his world view only because I love his daughter more than life itself. Angry at the men and women of my country who have acquired the reputation of being a bunch of immoral clowns and that it has all escalated to this disdainful bigotry that so many feel in the Middle East and around the world. Even feeling sometimes that I do not know what is real anymore.

The very next day I could not find Mahru during my lunch break. And Friday was the same thing. Not even her jacket or books were left inside of the office lounge. Even texting her there was no response. And not one word from her the entire weekend.

Monday it became the same thing all over again. Only this time the whole thing began to feel extremely concerning. Isolated from the reality of this imposition and this interference that is far from what I consider to be normal. Knowing only that I want to see her again. Fearing that my love for her is just some naive dream. And feeling a heaviness closing in around me. Still refusing to believe that she cannot commit herself to me. Almost wanting to believe that she is telling me that it is over. Thinking back and maybe refusing to see it in her eyes and as it comes off of her lips without her saying it. And then what hurts the most is me wondering where I went wrong. And then wondering what is wrong with me. Feeling the solidity of my being erode from the dying light of my soul. My living heart and substance withering with a paralyzing decay of mind.

Tuesday morning I wake with the eager intention of finding her even if it means driving by her house on Thirty-seventh Avenue. Assuming that Hassan and his parents have left already the thought again re-enters my mind.

Dreading that plans have changed I throw on my black t-shirt and light-wash jeans. Pulling the lip of my white canvas shoe around my heel I wonder if she has even been to school at all. And then I think about Wednesday being the last time that I saw her.

Stuffing last nights assignment into my notebook I then wonder if she could have even been put on the next plane to Cairo. Some far away place where I would never be able to find her.

Grabbing my keys and an apple off the counter I then step outside and lock the door behind me. Walking to my car as the sun is just barely rising I find myself still grappling with the parlous threat of a bleeding heart.

Hurrying to turn my key into the ignition I then turn my wet leafy car around and pull out of my uncle's quiet driveway.

Moving down Forty-first Avenue my mind feels almost asphyxiated with thoughts of her. Turning onto West Boulevard tears streak down my face and I feel left in the dark as an unforgiving world seems to be hurrying on without

CHAPTER THIRTEEN

me. Feeling in my heart each day like the world is leaving me behind.

Parking my vehicle outside of the school I contemplate doing whatever it takes to find her and then confront her.

Walking up to the entrance doors and pushing through a river of student faces I keep asking myself why she has ignored me for several days now. And then I question if she would even consider this tenuous perpetrator who she does not even love and wondering if I am wrong.

Walking into Mr. Petrov's class and sitting down I know that I want desperately to hear the sound of her voice. Simply to see her and know. And to know that she is okay.

After sitting through Environmental Engineering I then get up and begin to walk to the admissions office instead of going straight to Mrs. Graham's Earth and Ocean Sciences class. But peeking inside of the door she still isn't there.

Walking around the corner and down a glass hall that lets in a few feet of natural light I then step inside of the integrated café to see if I can spot her.

Maintaining a low profile I scan the crowd inside to try and find her. Discreetly standing behind an empty hot table that has been pushed into the corner I wait to see if I can spot her. But as swarms of students flood the large eating area I wonder if there is any hope at all in finding her.

Prepared to skip Mrs. Graham's class and to keep searching for her Mahru then walks right passed me. Not noticing me standing right next to her she keeps walking. Her black curls and dark eyes and smile are adorned with a silver lace scarf and fringe. Accompanied by three of her friends I notice two of them wearing a veil that covers the head and wraps around the shoulders.

Watching her socialize as she maneuvers in her slim fit straight legs and black long sleeves I feel my heart pound at the sight of her. Only I question if she has been coming to school everyday but just choosing to avoid me.

Being distracted by the conversation that she is having with her peers the four of them then continue to the other side of the plant divider where the bakery displays stand and where the cash registers are.

Carefully observing her from a distance I take simple pleasure in the way that she moves across the room with confidence and style, noticing how she seems to stand more alone than she does confide the way that her friends do.

Counting about how long it takes for one student to disappear behind the divider before walking away from the cash registers I then decide how I am going to get her attention. Barely able to see her in line walking behind the tall bowstring hemp I continue to wait patiently.

Tactfully walking over to the cafe registers all while trying not to draw any attention to myself I wait for only two seconds. Watching Mahru beyond the long box planter extending a tall and lengthy snake plant I then step away from against the wall to make eye contact with her in a quick attempt for her to follow me outside. Startled to see me face to face inside of the Coffee House she then stops and notices me walking away.

Still a little startled and knowing exactly what I want from her Mahru watches me exit the cafe as she waits for her friend, Zuzana, to finish paying.

Setting down her plate and green satchel bag at the table beside her friends Mahru then excuses herself and follows me outside with a nervous unease. And just as a few curious eyes begin to notice me walk passed them.

As Mahru comes around the corner into the admissions hall she then sees me open the same door that leads to Mrs. Johnson's office. And this particular door first opens to a dark and empty corridor.

Making eye contact with Mahru before the door closes most of the way I then listen to her footsteps coming closer.

As the door begins to open I then reach for the handle to help open and close it. Catching the door from making any noise Mahru carefully steps inside. Pulling her closer to me out of longing she embraces me. But clearly she has also feared this moment. Eyes that cast a shining doubt. Almost to say that she has forgotten. But still letting me know that she has not forgotten me as she touches my face in the dark with the blinds turned.

"Where have you been?" I ask quietly.

"My mind is a mess right now. I'm sorry it seems like I've been avoiding you. My friends that I go to mosque and halaqa with have been keeping me from seeing you. All of them heard that my dad has tried to pair me with someone. So now they're all talking to me."

"But Hassan and his parents have flown back?"

"Yeah, they flew back. They left a few days ago. I'm just still waiting for my mom and dad to stop talking about it. Everyday they keep bringing it up and wondering what I am doing with my time," she upsettingly voices, clearly pressured by the whole thing even though Hassan and his family are gone.

"I kept looking for you in the office. I kept waiting for you to call me."

"I know and I'm sorry. It's just that my dad has been spending so much time with me. And I've needed to keep appearances for reasons that you already know about. I've been so tired of people asking me 'So how long do you

CHAPTER THIRTEEN

have until you're finished? And do you know how to cook?' It's just like an interrogation that you never signed up for."

"So what happened to you Thursday and Friday?"

"I've just been going out to lunch with my friends that you saw. There's this place that serves Lebanese food right here on University Boulevard called Jamjar Canteen. I've just been letting them take me there since they know my parents. I didn't want to avoid them and then it be weird," she continues to forestall, still telling me about where she has been to lunch but not telling me why she hasn't been helping Mrs. Etienne inside the office.

"So what else has been happening with you? You know I was worried about you? I think about you all of the time," I remind her, wondering if I am losing certitude in her wanting to hold on to me.

"I'm sorry, Lucius. It's just all been so crazy and stressful. And I'm so sorry to put you through this. I told you in the beginning that you should stay away from me. I hope that you don't stay mad at me."

"But I don't want to stay away from you. And I could never be mad at you."

"It's overwhelming because I feel like I'm living two different lives. Trying to make my parents happy and then wanting to be myself. My dad keeps telling me that a daughter who refuses her parents preferred husband is perceived as disrespectful and disobedient. And that such perceptions will in turn bring dishonor. He keeps telling me that my mother was married at twelve years old and that it's time. He keeps pushing me. You can't do this and you can't do that. And then the constant monitoring of my behavior and what I'm wearing. Just all of the sudden. Even more than what he usually expects me to do."

"What about Hassan? Are you talking to him?"

"He and I never even really got anywhere when we talked. But he still thinks that he loves me. Which is weird because I never gave him any indicators that I liked him." She then looks up at me almost finding the act itself difficult. "I miss you so much it's killing me," she admits, wrinkling her lip and wiping her eye.

"I miss you too—so much," I tell her, in my heart feeling a near gust of despair as I grasp her arms with my forehead against hers. Rolling her mouth into my lips she barely kisses me. But only after thinking about it first. For a moment she then doesn't say anything.

"Listen to me though okay. Just because I feel the way that I do about you doesn't mean that you can just follow me around all of the time. This could really be bad if my friends see me with you. And my brother is supposed to be meeting me here today," she tells me, pushing her feelings for me completely out of the way.

"But I'm madly in love with you."

"I'm serious. My brother might have seen me walking out of the café to follow you just now."

"So come and live with me," I again offer, my eyes fastened as I bear a heavy storm beneath me that fears her resolution. I watch her become more anxious.

"You act like it's so easy to just walk away from your family," she says, looking at me as she keeps her arms folded in front of her chest.

"My dad would choke me against the wall when I was eleven years old. He would tell me all of the time that I am stupid. Grabbing my hair to shove my face into the floor. I love my mom. I didn't want to leave her there with him. But maybe it was easier for me to leave than it would be for you," I word carefully, sensing my heart shatter on the inside as the thought of not seeing Mahru anymore enters my mind.

Watching her eyes become vacant as she stares into the space down towards my chest I then decide to let her go. At least to let her feel that I am letting her go. Seeing that her face says it all and that she appears to have already made her decision. Me feeling that I've overstepped some sensitive space in her world of hiding from everyone and herself.

Grabbing the back of her neck I then lean her forward and softly kiss her forehead goodbye.

"It was not supposed to be like this. I wasn't supposed to fall in love with you," she stops me, her eyes still convinced that none of this is her decision.

"I hope that you find the kind of happiness that exists on your own terms. That you find what moves you and what moves your soul. The things that you deeply crave from this life. Because you deserve all of it. Someone who makes you feel less afraid when you fall. Someone who shows you how deeply you can feel. And something real. Because nothing is more beautiful in this life than loving someone who can love you back."

Watching her almost painfully look away I feel her avoiding me again. And just as I'm about ready to say nothing in response to her silence and walk out into the hall without even looking at her I feel her hand touch mine to pull me back. Grabbing my fingers she feels her face against my hand, drifting back in time to a place that seemed so much more simple, a not-so-far-away place

CHAPTER THIRTEEN

where she felt free and also loved.

Standing so close to me she is drawn by a magnetism that causes her body to sway and want to surrender. Her eyes wander my physique with an unmoving fixation that longs for what the body wants. But her heart stands still as if facing a fierce and torrid juncture. Deep eyes that rage but that are still afraid. Watching her heart being ripped apart. Cutting me to my core to witness her pain crawling out of her eyes and skin with the heaviest and most upsetting obligation imaginable.

Looking at her in the dark I catch her sad eyes turning towards the light as if to ask some higher power for help. I feel her pulling air into her lungs with a distressing cry that quietly sends chills down my back. Facing me while rubbing her head with both hands I grab her wrists and pull her closer. Sliding my fingers behind her black curly hair I rub her forehead as she gives in to a shaking sigh of relief. Hugging her I rest my face on the back of her head. Holding her behind a closed door while looking through the cracked blinds I feel what she feels. Having to love in the dark where no one else can see. The only place where she can really say what she feels.

"I'm sorry," Mahru tries to tell me, she looking into my eyes and seeing the beautiful way that I complicate her life.

"Don't be. I just miss seeing you."

"I know. And I miss you too. And I'm sorry that I haven't spoke to you. I promise that I'll call you tonight. Trust me. . . . But I need to go back before Zuzana comes looking for me. You know that I care about you," she tells me, wiping her face dry.

"Should I keep coming by the office to see you?" I ask her, my heart still drawn to her even as she confuses me to this point of near insanity.

"I always want you to come by and see me," she timorously utters, still refusing to tell me something.

Feeling emotionally exhausted I take a long deep breath and acknowledge her being at least somewhat honest with me.

Trailing my two hands down her waist she can trust herself no more to stand distant, clearly torn between me and this world that demands from her everything that she has. Still at present she finds a familiar silence and remembers my touch that she has tried so hastily to repress from her memory. Falling into my kiss and my arms with an upsetting uncertainty her lips again fall away from mine. Holding onto me for a few more seconds she takes one last look at me before opening the door to leave. Squeezing my finger so tight as if to ask me not to let go of her, she then walks out, troubled by her love and her loyalty to her family. Saddened as she fears her love for me being slowly torn. And once again me being left in the dark with hardly the frailest hint of solace.

Later that night Mahru waited for her family to fall asleep so that no one else could hear her crying in the shower. The one place where she can fall apart without being interrogated. The one place where her warm tears can blend in and disappear with the space and the water that dissolves her.

After getting out of the shower to call me all that she could dare mutter was just more of the same. And the call seemed to be over before it even began. Just a short conversation with several long silent pauses. And then after she hung up with me I only wanted to cry. Almost unable to make sense of why she cannot be here where I am. Not being close enough for me to touch. Not being able to just look into her eyes and feel better about the world and about myself. Hating myself and even begging god to somehow help me to be a part of her life. Knowing that I treasure her more than anything in this world. And yet still confused about whether or not she is within my reach. Feeling as if the devil himself has come to convince me of my worth. Reaching down into my soul with his glass-cutting grip to torque all of me into some excruciating reminder of all that I am. Tears streaming down my face like the slow drippings from a melting candle. Down my cheeks and neck as I try drying all of it with my hands and shirt. Rubbing my face in the dark of night. My heart emerging more fatigued as she continues to devastate me with her unfurling sadness. Seeing her coming to grips with the reality of this causing the life to be literally squeezed from my heart. Sensing myself to be weak in my sadness. Me having been strong for too long. Believing in my mistakes instead of my virtues. Feeling loathingly hostile to the thought of anyone else having her except me. And then me wanting to cry more often than not.

Lying awake in the night I wonder how I can ever show that I am grateful to the moon when she is yet farthest from me. If she still knows that I love her. Wondering if she will ever allow me to become the light in her universe. Wondering what her family would think of me if they dared acknowledge that I exist. If they'd still love her for choosing me. Apprehensive to the thought of forever being to her a dream that can never become a reality. Looking up through my window into those night stars and wiping my eyes. Asking the heavens if there is a chance that the two of us could live together with a love that will never die.

THE DREAD
CHAPTER FOURTEEN

The very next morning the pacific coast had become more laden with crisp carnelian and saffron. Giant drifting heaps of fall leaves crawling back into the earth from whence they came. I had all gotten ready for class with one tiresome thing eating at my every waking thought. And with a flustered dawn setting foot to this assiduous urgency of mine. Thoughts of eloping that pervade the wildest parts of my love and imagination. But still facing this moralistically myopic thing that grows more unbearable for us each passing day.

Back on campus from one class to the next it all of the sudden became time for me to sit with Mahru during my thirty-minute break. Stepping into the office lounge and seeing her look away from me is almost dismantling enough for me to change my mind and walk away. Only I know that I love her more than life. Her radiant fair ivory skin and clay lips too prepossessing for me to reverse my course. Far galaxies encompassing her dark eyes that are wrapped with illusive sin and passion. And seeing her in her pearl mauve scarf that wraps loosely along her visible neckline.

Talking with her I still want to believe that she loves me. Me watching her painfully ignore her faith in me. Even trying my very best to endure it. Watching in her eyes this awful pressure to confront me as she refrains from telling me anything. Talking to Mahru as if nothing is being wedged between us. Watching her desperately trying to hold onto something that she has already let go of. Me being perhaps too much in love to see that what she and I have

THE DREAD

can never work. Sitting and worrying that someone is going to walk through that door and see the love that she has for me reveal all over her face. She being part of a community that has eyes inside and outside of this school.

Helping to proofread her paper on the sofa I watch her keep busy as she edits her assignment from yesterday. Almost visibly tense she remains focused instead of being in the middle of a conversation that will only make her more uncomfortable.

Sitting alone with Mahru under a warm hanging iron pendant light my abiding love for her seems almost out of place. Everything left unsaid lingers in the forefront of my mind. Desperately trying to avoid this inner conflict that troubles me even more when I am alone with her. She being clearly torn and no longer able to hide it from me. And I mutter nothing only because I know that I would die if I ended up pushing her away. My mind obsessing over all of the reasons that she has tried to stay away from me from the beginning. Fearfully withholding all evidence of our love from her family. Even afraid of calling me and talking to me as our contiguous love inescapably evades this edging anguish. Incapable of going to her the way that an adult man can approach his lover unrestrained. No being out in public or with close friends. Only haunted by the reality of our indifference. This distance between our two worlds tearing my heart with dejection and confusion. My efforts to change everything already having been dismissed and ignored. Seeing where she is all over her face. And though I tell myself that she is the only one for me I worry about how that can ever be.

As the hand on the clock continues to move I watch her mind default and revert to some vexatious function as her heart throbs to avoid an opprobrious and scornful shame. Watching her rationalize her unpleasant position I can see eating at her this relentless belief that she can never choose me. Watching her accept this unfair responsibility without saying any words. Still afraid to disgrace her family in this fight for love. And knowing that she loves me. But also knowing that she seems to have already made her decision. The decision to do what she has been told. And to pretend that the two of us never happened. Feeling her moving further and further away from me even after we have shared everything. Our wildest dreams and kept secrets. A sacred trust and sharing of each other beneath my pima bedding that has not been warmed by her for already far too long.

Looking at her as time moves closer for me to leave I catch this look from her that I cannot even begin to describe. Sitting further away from me with

CHAPTER FOURTEEN

this look in her eyes that pits her stomach down into the darkest depths of her aching heart. A hollow emptiness of coming to terms with. Her deep brown eyes watering and red with a shortness of breath. Simply talking to me being something that has become more painful for her to do. She seeming to only think more and more about how it is all going to end between us. Filled with the disappointment of believing that everything cannot be had. My heart unable to escape the dread of this disparity every time that her eyes achingly fixate on me. It being incredibly unfathomable to even consider forgetting someone who has given me so much to remember. And me watching her shatter my heart as I keep on loving her with all of the little pieces that I keep safe with me. Walking out of that room with only a feeling. My mind and heart too numb to remember anything that was said.

Arriving home I begin to feel more that our love for each other is only a disadvantage to her safety. Finding my key as I walk to my front door my mind becomes completely paralyzed by the abnormality of such a foreign devoir.

Shutting the front door behind me I tell myself that I am prepared to do whatever it takes to ensure her happiness. And then I again face the frightening disappointment that none of it is up to me.

Gazing out of my cold window to the sound of nothing a setting sunlight begins to dull over the tops of the trees. And I know that I should not have to feel as though I am sliding down a rock face with my hands tied behind my back.

Starring at a loose picture of Mahru left on my coffee table I wonder why I can't just be accepted by her family and why they can't just let me love them. And I feel my heart being crippled by this seventeenth-century bullshit when husbands stopped dining with their wives, and when they refused to become companions, sequestering women to the harem. All of it seeming so out of touch with reality and the modern world. Feeling that my heart might stop beating if I ever find out that Mahru cannot be with me to love. And that is the part that scares me the most. Wishing that I didn't have to deal with whatever this is. Perhaps having kid myself all of this time. Feeling miserably cursed and wondering about what my existence means if it not to be with the only woman that I love. Even wondering if I should go to Khalil myself to ask for his daughter. Many cultures having done it this way for several millennia. But still she insists that I not get involved. Deep down knowing that she is being forced and torn away from me. And yet feeling that there is nothing

THE DREAD

that I can do. Wondering if what is now happening will change absolutely everything. Thinking about her knowing what we have and if she will still throw all of that away.

BREAKUP CALL
CHAPTER FIFTEEN

One week later my everyday visit with Mahru at school was becoming more intense and more difficult to face. Every day she being less talkative during my thirty-minute break and gradually responding less to my texts.

Today it became apparent to me just looking into her sad eyes that she is beginning to break up with me. But still I want her to tell me. Not wanting to play her cruel guessing game. Silent about the pressure that is always intensifying at home. Always looming some argumentative discussion or moral imperative at the family dinner table. Her mom passive but annoyed underneath the whole thing. Her dad quick to scoff at anything remotely indifferent to his own derisive bias. Talking about marriage like it is some cold colorless labor that must be done. Nobody expressing any warmth or joy. Khalil casually berating Madge and Mahru with his inelegant and nondescript worldview. Both of them careful not to provoke their dad as they can become easily corralled into an unpleasant conversation. Mahru feeling a subtle resentment as she sits being robbed of the most important decision of her lifetime. Khalil making them feel that he is quick to be disappointed while simultaneously being so quick to discard them. Handing her over to someone who says with words that he can love her. And Khalil the entire time demanding respect because of it. Guilt-tripping her with his self-righteous rant about what is honorable. Occasionally dishing out a claustrophobic tongue-lashing without anyone having angered him. Somehow even interpreting his daughter's silence as being combative. Even as she sits defenseless and defeated. And her love depleted. The pond to her desolate heart dried up by the heat of an imperious sun. Her flame washed away at the hands of a verbal flash flood. Khalil inherently a contentious man perhaps. But maybe just deeply concerned in finding for his daughter someplace good enough for her to live her life. I think a man who loves his daughter. Choosing Hassan who is close to him because he cares so much for her. But already there is someone. Someone who can love her more fiercely than anyone else can. Someone who has already captured her heart.

Arriving home frustrated after having talked earlier with Mahru on campus she surprises me with a strange call. Sitting in her truck outside of the school after most everyone has left she waits for me to pick up. Having just barely taken off my shoes I answer her and almost immediately realize why she is calling. Knowing as soon as I heard her say hey to me. Listening to her hesitate at first—quickly forcing herself to tell me.

"Hey," Mahru says to me, worried for me and more hurt than she can bear to acknowledge in telling me this over the phone.

Trying to hide my being worried and even a little apprehensive I calmly answer her.

"Hey. . . . Are you okay?"

I hear Mahru trying to constrain the emotion of her being cut in half, hearing in her throat the sound of her toskal agony.

"No. . . ." she says, with a loss for all hope that does infringe upon her sweet voice. I then hear a subtle clearing of her nose and can tell that she has been crying.

"Tell me what's going on. I'll come and get you right now. If you can just tell me—"

"Lucius, listen to me. I cannot keep talking to you. You have to stop talking to me. It will never work between me and you. I am really sorry. So please don't expect me to keep calling you anymore. Please don't call me or text me anymore. Okay?"

Listening to how upset she is and not knowing how I can change her mind before I never hear from her again I pause for a moment.

"I thought everything was okay. Why did I think that?"

"It's not your fault, Lucius. You know that. . . . And you have always known that we were never going to be anything more than what we were," she says, me hearing over the phone how hard she is biting down as she finishes her

CHAPTER FIFTEEN

sentence.

"Yeah—maybe. Or maybe I just wanted you to love me just as much as I love you," I almost hastily reply, realizing that there is probably nothing that I can say that will get her to change her mind. Me realizing that I have seen all of this coming over the last several days.

"I'm sorry that it has to be this way. But there is nothing left for us to talk about. I need for you to let me go, Lucius. Promise me," she insists, almost hesitating.

"Do you love me?"

"No—I don't," she painfully tells me.

"You don't what?" I ask.

I then hear nothing from her as she finds it increasingly difficult to respond.

"You know that I am very much in love with you. But I promise you," I tell Mahru softly, with tears drawing near to my lips. "I promise you that I will let you go," I mutter, trying to conceal my frustration from her ears.

"Thank you," she tells me.

"Yeah. . . . Okay."

"Goodbye," she then faintly voices, heartbroken from having to accept this decision that has been made by her family. Feeling that there exists some all-seeing cosmic punishment for her simply being a woman. Afraid and feeling that there is no way she can escape this bitter arrangement that has been sloppily pieced together.

Mahru then hangs up.

Understanding that she is gone I begin to feel that there is no way that I can ever overcome this phthartic heartache that is now beginning to take shelter inside of me. Feeling everything that I love being torn from me. And without any good enough explanation as to why as I face this hellish downpour of rain inside of my heart. The sudden fear of not being able to feel her kalonal touch torments me. Fearing that it is only a matter of time now before she becomes just a precious memory. Feeling that I will never again experience her tender lips gently pressed into mine. Every image of her and coming to grief with draining my soul of its living warmth. Having taken from me all that I love and worship. Every hair on my body acknowledging my vacuous disillusionment.

Lying down on my pillow-swallowed sofa tears from my right eye spill over into my left. I cry knowing that my idea of heaven can never be permitted by

God so long as I am prisoner to this mirky place. Me believing that she has chosen this man who her father has chosen for her. And knowing that it is all an awful lie. And dead I now am.

Thrashing through the guesthouse looking for everything that belongs to me I think to leave in my car tonight for Seattle. Pacing across the wood floor I grow afraid of becoming unhinged and broken. Stopping myself I imagine her changing her mind as I face this aching inside of my heart. Still desperate to believe that she is fooling me and also herself. Miserably encumbered by this heart-rending trauma.

Walking into my sun-lit room I crawl into bed and try to lie still. Feeling my chest want to cave in I stop and take one great gasp of air as I face the wood planked ceiling. Feeling my tear-soaked pillow behind me I want her to feel my razed heart crumbling. Irremediably disarranged by those feelings of separation that have overcome me. Afraid to see her face again even in passing. Feeling afraid that all of the love that I have for her will surely destroy me.

Lying still to try and compose myself I listen to the air that is taken in by my lungs before it escapes. And I pray that my heart survives this shadowy hand that pursues the living part of me. Pushing myself from this pain that I want buried. But still finding this part of me that is stubborn and unwilling to lose sight of her. In my heart knowing that I love her too much. Wondering how I can let go of her when clearly I am reminded of her deepest affections for me. Wondering how I can let go of the one person who causes me to become curious through every facet of the conscious and subconscious sphere. Questioning if I am even a real person I feel a part of me beginning to lose it.

Lying on top of my made bed I think about how she is genteel and respectable. And then I think about how I am everything else. Pulling the soft sham behind my head I wonder if her dad will inflict some type of misery over her for having been with me. Crumbling without my other half to comfort me. The amount of earth between us crushing me and leaving me for dead as I suffocate under a slow moving stream forged by my own tears. Thinking about her belonging to a family that does not want anything to do with an outsider. Since that is what I am. She being an Egyptian princess and me just an unwelcome stranger who thought that he could love an angel like her. Knowing that I love her and knowing that she is worth every bit of the risk. All of this perhaps not being so much a cultural thing as it is that she is a rich man's daughter. Wondering if he would try to hurt me just because I love her. If he would really think that I am a bad person. Just because I was born in

CHAPTER FIFTEEN

America and lay claim to nobody's god. And her protecting me I'm sure. But only ever having wanted to protect her. Only ever having wanted to love her.

Fretfully I then ponder how I myself could ever take care of a woman. Afraid of not being able to adjust to the responsibilities of loving anyone other than myself. Afraid of what I might become through her eyes, and through the eyes of a child. Trying to convince myself that all of this is probably best. Afraid to disappoint her. Something that I know I could never bear. Knowing that it would destroy me. Wondering if my fear could compromise my relationship with the only woman that I have ever loved. As if she is even still possible. Fearing being like my dad. Knowing already that I am nothing like him. And still a part of me wanting to confirm that there is no trace of his cruelty swimming through my veins. Feeling that not being there for her is crippling me. Always this weighing on me. And me still wanting her even though she is gone.

Pulling some plain paper from my bedside drawer I begin to write Mahru one last poem. Easily extracting the words right out of the ether I use the twenty-seven bones in my hand to write to the woman that I love. Not sure that it really even matters anymore. Writing it with the last little bit of sun light that is left. Me knowing that only sadness can come from it.

Folding the paper into an envelope with her name on it I then set it aside for me to take with me tomorrow. And knowing that I cannot change her decision. Only wanting to exhibit my relentless endeavor to dismiss what she says to do. Just as I have done from the first day that we met.

> *Belong I do and yes to you my love for you is blind*
> *blind from seeing anything that isn't you and I*
> *me and you on separate sides of this scalding gate*
> *bathing in sun rays covered by lines of shape*
> *touching my hands and lips through woven steel*
> *the need to go over top or bottom my flesh would peel*
> *please love stay and guide me another way*
> *love stay I say that gates must have a doorway*

HOPE FOR A LAST

CHAPTER SIXTEEN

By morning I still hadn't fully grasped the fact that everything that I love is gone. Lifting my sage bedspread to a cool brisk sunrise my hands feel the chill in the air. A faint morning frost is visible at the edge of my large window. My feet shuffle across the cold wood floor. Weary after battling a piercing sadness all through the night.

Grabbing my chilled Darjeeling tea from the fridge I then grab my letter to Mahru to take with me. Seeing her amble across my floor in my mind as I prepare to leave and head to class.

Walking outside beneath the beautiful fulvous colors of fall I still can't help but feel terrified. Nervous that I might see her.

Waiting for a minute inside of my car I wonder why I should even turn the keys. Wondering if I even want to finish school. But maybe really hoping deep down that she will want to say something to me. Anything but this sickening silence that keeps ringing in my ears and tearing the flesh to my heart.

Twelve minutes later I find myself trudging up the back way to class where a nearly hidden path remains covered by changing shapes of sunlight that flicker down from the trees. In through a side door that is mostly used by administration. With each footstep becoming more aware that I haven't yet embraced the full impact of my love being deprived and dejected.

Moving through the hall I see only her face. And she stares right back at me until her eyes turn away. And until I notice that it is just someone else.

CHAPTER SIXTEEN

Feeling the red sand seep down through the hourglass that belongs to my heart. Adoring her breathtaking smile from the still fresh shards of memories left scattered in my mind. She being opium to my eyes and part of a power that reaches down into the deepest darkest corners of my soul. Likened to a brilliant light that uncovers all that is beautiful. Offering me warmth when all is dark and forsaken. Like the rising sun over a darkened landscape. Ripped apart by something so abstract and putative. And me feeling like I just want to die.

Not seeing her all day was intentionally my safer objective. Acknowledging that passing each other in the hall would be far too excruciating for us to bear. During each tortuous lecture I somehow was still able to focus and take notes. Still listening in class and doing only what I had to do to get by. And then when it finally came time for me to leave my letter with Mahru I simply just left it inside of the office lounge after she went to lunch. Conveniently seeing that Mrs. Etienne was preoccupied with a visitor. Placing my letter inside of her winter jacket in the corner of the seat cushion. And not picking up her jacket to smell her scent even though I wanted to. Leaving only my unsigned letter just incase somebody else found it before she did. And then of course leaving the admissions office discreetly without anyone having seen me.

Getting home after class I quickly move to dull the gnawing torment brewing withinside of me. Refocusing my attention by redirecting my many frustrations.

Not needing to get up early the next day, I pull out my paints and my brushes, driving the noise out of my head with some Nirvana and Mr. Gnome in the background.

Mixing my paint and wiping my stir stick into the fabric I begin to mix in some varnish with my colors arranged from light to dark. The routine cementing my heart from this pique enigma. Layering one area at a time. Preparing myself to stay up late if need be. And only finding it difficult when I stop and see her looking back at me. Learning to breathe as my tears flow. Still keeping my paintbrush steady.

Faintly hearing my phone ring with my music playing I then look down to see that Mahru is calling me. Feeling tormented but still buoyant just seeing her name I answer without speaking into the phone.

"Hey. . . . I thought that we agreed." Mahru contends, wondering if she has lost her faith in me to leave her alone. Still hearing in her sweet voice her maybe wanting to hear from me.

In the middle of a six by ten area on my canvas I place my brush down on the table. I then turn my music down before sitting on my paint stool.

"I know I said that I would let you go. I just needed to defy you one last time. And you did not specifically cross out me writing to you. But I promise now that I will leave you alone."

"Yesterday I hope you were listening to me. I just really need you to understand."

"And I do. I will leave you alone," I tell her with difficulty, deep in my chest feeling my heart cry out inside of me.

"I'm sorry for what I've done to you, Lucius. I'm sorry that I allowed you to believe in me. Knowing that I could never give you what you deserve. I'm not sorry for loving you. I'm just sorry that I hurt you."

"It's not your fault. You don't have to be sorry to me. I just still wish that you would let me change things. Like you saying that you thought about coming to live here with me. I could take care of you."

"You can't take care of me, Lucius. It was never going to work out. And my dad will not like the fact that I've been seeing you. He will not condone us marrying. My father doesn't want to listen. My family will never understand you and me. And when all they want to do is fight about it. Back home in Egypt people have different views about marriage and family," she painfully reiterates.

I don't say anything, feeling forever powerless in my efforts to stem the tide to her ever-growing fear.

"I know. . . . It's okay," I tell Mahru, achingly enduring this cimmerian spear that pierces my bone and touches my heart.

"No. It's not," she tells me, feeling again her being ripped apart from me. "And I don't know what to tell you anymore. I love you so much and I love my family too. I'm not ready to leave them and never see them again."

I say nothing in return. Only drowning in my own silence. Hurt being the only thing that I can feel in my body.

"Are you there?" she asks.

"I'm here . . ." I tell her. "Sometimes I just wonder if a part of me has always known that one of us would end up being disappointed. Not with you. Just this dumb thing between us. I feel like I've been going crazy always thinking about it."

"You forget that I'm disappointed too. But I can't say no to my family. I

CHAPTER SIXTEEN

never wanted anything like this to happen to us. I tried telling you when we met," she says, trying to conceal her aching sadness.

"I love you, Mahru," I painfully remind her.

"I know that you love me. But you have to let me go," she whispers thin, me fighting inside of my head what I want to believe.

Listening to her breath on the phone her tears push to the edge of her watering eyes. "I want to see you. But I can only see you one last time. And then you have to promise me that you won't talk to me anymore. Maybe I can come and see you tomorrow," she says, hoping that I will want her to come over. Me knowing that I would never deny her coming to see me.

"I'm free tomorrow so . . . you're welcome to come over."

"I will come over in the morning about nine. I just need you to remember what I'm telling you. After tomorrow you cannot text me or write me anymore."

"I know," I tell Mahru, listening to her heart falling down inside of her chest.

"I never meant to hurt you, Lucius," she tries to convince me.

My chest begins to tighten as I listen to her. I want to tell her that everything is going to be okay. But I don't. Knowing that she has fallen powerless from her own free volition. Succumbing to an invective and dehumanizing form of duress.

"I know," I tell her, almost unforgiving as I try to hang strong, praying in my heart that Mahru will come and find me one last time so that I can at least say goodbye to her.

Speaking with Mahru, I quiet my tears, pressing down on this wound to try and keep my heart from bleeding to death. Still clinging to this fool's hope. Knowing that I cannot cause her to feel guilty for this thing that I've created and that I am responsible for.

"Are you still there?"

"Are you scared?" I then ask.

"I'm just tired. I was arguing with my parents earlier. I was actually trying to talk to them about even the idea of being married to someone outside of Islam. My dad went crazy. He became so angry that he yelled at my mom," she says, fighting back the torment that again reaches to grab a grimacing hold on her heart.

"You're gonna come see me tomorrow?" I then ask Mahru, praying with all of my heart that I might get to see her one last time, tormented by that same torment that ravages the heart, leaving what is left of me in nothing but ruin.

"You have to promise me what I said. Can you do that?"

"Yeah," I tell Mahru, part of me believing that I should just let her be. And as painful as that would be for me. Feeling my heart being ripped from my chest as my words slip from me. Pushing from my mind this devastating bind that forbids us to shamelessly be together. Knowing that she could only temporarily wound this beast that keeps us from fully surrendering our love. Knowing that I am giving in to this love that has no name. Delaying the inevitable with this toilsome attempt to cure a cursed love. Like a maimed soldier left to die. Only thinking about that nurse who sometimes comes to care for me. Knowing that I will not be dead so long as I hope to see her. Sharing with her my one heart-twisting hope that I know before long will destroy me.

As Mahru prepares to hang up I feel my soul beset by the howling of beasts that create a trembling in the ground beneath me. Finding myself partly angry and partly trying to keep myself from extending this hurt that tries digging itself deeper into my heart. It being clear to me that she isn't ready to leave her family even for love. What little time I have with her being all that I can seem to think in my head.

Finally hanging up with me Mahru closes her phone as her silent tears roll over her lips. Falling to pieces she then turns in front of her bed clenching the bed linens. Her heart crumbling as she can only remind herself of what her father might do to her if he ever finds out. Pulling her bed blanket closer to her eyes she tries to quiet her crying. Knowing that she can never fully empower her love for me so long as this ignominious fear is present inside of her.

After hanging up the phone with Mahru I face my canvas. I feel all of my body's water spill from my eyes. Knowing that we would not be here if it weren't for me. Me being the one who wouldn't stop talking to her. The one who wouldn't stop writing her. My kiss being the spark to all of her lust. Genuinely hating all unintelligible men who claim to know anything at all. Hating them because I feel that I am no different from them. Marked by this stomach-churning gimlet that causes this unseen despair. Knowing that I cannot live without her. Ashamed for failing to eliminate in her mind this cultural dictum that weighs heavy on us both.

Tears smear into the paint that is left on my hands. Our love shaken by fear. Unable to believe that we have really come this far only to find ourselves defeated by some bigoted edict of tradition.

A LONG KISS GOODBYE

CHAPTER SEVENTEEN

Opening my eyes to the morning a soft blue draws a blanket above the silhouette of dark trees that skulk before the sun's rise. Through the window barely cracked I hear the soothing sounds of a gentle wind caressing the leaves outside. Wondering if she is getting ready to come over I then crawl out of bed to see that it is just eight a.m. on my phone. Cigarettes After Sex plays on my Bluetooth as I migrate into the bathroom to pee and brush. My deepest emotions stir inside of me. Feeling her abandoning me. Feeling her cave to this ideological detriment and this marring of the soul.

Changing the temperature on the thermostat I begin to warm a pot of water in my black split-leg shorts and t-shirt. Pulling my hair back into a bun I look out my front window and imagine her pulling up to see me. All of the space inside of the house brings to mind the times when she was here with me. Thinking about of all the times when we have been completely lost in each other. Her sex and her touch being medicine to my numinous depth. She being the other half of me that I have now been watching die a little each day.

Leaning into the deep wood ledge of my window with my warm cup I think about her wanting to say goodbye to me. Feeling in my heart that she doesn't really want to say goodbye. And I ask myself if she will actually submit to this malefic and manipulative marriage.

Looking over the condensation forming at my window I eagerly anticipate her appearance, flustered between my many frustrations and my exceeding love for her. My every effort stays focused on trying to keep still in my mind. Already having this feeling that losing her will destroy me. Admitting to myself that I am a part of this extremely sad story. And not for one second wishing that I never met her. Only ever having hoped to wake each morning beside the one I love. A part of me feeling like I still have her. Bewildered as to how a beautiful and unmistakable thing like love can still escape us. Fooling myself in thinking that she will continue to come to my door. But really and truly knowing that this will be the last time.

Hearing my phone vibrate on the kitchen counter I then read her text.

"I will be there in ten minutes."

Texting Mahru back that I'm awake I then feel more this bogging back-and-forth more than ever before. Hoping that she will stay for more than just a few minutes. Hoping that I can forgive her. Thinking to myself that I know too much about her home life to be angry with her. Even still foolishly thinking that she could run to me if she wanted to.

Hearing her old vehicle door shut outside I glance out of the window and see Mahru carefully walking up to knock. My heart anxiously pumps my lifeblood through every detour of my nervous body as I move closer to the door.

Parting the door open her loving presence causes me to tremble as always. There she stands with her love for me seeping from her sad eyes. Piling high the sand bags to the emotional flood of her immurement. Almost overflowing with a love that has been walled up inside of her since before Halloween. Wearing her laurel colored cardigan over a hazel wood top that presses firmly against the curvature of her elegant lines. She drawing a faint smile of affection as I welcome her inside. Her tight black pants high above her waist with her belted carob boots and her striped canvas tote bag. Her lush black curls contrasting her vibrant natural skin color. Me feeling myself moving around her body in spirit as I follow her hard eyes.

"Hey," she says softly, the low pitch in her throat revealing to me the soreness of her having cried plenty. Comforted in hearing her voice as she waits to see if I might smile back at her.

"Hey," I try to smile, showing her that I am not too hurt to still be happy that she is here. Gathering a tear in each eye I see her uncomfortable unease.

"Let me get you some warm tea," I tell Mahru, me being certain that in five minutes I will never see her again.

"Thank you," she says, hesitant for a second, she feeling her heart relish in the tenderness of my kind hug.

CHAPTER SEVENTEEN

Looking back at her I am sad that she has come to say goodbye. Knowing that I can never be permitted to marry her and be there for her the way that I have been and more. Encountering a soft yearning in her voice for me I continue to observe a sadness in her. And I watch her eyes move back and forth in my direction as I hand to her a cup of black tea.

"So are you able to stay long?" I ask, feeling an endless tenebrous pit growing inside of my stomach.

"If that is alright. I have the whole day so," she says, her deep dark eyes still looking up at me.

"Good. Me too," I tell Mahru, finding an amiable comfort in her setting aside this final tryst between lovers.

"It will probably be the closest that we've ever had to spending a real day together. Maybe like that time that you took me to see the waterfall," she says, her love quavering a little as she holds intense eye contact.

"Yeah," I acknowledge, burying my hurt emotions, seeing her weighing veneer begin to unmask as the world seems to desist from its natural rotation. Seeing in her this heartbreaking sadness that still wants to love me and that still wants to fuck me.

As Mahru touches my hand a long tear falls down the side of her face. I move closer to her. Opening my arms she moves her hands up my back, she feeling herself be where I am, using me to calm her aching heart as she cleaves to my gentle touch. Her tears silently spill into my black shirt. Holding Mahru she grabs me tight as her lungs expand against my chest. She wishes that I will forgive her and for the heartache that she claims to have caused. Her eyelashes are fixed to a damp mold and her nose still wet. Feeling in my heart the saddest most aching pain that I have ever felt. She still believing that she must submit to this absurd marriage. She kidding herself that her heart will mend and that she will forget me.

Holding Mahru tight I remind her that I cannot forgive the woman who loves me still. Knowing her love exists as the counterbalance to any pain that she has caused. And the way that she looks at me being even more painful for me to admit. Knowing that she wants my love and knowing that I will give it to her.

Feeling her slender fingers comb through my natural blonde curls Mahru hastens me to taste her sweet mouth. She then touches me and holds me with a grip that anticipates my rousing affection. But before our lips touch I look into her eyes with a love that kindles her utmost desire to feel me love her again. And her dark eyes and smile possess me with her tantalizing alchemy. Charging her lowly spirit my lips taste her lustrous mouth that glissades utterly over mine. Feeling a subtle terror she feels for my kiss to try and relish the taste of her thirst. Her last wish for me to give it to her nice and slow until there is nothing else left of her. And knowing that I will stay inside of her from morning 'til night. An all-day way of worship like venturing a psychedelic journey to sushumna. Breathing in and out our souls inside of this hot wet place that is always anxiously sought after. A place of mystical love and our wild effort to be with each other for as long as we can.

"Today is the last day that I can see you. So I want it to count," she tells me, with a heartbroken criticism of self, looking up at me as her dark brown eyes begin to water.

"Okay," I tell Mahru, taking into account how difficult it must be for her to speak to me this way. Caressing her with my hands and my brow to her face my heart sinks into a crushing slow cooker, me desperately trying to understand her without letting the flame to my heart burn low.

"I will make today the day that you always remember," I then gently voice, comforting her with both my hands over her face to where my thumbs surf the lines above her eyes. Trailing my fingers down below her cheekbones Mahru shakes her head yes with a still dazzling smile and as a single tear rests underneath her eye. Carefully I then kiss this tear from her face. Kissing her with a romance that I know will soon ignite into a delirium of sweltering sex. Knowing her love will momentarily cure me of this disease that causes me to question as I breathe in and out this beautiful love that comes to fill me wet before it leaves me dry.

Feeling her fingers crawl down my stomach to the base of my shirt her tender eyes smile back at me with an incandescent glow. Leaning into her she slides my shirt over the top of my curly head as I kiss her again after coming out from underneath my shirt.

Taking Mahru by the hand I lure her to the upstairs room with my kiss. In my heart knowing that I would never thirst if only my lips could be there to always satisfy her. Holding her ever so gently. Her last wish granted as I compare the sweet surface of her lips to the effervescent succulence of an exotic fruit that has been squeezed into my mouth. She weaving her hands up my back towards my shoulders in a beautiful physical connection that sends shivers down my entire body.

Advancing down the front of Mahru with my lips pressed firmly against

CHAPTER SEVENTEEN

her stomach, my hands move up underneath her shirt, looking up into those eyes that long for me as I plant my lips into her. Removing her tight pants legs she leans back onto my bed as I pull the material away from her ankles.

Traveling her long thighs my hands move with a subtle sophistication that sends shivers round about her. My hands and fingers inching all the way up under and passed her buttocks as they climb over the top of her black panty line. Like a feather broom to a silk web her laced lingerie slips down her legs as her hands and fingers comb through my hair. She moving her hands up the back of my head as I remove her sandals from her heels.

Drawing a V below her abs with my fingers, my lips then slide between her libellule, still looking into those eyes as my perfect hands strum down her back end, and she still gazing down at me with a still attraction.

Climbing up to kiss Mahru I cling to her lips with an intensity that shakes her entire body with a paralyzing calm. Carefully she pushes my shorts down around my thighs while holding on to these lips that have proved to be perfection. Easing the edge of her form-fitting top up around her frail torso she struggles to get her arms around my neck and chest after lifting her shirt over. Moving her thigh up underneath my arm I hold on to her as her other leg follows. And like a steady freight crane carefully I move her onto my bed to that beautiful supine position. Aroused beneath my waist then comes that part of me that does protrude, my love causing an effluxion of vitality to commove down my entire vessel in a slow whisper that moves over my entire body towards my legs and toes.

Stitching up my torn heart her smooth lips fall upon my face as she gives heed to my inhumed existence. Wishing only to free her I seize her lips with an upward nudge of passion that educes a sort of ethereal beauty as we lie within the soothe of each other's company. Like a budding flower each time coming into existence. Moving across the surface of her entire body the way that a dragonfly wets its tail above still water.

The faintest cry is then loosened from her in a lucid expression that does announce her bestirring itch for me. Pouring a bottle of liquid coconut oil over her and on my throbbing nerve, I then place myself inside of her, falling into Mahru with all of my love. Watching her fall into this serene state of awareness her eyes traject to me the absolute beauty of a jungle mist that I do crave to lose myself to. Like swimming up for air life pulses through me. There still being love and joy inside of this certain darkness. Inhaling her ma-li scent through my nose I push deeper. Tasting each second I have with her and putting from my mind her fear-based resolution. Determined to let her feel me one last time. My mind, body, and spirit like the petals of a wild flower floating over sublime lush lands with hills and valleys. Lips that conjoin like the glittery coils of a wet snake dancing in the amazon. Kissing her sending me into a savoring affair for that which is most delectable. Always tasting the delicate layers that exist in her myriad of emotion. Opulent lips that gratify and subdue. She dragging her fingers down my stomach like a tree scattering its roots. Brushing my lips over hers as I dip into her mouth. Osculating under this euphoric form of affection. Traveling back and forth the silky inner-walls of her vaginal hollow.

Over and under her perfect naked body we find ourselves salivating beneath this recalescent and inundated Elysium, turning about as our hips move in a natural sequence that gives sentience to the repressed soul. The soused surface of her rare figure displays her extreme urge as she trembles and fluctuates excessively. The stroke of the clock subsides more each second as if a puissance emanating from the soul is causing its mechanics to cease. The tenderness of her small hands move gradually along my stomach as she feels for my kiss. Hands that possess god's love for me. A slipping of the hands that mesmerize me with a truly hypnotic array of affection. Always moving my hands over her oily figure as if to mold her inner spirit into that of her outward beauty.

Feeling the weight and motion of her body like feeling each wave as I swim out to sea I watch her taste that sweet spot where everything else melts away. Moving to revive in her a fully climatic experience that forces her into a restful and suspireful awakening, the pendulum-like motion of her bridge between heaven and earth slides over my engorged pileus vein. With a bleating cry in feeling this state of elated bliss her seashell pussy then feels an orgasmic našwa. A filling and peaking drug of choice with a sudden rush separating the spirit from body.

Drifting further from this realm I still reach for her masala lips as I feel her beautiful legs wrap around me from behind. Turning my face adjacent to her lower abdominal center I absorb for myself the memory and sensation of her. Lying and thinking only of her as my hand moves across her chest. Our bodies dripping wet from our warmth. Turning my face into her stomach with my nose and lips prodding her oily skin. Caressing and alleviating from her this heartache as I kiss a tear that escapes her eye. Making known this love of mine in all flesh and spirit. Vowing to never forget the love that she still shares with me. Hoping that there is still somehow a way and that she will utter some-

CHAPTER SEVENTEEN

thing to break this sad silence.

As her fingers prowl through my hair I lie silent inside of this ephemeral paradise, and as I try to remain still in my heart, she caressing my shoulders and arms from underneath me. Thinking about how much I need her and how I still want to spend forever with her. Burying my face in her arms I pray that she will change her mind before I climb up to inject my kiss into her head. Brushing from her face those black curls that I adore as I look into her full dark eyes. Smiling hopelessly, I receive no returning word of comfort. Only a look in her eyes that refuses to ease my soul. She lowering her gaze and holding this belief that she must suffer. And so I comfort her the way that she has sought and asked to be comforted. Still drawn to her mere presence being so breathtaking. As if the tortured beast inside of me has become sedated.

Peacefully rested alongside of me I turn to hear her heartbeat, brushing my knuckles against her face as she breaks a smile. And she has that beautiful and benevolent smile. Knowing that she can never see me again after today. Losing me being all that she can seem to think about as she lies touching me. Her eyes afraid of letting herself deserve me as we lie inside of this naked embrace. Almost as if she cannot believe in what she sees. Desperately wanting to believe that she can run. She being the butterfly that escapes my chrysalis heart. The one creature that god has created for me. And not being able to convince her of this simple knowing. Wondering how I will ever taste the lips of another. Wondering how will I ever come to love myself again the way that I do now. Questioning the value of the human heart if the body and the spirit cannot love the way that nature intended. Wondering if the bitterness of this world will pull me down from heaven. Knowing that without Mahru to hold and love that I will surely die.

Recognizing this torment that I have to bear Mahru tries to remove it from my thoughts with her kiss. I kiss her back knowing that she bears this same torment. Here being where we have experienced a kind of energy that is not of this world but of that place that testifies of itself and of that infinite power. Call it god, love, the great anima mundi connecting us to all, or that spirit that only we can allow to let live inside us. And I ask god why she has sent me into this world to be cursed by keeping me from the only woman that I love. Trying to wrap my brain around why we have crossed paths if her love is only illusive to me. Lying here with Mahru in my arms wishing that I could spend just one more day with her. Wishing that I could feel her beside me for as long as there is time.

"Where are you supposed to be right now?" I then ask, gently moving my hand across her face as her blearing eyes look up at me.

"With Zuzana," she replies, brushing my thumb against her lips.

"I'm happy that you came," I express, carefully suspending myself above her, remembering that she is in just as delicate a place as I am, me communicating with my kiss this precious adoration that I will always have for her.

"Me too," Mahru tells me, allowing me to see the unaffected sincerity in her eyes. She still leaving out the minutiae of her day-to-day life. Me feeling a tacenda of silence amidst her sore eyes.

"Just know that the love that I have for you will only be locked away for safe keeping. Should you decide to change your mind. Okay."

"Okay," she says, her response making her hand twitch nervously as she rests it against me, she shying away from my ability to cure her of every heart-aching torment. Sadly smiling at me and shaking her head yes she tries to come to grips with how hard this is. Our undying love denigrated as something that is so abhorrent. Feeling her heart breaking as she shares with me this agony and this love that we have both nurtured. Still barely shaking her head yes and reaching for her breath as if to suggest that she might die.

"I can't begin to tell you how grateful that I am for you. You are a beautiful gift to me. You are the most loving and most caring person that I have ever met," she says to me, burying her face into my chest with her arms wrapped around me. Me feeling her tears crawl across me and onto my bed.

"If only I could make you stay," I try to interject.

"Please stop," she whispers, still lying there with her head nestled between my neck and chest.

"Okay," I indistinctly mutter, feeling her entire body hurt as she bites her lips. Touching Mahru's face she lies there touching mine, she still allowing her hands and her body to feel all of me.

"I guess I sort of always knew that this would happen. And I haven't dealt with it yet I know. And I feel like it's my fault for believing that I could have you," I gently confess, feeling more hurt than I care to express, grinning my teeth and licking my tears. "I will always love you, Mahru."

"None of this is your fault," she then tells me, shedding a single tear in the fore of a mental brume as if lost in a blurring mist, hushing an impuissant suffering that pounds as it tries to escape her.

Lying with my nose and lips to hers I gaze into this creature who has always altered the beating rhythm of my tender heart. I listen to the gentle sound of

CHAPTER SEVENTEEN

her soft breathing and grow more afraid of forgetting what it feels like to hold her close to me.

Looking up to wipe a falling tear that escapes me Mahru reaches for my face. I gather every bit of strength in me to make her not feel so responsible. Clenching her fingers around my waist she pulls herself tighter to me in fear of letting me go. Knowing that she will go even though she carries in her heart the strongest feelings of love for me. Me trying to make the best of her being here now. Watching her study my face as I look away from her. Gently moving my hand down the way of her tight curling hair as my heart tries escaping this slow and awful torment harboring within my chest.

Realizing that I am being forced to let go I then try and ease this abyssal suffering of ours. Leaning just past her ear I then gently whisper my only instruction of solace.

"In your travels do not draw your attention to those stones in the dirt that cause your feet to ache. But rather draw your attention to the loveliness of all that does surround you. Marvel the blades of grass that seem to turn silk under the loom of golden leaves that share with you the sun's warmth. Find the kind of acceptance that shakes you to your bones and that offers your heart unbound joy. The kind that quiets the voice inside of you telling you that you are not good enough. Forgive yourself for the mistakes that you've made. Remember that your spirit is not a mechanical device that heeds to walls and streets that tell you where to turn. You will always be beautiful because this is who you are. And bask in those moments that take your breath away and that make you happy to be here. I will always love you. And you will always be beautiful to me," I gently voice, stifling back the tears that escape my aching expression.

"I will always love you. And you will always be beautiful to me," she then tells me, her inner frustration moving inside of her as she tries smothering every emotion.

With tears bleeding from my eyes I taste her precious mouth. Touching her I search for a comfort that comes from her still being here. Grasping her with my last dying wish to remember her.

"I have something to give to you. I'll be right back," she then says, getting up from my bed as I watch her walk naked behind the wall that leads downstairs. Hearing nothing for a moment she then walks back into the bedroom with a red envelope.

"I want you to have this," she says, moving her hair out of the way as she lies down with me.

Taking the red envelope I notice the flap is unsealed and tucked inside. Unfolding it I slide out a gold perantique ring with a chain of similar antiquity. Turning the ring over in my hand and seeing an engraved scarab I then realize that it is her grandmother's ring. A strange and draining emotion falls over me. Drying my face in silence I then fear what will stem from our love being kept so secret.

"I don't think that I can accept this."

"I want you to have it. It is important to me that you have it because of what it signifies. Do you remember the story behind it?"

"Yeah.... I remember," I struggle to voice, holding her ring in my hand.

"Since I know that you do not like wearing anything on your fingers while you are painting I thought that you could wear it around your neck."

"I know.... I love it.... I will never take it off," I try to smile, with a broken heart.

"I always loved you," she then says, trying to conceal her torment.

"I've always known," I gently retort.

"I'm so sorry, Lucius," she almost whispers, using both her hands to quietly wipe both her eyes.

Nodding my head and feeling my breath I turn to look towards the light of the window. Feeling her veneficus touch I watch her fingers slide up my arm as my blood runs thin. Watching her move closer to me I swallow my newfound nullity with a painful grimace. Feeling her move further from me as we lie in silence and as I turn her black curls between my fingers.

"Now that we've seen each other this last time we cannot see each other anymore."

"I know," I acknowledge, feeling a dried emptiness and almost fidgety as I grow more fatigued with a heavy heart.

"You will always be beneath my skin," she then expresses with an undeviating snivel, she knowing that she can never again feel what she has felt with me. Wanting to die as I watch her rub the tears from her eyes inside of this final goodbye.

"And I will always love you until the end of time," I tell her back, desperately wanting to shake from her this squalid spell that lays waste to her heart. Like the wild wolf who cries to his lueur love. Feeling her grow more reserved as I am left alone to the dark of the woods. Feeling the onset of this sulky sickening sensation, and furthermore confused as I draw each breath with a

CHAPTER SEVENTEEN

soreness.

Pressing her face to my neck she hastens me to taste her lips once more. Tears roll down my face like large rocks tumbling down from the side of the mountain. Seeing this intangible thing called fear become the wall that separates us. In our warm embrace finding the only way that we should have to say goodbye. Her soft utterance still music to the dying light of my blackening heart. Me sharing every beautiful second that her heart beats with mine.

Thirteen hours passed before a soft midnight plum deepened over a starlit sky. Satisfying every part of our love with the alleviating sustenance of each other's grasp. Hoping that time might cease to be time as she tarried and with every heart-rending pain amplified. Hidden to a place where her lips became my lips as our hearts did measure simultaneously in tandem. There being no place we did not travel to in those final hours. Knowing that we would never see each other again. Time passing too soon when it then came time for her to leave.

BLACK BIRD

CHAPTER EIGHTEEN

Watching Mahru turn out of my dark driveway it then dawns on me that the one keeper of my heart is now gone. Standing in the dark for a moment I see that my love is like the flower that blooms before the frost.

Closing my front door I then become emotionally clobbered by the reality of our affair. Here and now where there is no pain more perfect. Ailing with a hurt that was previously unimaginable. Feeling as if my eyes and heart have been removed and left to wander the dark aimlessly. A place where black birds feast upon my heart's love and tear at the flesh of my happiness. Under a moon covered by a dark haze that smudges its shine into the dirt that darkness has risen from. Me feeling the onset of this awful emptiness as I lay over my sheets clinging to the lingering redolence of our affection. Wanting to question everything that she has shared with me. Feeling all of me reject myself. Doubting that I have ever known love. Asking myself if I ever knew her and wanting to believe that death can be my only cure. Death smelling so sweet and almost dying to taste it. Existing without a shred of power to alter the course of her fear-based decision. Drawing nearer to my death as I wrap my body into the fibers that still bear her sweet smell and warmth.

Struggling to sit up in bed I torture myself by staring at my unfinished painting of Mahru. Her gorgeous face seen on my forty-eight inch canvas that hangs on my bedroom wall. Most of the painting finished except for the left side of her cream gamboge body and the dark silk that falls from her

CHAPTER EIGHTEEN

shoulders. Looking into her painted eyes I ask Mahru if she will ever come back to me. My heart stops in the time that it takes for a single tear to pass my face. Turning inside of my torment I acknowledge my always seeking what is beautiful, wondering why I chose her in the beginning and why I thought that we could overcome what was inevitable. Even asking myself if I knew that her love would one day be divided from me.

Needing to get up and just be somewhere else I slide on my Sorel boots with a thick sweater under my wool mountain jacket. Grabbing my grey wool beanie I then step outside to get a little fresh air and to spur the dead fluid that rests in my veins.

Feeling my wet cheeks touch the cold air outside I trudge towards the road. Looking up and noticing that my uncle's house lights are still on I then see the silent clouds above my head, and I wonder if it will rain, there being nothing too grim to deter me as I stumble onto the sidewalk in front of the house.

Wandering north on Granville I notice the traffic at this hour beginning to dissipate. Passed the quiet quaint homes at the edge of Shaughnessy. Passed the Persian ironwoods and katsura trees. Not thinking about how far I plan to walk. Only wanting to numb my gnawing pain to this cold night.

Stepping closer to the frivolous commotion of patrons leaving their fine restaurants in Fairview I relax my detached pace a little more. A sadness stirs in me just a few feet from the decorative dilaab of twinkling lights. Unable to bear the sight of a pretty face I want to cry each time that a smile is passed to me. Finding myself unable to even look at a small child without thinking about what could have been. Embittered and dispirited from having lost the one person that I love most in this world. Feeling my nose getting cold. Walking the streets tired and looking every which way as if on the verge of an idea that might satisfy the rescue of her. Even more concerned with what is happening inside of my head than I am careful with my step.

Drifting further from myself I grow unaware of the time that is passing. Arriving to an unfamiliar viewpoint I stop to admire the city lights from a street bench that sits on Cambie Bridge. The light of day has long faded like a flickering bulb beneath the floorboards of an empty basement. Overlooking the city I begin to feel my heart rend with a morbid kind of neurosis. Feeling something unusually menacing buried beneath me I gaze at the warm glow of the city as if home has suddenly caught fire. Standing above Quayside Marina my mind suffers this stygian malaise that has plagued my existence. Trying to understand this lover's tragedy I contemplate going the way of all flesh. Disenchanted as my insides knot with a heart wrenching nausea. Even convincing myself that I wanted Mahru just so that I could lose her.

Pulling from my jacket pocket a piece of paper with my handwriting on it to her I then open my hand to let it roll away from me. Drying with my fingertips the tears that spill passed my cheekbones I then try to not let my losing her encourage my taste for being dead. Knowing that I have no feelings of resentment towards her. But maybe thinking that I do. Feeling awful despite her having warned me. Sad that she did not go to war for this beautiful thing that her and I have. Realizing that I am not as strong as I pretend to be. Watching my warm breath separate from my body with a floating wisp. Breathing in and out this dancing disappearance. Knowing that it had to be because of me as I tuck in and hide my cold fingers.

Standing up right to keep moving I now really feel that I am losing my mind. Wandering the streets tired. Emotionally too heartbroken to sleep in my bed. And already feeling the tragedy of having to wake up tomorrow after seeing her leave.

Smelling the ocean coming down from the bridge I glance beyond the walkway railing. And then down a spiraling footpath beneath the bridge through a well lit waterfront park. Trailing the edge where the skyline fills the water with a gold foiled sheet like desert stars over a wine berry blue. Passed the Marina Plaza and through an empty parking lot. A busy city distant to the wandering idealist but convenient for anyone looking to play the game. An unresisting society sick with a fear that becomes a sadness. Feeling society torn from what it means and feels to be human. Or perhaps it is only me. Separated by a belief. Our beautiful love like a broken bottle. My spirit trapped in the flesh like my soaring love to a birdcage. Something real beset by ideas and words. And all when words have no love to give and no skin or lips to touch.

Walking tired I slum the edge of Yaletown with a crippling sadness, inebriated to my soul's core as I question how I've sustained my body from shutting down. Advancing down a path of concrete and glass I am confronted with a pain in my heart that begins to deteriorate me physically. I think back to when I slept outside under the expressway after I got in Damien's face for yelling at my mom. Still this breakup with Mahru is undeniably the most nightmarish thing that I've ever had to endure. Passed the setting sun and beclouded by this westward crawl towards my grave as I become heartbreakingly disemboweled.

Under the Dunsmuir Viaduct crossing into Chinatown my body reminds

CHAPTER EIGHTEEN

me of the stiff and irritable muscles that cling to this dead thing that once housed my soul. Every street now leads nowhere as the dark of night offers me a protection from being seen. Vagariously I stagger through a stone and brick alley that smells like burnt rice. Passed the closed iron gates and tawny blood cider bridal wreath shrubs. City lights form an amassing glitter of distraction for meddling persons and scouting police units. My body now an unrecognized silhouette amongst the dark shapes that stand still in the black of night. Knowing that there are so many ways for me to die as I battle my feeling dead. Feeling my body turn ill as the temple to my frail heart becomes demolished.

Shuffling along the edges of shadows that conceal a path to an undiscovered fortress of space for me to rest my delicate eyes open and close with every succiduous step. And then like a gutted fish railing in puke amidst a distressing marmalade color from above I am left to the shadows of a stairs crawl space.

With my being tired combined with the reality of our illicit love affair sleep consumes me without having even the slightest idea of where I am. Dirty crows cackle at my defeat wishing me dead for their pickings. And with my eyes closed I ask god to forgive me for letting her go and for my being tempted. Knowing that I could die now and knowing that I will never have her to care for and love. Accepting that should the black horse and carriage roll up alongside of me that I will know that it is my god who I belong to and not to this world. Knowing that I cannot be broken anymore than I already am. My tears fall behind my ears and curl my hair into the rubble of a hole that I have named. The overgrowth crawling from beneath the earths' darkest inhabitants reach for my heart to clutch it clean of its oxygen. And finally falling asleep from exhaustion I pray that I may never see the light of day.

Before sunrise I awaken to the prodding shove of a street sweeping man who presumes that I may be dead. The man even trying to push me over to see if I am in fact dead.

"Hey man, you can't sleep here anymore. You have to go," the man says, staring me down with one eye in his denim uniform. Looking over my shoulder to respond I then see no one standing there. Looking up through a cloud of steam while lying down I then make out a man sweeping garbage at the other end of the street.

Standing myself up and brushing off my plush walnut jacket I glance around and realize that I don't quite know where I am. Remembering that I left my phone at home I then check for my keys inside of my zipped pocket.

Snaking wistfully under the small sidewalk maples on Beatty Street I then realize how far away from home I am. Sore and cold I walk down a few more blocks to Seymour Street, admitting that I am not quite ready for home. Feeling an emotional pileup inside of me as I contemplate leaving this beautiful Manhattan surrounded by mountains. Trying to better visualize my next step. There being nothing else left of me but these sad and dirty broken pieces.

Moving through downtown I feel like a hard piece of gum scraped up from the cold gritty pavement. Shaken by this agony and this heartache as I stand surrounded by the stir of morning traffic.

Heading west towards Stanley Park I maunder to admire the last of this vibrant fall that will always remind me of her. Putting space between me and the one place where we have spent most of our time. Torturing myself with a sadness that knows no lights at the end of tunnels. Feeling myself begin to decompose from my turn in the light. A sadness that chooses the dark path instead of seeking solace in the eyes of someone that I know. Staring into space just so that I can see her smile back at me. Tasting in my mouth this exquisite horror as I feel myself sinking into the darkest ocean.

Watching heavy traffic back up along the coastal framework of a sea glass city I can smell the salty water on the cold English Bay. Feeling her still holding me I keep walking beneath an overcast sky and under a rufescent autumn canopy. Feeling her close to me as I move passed the pure rich entrance of the park. Through a dappled evergreen forest surrounded by western red cedars and moss-dripped bigleaf maples. Catching sight of a great blue heron perched below an acid yellow exhibiting spatters of ladybug red and scarlet. With each step along the damp park trail vowing to never forget what she has shared with me. In my heart there being no doubt that I will always love her.

Beneath the giant emerald conifers high up in the chalky clouds I spot the beautiful bald eagle from under a stone bridge covered in vines. And right before approaching the famous Lions Gate Bridge with its mythically colossal ocean green towers extending a path as if it were the entry of the gods.

Beneath the bridge cables I stop to admire the streaky tree green water reflection along the Stanley Park Seawall Path. Moving towards the bridge deck peels away a water to mountain landscape with storm clouds rolling off of the aegean blue peaks. The silvery translucent view of vast water to sky so stunning and yet still unable to ease my troubled soul. Missing those eyes that take away my pain. If only her being here could grant me this simple cure. If

CHAPTER EIGHTEEN

only her love for me had not been fashioned with a seam that sunders.

After a three hour walk home I pour a tall glass of water to try and remedy the pain shooting up through the back of my head. Believing that I am dehydrated I turn on my black sink knobs to wash the filth from my hands. Looking at my phone I think to call her before reminding myself that I cannot. Struggling to keep my promise I take all of my clothes off at the door before walking into the bathroom. Hoping to try and wash away my sadness with a lengthy shower. Pulling the vinyl curtain closed from the copper ring above I sit in the tub so long that I almost fall asleep after washing myself. Hardly even noticing the water turn cold before the water heater is empty. Turning off the shower to grab a towel I then withdraw myself to my dark and dreary shelter of seclusion.

    Walking in front of my open window I turn back the saddle-brown lip to my bedspread before climbing into bed. Part of me wishing that she will come and find me still lying in it. Feeling for my naked skin that is dry to the touch. Believing that there is no place for me now as I find myself with a love that is no more. Lying alone in my bed and seeing her face. Missing the impressions made into the blankets and pillows. Missing the way that her hands move up under my chest and the kisses that she would place across the back of me. Lying in bed running my hands down through my hair I remember her love. Pulling my hair down over my face feeling her lovely fingers and hands streaming through mine while all of my troubles dissipate into some nonexistent form. Rubbing my thumbs over the tops of my nails in memory of her smooth skin that was once close enough for me to touch. But she is not here and I fear that my heart cannot bear the thought of her being gone. Truly believing that I will never love again. Clutching my heart where the air pushes out through my lungs and where the weight of this storm shreds apart the hull to my soul. Realizing that my love has only ever endured this extraordinary torment and cultural barrier that bleeds dry this heart of mine. Being only here where the taste of life has vanished and where the well is dry.

    "And now my love is dead," I tell myself, observing the cold light that shines into my window as it slowly becomes swallowed by a leaden cloud.

    Rubbing my wet face into my soft ash linens I acknowledge that she has ruined me entirely. Having given me all that there is to be given and only to have run away with it all. What I must now live with and die knowing. Seeing in my mind her deliriously happy the way that she first was. Seeing her sitting beside my warm fireplace that I have never lit. Wrapped in a cozy blanket and reading to our beautiful children. And then I see her with this man who cannot even give her what she truly needs. And more than material. Facing this relentless storm. A storm that causes my heart to panic. A storm that destroys my desire to better live and love. Casting me into this battle for survival where I am left thrashing in a sea of sadness.

Suddenly my crying tears stop and my troubled mind is still. Distracted by a mental haze that suffers me to become nearly delusional with humor. The day seems to escape me as daylight now recedes from the windows. And then I remember my unfinished painting of her. Realizing that nothing can rescue me from this cruel ugliness that wreaks havoc in my head. Tears dripping down my face as my mind begins to drift into a place that is called no place at all. Looking back at the things that I miss to try and create a distraction that keeps me from brooding so heavily. Missing that six-in-the-morning feeling in South Beach. A cool air dripping from a brittle white and burgundy brick beneath the towering pines with a morning scent welcoming the eastern sun. The sun peering through a bone painted cityscape giving humidity an invitation. Tropical pine needles dancing on a floor of tree crumbs before the slight stir of morning. Leaning over that wide cement staircase downward into a warm abyss of small alley patios and confined space divided by more coconut trees having soft conversation in the sky. Walking a worn path under an arbor of more suffocating pine. Overlooking the bridge east of my aunt's home to a beautiful glass city floating on the water. Trying to remember what it was like for me the day before I fell in love and trying to remember simplicity as it once was.

Finally feeling that I have mastered a moment of peace the thought of losing her again comes crashing down into my head leaving me only where I started the moment she was gone. Searching for her scent in my sheets the moonlight shines onto my bare back. It is that same light that casts my dark reflection down in front of me and that reveals all that is left of me. Coveting the dead and miserably unaware I tell god that I do not want to die even though it appeals to me. Staring off into space with still no food in my stomach sleep consumes me. Crying for her after the baby angels above have long blown out that large candle that burns in the sky.

MORIBUND

CHAPTER NINETEEN

Waking up a little before noon after already deciding to stay home from school I begin to fall right back to sleep. A light rain trickles outside of my bedroom window as her fingers reach over and play with my tight wheat-colored curls. Turning to see her face I touch her ringlets of black thread and shining pearl. Her skin like a sun-bleared mist above the golden Iguazu Falls. Loving her beautiful smile she looks up and then grabs ahold of me. Observing this brill morning as it rests upon her face I then catch in her perilous eyes an entangled tiresome gaze. With my attention drawn to someone else sleeping on the other side of her I then recognize this man to whom she is betrothed. The man reaches over to move her black hair from her hesitant face. She then looks at me and tells me that she is okay when I know that she is not. Wiping her falling tear with my finger I then see his hand move down the side of her.

Confused by this nightmarish prescience I then wake up and realize that it is just a dream. Enfeeble from this bleak isolation my agony sleeps in the blood of my veins like a poison waiting to suffer my pillaged heart. This jarring absurdity desiccating our love and leaving me washed-out and displaced as the light inside of my chest wanes.

Pushing my bedspread away from me I rub my face confused as to why so many cannot open their hearts to see this beautiful world that we live in. Instead wanting to control everyone and everything. Emotionally battered by this bid-rigging of the heart. Her love for me likened to a perfect limb that has been amputated. An unnatural betrayal impinged by this ideological decadence. Not acting on the belief that we are defined by our compassion and kindness towards each other. Too afraid to propose even the idea or wish. And all to avoid a familial friction for fear of things turning vicious. Enduring this torment because of her tentative efforts where from her there has been no upheaval. Our nonpareil love being the only thing that should warrant such disobedience. Being told no when only we know. And believing it to be further a crime to reject and disobey the heart. Feeling my muscle and bone flood with a heartache that knows no repair.

Feeling hungry for something that I do not have to prepare I then think of the café near the edge of Shaughnessy. Watching the rain die down outside my window and knowing that class is about to end I then think to ready this truant before this invasive sorrow enters me.

Crawling out from my brown bramble bedding I turn on some music to distract me from this gut-wrenching sadness before it gets to me. Hardly letting go of a whimper while my teary face seems to melt from my skull. Struggling to brush my hair and even look at myself in the mirror. Following through with my normal morning routine I then slide into something warm to wear. Making sure that I have a few dollars in my pocket I then grab my warm jacket from the coat rack downstairs.

Stepping outside and locking my front door I begin to mosey down to the café around the corner. Taking a deep breath outside in the crisp fresh air I am still consumed by the puerile prejudice of such a suppositious polarization. Khalil assuming some menacing disadvantage to Mahru when I truly love her more than anything. Wishing that I could have looked Khalil in the eyes and professed to him my love for his daughter. Wanting to share with him face to face that I want nothing more than to provide for her every need and to love her better than any man can. Feeling this massive scab upon my impoverished heart become thin. Having heard it in her voice that nothing can be arranged. Still wanting to relieve Mahru of her ties to home. And she clearly forewarning me that she has no courage to elope. Hardly able to make it down the street without feeling that I'm about to lose myself. Watching the people happily together as they walk by me holding hands and in love. Making it seem so easy the way they do it. No fear hiding behind their eyes. There only existing a love that seems so free from this complicating world.

Walking into the Pergamino Café I then walk right back outside with my cold tea and my avocado toast tartine.

CHAPTER NINETEEN

Sitting under the outside arrangement where the blonde umbrella tables are all crunched together with metal chairs I observe the coffee drinkers perched with their legs crossed. Nearly everyone is talking to someone across the table or reading the paper. One man chewing the end of his glasses while staring at his tablet. An annoyed woman's miniature dog wraps itself around the bottom of the table as it tries to leap towards the edge of the street, the tiny dog lunging its little body at everything that moves. Oddly enough any noise that the dog might be capable of making seems to be coming from inside of the café. And luckily for me I arrived just before the crowd began to form. A crowd that sits like pigeons huddled closely together as they eat and drink. A family of eight is waving down someone they know from the edge of the street. And then I grow uncomfortable noticing two couples smiling and holding hands. Looking away I try to admire my surroundings as I grow torn between the pleasant atmosphere and this suffering instilled in me. Trying to remain unworried in my heart beneath a patchy overcast sun.

Having shared with her my whole heart I still doubt my own worth hearing Damien's eviscerating earful in my head. Doubting everything that I am as I feel in my bones his pugnacious haranguing and ill-tempered derisiveness. Knowing of nothing that I can do but to run and cut myself off as I sit convinced of my inadequacy. Feeling the memory of him always looking for an opportunity to belittle and upbraid me to tears. Always hawkishly goading me to attain a sense of disunity to satisfy his own insecure jealousy. Alienating my mom from her siblings. Grabbing my neck and shoving my face into the floor. And all for trying desperately to defend my mom. Even taking a beating from him just so that he wouldn't touch her. Watching Damien come home drunk and seeing the devil in his glowering eyes. My mom and I always living in fear. And now I am afraid for Mahru. Feeling her love being ripped away from me. Khalil's incessant sermonizing rigged with hostilities for fear of a certain stigma. Always imposing a debilitating bombardment of fragmented truths. Allowing no protest from a daughter that he loves. And not for one second wanting to vilify Khalil for driving this wedge between us. It being hardly a reasonable thing to judge when he does not even know that I exist. Even thinking that all of this could be different if he just knew who I am.

Turning my attention to the casual activity around me I am caught off guard by a pretty face that passes me and says hey. Only I cannot respond. Watching her continue to her table I then want to say something. But then I realize that it is not Mahru. Still silently praying for a peace that I know exists.

Tilting the bottom of my glass I then acknowledge that I am too torn to be sitting here.

Thinking that I am ready to stand up and leave, Mandy from Mr. Petrov's class then says my name before sitting down in the chair next to me in her slouchy turtleneck. Right away I notice her cool smile and the raw umber and russet in her hair. Feeling startled and trying not to appear so traumatized I give Mandy a quick glance only to acknowledge her.

"Hey! Are you alright?" Mandy asks, seeing that I am unhappy and hoping that I will talk to her.

"Yeah. I am just sitting down for a minute . . . thinking. . . . What are you doing here?" I then ask, trying not to sound hopelessly frustrated.

"I'm just with my friend Kayla over there getting some coffee. I saw that you weren't in class today. Are you doin' okay?"

"Yeah," I nod, mostly looking down at her feet so that I don't have to look at her in the eyes.

"Well, okay," she tells me, disappointed that I'm still not much for words. "It's just that you were looking kind of sad. And you can always tell me anything," she adds, persistent in getting to the root of why I am unsettled.

"Yeah. . . . It's just . . . thinking about someone. A girl that I am never going to see again. Her parents have coaxed her into getting married to a man who she doesn't even love. And nothing makes sense anymore," I come out with, at a near whisper.

"I am sorry, Lucius. That is so sad," Mandy says to me.

"It is," I mutter, touching my lips and staring at the table in front of me.

Kneeling down next to me to try and get me to look at her Mandy then puts her hand on my knee.

"Well if you ever need or want someone to talk to you know that you can always talk to me," she then says.

Finally looking at Mandy I acknowledge her. Hearing her friend Kayla call her name I then look out over the guardrail and then back at her with eyes that tell her I am finished talking about it.

"Maybe I'll see you tomorrow," she then says, standing up and running her fingers through my curly head before walking away.

Watching her disappear through the café entrance, I then stand up to leave, throwing away my garbage before walking back the same way that I came.

Arriving back home I then carefully assemble my paint area to begin finishing

CHAPTER NINETEEN

my portrait of Mahru. Wanting to evade this suffering in my heart I separate each tube of color according to what I need. Slipping on just a pair of shorts I set aside my cotton rags before turning on my warm lamps. Squeezing a small dab of each pure pigment onto my palette I work fiercely to tap out of this emotional frailty. Applying my two base layers to the surface I begin layering up from light to dark. Every application of paint sweeping the canvas with a hypnotic maneuvering of the brush. A persistent caressing of colors like fingers that never tire from the strings of a musical instrument. Every stroke hammering the release valve to my quiet suffering as I become possessed and consumed by my process, standing and working patiently as each hour passes.

Nearly finishing her left side and only one layer away from my session being complete I now fixate on the memory of her love and become hopelessly distracted. Setting down my brush I look at Mahru gathering fresh tears in my tired eyes. Wanting to deny what we had I question if I can endure as I feel my physical and mental state begin to waste away. Hearing thunder approach outside I stand unconvinced that this merciless heartache will ever end. Dying inside of myself I still desire to see her. My every exertion of passion threatened by the depths of this struggle and privation. Feeling myself stretched by this searing of scars. Baffled by how God has interceded himself in the way of our love. Bearing the sharp end of her dad's fear for the unknown. Dogmas and conceptual prisons isolating us into this fear and anger that exacerbates this confusion and suffering. Still feeling the tips of her fingers locked into the tissues of my heart as I hesitate to pick up my paintbrush.

Looking at my unfinished painting of her I accept that I cannot bring myself to finish what I have started. My hands and arms become heavy from this perplexing disappointment that truly suffers my heart. Deluged with tears and standing against my anguish in front of my painting I struggle to make myself still. Too frustrated and heartbroken to pick up my brush I begin to loosen the wet paint from a portion of the canvas with a tall bottle of thinner. Watching the many layers washing away until its primed threads are bare and again visible. Standing myself up with a drenched face and in complete agony I wipe my canvas down with a dry cloth. Hoping and praying that Mahru will reach out to me and that my heart will not be cast adrift into this inferno where I am left decimated by these feelings of gloom and abandonment. Feeling this foolish longing to hold her in my arms despite what I know is certain. My self-criticism bordering being self-destructive. Feeling as though my soul has irreversibly detonated from these tears weighing the release to my love's end.

MORIBUND

Wracking my brain to shake this cowardice from me before my heart mirrors this black brush whose skeleton feels none of nature's warmth. And just like a cold tree in fall my color feels torn from me until I am leafless under a heavy snow that burdens my soul.

Pouring an odorless turpentine to carefully remove the oil paint from my well-kept brushes I can taste the sadness falling into my mouth. Tears falling down my cheeks and mixing onto my palette as I try to remove each daub of pigment. Her paralyzing affect still so near to my senses and my immediate mindfulness. Feeling like I have lost a part of me that I will never get back. Finding myself back and forth between the space that surrounds me. Perplexed as to why no one will let love conquer their heart and mind. And as if it would be such a scandal. These beautiful matters of the heart being for no hucksters of thought. Khalil shadowing her as if she were some wayward dunce. Believing that his daughter is uncooperative and that she could be potentially unpredictable. Trivializing our anomalous love with his tepid and inauthentic disaffection. Him smoldering with a superstitious spiritlessness as if I were some impious scoundrel. Never knowing my inimitable love that exists only for Mahru.

Feeling my strangled heart twinge with sadness I turn my hot lamps off and disappear into the shadows of my moonlit room. Venturing into the dark doldrums of my sorrow I tend to the silent echoing of my war-ravaged love. The inner light of my luscious sun washed away by the downpour of this storm. Like the rich sycamore fig whose sun has been deprived by that merciless vine that suffocates. Traveling through madness as time and strategy weighing heavily on my mind.

Taking all of my clothes off I lie down in bed pressing my face into my sheets and blanket. Smelling her in my bed my pain for once makes a terrifying sound. Feeling her close to me I know that she is far from me. Afraid that I have conjured this dejection and utter torment. Falling by the way of my tears that seem to have no end and conquered by this misery that has sought my name.

THE WANDERER
CHAPTER TWENTY

Fourteen days from the day that she came to see me and each breath still suffers this searing agony in my heart. And when I am not thinking of her she is still in my peripheral subconscious. Already antisocial I still struggle to be aware of my unhappiness to avoid the prying eyes of my classmates. The classroom being a place where my mind wanders and where the spoken word does reconfigure before my ears.

Every day my mind is clouded as I distance myself from those who would appear to know and understand me most. Even my mother wonders how come I do not seem to exist anymore. Me hardly knowing why I hang on to this latently forsaken love that suffers me to this degree of insanity. My mother sensing my disenchantment when she calls me and when I happen to answer. Remembering last week her calling to tell me that she is not with Damien anymore. And granted that I am happy for her I still cannot latch on to her bubbly enthusiasm. But I am happy knowing that my mom has made mention of coming up to see me for Christmas. Knowing already that she hears it from Louis that I am no longer seeing the girl who I met on campus. And I kindly refuse to tell my mom anything about it because of how much it still hurts. Feeling like a foolish boy. And unable to help feeling that I have somehow let Mahru down. That *something* must be my fault. And believing that if I try anything that it will only make things worse for her. Falling a thousand feet to my death all the day long. And every day following through with what she has asked of me. Ill with a longing for her when I am not even sure that she wants me. Wishing that I could love her and care for her. Even wishing that I could love her mom and her dad. And her brother Malik and her sister Madge. Wanting to love them all. But thus far believing all of it to be impossible. Feeling with every fixed second that time is running out. Having given Mahru all of me and only to be left this way. Afraid that this awful torment will never let go of me. And knowing that there is nothing that I can do to get her back.

Each day my studies continue for me with no real purpose other than to get at least a passing grade. Walking the halls is strangely despairing loving this pain that she has entrusted to me. This pain in my heart being all that I have left of her.

Mandy in Mr. Petrov's class appears disappointed because I still will not speak to her, still holding Mahru close to my heart and ignoring the say-so of anyone telling me to let go of her. Still thinking about her every second of each day. Even when I think that I am not thinking about her. The sidewalks and streets here on campus all making the image of her appear so clear in my mind. Feeling her so close to me each day when we are so very far apart. And each day surprised by how our paths never cross. Always hoping to catch a glimpse of her by chance. Her spirit like the ethereal hummingbird that you can sometimes hear but not see. And knowing that after she graduates in just a few more weeks that she will soon be married and living her new life on the other side of the world. Every day wishing that she could just finish out one more term and wishing all of the time that we had more time.

Each day in class and at home I see her always. And still each day I die a little at the thought of losing her. Having lost her to some pretentious knave. Somehow able to manage each day knowing that there is this pressing need in my soul. Darker than the deepest sea my heart still reaches for air. Each day holding sacred to me this precious memory of her. Wanting to believe that there is still some chance. Haunted by having ruined something that has been shaped to perfection with both our efforts. Wishing that I could affect the difference between what survives and what dies. Nature and love being the most sublime of all design and forever existing as that one abiding force. And yet still I fear for her. Wanting her to come away with me someplace far far away where these lies cannot tempt us. The concept of dishonor strategically reflecting and reinforcing the subordination of women to men. The hierarchical organization of the written word suppressing the divine feminine in us

CHAPTER TWENTY

all. Khalil so regressively maladjusted and ready to excoriate her with moral intimidation. Blaming these divisions that deprive us from being human and from expressing love. Feeling unforgiving towards everyone and everything that keeps us from expressing ourselves as being divine.

Leaving class quickly after it lets out I still look to try and catch Mahru walking to her distinct sea-green truck in the parking lot. Not wanting to wait around and make her tense I continue to drive straight home to have dinner with my uncle Louis who will not take an unconvincing no for an answer. It being pretty obvious that my uncle is worried about me. He then texts to tell me that he is stopping at FedEx before he picks up an early dinner.

Turning onto University Boulevard, Louis texts that he will be home in about forty-five minutes, still turning out of the campus parking lot where the old purple-leaf plums line a still pear-green landscape.

Arriving home and parking behind Louis's house I walk the brick walkway that leads to the backdoor that is always unlocked. Taking my mesh running shoes off in the mudroom I hang my seam-taped jacket by the backdoor. Washing my hands and face in the bathroom I next take a seat on my uncle's pecan Berkshire sofa.

Facing the tall arched window overlooking Forty-first Avenue I then begin to drift off into a miserable silence as I wait. Straying into the fiery abyss of a dream world as I stare into the copper Burchiellaro table in front of me.

Taking out my phone I then delete her number from my mobile contacts. Feeling my sadness intensify from the thought of her parents having to be the ones to stand between us. And all when I could have loved them so easily.

Distracted by a dark cloud blanketing the evening light from the window I then begin to feel that something must be unfavorably wrong with me. That I must be somehow bad. Still believing that for the most part most of us are not really bad actually. Most of us living our lives confused and afraid. Telling myself that I should not have listened to her and that I should have talked to her dad. Even wondering if I should keep my promise if only it would mean being with her. Thinking of her causing me to feel even more pain than I am able to bear. The last couple of weeks feeling like two whole months since I last saw her.

Grabbing the TV remote the Arabic folktale movie Aladdin blares loud in my face before I can flip the channel. The royal guards of Agrabah are chasing Aladdin with their swords and calling him a street rat. Finding nothing I want

THE WANDERER

to watch I turn off the TV just as Louis is pulling into the driveway outside.

Sliding into my shoes and stepping out back to help my uncle I see him in his shearling jacket carrying a hot bag of Kosoo Korean. Greeting me with a warm smile Louis tells me that he can carry it as he voices for me to head back inside.

"I got you that soup you like. You doin' alright?" he asks, sliding off his boots.

"Yeah I'm good," I tell Louis, trying my best to smile without revealing to my uncle how I really feel.

Unpacking the styrofoam containers of food in the kitchen and thanking Louis he then urges me to instead sit down in the living room. Sitting on the sofa that sits facing the large window Louis eagerly begins to devour his meal.

"I sold ten designs of yours with that new 3D printer. And I got them all mailed out before I picked up dinner," Louis says, rolling his sleeves up and being reserved about his date last night, my uncle still teeming with a reticent sort of joy.

"How much did you make?"

"Almost three hundred dollars. I am also raising your pay to eight hundred and fifty dollars a week. Right now is the best time of year for us. And our sales will increase more after January and February."

"Thank you," I tell Louis, reaching for a square of jeon. Taking a couple of bites I then set the rest down in my bowl.

"It's good isn't it?" Louis seeks to confirm.

"It is. Thank you again," I answer, trying to enjoy our time together without talking about Mahru. He then watches me take another bite.

"You know I have been worried about you. I have never seen you like this. And you know you can always come over anytime and talk to me. . . . Are you still seeing your girl?" he then asks, his kind eyes visible beyond his hard scruffy face.

Seeing the evidence of hurt still glazed over my eyes and face, Louis looks down and nods, him witnessing this ruinous beast that suffers my heavy heart. And still as hard as I try to free my mind of her there are times when I cannot escape this heartache that wakes inside of me like a waking virus that lives and thrives with a mind of its own.

"Man, I'm sorry," Louis utters.

"I promised that I would stop talking to her. She is getting married," I try to answer with difficulty. "Everyday I hate myself for letting her go. And some

CHAPTER TWENTY

days I want to be angry with her. But I also know that she wouldn't be doing any of this if her parents were not pushing her so hard."

"Well I think it is a shame that her dad never had the chance to meet you face to face. I think that he would be pleasantly surprised. Especially when it comes to finding someone who is good enough to marry his daughter," he says, him being as sincere as he always is.

"Maybe he would have been happy knowing that she was happy. But she was never mine. And it has been eating at me for some time now. Unable to even fathom what just happened. It's fucking all so stupid."

"I wish that I could do something or tell you something. But all that I can tell you to do is hang in there. You are my favorite nephew. Just maybe try and give it time. Maybe even see other people. I know all of the girls have an eye for you. You could be like the bumblebee crashing into all of the flowers on top of the mountain," Louis tries to enliven, attempting to uplift me from my despair to no avail.

"Forever may pass before this love leaves me," I return, feeling downtrodden, my body language displaying my internal conflict as I pick through my soup.

"Maybe just try and stay busy in the meantime. And be easy on yourself."

Nodding my head I tell Louis that I appreciate him trying to put my mind at ease. Still foolishly hoping that she might be fearless enough to come find me and run away with me.

"I got something else while I was out. Something I usually keep a secret. Just don't tell anyone," Louis then offers, pulling a baggy of cannabis from his pocket with some rolling paper. "I am worried about you drifting away into a place that will only destroy you. Maybe this will help."

"No thank you," I respond, watching Louis roll his joint as he hums to the swamp lantern fragrance of his flowers.

"I read this story about a man, a stockbroker, who decided that he would travel the world by walking on foot. He said that in every country he visited all the people were the nicest people he had ever met. But still in each country someone would warn him about entering the next country. Everywhere someone would warn him and say that over there you might be murdered or something, even through all of the Middle East. But everyone was the same and everyone was nice. Even though they all pointed their fingers at their neighboring countries. The bottom line is that people talk shit about people they don't know because they are afraid. It's not because they are bad people.

Even the Arab world was once accepting of different religions and ideas. Once on a quest for knowledge through science and study. And then war and fear changed people. And so it is sad that Mahru's ethnic tradition continues to link her dress and demeanor to religious piety and political regimes. Subjugation and segregation. All of the inaccurate things connected to islamic teaching or any religious teaching for that matter. If only we knew better. And if only we knew each other better."

"Yeah but what can you tell someone who believes what they want to believe?"

"If people really believed and loved God the way they claim to they would love more. Belief to me is the death of freedom. I think that people should know. Not accept. The worst deeds in history have been carried out by those claiming to act in God's name. All of them wanting you to believe this, worship this, and externalize your power. Forget about being your own savior through your behavior. No—you have to accept our ridiculous dogmas and somehow the world will magically change for the better. And forced marriage is an unethical violation of your human rights. It is a form of violence against girls and women. But maybe there is no hope in changing people's minds. The Christians do not even realize that the holy cross was first an Egyptian symbol—a Pagan symbol. But how do you explain to people these things? You don't. There is love and there is fear in this world. And I pray that love favors you," Louis sagaciously tries to comfort.

Watching Louis blow smoke rings like he is planning an escape to the moon I follow his thick disappearing circles. Following his skunky cloud of smoke to the window I think about maybe reaching out to Mahru. Only I do not see how it would benefit us. Believing that I can only cause her more heartache. And knowing that reaching out to her would mean breaking my promise.

Watching my uncle begin to sail the quiet and murky sea I suddenly recall a student in Mr. Wong's class all turned out in his soccer garb. Having seen the rest of his squad decked out in their threads on campus I then remember this same student mentioning a game that is scheduled for this evening. Knowing that her brother Malik is on the soccer team the thought to see her from a distance then enters my mind. Knowing that she has attended games in the past to see Malik play.

Wrapping up the rest of my food I suddenly inform Louis that I have to head out to a soccer game. Feeling too good to question my intention and

CHAPTER TWENTY

motivation he lifts himself up to his feet to hug me. Expressing my love for my uncle I communicate with him that I will come back over in the morning. Thanking Louis and apologizing for leaving I then urge myself to grab my jacket and head out the backdoor.

Driving up behind the stadium I notice the parking spaces filling in heavy with people crowding the north gate that leads to the soccer field. Parking on the south end close to the concession tents I walk behind the outdoor seating thinking that I might not be able to get close enough if she is with her mom and dad. Under a lavender grey sky the brush-dotted clouds begin to dim above a lit green field. The school colors blue and gold are painted and hanging from nearly everywhere. Behind the stadium floodlights and bleachers I can hear the people shouting and chanting "Olé, Olé, Olé!"

Wondering if Mahru is already seated Madge then walks right by me. Stopping dead in my tracks I then notice her mom Ianna and her dad Khalil. Carefully observing through a dense crowd I recognize Madge and Mahru standing in front of their mom and dad as they wait to go up the stairs. And then I see why Mahru and Madge do not want to upset Khalil. A good looking burly man with some facial scruff in his tan muscle-fitted sweater. Like lava rock to a hiker's feet his face is hard and rigid. His irascibly waspish face making him a difficult man to approach. Khalil appearing to have almost no visible joy. Standing large and fierce as if a demolisher of love. His large build and averse bearing being enough to intimidate most men. Especially this twenty-one-year-old boy who is madly in love with his daughter. His dark eyes so serious and fixed. Everything about him bringing to memory what she has shared with me. His nescient quarreling compared to that of an ill-tempered sectarian with his hubristic posturing and ideological pervasiveness. Believing him to be just like the Christians, atheists and others who have all poisoned the well of love with their asperse divisions.

Watching Mahru's mother Ianna turn to look at them both I imagine her obverse to the aggressive disciplinarian. Her watchful eye reminding me of Mahru in her sapphire chiffon scarf that mirrors the inner turmoil of a stormy day at sea. Her braided silk falling over her long blue tunic that sways over her tight white leggings.

Watching Madge suddenly split off to speak to her friend twelve feet from her parents I look back at Mahru hoping that she will shift her eyes and see me.

THE WANDERER

Waiting for the crowd to dissipate over the stairs she watches her sister all glassy-eyed with her hands inside of her jacket pockets. Standing back against the wall and wondering if she is thinking of me she then makes eye contact with me. Any natural joy likely or ready to surface from her surprised face is quickly quashed by fear. Afraid of locking her eyes with mine she surreptitiously shifts her attention as if to repress her errant ways from being discovered, still afraid of parting with any evidence of emotion that might lead to suspicion. Following her eyes that glance back at her mom and with me feeling nearly wrecked with heartache I then make sudden eye contact with Ianna. Lost in thought she catches me staring and stares right back at me. Every emotion stirs inside of me as she makes little effort to connect any dots. Realizing that I am grievously in the wrong I refocus my eyes elsewhere and quickly disappear into the crowd.

Standing further back and watching Ianna turn to walk up the steps Mahru glances back to make sure that I am not following her. Watching her turn and look away I wonder if she is terribly disappointed by the fact that she is crushing us both. She still making no effort to communicate with me as we move further away from each other. She quickly adjusts her line of sight once she glances and notices where I am. Feeling no effort from her to again look my way I can then tell that she knows exactly where I am standing.

Watching Mahru follow her parents up the stairs she confirms with me everything that I needed to know. I watch her walk away from me as if she is more indebted to her family than she is loved by them. No more looking in my direction to see where I have gone. Still agitated by the thought of never seeing her again as she walks up the steps.

Stepping closer to the bottom of the staircase that leads to the upper seating she continues to walk up with her back facing me. Watching her parents disappear around the top of the stairs I then see her disappear behind them.

"Hey Lucius," Madge smiles at me nervously.

"Hey," I respond, taking my eyes off of the top of the stairs.

"You know with my mom and dad being here it would not be a good idea for you to talk to my sister. It will just make her get in big trouble," Madge warns, reminding me that nothing that I want will work. Giving Madge a slight nod I attempt to mask this gloom that I feel has already completely robbed me of everything.

"Yeah. . . . I know," I return, trying not to appear so broken up while making eye contact with Madge. Quickly she puts her arms around me and gives

CHAPTER TWENTY

me a hug. She then walks by me sadly knowing that her sister and I can never see each other again.

Grabbing her girlfriend who is wearing hijab she then quickly walks up the stairs. The crying sound of excitement fills the back of the stadium and drowns out the instruments that have begun to play out on the field. Watching the people at the end of the line trickle up the stairs I then sense in extremis my heavy heart. Fighting to honor her wishes I withdraw my efforts. Knowing that I do not want to make trouble for her. All over again feeling hopeless in knowing that she can never speak to me and knowing even further that it would be unwise for her to try.

Walking up the cement steps to have one last look at her the crackling sound ringing in my ears pierces from the raging crowd. Inconspicuously I observe Mahru gathered with her family at the bottom of the bleachers. Remembering everything that we have felt and shared the crowd again cheers as they call out the names of the players. Watching her cheer as Malik runs out onto the field my heart aches with a thousand holes in my chest. Seeing her so unannounced releasing a hoard of disease carrying wolves howling through the caverns of my soul. My heart likened to a snow-caked carcass as dead leaves and spring weeds consume and dissolve me. My love and my flesh turned to dust. Something so beautiful *gone* that nobody can understand. My Shangri-La ablaze beyond this dark horizon. A smoke filled sky above the deep blue. Every turbulent emotion lost swimming in the empty space that surrounds me. Derailed to the shadows under this black sky where the light follows only her. Itching to be lost to the dark of the woods where there exists only a silence. Thinking it to be a lovely place to die. Swirling in a sorrow that cuts like daggers. Every beautiful unspeakable truth shattered.

Heading home in hopes that my heart can be rid of her I make my way passed the gardens onto the south side of the stadium. Traipsing behind the tennis courts I struggle with being an emotional wreck as I work desperately to pull myself together. The chill in the air stabs me with just as much thrust as I contemplate this kalopsial affair. Feeling the life being pulled from my heart and lungs. Feeling that my ruling self wants Khalil to know. My menacing heart driveling on about having done everything that I can. Feeling overcome by this sense that she still loves me despite her choosing this obligatory custom that serves only her family's prestige.

Unlocking my car I begin to drive home trying to see the road in front of me. A thick mist seeps down my lane and whispers to me the eerie shadows of my sorrow. My eyes saturate with wet shapes that separate into different dots of light as I adjust my windshield wipers. My murdered heart begins to dissociate my mind from my body. Feeling this avalanche of hurt striking me deep in my chest. This disturbing howl in my heart tearing at the flesh of my resolve as I park down my dark rainy driveway.

    Entering my front door a familiar sadness like a squirrel burrows itself inside of this hole in my heart. Shedding my clothes and crawling into bed an excruciating sadness thrums through my blood as I unsuccessfully attempt to pull my hair from my head. Wanting to die I ask God and I even ask him please. Disheartened by this separation and this gnawing incognizance as another tear crawls across my worn face.

THE MISSING RING

CHAPTER TWENTY-ONE

Six days until Christmas with two days left of exams and it really begins to dawn on me that I am never going to see her again. Still wanting desperately to be with the only girl that I have ever loved. The sweet satisfying memory of her pervading my thoughts each day. Her soft skin and her touch still so near to me. That smile she gives that always brightens my face. Only she is not here. Sad as this frigid hibernal air draws near. Knowing that she will never share with me the warm festivities of the solennial winter solstice. No enjoying the gentle sounds of Jack Jezzro and Bob Brookmeyer. No looking out of the window together at a winter wonderland. No homemade cider and lo-fi Christmasy tunes. Decorating only a little with what Louis has left over from the attic. Red and gold glass ornaments fill the length of the garland on the oak fireplace mantel downstairs. No Christmas tree only because I do not see the sense in me enjoying it all by myself. Feeling sentimental about the holiday season as this sunken downslope bleeds from me all gratitude and discernment.

Ever since it has turned cold I have been painting rigorously in tribute of my love that still exists. Thinking of her each day as the snow begins covering the perse blue mountains. Mahru still breathing life into my soul despite her getting ready to be married. Each day feeling her aurulent ring sway back and forth from her necklace as I create something inexplicably rare. Capturing her in such a way that her beauty can never escape the heart as it climbs into the soul. Having made it my goal to finish the painting before Christmas. Already having all of the lighting that I need I only had to make a digital scan of the work myself. And sending her this file I knew that it would be the last time that I would ever contact her again. No sweet words with the attached file. No *who* the email was from. Hoping that by not saying anything that she might contact me instead. But all that I got yesterday was a return message with a simple *thank you*. Only two modest words. And perhaps fitting for me since I wrote nothing to her. Not writing her being the safer bet incase of prying eyes. Convinced that the stories about her dad checking her texts and emails are true. And then of course me remembering to keep my promise to her.

With her portrait finished I haven't sought out much else to do except stare at my painting of her. Mostly imagining what it would be like having her here as I sit solus by my window turning circles in my head. Thinking about her graduating from university and being married so soon. Less daring when I read on the events calendar what day she would be having her small ceremony. Feeling it would be a torture to us both like that night Malik played lead striker. And then me not wanting to risk being seen by *both* her parents. Thinking it better for me to avoid this emotional torture. A merciless and unrelenting anguish that still tears at my heart and soul.

Sitting in my chair beneath her painting like I am guarding it I question how she could ever trust this stupid boy from a broken home. Ruminative speculation leading me to believe that perhaps her loving this boy who is beneath her is the reason why she is gone. Reaching for a fresh fig from the wooden tea tray on the console table my eyes follow the tiny copper lights that I hot-glued around the window frame. Grabbing a slice of orange the flame on my woodwick candle flickers like the sound of a miniature fireplace. Looking out my window at the mottled clouds above the great red cedars I give no thought to moving back to the States having only two years left. And this shred of hope still leads me to wonder if she will change her mind. Believing once that I was the only love that she wanted. Everyday I wonder if she could ever love anyone else the same way. Confused by her throwing it all away for fear of being judged or politically incriminated. Afraid of being told that you never want to be seen again or spoken to. Being told that you can no longer be with god when god is love and you are made of love and therefore will always belong to and be a part of god. Always perfectly imperfect. Always closer to god than anyone who may seek to judge otherwise. Visualizing her family talking about honor like it is something beautiful. But what is beautiful about stopping love or being too afraid or ashamed to admit and discover that love exists? Still doubting if this impecunious tramp could ever amount to her expectations. Still questioning how this perfect girl could ever love this simple boy. Each day feeling alone. The feeling of her being here in these walls making me wonder if I will ever want to leave the guesthouse. Always in the clouds with her on my mind like the hum of a gong constantly tuning out into space.

Standing up from my leather chair to lie down in bed I feel torn about not knowing what really happened. Tilting my head back and staring up at the dark wood planked ceiling I close my eyes and wish that she could be here right beside me. Running my fingers through my hair before sitting up in bed I rest my elbows over both knees looking at these hands that she used to say are beautiful. Doubting if I could ever make her happy I convince myself that I could never belong to someone as wonderful as Mahru. Feeling a tear slip from my eyes I place both hands over my face. Rubbing my face wet through my hair I turn to see the natural light flooding into my dark room. Distraught and nearly plunging into insanity my heart flutters from the effects of this torment. Crushed to pieces by the thought of her being gone. Overwrought facing the reality of her love being abstracted from me.

Turning underneath my saddle-brown bedding I cannot help but accept that it has begun. I begin to dread the unbearable truth that I will never hear from her ever again. Knowing that she will soon be married to a man of whom her father approves—including all of her mosque congregation and devout relatives back home. Repeatedly warned against speaking to her obsessively conventional father. Telling myself that there is nothing else I can do after I have given Mahru all of this time. Still I keep thinking that she will call me again or come to my door. Still I keep thinking that she is somewhere thinking of me just like I am here thinking of her. I convince myself that her decision was only for the best. Still feeling that she is being punished for her simply being a woman. Visualizing Khalil in my mind intimidating her with an interrogating light. So quick to claim *disrespect* all the while dismissing the disrespect *to the self* inflicted. Tendentiously indoctrinating her with some honor-bound bullshit about covering up her skin all to later be objectified by way of imposed marriage and coercion.

Sitting up in bed heartbroken from having to accept her being gone I visualize myself banging my head against the bathroom mirror glass covered in blood. Alack seeing her sad eyes in my mind my razed heart crumbles. Feeling ripped apart by this poisonous and cruel exile that is cutting. Irreparable I question her father's thinking as I revisit in my mind the great Kahlil Gibran and his parenting advice on children. How we are the sons and daughters of life's longing for itself. How our souls cannot be housed because our souls dwell in the house of tomorrow. Feeling angry that she does not listen to her heart as she destroys ours.

Lying back down in bed I wonder if I can sit up and write what is in my heart even though she can never read it. Lying down in bed staring at the paper and pencil on the edge of my bedside table I want so much for her to feel what I feel. Knowing that I will have to turn on the light if I mean to write to myself *the emotion* of a nequient love.

As Mahru lies down in her bed looking at my name on her phone she thinks of me. But she is disappointed in herself. Her loving thoughts somehow reaching me unbeknownst to her. A telepathic wave still relaying messages into the great cosmic ether. But she is severely saddened as she thinks to press my name and call me. Unsure if she would listen to her heart and if I should want to speak to her. Painfully trying to tell herself that she is to be married in six weeks' time. She lying still with her head down on her tear-drenched pillow. Crying because she knows that a most precious part of her will soon be erased. A havoc that consumes her. And so afraid of upsetting her dad that she forgets herself. Feeling claustrophobic and infinitely trapped as this nocuous toxicity encroaches upon her natural discernment. Denying that she already loves another with enormous tension. And already accepting that it is all too late for her.

Wanting to hear my voice she plays back my old message on her voicemail. She then plays it again. Lying in bed bathing in her tears that carry the memory of my touch and my kiss she forbids herself again that she cannot continue our love affair. Feeling in her body and in her heart the way that I love her she argues with herself that she cannot run to me. Afraid that it would leave her and her family in ruin if she disappointed her mom and dad. Reminding herself that our love is a danger to her and a shame to her family.

Crying more than she has ever cried before she exists in her heart, alone, afraid, and now more miserable than she can bear to stand. Dying inside of her afraid world and wishing that she could go back and say yes to me. Tangled up in her fear and indecision. Wondering if I could ever forgive her. Deciding it best that someone else make her decisions for her for fear of a hidden consequence and being shamed. And all when real love knows no shame. Still lying there with her last desperate attempt to try and free herself of me. Sad knowing that soon there will be no more door for her to knock and no more to all that she does truly love. Heartbroken and beyond remedy. Aching with a sorrow that comes from knowing that she will soon lose forever the one person that she truly loves.

Falling asleep just barely long enough for her tears to dry her mother enters her bedroom after a light tap on the door. Seeing that Mahru is asleep Ianna steps inside to quietly put some of her things away. Kindly putting away Mahru's necklace that was left on the picture table downstairs with some folded shirts and socks.

Setting the necklace down inside of her jewelry box Ianna notices that her mother's ring is missing. Having also noticed that Mahru has not worn it in weeks she begins to thumb through the little miniature drawers just to be sure that it is still there. But she does not see it.

Glancing back at her daughter resting in bed she then turns around and quietly places Mahru's socks in her chest of drawers. Pushing the socks into the back she then catches her ring on a different pair of socks as something that sounds like paper catches her subtle attention. Feeling her hand in the sock drawer and finding nothing that could have made that sound she then feels around for the roof of the top drawer. Hearing it again and feeling a small stack of papers move tucked behind the frame inside she then becomes curious. Fetching the papers down she discovers a neatly kept assortment of substrates, some on plain college rule and some on finer more intimate paper. Deciding not to intrude on her daughter's privacy she then cannot help but notice the careful writing on the back and the few words that intrigue her. Sliding off the hemp cordage Ianna begins to read the first letter and then the second. Hurrying and trying to read them all she becomes more curious. Drawn by the intimate beauty of those words written to Mahru she is then questioned by a voice behind her mid-read.

"Mama. Madha tafiel?"

"Who is Lucius?" Ianna returns.

"Mama. He is just a boy from school. I only saved these incase he became trouble for me. I was just about to throw them all away," she says with disbelief, hurrying out of bed for her mom to hand the letters to her.

"Tell me that this is not what it looks like. You know that you are not supposed to be talking like this to boys at school," she fearfully exclaims, grabbing Mahru by her chin.

"We have not been talking. He stopped talking to me a long time ago," she counters, covering up her heartache as she again reaches for her mom to hand her the letters.

"You know what your father would think of this," Ianna sternly warns Mahru.

"I promise you it is nothing," she sighs, as Ianna hands them to her.

"This Lucius is talented in writing all of this to my precious daughter. And for that I can see why you have kept them. Let's not tell your dad about this though okay. I do not want your dad getting upset at us again," Ianna tries to alleviate, feeling secretly torn about Khalil and herself arranging their daughter's marriage.

"I told him not to talk to me. Then he would not stop writing me. And anyways Mama I'm telling you it is nothing."

"Okay then. It's nothing," Ianna repeats, for a second noticing Mahru unexpressive and emotionless as her eyes wander off. Mahru masking her feeling untenably torn in torment from not being free to express her love.

"I am just nervous about if Hassan is a good fit for me and then living so far away from you and dad—and Madge and Malik," Mahru tries to deflect.

"I was nervous too after my parents died and I was married to your father. That is just how it feels at first. You are so beautiful. You don't have anything to worry about. Hassan has his own house near the city. You and him will have a beautiful family together. And your dad and I will be moving back to be close to you before you know it. And soon everyone that we know will be congratulating you on your wedding."

"Mama. . . . Do you love dad?"

"When your dad and I were both in school and the other girls saw a photo of him they all became jealous. He quickly asked for my hand then. He was the first man in my life. And hopefully he will be the last," she averts, surprised that she even had to think about it.

"What if someday Hassan wants to marry another?"

"Your dad and I have spoken to Hassan and his family. He would never burn your heart with a second wife. Stop worrying so much. In four weeks we are flying to Cairo and you are getting married. You need to think about getting ready."

"Okay . . . ," Mahru dispassionately tells her mom, feeling nervous.

"Alright. . . . And by the way what happened to your grandmother's ring that you are always wearing? You have not worn it in a while. And it is not in your jewelry box."

CHAPTER TWENTY-ONE

"I am still looking for it. I may have misplaced it."

"What do you mean you've misplaced your grandmother's ring? That was one of the few things that I had that belonged to her. I hope that you find it. . . . Hey . . . ," Ianna then says, lifting Mahru's face from under her chin. "Everything is going to be okay, you will see. Hassan is a good man for you."

"I know. Everything is fine."

"Four more weeks. My sister and your entire family will be there. You should be excited," Ianna says, leaning in to kiss Mahru on her head before getting up to leave. "You need to get rid of those letters before your dad gets home," Ianna lastly warns.

"Bahebek."

"I love you too," Mahru tells her mother.

When the cricket plays its tune under the yellow moon, there is only a longing, a need to hold her close. Darkness drinks warmth from the lonely. The absence of her body expanding and contracting each breath worries the heart that has no beat to dance with. There is only time which to the learned means nothing. Time that corrodes. Time that washes away meaning. No calm. No drifting in the deep mass of space that exists out there when she is in my arms. Stars dim in the fog of my mind. No part in the sky that sees into heaven. Only alone. Still dreaming with an ear to her long awaited presence. Cast a spell upon my heart and mind for a peace that I long to find. For love to be here instead of there.

No sweet scent to covet from a tender beloved. No warm lips to melt my heart into nothing. I am just a wanderer who travels alone. No heart to aid my aching bones. I am the wanderer and the shadow in your midst. The thirsty thing that wonders if he exists. Cry no more when for the dead all is dried up. The empty heart to the old and worn empty cup. No warm lips to clean this dry blood from my heart. No feeling from the soul who trails the dark. No sweet scent that gives meaning. No touch and no feeling. No hope for the day tomorrow in a world so sick with sorrow. Hang death from your garden pot where the sun doth yet to feed. No desire in the belly of loves longing that allows the soul to breathe. If only love was as wild as the very forces that hold atoms together perhaps love would come easy without being bound and tethered. Find heaven with your heart above your mind that does deceive, where there is only truly knowing and no need for your heart to bleed.

CHRISTMAS DAY

CHAPTER TWENTY-TWO

Standing up from bed to look out my window the snow on the trees and the light shining through them would normally be to me a beautiful tonic. The mild climate allows the thin snow covering the driveway to recede. Wet enough that the snow is already falling from the branches. Its vanishing beauty leading me back to this vacant corpse of mine. And my heart withers with an unusual sorrow as I attempt to embrace the happiest time of year. Feeling the cold air touch my skin I close my eyes with a tender longing for her. Veiled behind the wet frost on my window I stand naked, feeling her ring around my neck, wondering if I will ever be free of her.

Walking out in my cable-knit pullover sweater onto a slushy footpath in my slippers I mosey to the backdoor behind the main house. Kicking my slippers off inside and walking into the living room Louis is already putting more gifts under the tree for his girlfriend who is still sound asleep. The Christmas tree nearly touches the lofty coffered ceiling with its giant burlap ribbons swirling down to the floor. Large twine balls and pinecones clutter the tree as more ornamental baubles catch the light shining in from the arched windows. Dried myrtle twigs and curly willow branches burst from its height. I also notice the sizable script reading the word *joy* near the top of the tree. Again I observe the beauty of this unrivaled morning apart from my feeling drear and empty. Feeling my heart sulk and pine beneath this charming mask. And in front of my uncle I pretend that I am not just here to endure this spacey sense of disappointment.

My young aunt Lina with her warm smile waves for me to come and help her chop fruit as she plays her soft Christmasy jazz-hop in the kitchen. The sparkling tablescape has been set with crystal goblets and small twig trees made from grapevine and copper-wire lights. The table sits cluttered with berry sprigs and whitewashed pinecones studded with tiny silver orbs. The three-tiered centerpiece filled with gold hammered and glass mosaic balls sits enwreathed by birch tree candles and small ceramic tealight owls. A wooden bowl filled with coconut curry soup sits beside a 19th century copper pitcher filled with homemade cider. The serving plates are filled with banana dark chocolate crepes, pumpkin pie bars, dragon fruit, and fresh-pressed strawberry waffles.

Watching my mother and Camille then come down the stairs together it quickly becomes time to open up the presents under the tree. Camille is the petite short-haired blonde who my uncle Louis met at the gym over a month ago. The two of them are kind of a surprise since we all thought that my uncle Louis was a skirt-chasing hermit or Romeo. And so we all know that it must be a pretty huge deal for Camille to be spending the weekend with us. Louis having finally met someone who he wants to spend every waking moment with. Watching him wake up so early just to construct a model Christmas that is incomparably exquisite. And then of course it also comes as no surprise that my mom and Lina really like Camille a lot—myself included.

Everyone tries to take a nibble of something from the kitchen before coming into the front room to sit down. As Louis hands each of us a shiny package from under the tree I sit next to my mom on the end of the sofa where I can watch everyone else open theirs first. Watching everyone sit close together in kind celebration I keep wishing that she could be here sitting beside me. Almost sensing her luring magnetism and her loving hand in mine. Our two hearts floating above the alpine feeling the soft music, the smells, and the taste of Christmas. Distracted, my eyes glance at the snow melt outside before again sensing the warm smiles and faces that surround me. Still feeling the laughter and the love as I gaze at the soft glow coming from the fireplace. All of us feeling that we are a divine part of what god is. All of us connected to each other in some way as we all celebrate the birth of a new sun or *the return* of the sun. The victory of light over dark that happens each year right before Christmas on the path of the ecliptic. Each of us sharing in the ritual of gift-giving as the scent of pine permeates the air. All of us sensing a oneness

CHAPTER TWENTY-TWO

during this time of solstice. And sometimes all of it just feels like money wasted on unwanted gifts. Different people all over the world celebrating the same thing in many different ways. All of the different gods. All the same. And even if the tradition is silly it still makes us all feel closer to home and each other. And I can say that a day like today feels pretty good after feeling so heartbroken and even still discouraged. The soft gentle music playing behind me and seeing my family being my favorite part most of all.

After a round of coconut egg nog the excitement begins to die down to a more leisure crawl. Hearing my aunt Lina talk about the family who could not make it somehow hits in my heart a sensitive nerve. An almost flush-like feeling like small blood vessels dilating moves up my back and shoulders and face. I think about being here *without* the one person I care about most. Still wishing that her family could meet mine and thinking that mine are not all that bad. Fantasizing about how fulfilling it would be if both our families could just be here to enjoy the different company. All gathered around uncloaking the divine spark in every soul and feeling what it means to be human. Undivided by all illusion and the erroneous dictates of men. Finding it sad to think that it has now been six weeks since her and I last spoke to each other. Beginning to feel dewy-eyed amidst this lovely day I struggle to be fortified against every despairing emotion. Feeling the more I miss her the more that I find myself just wanting to be alone.

As the morning shifts into the afternoon talk begins to build about going out for a drive into the mountains. A torpid spaciness overcomes me as I briefly become bemused by this strange joy that is swelling in the room. Suddenly I begin to feel in my heart that I do not even care. Not caring about what is being devised or proposed around me the more I think of her. Still seeing her eyes and her face and her smile so clearly. Her voice just as clear to me as any voice.

Deciding that I need a moment to breathe before getting pulled into something that might trouble me even further I quietly sneak out the backdoor. Luckily quiet enough for nobody to notice and disturbing nobody who might try to make me feel guilty for leaving.

Walking outside and upstairs to change clothes I begin to think more about going somewhere to be by myself. Throwing on a knitted long sleeve I for a moment pause to see out the window the niveous snow-capped mountains in the distance. Grabbing my wool jacket and grey knit beanie by the backdoor I decide that I want to check out this diner that is a fifteen-minute walk from

CHRISTMAS DAY

the house. It is the place with the royal blue entrance and all of the window seating looking out onto Cambie Street. Simply wanting to be somewhere where I can contemplate what I am feeling.

Texting my mom while closing my front door and walking down the packed driveway I tell all of them to go ahead without me. I also lie and tell my mom that I am meeting a friend who would be spending Christmas alone if it weren't for me. Really just wanting to be alone and not spilling tears in front of everyone. I then end the text by telling my mom that I will meet back up with them after they all return home from their drive.

Sitting alone at the diner I wonder if she is even thinking about me at all. The Paraíba tourmaline color on the concrete wall hints a faint reflection onto the white button-tufted booths by the window. Touching the candle on the wooden table I notice the place is only half packed as my eyes follow the oyster bay brick up to the exposed ceiling above.

Smelling the large bundles of cinnamon near the entrance behind me I make eye contact with the waitress and nod for her to come and take my order. Asking her for just a green tea and noticing her kind smile she begins to ask me *why* I seem to be alone on Christmas. Her pleasant features remind me of a girl I once loved. Her long dark ponytail behind her white scoop neck shirt and striped apron with the leather strap around her neck.

Slow turning the table candle in my hands I cannot help but feel apathetic conversing with and observing the opposite sex. Perhaps for fear of feeling too much and remembering how much love there once was. Surrendering only a single explanation and watching her lip curl under her soft eyes she then offers to make my tea at her apartment. She reminding me of this love that I still feel as if Mahru were sitting right here next to me. Being compassionate and considerate with regard to her being alone today I turn down the hopeful advances from the waitress. Thinking only about the one girl that possesses me each moment I still receive her kind complement.

Watching the waitress walk away I begin to feel pretty stupid and even worse—lonely. Still disappointed and broken up as I think about missing Mahru.

Turning to look out the street-side window subtle movements come to life like a canvas followed by a beautiful idea. Traces of snow with red and gold seem to soften the busy conditioning of man.

Looking down at my phone I then see that my mom has tried to call me.

CHAPTER TWENTY-TWO

Suddenly I then feel bad that I lied about where I am. Still content though not being told how depressing it is to be alone on Christmas.

Being handed my tea with another warm smile I still find it hard to dismiss Mahru as the peaceful beauty of this season reflects to me the warmth of her spirit. Watching the waitress walk away I keep wishing that I could somehow see her again. Thinking that maybe I was not persuasive enough. Feeling now like she is already long gone and moved on.

Turning to look outside again I admire the beautiful evergreens and the garland that are filled with the magic of tiny gleaming lights. Something about it bringing with it a sort of relief but also a sadness. The dark evergreen and luminescent bulb sharing a magical color and warmth. A warmth that stands against the glittery frost of winter making its magic all the more meaningful. Scenes like this one pulling me through my darkest hour or just the typical inconvenience of everyday life. The frosty air of winter examined by a curious sun through a small opening in the sky where tiny pieces of glass melt on impact. The hurried pace of everyone rushing to be indoors from the cold. Holiday wreaths warming the streets with holly berry and ribbon as the spirit of giving a gift is given. Where candle lights burn warming each and every color and where all through the day we yearn for our lover. Where some return home by the wood-burning fire and lie bundled together by the one they admire. It is this warmth that reminds me of my love for her lips and the fire in her that causes my heart to burn. It is the kind of magic that is always seen in the eyes of the one girl who I can never stop thinking about. Thinking about the first time that I saw her and the first day that we made love to each other and how she was so ready to trust me.

Noticing the sunlight begin to dim I leave a tip and pay my check before stepping outside to head home. Turning to look down the sidewalk to see who else is still open I then spot a bundle of fresh haidemorala roses inside of the pharmacy next door. Brilliant splashy petals ranging from a persimmon pink to a milky cream color.

Wondering if my number could be blocked on her phone I also then think to ask myself if she might refrain from reading anything that I send through text. Tired of second-guessing her love for me and wishing today to disobey her once more I finally convince myself to do something positively *foolish*. Tired of wanting to know if I have done everything to express my love for her. And every time despite her unfortunate fears. Already knowing that if I refuse myself that I will never love again.

CHRISTMAS DAY

Clearly acknowledging that my plan involves breaking my promise to her I open the glass door hearing the bells on the handle clank behind me. Purchasing the roses before the store closes and getting them all wrapped up I leave just as quickly as I stepped inside. The lady working the store flipping the closed sign on the door right behind me after walking out.

Walking home with flowers under my arm a nervous prickly feeling tries to forewarn me. Only I am too distracted by the cold and how beautiful the night is as the sun begins to set. In my mind I keep thinking about leaving the flowers and a letter on her doorstep before the sun rises in the morning. My only hope and reservation being that Madge will still get up to leave for work before dawn. Hoping that Madge will see what I am leaving for her sister before anyone else wakes up. And I know that my plan is far from genius. And I know that I am becoming desperate. But I also believe firmly that it is my desperation that defines what true love really is. To be completely reckless in order to find a love that is more rare than anything that I have ever felt, seen, or touched.

Nearing my driveway as I observe the sparkling streets of an enchanted spell bulbs fuse against the shadows of the moon. Seeing that everyone is back as I spot Louis's truck in the driveway I walk towards my front door behind the house.

Taking my warm clothes off at the door before walking upstairs I begin to look carefully for something stylish to write on. The magical ambiance of my cozy oasis still not enough for me to find comfort without her. Finding some tea stained paper that I made myself I pick out some decorative rope from an old box of stuff that belongs to Louis. Using the rope to secure her bundle of flowers the beauty of all that is done carefully is what begins to mean more to me. Changing into some more comfortable clothes I look up at her painting already beginning the words before I sit down to write. This being my one last act of defiance to commemorate our forbidden love affair.

Writing on some scratch paper I next try to write as neatly and as elegantly as I can. A part of me feeling that this last attempt to communicate will be unsuccessful. Hoping that by only signing my name that she can deny knowing who it is from if it gets her into any trouble. Knowing that I do not even have to sign my letter for Madge or Mahru to know who it is from.

Continuing to fashion the most telling symbol of my love's obsession I add the element of fire by carefully singeing the edges. Rolling her letter up with cordage I accept that Mahru may never get to read what is written inside.

CHAPTER TWENTY-TWO

Staring up at the lights that are strung over the exposed rafters down to the floor I come to terms with having satisfied my efforts. Knowing that I will have to leave the house in seven hours so that I can get there while it is still dark outside. Praying only that I am right about Madge getting up to leave early. There being no more tears left to cry as I lie awake in bed and imagine her surprise or saddening dismay.

Unable to sleep I then get up to sit in my chair and to watch the clock. Afraid of not getting up early enough I glance at my phone every time that I want to fall asleep. Resting my eyes mostly I can feel the tension curl in my muscles as I sit thinking about how afraid she is of her dad. I also keep wondering if what I am about to do will leave her vulnerable and unsafe. And I wonder if she will even get the chance to hear from me if my little message is not thrown into the garbage first.

One hour before the earliest noticeable light I pull onto West Thirty-seventh Avenue with my vehicle headlights turned off. Parking two houses down underneath a big-leaf maple near the edge of the street I try to avoid being seen by anyone who might be home.

Stepping out of my car I walk the long wrought-iron gate with its stone supports that row every inch of the property along the front of the house. Being careful not to slip on any ice on the brick sidewalk I step closer to the lantern hanging from her gated entrance. All lit up in the dark her large home stands tucked away behind the gate and the three hundred-year-old oaks that tower over the spacious entrance. Her beautifully lit home appearing to melt the light traces of snow that are scattered where the sun does not touch.

Surprised to see that the gates are opened I hurry down the winding cobblestone path smitten by the beauty and monumental size of her French Renaissance style home. Walking up to the twelve-foot double doors at the front of the house I feel as anxious as I sometimes become when I feel her close to me. And not just because I am risking so much by leaving her my letter. But because I still love her with all of my heart. Quickly and quietly leaving the flowers and letter on her doorstep I hurry back to my car walking as fast as I can. Turning to look back at her front door I quietly disappear into the cold thick fog that blankets the street to my advantage. I walk away from the front of her house saddened by a second glance. My head flooding with every memory that I have of her known and forgotten. Knowing that I can expect no return response should Khalil see my letter that I left for his daughter. And

CHRISTMAS DAY

I leave knowing that I have seen only something that belongs to her. Perhaps the last image or thing that will ever satisfy the pain of never seeing her again.

Sitting on the cold leather seat inside of my car having one last look at the street where her house sits I again begin to feel a sadness. Feeling the heater vents finally start to warm up from behind the wheel I then turn on my lights and drive away knowing that I have seen enough.

THE MORNING

CHAPTER TWENTY-THREE

Shortly after leaving Mahru's house Madge steps outside of her front door in her white poplin shirt and button down waistcoat to leave for work. Rummaging through her small leather backpack for her car keys she looks down and sees a bundle of beautiful flowers and a letter neatly seated at her feet. Quickly identifying who the letter is from she then quietly peaks back inside of the house to see if anyone else is awake. Not wishing for her sister to get into any trouble Madge carefully tiptoes back up the stenciled staircase to deliver the roses and the letter before her dad wakes up.

"Mahru," Madge whispers forcefully, shaking her sister to take notice. "I found this at the front door. This was left outside for you."

Seeing a bouquet of bright roses and realizing what her sister just said she immediately sits up in bed surprised and terrified.

"Did dad see this?"

"No. Everyone is still asleep," Madge answers, handing her sister the surprise flowers and letter. Mahru then pulls the letter from the envelope to read who it is from.

"It's from Lucius," she says, with a smile.

"You have to let me read it when I come back. I have to go," Madge tells Mahru, her face beaming with curiosity.

Both of them then pause hearing a faint disturbance downstairs. Parting with a kiss on her sister's forehead Madge then tells Mahru to be careful. "Maa salama," Madge whispers, quietly closing the bedroom door before walking back down the staircase.

Quickly getting up from bed and hiding the flowers inside of the wood chest in her closet Mahru then lies back down with my letter under her linen pillow. Her heart pounds over the moon with excitement as she anxiously lies in bed waiting to read my handwriting. Listening to the faint hum coming from the coffee grinder downstairs she waits for her dad to leave the house before attempting to read it. With an endearing smile she ponders the few words that caught her eye before she hid the letter under her bedding. Lying underneath her comforter she senses my abiding love for her like a brightness that will never vanish.

Waiting for almost an hour Khalil then finally leaves and heads downtown to pick up breakfast for his family from Café Medina which is almost twenty minutes away. Watching from her casement window Mahru crawls out of bed knowing that her mother is still asleep and that her brother most likely will not be up before noon.

The lucent fog outside dissipates as the first light of morning finds its way shining in through the window. Locking her bedroom door Mahru flips her warm toffee-colored blanket around her shoulders. Pulling out my letter and the roses from her chest of drawers she places them on her bed admiring my message just the way I left it. Anxiously opening my letter she begins to read. A tear falls down her cheek reading the first three lines. The fourth line lures from her another tear. Absorbing my words with intrigue she reflects back on a love so unforeseeably irresistible and wondrous. The ink on the paper dances circles around her heart like a small vortical pillar of swirling leafage. That unforgettable summer to our last goodbye mesmerizing like a stream of emotion bathing each soul in truth. Mahru then realizes that she is not ready for it to end.

Her eyes doubt and yet bear a curiosity. She wonders in her mind even when thinking of what she wonders is already known. Cautious and shy she dances around the shining water that calls for her lips to taste and her feet to feel. The man in the water tempts her lusts and still she walks by—still smiling and still staring. Only in her dreams can she imagine what the man in the water would have given. What he would have shared with her. Only in her dreams can she imagine that feeling when

CHAPTER TWENTY-THREE

spring has sprung. Where life is filled with the gift of color and a light that changes all of them at once. A taste that satisfies the soul. There being only the memory of her haunting eyes that yearn but do not touch. Her angelic stride shifting above the reflection in the water. Her soul trapped in her body as if careful to damage her skin that expires under the duress of time. Her soul held hostage in hopes that her skin and image will glow vibrant for just one more day. And so the man calls for her once again hoping that her being able to trust will free her from death. Hoping to love her. Hoping to taste the nectar of her soul. The part of her that hides behind the her that is visible. The part reflecting the depth in her eyes and the part that powers the heart. And losing myself to all of her.

Lying in her bed and remembering how important that I am to her Mahru then feels a frenetic naz radiating from inside the core of her heart. Smelling her roses and holding my letter close to her she ponders every sweet impression that resonates from my correspondence.

Climbing out of bed and placing everything back inside of her closet drawer she then uses her hands to dry her face. Throwing on something warmer to wear and grabbing something to write on she then grabs her car keys and runs downstairs quietly to exit the front door.

Stepping up inside of her truck and admiring the morning being so beautiful Mahru then drives down to the ornamental grounds in the neighborhood. Into an undisturbed lower valley encircled by large homes that stand lit above a cloudy hill she makes her way into the parkland of gardens.

Parking her truck she sits beneath a row of winter trees that have become wet from the temperate mist that cloaks the cold air. Leaving the heat on with her vehicle running she cracks her window to enjoy the slight chill that blends with the fragrance of morning. Seriously reweighing everything and abandoning in her heart every coaxing pressure and being steered to be married she recalls the simple joy and the love that she once had as she anxiously then dials my phone number.

Having already gone back to bed I then hear my phone vibrate on my bedside table. Motivating myself to move and see if it could be her I immediately recognize her phone number. Nervous my love begs all hope feeling my heart muscle accelerate before pressing the green answer icon. Holding my phone

THE MORNING

close I wait for someone to speak on the other end.

"Hello," a soft familiar voice says to me, her sweet golden sound pricking my ears.

Knowing who it is, I am surprised and overcome by her sudden phone call. Mid-hello I discover something darling in her voice that uncovers her appetency for my love. Paying careful attention I hear her smiling as she repeats herself.

"Hey," I nearly hesitate, hoping that I had not caused her any personal distress or grief with her dad.

"Mmh-hhm," Mahru softly chokes, her smile gleaming with an affectionate trail of tears below her gleeful eyes—the sound of my voice touching her ears like a magic panpipe from an old folktale or myth. "I read your letter and I love it. Thank you," she then says.

"I've missed you," I smile, wiping my eye with the inside of my thumb.

"I've missed you too," she tells me, her heart swelling with a tremendous joy that she cannot even begin to describe.

"Did your dad see the flowers?"

"No—Madge brought them up to me before she left for work. My dad would have killed me if he had seen them. I cannot believe that you did that," she says, being both disapproving but also soft with a tender affection.

"I won't do that again—I swear."

"Good," she smiles.

"It's just uh . . . I had to write to you . . . just one last time."

Not hearing Mahru say anything I offhandedly think of something else to say.

"Did you have a good Christmas?"

"Mmh-hhm," she then faintly comes out with, her heart pounding firm with an intensity unknown to her, me still confused about her silently toying with me.

Waiting again for something to be said I realize that she must also be waiting for me to do the same. Suddenly she resumes our diffident conversation.

"You know I have thought about you everyday since I last saw you. I never wanted to say goodbye to you. I never wanted any of that to happen—what happened to me and you."

"I know. It's okay."

"No. It is not okay. Not when I know that my heart belongs to you. From the very first day that I met you and you wrote me that letter. You were always everything to me, Lucius. I couldn't even believe that you were real you were so perfect."

Feeling my heart stimulate from the prior obstruction of blood flow Mahru can hear and feel my emotional sentiment getting to me.

"I loved you too the first time I laid eyes on you," I tell her, wiping my face and expecting her to come out with why we still can't.

"Do you think that you could forgive me?" Mahru then asks, holding back soft tears with a calm sweetness about her voice.

"I forgive you," I try to console, grinning my teeth with discomfort.

"Are you sure that you still want to lose yourself to me?" she then asks, anxiously anticipating my answer.

"All of you—Yes. Each day awake and each night asleep in my dreams."

"I do not want you to be just a dream to me anymore," she returns, all but trembling.

"Let me love you," I about whisper.

Listening to the relieved thrill of her delicate laughter, she stops.

"No. Let me love you. Let me come into your shining water. Let me taste the nectar of your soul," she reflects softly.

"Okay," I inwardly chuckle, still unconvinced about her being serious.

"Except this time I am not going to let go of you," she willfully asserts, grabbing my attention.

"I never want to let go of you."

"Are you at home?" she then asks, a sweet thirst moving from her lips as she shifts the conversation.

"I am."

"Can I come and see you right now for just a few minutes? I can't stay long because my dad will be back and my mom will be waking up soon."

"Yeah—you can come over. The driveway is full because my mom and my aunt Lina are here. Just park behind Louis's truck."

"Okay I will be there in ten minutes."

"Okay."

"K—bye," she hangs up, her love for me still curling off the end of her tongue.

Setting my phone down at my bedside table my heart feels reinvigorated by this lost taste for her love. The gentle vibration from her voice evincing an intense anticipation so lovely that there can be no mistaking her joyful delirium. Already sensing something different about her that has changed. As if no

THE MORNING

more burdened by the agnatic dictates of what is said to be honorable. Like a warm shifting wind in the change of seasons. Only wondering now how long this will last. Wondering if she can love me enough to make this fierce leap into the unknown. This place that I know to be dark without her radiant light. Kind words like tender mercies no more befallen by persuasive obligation. Our loving entanglement no more swallowed up by the pious self-deceptions of our time. Honestly hoping that she has quashed this fear to love me.

Sitting up in bed my slubbed comforter then slides down my back and shoulders as the cool air touches my skin. Again waking up to the fact that she is coming over I spring from my bed across the cold wood floor. Touching her ring dangling from my neck I dare imagine her wanting to make this work between us. Throwing on my thickest pair of sweats and my quilted pullover sweatshirt I then quickly slide into my loosely tied tall boots.

Hurrying to brush my teeth in the bathroom I next head downstairs to sip my herb tea to throw off the minty taste in my mouth. Feeling the warm light shining into the guesthouse I then set my cup down above the barstool.

Stepping closer to the mirror behind the coat rack near the front window I then stop to run my fingers through my thick head of hair. Remembering the joy that it brings Mahru to touch and smell my golden curls I instead choose to leave my knitted beanie behind. Understanding that she should now be arriving at any moment I then reach for the door handle to step outside.

Seeing the back of the main house all lit up I absorb the crisp Tiffany-Blue sky and the twinkling sunlight shining through the weeping white spruce and western white pine. Smelling the cool hiemal air with my hands in my pockets I then notice Mahru pulling in to the end of the driveway. Eager to catch up with her I walk towards her truck. Her wet tires halt against the drenched pavement along the melted snow. Feeling her close is naturally enchanting. The tenderness in her eyes and her smile being enough to soothe and extract the bitter poison that still stirs in the blood of my heart.

Walking around the front of her blue-green truck I see Mahru sitting in her driver's seat watching intently with a delightful grin. Stepping closer to her I can feel her heart pounding as she props open her driver side door.

Following her eyes that fixate on me I again catch her smile as I walk around her door to where she is still seated. Pulling her emergency brake she then stands up outside of her antique defender to greet me all dressed in her modishly stunning car coat. She immediately shares with me that smile that belongs to only her. God I love the way that her skin pulls against her

CHAPTER TWENTY-THREE

face when she smiles. The festive colors of the harvest still reminiscent in the warmth of her skin. The lush moire of her ravens hair falls alongside of her face complementing the definition that is seen beyond her luminous gaze. Stepping closer to her I become spellbound by the phosphorescent glow around those castaneous eyes that still adore me.

"Hey," I mutter, still having mild reservations about her coming here to break my heart.

"Hey," she returns, stepping closer to me as every part of her seeks to feel again as beautiful as before.

Without words and with a focusing of the eyes on each other everything needing to be said or known becomes so as we move to hold and feel each other so closely. Her arms and her face and body hold tight inside of mine. Pulling on the ring inside of my shirt she again seeks to feel those things within her that can be felt no place else. Holding her close the tense weave of my muscles break free and give warmth to every part of her. For a moment her need for my warmth stands contrasted against the brittle branches that hang from the dawn of winter's turn. Her eyes enchanted as if it were I whom she has been waiting for her entire life. Seeing her look at me this way causes my soul to leap from its rest and to give of what I too am feeling. Eyes like a still river raising light from the moon that passes through the sky. My emotional fragility unnoticed as she reaches for me to hold her tight. This burning inside of me initiating a pure joy and peace that I thought would be forever lost. To love and be loved manifesting to be the most incredible experience ever granted unto me. Feeling her now to be my every breath and the very beating of my heart. Her lips like the wild meadow awaiting the lonely traveler to experience her rich redolence after a heavy rain under a vermilion sky.

Before I can think to doubt her for whatever reason she hurries to charge my lowly spirit with her succulent lips. Reaching for her waist my hands feel for her flesh beyond her grey ribbed sweater. More to me than the beauty of the earth it is even her name that causes me to tremble when I am close to her. The propinquity of her lissome figure arched against my body is now soup to my broken heart. Her kiss and her touch allowing love and blood to again souse the channels hastening through my vascular body. My arms hold on to her like I can never let her go. Warming her nose against my face she again offers me those lips in that sure way of which I am familiar. Knowing now just as I always have that there can be no love worthy or memorable enough to ever take her place.

THE MORNING

"You are still wearing the ring that I gave you."

"I've missed you," I tell Mahru, holding her along a wet and misty driveway that absorbs the morning sun, still finding it hard to fathom that she is close enough for me to touch.

"I've missed you too," she smiles.

"Did you mean what you said about not wanting this to be a dream? Are you sure that you want me?" I ask, nervously.

"Never have I been more sure about anything in all of my life. I want to be with you, Lucius," she comes out with.

Feeling a warm happiness brim at the canthus of my eye I feel weightless from the sight of her. Kissing Mahru the lilt amalgamation and assemblage of our imbricating magnetism charges the stimuli within our souls merging us into a mellifluous bond. Her desire to please secures my imprisonment to her gladly. Again suddenly feeling like I belong to her I begin to grow increasingly confident that her kiss means that she has truly changed her mind. Her mind and her eyes now shifting into deep thought as they stay fixed to mine.

"I feel now like I was so wrong to be afraid. So many things preventing me from acknowledging the truth and the fact that I can choose. It was never about you. You are perfect. I just know what I want now. I never want to be anyplace where you are not with me. Understand that I always loved you."

"And I have always loved you. From the first time I saw those eyes and that face. I would be sad for a thousand lifetimes if I knew that you were unhappy. And I will never stop loving you," I remind Mahru, holding her precious face with both my hands and following her passionate lips along the tall Portuguese laurels.

"I am so sorry about before. I was afraid. I do not want to be afraid anymore. And I do not want to spend my entire life with a man who I do not even love. A man who I know could never love me the way that you do. I want to be free to love who I choose," she almost cries, her smile and voice lifting me from this sufferable realm of doubt.

Following her eyes and moving my face closer to hers she unveils her deepest feelings that were left buried and kept secret. Yearning to taste my love her lips fasten to mine aching to fill up and replenish her starving heart. A heart-hunger dying to again taste what was and still is. Like bare skin seeking to love extravagantly and to walk between worlds. Her kiss melts me into poetry that I know will never be written down. Still tasting on her lips an eternal desire unquenchable. Gazing into her eyes I know love to be the lens

CHAPTER TWENTY-THREE

that sees into heaven where one's eternal breath is granted and taken. It being obvious to me as I stand brushing my thumb against her lips and looking into those eyes that she is the one who conceals the road to my freedom and my happiness. Pulling Mahru close to me beneath the fragrant cool of morning her eyes shine like dew over morning clovers eager to bear the weight of this weary traveler. And even more in love than she was the first day that we met.

"I never thought that I would see you again."

"Neither did I," she says back, with a smile.

"You know that you don't have to go back home. We can drop your truck off and you can come back home with me."

"I need time to tell my sister goodbye. Also my brother. And I need to figure out how to explain this to my mom and my dad in a letter or something. I don't want you to worry though. Okay?"

"Okay," I return, pressing my forehead to hers.

"Are you sure that you still want me?" she still asks, unforgiving of herself.

"Never doubt my immense love for you. Even A thousand lifetimes spent with you would all be over too soon," I wholeheartedly express, catching her relieved smile. "Should we go inside where it's warm?" I then prod, feeling the cold wind blow up the driveway.

"Yeah—for just a minute. My dad will be back soon and he will be wondering where I am. But I promise that I will text you later today okay."

"Okay," I voice, altogether grateful just to see her as I begin to steer us both towards the guesthouse.

Further back along the snow-melted driveway small beaming rays of sunshine poke through the wide variety of evergreens.

Stepping inside my front door Mahru stands still to admire the decorative work and the lights strung throughout my small cozy place. Keeping her car coat on she turns around to again reach for my kiss. Staring those lovely eyes into my soul with her arms wrapped around me tightly she knows that she desperately wants to stay. But she also knows that it will not be today and that she must get back home.

Still satiating her thirst for my lips and my kiss she wraps her heart up in the warm swirling blanket of my tongue. She uses her gentle fingers to touch my skin with all of her love. Her touch feeling for me like waves pushing and pulling in a shallow sea. The most beautiful silence wrapping us both in the memory of what was and is now.

Aware of the time Mahru steps back to pull something from her wool pocket. She then hands to me a red envelope with my name on it.

"I took the pleasure of writing you something like you always do for me. Loving you has irrefutably been the most beautiful experience of my entire life," she admits, standing so free and liberated in knowing exactly what she wants. Her focused eyes no more vague as her written letter passes from her hand to mine. And then that perfect smile.

"Thank you," I tell Mahru, my heart still tossing in the wind as to how she is even here right now.

"Wait. . . . Read it after I leave. I'm sorry but I have to go home. I will call you later tonight," she says, taking my hand off the seal.

"You promise?" I return, she sensing this dread of losing her again surface in my eyes.

"I promise you I will. My mom and dad are also leaving in a few days to go to a Lake Washington retreat near Seattle. I promise I will come and see you every day after they leave."

"Okay."

"I love you, Lucius. I have to go," she struggles to repeat.

"Okay," I swallow, still afraid that she might not come back.

Holding her hand to walk back outside she reaches up to kiss me with those dark luminiferous eyes. Her honeyed lips caress my heart and my soul with a confident knowing. Feeling her gentle embrace her lips then pull away from mine.

Walking all radiant back to her antique turquoise truck I recognize the light in her eyes that I first discovered at the beginning of the semester. Her decided smile glows with a happiness that she must now ready herself to conceal.

Quickly climbing back into her truck I then reach to tell Mahru goodbye with one last kiss.

"You're gonna call me?"

"Yes. Maybe eleven o'clock."

"I love you."

"I love you. I'll call you," she smiles.

Carefully backing down the driveway I watch her wave to me before she then pulls out onto the road to drive away. Surprised by how different it feels this time I smile at all that has changed in such a short amount of time. The last time she said goodbye and the aftermath of it all quickly fading from my memory. A familiar warmth reappearing and with a replenishment of love and

CHAPTER TWENTY-THREE

promise that I believed to be dead.

Glancing down at the red envelope in my hand I then walk back to the guesthouse to go inside. With my heart still spinning I open her letter to me. Carefully reading her handwriting I finally let go of everything that has tortured me throughout this excruciating heartache.

Dear Lucius,

I truly want to say thank you for being the wonderful person that you have been for me and for the love that you have shown me. I am so grateful for you and I am always touched and moved by your tenderness and compassion. When I look back I regret having made you feel so awful because of me. All I could think about is that I did not want to hurt you. And I know that it has been difficult for you because of me. I know now that you are the greatest person that walked into my life. I know that someone else in your place would have given up easily on me. But it takes a person like you with a very kind and gentle heart to not do that. And for that I want to say thank you from the bottom of my heart. Even sometimes I feel like I do not deserve you. And this letter can go on forever because if I wrote down a million words that would still not be enough because you mean so much more to me than just words. And from the first day that I met you I never stopped loving you. If you could still give me one more chance I promise you that you will not regret it. And what I really want to say is that I hope that you can forgive me. I miss you and I never stopped loving you.

All my love,
Mahru

RUN AWAY WITH ME

CHAPTER TWENTY-FOUR

Walking back up my frosty driveway after wishing my mom and my aunt Lina safe travels I think about them making that two-and-a-half-hour drive back to Seattle. Both of them heading for those same coastal mountains that lead me here to this seaside neighborhood outside of Vancouver. Already missing my mom I feel terrible after confessing that I have not thought about moving back to Washington. Admitting to myself that I do not know much of anything the way that things are turning out and changing so suddenly. Still feeling that it might be too premature to be filling my family in on the details about me and Mahru. Louis being the only one who was up early enough to see her distinct sea-green truck parked behind the house just a few days ago. Him later making discreet mention of it when he asked me in private if we are getting back together. Only feeling like I know the answer to that question more now than I did then.

Stepping back inside the guesthouse to put away the dishes sitting on my dry rack I greatly anticipate Mahru being on her way over. Still wide awake after having talked to her most of the night. And even now remaining confident about her feeling ready to make this dramatic change in her life. Still mulling over in my head what to do if things escalate with her family. Even having already called my aunt Lindsey just incase we need to disappear for a little while. And already familiar with the drive down to VaHi, in Atlanta, Georgia.

Putting away my clean clothes from the dryer I think about her never

CHAPTER TWENTY-FOUR

having been anywhere alone without her mom and her dad. Knowing that they will no longer be there to watch out for her I understand that this must be the biggest leap of all to run away for love. Still sad in my heart that we should have to find love this way. Still touched by her love for these perfect hands that care for her and that have made her immortal across the canvas that marks these walls. My heart and soul imprinted on the scribbles of ink and paper that clutter her keepsake box. Everything that I am all belonging to her.

Hearing the deep soft hum of her truck engine I step outside brushing my gold curls away from my face to find her driver side door already opened. Behind the main house she looks at me like I am the brightest thing that she has ever seen. Stepping down from her truck to grab ahold of me, I reach for her, kissing her perfect lips. Pulling her button-down coat around closer to her neck another gentle kiss warms us both as the winter sun moves behind the blond white clouds. Removing her cream wool scarf she smiles at me finding my loving tenderness irresistible to her. Pushing her fingers up the sleeves of my sweater there is nothing grave nor troublesome that threatens our love to feel unsure. Each second living for each other as we do live for the air that we breathe. She still lolling in the energy of my allure that has swallowed her completely.

Falling from that beautiful dark sky inside of her eyes the dripping conifer trees all stand still to adore our awe-inspiring presence as I hold her close to me. Her face and fingers softer than fine chambray as my hands feel for her warm desert skin beneath her alpaca pullover.

Slowly kissing her blush lips our two souls mesh and mend in pursuit of that sweet rapture that causes the entire body to ache. My kiss still swimming underneath her skin and seeping into her bones as she hard plummets further more towards this impavid love. The receptive selvage of her turning aurorae lips being to me that styptic dressing that remedies this agonizing anxiousness.

"Come on," I whisper, reaching for her hand.

Taking Mahru's coat at the door she then takes off her boots and makes herself comfortable atop the cloud daybed along the deep window ledge. Grabbing her a cup of tea from the kitchen with a fresh bowl of fruit in my other hand she then curls up in my shaggy blanket.

"I am sorry that I cannot stay long. My parents are only getting an oil change and some groceries. I know that they will be back soon," she regrets, tugging on her Andean-festival sleeves.

"I understand. Are they still leaving tomorrow?" I then ask, leaning into the cluster of sofa pillows behind me.

"Yes. Tomorrow they are driving to Seattle just to get away for a little bit. Just for five days. But I kind of want to spend most of that time with my brother and my sister. So maybe Friday morning you can come and help me grab most of my stuff while Madge and Malik are at school. That will be three days before they get back. And then Sunday morning if you can park one house down away from mine I will just have my school backpack and leave hopefully before my brother wakes up."

"Okay," I carefully listen, making note of those two days. She then scoots over to sit closer to me.

"I cannot believe that I am actually doing this. I just know that I want to be with you."

"And I just want to be with you," I tell Mahru, seeing in those brilliant earthy-brown eyes of hers that she is really ready. Still somewhat nervous as she looks down smiling at her hand inside of mine.

"My parents reminded me again this morning that we are supposed to be flying to Cairo on the fifteenth. And then the twenty-fifth is the day that I am supposed to be getting married. Hopefully my parents can refund their plane tickets. And I feel bad but I know that this is the only way."

"I wish that you didn't have to separate like this from your mom and dad. And I am sorry that today is the last day that you will get to see them."

"Me too," Mahru mutters, burying her face into my chest.

"I really did want to know your mom and dad and the rest of your family. And I wanted to love them because I love you. . . . Are you sure that you still want to run away with me?"

"You already know the answer to that question. And I am sorry too that they will never know how wonderful you are and that we have to be together like this."

"Are you going to resent me if you never see them again?"

"I will never resent you. The way that my parents are is not your fault. And I know that once this is done that there is no turning back. And I know that I can live with that. Just as long as I have you."

"I promise you that you will always have me," I assure her.

"Let me live and die right here in your arms," she then says, hiding her face into my neck.

"Okay," I assuage, holding my love tighter, acknowledging her every wish and knowing that I would stop at nothing just to be with her.

CHAPTER TWENTY-FOUR

"And you will love me forever?" she then asks, moving her hair from her face.

"There will never be an end to my love for you. This magic spell that you have over me will traverse far past the ends of forever."

"So is my love for you," she affirms.

Sitting up to kiss me her honeylove lips rush me with a calming fix that leaves me spaced out and forgetful. Pressing her perfect forehead to mine my fingertips travel her cheekbones before cutting through her thick black curls.

Grabbing Mahru where her fine woven blouse hugs tightly against her thin torso her back arches forward before lying back down to lounge with me. Sharing with me her subtle kiss that seems to unravel without end her fingers spin my locks into gold as she surrenders to me with every portion of her pliant body. Every inch of her warmth offering me sanctuary with her golden touch and her coral lips. Her perfectly sculpted hands drawing around me an invisible circle of protection to remind me that I am loved.

Holding so intimately dear the one girl I love more than anything I consistently begin to feel that nothing in this world will ever again come between us. Adoring her keen sensitivity to my every touch as my fingers travel her body inside of her boatneck sweater. Trailing her travertine skin I long to taste her again. Her small hands squeezing my chaotic curls as she bends closer to kiss me. Holding Mahru in good faith that she will not leave me devastated as I gaze into those dark magic eyes that have sought me out.

Startled by her phone alarm Mahru reaches across the coffee table to turn it off. Rolling her eyes and falling back into my arms she groans over the thought of her having to leave. Turning her head to look up at me I see the determination in her eyes to tear down all dividing lines and restraints. Still wanting to stay holding her as she grounds herself to the warmth of my body and as my fiery kiss culminates within her. Grateful to have heard the sound of her voice and to have felt her magnetic touch as I press her for one last kiss.

"I will call you tonight. I am sorry that I have to leave," she says, hearing in her voice her concern for time as she reaches for her phone.

"What about Madge? Will your dad be angry with her? She could come live with us."

"I am sure that Madge will be fine. My sister has never been one to disappoint my dad. The only thing that matters now is me and you," she says, her eyes and her voice still soft for me.

"Sunday?"

"Sunday," she smiles. ". . . My parents will be home soon. I should go."

"Okay."

"Just five more days. And I promise that I will come back. As soon as my parents leave tomorrow I will come and see you. I am so happy that you love me," she then says, sliding into her wool seam-sealed boots.

"I do," I return.

"You are my home now."

"And you are mine," I remind Mahru, sliding into my sheepskin slippers.

Walking over to the front door to put on her grey button-down coat I detect that it is just as difficult for her as it is for me to see her go. Moving the two of us along I reach for the door handle mindful of her not wanting to be late.

Walking to her truck she turns back for me once more before I let her slip away from me. Once more a kiss before she finishes climbing up into her truck. Helping to shut her driver side door she then backs down my driveway before disappearing beyond the tall frore laurels.

Standing bundled up in the light cold I miss her already and wonder if she will make it tomorrow to see me. It still being difficult for me whenever her warmth escapes me. Subtle distressing sentiments besetting this newfound love and joy when I am not alone with her. And then again watching her slip away from me as I know that she must.

Walking back into my lonely guesthouse I begin to process everything *and nothing* all at once. Knowing that this love of ours still blooms even in the midst of what she herself has feared most. Our love being in fact *more* than what some will try and say that it is. Our beating hearts calling for each other the way that Mother Nature leaves a trail for him to find her. Her love ensnaring me so that I would be willing to die for her. Knowing that I would die if it pleased her and that I would die if without. Knowing that nothing else matters and that no other woman will ever be able to take the place of my love. Mahru being the only one who can reach through to my heart. Telling me that it is okay with her eyes and her lips and her touch. Voicing to the heavens that we have endured and that we are still here. Our love like the two intersecting mountains that never move. The two initiating the one and standing forever as a symbol of that joy and that freedom. Still wishing that her family could feel our immense love like the blades of grass and leaves that fall from the sky which are as numerous as the stars. Her love and determination more empowered and more careless than ever before.

BLACK LOVE

CHAPTER TWENTY-FIVE

Spurred awake by the winter sun brightening up the guesthouse I promptly set about my early-morning routine anticipating her arrival. Connecting the musical artist Bien to my Bluetooth speaker I then make for the bathroom to freshen up before migrating downstairs. Crumpling an article of mail under a few oak logs I then forge an ambient glow inside of my brick fireplace for warmth and aesthetic.

Lighting my musk teakwood candles I next hurry to throw some fruit into the blender for myself and for her. Pouring a raspberry-orange smoothie into two glasses I stand still dreaming about her being in my life like normal people. Always dreaming about her being out with me on the town or waking up next to me without feeling tense or worried about what her family may surmise.

Walking barefoot back up the stairs to make my bed the doorbell then surprises me. Turning back downstairs to peek out from behind the sheer linen curtain I almost do not see her standing up so close to the door. Stepping back a little I then see her angora camel-colored top that is made of a raw woven beaded material. Her natural pullover top hovers above the rim of her pants waistline revealing her navel ever so slightly between standing up straight and motioning to move her hair from her face. Her black pants hug tight around her tender thighs where the bold seams and stitches complement the curvature of her perfect legs. Her beautiful cold feet shuffle slightly in her black open-toe sandals as she zips up her keys into her purse.

Unlocking my front door to open it my heart falls ensnared eyeing her distinctive beauty. Holding her enormous gaze I am taken by her entranced fixation and moon-eyed expression. With an anxious step in her stance she half smiles at me shedding that magnificent grin from the edge of those sakura-cream lips. Smiling back at her I do not recall ever having seen a face so beaming and so happy to see me. All of the colors bleeding into that white light that is marked across that morning sky in those telling eyes. And I evince never having known what love was until I first saw her. Endlessly loving this illusive and eluding creature who could still change her mind.

"Hey," she smiles, her sweet voice filling my heart with this thing called love that evokes in me such passion and zest.

"Hey," I break silence, reaching to shut the door as she slides into my other arm.

Feeling her step inside my hello is immediately substituted with a rich kiss bringing all that is a part of discussion up to current. Inside of her candid kiss I am answered with more than could ever be conveyed by mere words. Feeling a sense of exhaustion from the power of her single kiss that leaves me to be still only thirsty for more.

"Did you miss me?" she then asks, her dark orphic eyes like something from a fairytale book, every part of me markedly coveted by her yearning.

"I never stop," I differentiate, pressing my lips to her glabella.

"But not for much longer you won't have to. It will just be me and you in three days," Mahru comforts, sizing me up with her mouth slightly parted, conveying to me with those eyes precisely what it is that she wants.

"Running away with you is the only thing I dream about. The sacred synchronicity of our souls twirling in the sunlight that shines in from my window. The memory of you in my bed and touching you. Every day all day thinking about the million different ways that I want to love you."

"You are my kara sevde," she then smiles at me.

"What does kara sevde mean?"

"It means black love. It is a lovesick term for feeling so passionate about someone. It is a blinding love for another person. Kara sevde."

"And you are mine."

Watching Mahru smile almost sheepishly I reach for her lips. Following me further into my tiny home the wood floor feels just as warm to our feet as our love is to the touch. Her lush smooth lips contort up and down mine as

CHAPTER TWENTY-FIVE

my hands move up the curvature of her back from underneath her crumpled blouse. Tasting her peach water-lily lips I pore over her savoring love feeling from her that she is now free. Mahru allowing that gorgeous smile to escape concealment as her shyness and unease dissipate like smoke to a heavy rain.

"Love me like nobody else can," she tells me, the word please still curling off the end of her delectable tongue as her black chanterelle eyes lock with mine. Squeezing my curly chin-length hair Mahru kisses me once more.

Peeling my shirt all of the way off her eyes follow my body as her fingers move down my stomach. Feeling her lips take shelter in me while holding her she falls far beyond this physical realm of existence. Swaying in front of her voracious lips she smiles at me as my perfect hands move down around her body the way that she loves. Feeling the ludic vivacity of her aura another kiss is made soft and slow as she discovers her bare feet touching back down to the wood floor.

Reaching our bedroom everything becomes slow motion feeling it in her fiery blood and soul that nothing can keep us apart. Slowing her down at the edge of the bed her flush irises radiate like satiny seed scales catching light in the dark. Like glowing tiger eyes the rutilant mångata of her boulder opal gems instill in me this inevasible desire. Itching to taste her alible figure spilling over my sturdy physique I proffer Mahru my whole heart.

Feeling her feverish desire to undress I gently pull on the edge of her slouchy wool shirt. Following her fire-lit eyes her thermic body ecstasiates to thoughts more intense than any heaven. Our clothes then slowly come off like a snake delicately shedding its beautiful skin. In sensuous motion and in passional intimacy her naked body is over-intoxicatingly lethal in its confident ability to seize my love. Gesturing for me to come and lie down with her she relishes in the deep-dyed satisfaction of making my home hers as she touches my lips with her kiss.

Heaving my thick bedding to the floor my vim heart like a fountain of love beholds her wondrous beauty. Her owl-like eyes penetrate my being with a vigorously inductive aim as she reveals to me her every sensual intimation. My lips and my tongue fill her suprasternal notch as her smile paints a picture that will forever be engraved into my mind. Earthing my solid body to hers like a barefoot walk in the woods I feel her warm abiding love in my veins.

Glowing with a pleasurable subtleness Mahru compliments me with every inhale and exhale as our bodies move. Her beautiful hands drag along the sides of my torso from my buttocks to my shoulders. Down and up again she strokes and caresses me without missing a tune as if I were a beloved instrument played by its master virtuoso. Her long adagio legs gently wrap around me seeming to revolve as they knead against me. The elemental sounds of Flaer Smin chime and resonate as her soft cloudlike lips take me to places that I have never been to before. Admiring her every mesmeric feature tiny little bumps on her breasts and stomach surface from me slowly moving my hands over her.

Climbing up inside of my arms her mesial curve twists into me with an elapid curl. Her lips are what I can never get enough of and with each kiss I see beyond the veil of mortality. Loving Mahru my body feels like a reflection beneath the marbled liquid contours of a giant glacier. Her hourglass figure presses firmly against my breast and thighs formulating a series of minor convulsions that peregrinate throughout my entire being. I am transcended even by the feeling of her black curling hair gently falling over my face and neck. Bathing in her scent her Al-Khazneh-tinged skin presses against my body as we fall hopelessly to a bottomless love. Every hidden gem of hers loved by my lips. Feeling all of her all at once as her body moves like the northern lights— the aurora borealis. Our hands exchanging hearts like intimate letters that have traveled over seas.

Searching for her soul between her legs a deep resounding moan escapes her. Kissing the lips of her basial bull her esculent slit quickly turns wet red with desire. Unable to restrain herself from smelling my sweet scent her limbs tug and twirl around my hygric body as she reaches for my lingam. Unveiling my preputial flowering ignites her secretions and primes her obsession as she places me inside of her dripping pomum. Penetrating her mussel shell with my membral lun I ease carefully passed her mellaginous lips slowly sinking into her pink Arabian Sea. Gently kissing Mahru our waists adhere following her selenic rhythm. Enthralled by the motion of our collaborative bodies moving in ways that are beyond my capacity to interpret. Always fueling her skyclad body with a spiraling plethora of sucking, twisting, and licking in a beautiful ritual that involves every act of love and pleasure.

Filling in her empty spaces I feel the soft knocking of her teeth in my neck as her dark eyes roll into the back of her head. Whelving my swollen nerve inside of her I escape beyond the rubescent entry of her superlunary yoniverse with a mizzling avolation into the vast ether. Two hot-blooded electromagnetic forces diving into an infinite ocean of intelligence. With a flammiferous filling of her cup her arcate back begins sculling her clysmic lips over my

CHAPTER TWENTY-FIVE

sun-reaching linga. Briefly I question if I can still feel my body as a controlling wave of this gratifying force travels from my toes to my face.

Feeling her pleasure pressure reach maximum satisfaction I recognize that her cup is ready to spill. Squeezing her gateway between worlds tighter around my thick pulsing vein the sweet pulling of endorphins set into motion this quavering thizz that achieves pure tao. Feeling her fluvial body cum with me inside my venous swelling tastes deep cosmic orgasm plunging into the innermost celestial sphere of her ecliptic. Dying and coming back to life in short rapid breath she expels a roil fluid splashing and squirting from her seawall. No more holding her breath as she releases her divinity that lies within. My deep-rubbing efflorescence still filling that empty space in her oceanic trench. Electricity still pulsing through our blood as we fall immersed to this tranquility during chaos. Feeling that imponderable prismatic thoughtlessness that one experiences at the peak of a thunderstruck orgasm. Floating in space like a silent ripple stretching out across the water. Our serous fluid running down her guttiferous orifice like a soft trickling spring over desert rock.

Never having felt her so close to me Mahru then lightly strokes my beautiful body. Feeling her fingers touch me I lose all sense of time. And then forgetting where I am for a second I quickly swim back to the surface to find her. Anchored to her sure-fired eyes I am then followed by a thirst in her that she is still craving to satiate. Grabbing ahold of me upside down with her mesic grasp she warms her sienna-sand skin inverse to me. Feeling her seize my sacral nerve she maneuvers to carefully empty me again. Like brontide building up to a cloudburst she absorbs me drawing a deep squeeze upwards consuming every ounce of my sucré crème. Effleuraging the soft soused petals of her poporo she braces herself feeling an apical and phreatic trembling inside of her. Feeling her squeeze that last lick she cums again into my mouth. Feeling me swill that nectarous haoma sluicing from her pink pearlious clam. Candy flipping her clitoral shaft and tasting the pomaceous pabulum of her inner goddess. Beholding in part that celestial diluvium by which all creation is bathed. Feeling her exultant joy and tactual grip as she releases a beautiful freeing cry.

An anthelion ring illuminates around her chocolate-colored eyes as she then runs her tongue over her crystal pink lips. Alluring and lovely-eyed she expresses a satisfaction beyond love and gratitude.

Following her eyes as they move through that last ray of sunlight I am transfixed watching her snakelike twist prowl for my attention. Like smooth desert limestone warmed by the sun she lies over top of me feeling an agravic nubivagant satiety. Filling me with this fathomless taste for her as our love thrives like the beating of the earth. With every one of her fingers her touch does complete me. Rubbing her slender fingers inside of mine as I follow her parting lips. She tasting my belle âme, her raison d'être.

Grazing the smooth surface of her statuesque figure I fulfill her every wish as the sounds that escape her enlighten my senses. Her love reminding me of the eternities that give birth to all of creation. Her love for me like the orbiting of that pure and incessant force that was born before the beginning of time. Bathing in beautiful unparalleled sex when so much of the world has lost all taste for anything subtle. Nestled alongside this nefelibatic nymph and by the flexuous plexure of her physical entwinement. Our firm and daring love proving that our hearts will live on for as long as there is time. No more divisive voices dragging the soul down into sinfulness and guilt. No more abandoning love over *the idea* that the soul is something noble and pure and the body somehow inferior. These fabricated sophisms no more a dividing ruse inside of this rebirth. Our natural love connected to the Most High of Creation and no less spiritual in our yearnings. There being nothing else that seems to matter as I blissfully lie here being gentle with her. Forever determined to please her. Always changing and never changing. My love always and forever being her greatest adventure. She being all that I need and love now and forever.

Feeling her naked weight on top of me the cloud-white light outside becomes more murky and overcast with rain starting to trickle onto the roof. A muted peace draws us even closer listening to the sounds of rainfall as a calm comfort cloaks our minds from all else. The raindrop sounds outside seem to perish into the distance as we lie in awe of each other. Too in love to let go. Feeling her heartbeat knock against my bare chest. She watching me quietly study her and the way that she exists when she is with me. Still staring into those eyes with our limbs entwined and answering her with my gentle traveling touch. Her small hands reaching up to run across the bottom of my face and neck as my hands move down her chest and stomach. Falling for her each time that she looks at me. Still holding on to Mahru like I will never let go of her.

"I can't tell you how good this feels," she enthusiastically hints, curled up inside of my arms.

"A feeling far removed from everything that we know to be truth," I attempt to describe. "Knowing what people are talking about when they talk

CHAPTER TWENTY-FIVE

about heaven. A singular solidity more immediate to god than what any poet could articulate. The center of the universe."

"People thousands of years ago said that god lived alone. And then god divided himself, or herself, to experience a togetherness and unity and love. To experience *this* what we have now. Love being the most beautiful thing that we have to give. Our reason and purpose being to love. Sometimes I still cannot believe that you are real. Since I can remember I always wanted this. But never in my life did I ever think that I would actually have what we have," Mahru tells me, her curvaceous body pulling me closer with a fiery yearning as strong as my own. Her hands rising up behind my back and over my head as I taste her nipples and neck.

"I have a weakness for you, Lucius."

"Love me forever," I utter softly, locked into her chocolate-orchid eyes as I see who she loves.

"Your wish is my command," she returns, tenacious with delight as she moves her mouth along my chest. Smiling an even greater smile she wraps her eburnean body around mine. Holding me where my heart discovers love all over again. Absorbing my masterful touch as her black candle-lit eyes drift into oblivion. Still speaking to her soul with my body the way that a finger draws a message in the sand.

Watching her rest peacefully in my embrace I am reminded that it is the woman who is marveled upon, where man kneels in silence to honor and respect; and that it is this same marvel that cures a good man into being a better man if not the world.

Kissing her face and neck with my lips her fingers grab my golden curls. Always being all that she has wanted from the day that she first met me. Still feeling myself becoming a part of her with every breath and every kiss.

"Ever since that first Saturday that you and I met to go swimming I have longed for your touch. And your touch is just as beautiful as the things that you are always writing to me," she voices, purring a melodic cadence.

"Pardon my desire to encircle you with a fire, so light, like the touch of my finger to your body that I much admire. I am a sinner of the flesh when I thirst for your sex, your love, and your body that has me more than obsessed. Friends are for establishing trade. Lovers are meant to behave in ways too beautiful to be conveyed. Inside of your mysterious gaze I am lost to a maze that labyrinth of a place. Now let go of your fear and allow your heart to trust. Let yourself die and reap the fruit of my lust."

"Don't stop," she softly whispers, almost asleep with her arm lying gently across my chest.

"Sleep in the peace that some call heaven when your heart kisses your mind's thoughts. Where dreams become real and you are not afraid of what you feel. Sleep to the gentle sounds of crickets and trickling streams as you wander through your peaceful dreams. When I am not there to press my lips to your precious face sleep in that gentle place and dream of my gentle ways," I extemporaneously compose.

Bewitched by her aureate touch and by the suspension of time and space I open her mouth with mine feeling time become meaningless. Nuzzled alongside of me I hold on to her with every effort to stay awake. A benthic comfort envelops my mind, body, and soul as a shadowy-white light finds its way inside the large window. The wet-weather clouds doing their best to protect our weary eyes with a thick mist of fog that blankets the outside. Noticing above my head the western red cedar branches all bending and heavily drenched from a rainy day.

Under our sage saddle-brown comforter I am completely fascinated watching the natural light touch her as she pretends to be asleep. In love with all of who she is I contemplate the simple fact that we are just two people trying to find our way in this strange world. Two souls who have taken refuge in the other's embrace as the war inside our heads moves passed.

Feeling her body pressed firm to me I let go of all unrest surrounding the previous matter of her yielding to family pressures. Surrendering all heartache about her feeling apprehensive and my prior inability to cope with it.

Laving in sweet serenity I close my eyes still curled up under the covers with her. Her familiar warmth like a summer breeze reaching in from a cracked window to kiss all of me goodnight. Beneath my tiny delicate lights that hang from the exposed ceiling I am comforted in knowing that she is where she belongs. Feeling her arm fall down behind me she displays to me the stillness of her soul. Here and now having both found a way to see into heaven. Taking shelter in her and being away from everything that is loud and suffocating as her tender ways educe in me this lazing comfort. Bundled up under a plush oversized blanket with other cluttered sumptuous layers falling over the upholstered bench at the foot of our bed.

Almost immediately an alluvion of sleep floods my body and mind leaving me completely blissful in my keeper's arms. My woodwick candle still flickering at my bedside table as I quietly fall asleep inside of this new beginning.

CHAPTER TWENTY-FIVE

Her ear firmly presses to the sound of my heart as she moves from one dream to another. With my eyes closed I absorb and fathom the incredible feeling of never having felt so close to home. There being nothing else like it in all the world what she gives to me.

Opening my eyes as day descends into night I watch Mahru wake up searching to see that I am still right here with her. Above her dimpled smile she expresses a natural thrill just from seeing me as I am. Gazing into her owl-brown eyes I am taken by the fire warming in her heart as I lie drawn to her wanting all of my attention. Still expressing with her eyes and her kiss how sorry that she is for denying her love. Holding her tight I feel her asking me again to forgive her. And I forgive her with all of my heart because I do love her. Indulging myself in her sincere love. Her touch alone being enough to set in motion this human awakening of mine. Her unearthly love being strength to my spirituality and knowledge infinite.

Watching her lift her naked body from the bed she like a goddess moves across the room with a stride that gives complement to every curve of her figure. Her nymphean physique meanders passed the six-foot standing mirror near the edge of the bed. Gesturing for me to follow her I get up to walk downstairs to make something yummy to eat.

Pausing in front of my woodsy view I observe the cold rain beginning to crystalize before hitting the ground outside. Slushy raindrops suddenly becoming featherlight snowflakes as the man in the moon licks his finger to the candlewick.

Lying down on our blanket-cluttered sofa I watch Mahru lean over the coffee table to strike a match that breaks the light of night that clings to her. One by one she lights each candle in perfect form as the glowing contrast of light and dark dances around the edges of her beautiful body. Watching her look back at me I see this magical creature who has given me life to every body and realm; and oh how grateful I am that she has found me and that she has reclaimed her love.

Feeling her curl up into my arms under the mixed blankets I hold her close withdrawn to a lucid stillness. Feeling a beautiful emptiness of mind we lie wishing that now had been then but still being grateful for what is now. Holding Mahru she rubs herself warm between me and the large mohair throw and chunky chenille knit blanket pulled from the coffee table chest. Together again on this enchanted evening that seems so very far from the rest of the world. Spending today without a single care in the world. And no more are we afraid to be simply as we are.

Softly and almost imperceptibly she skims her nails across the skin of my back. Paralyzed lying cozily up against her warm flesh I am unalterably indebted to this peacefully persuasive art. Feeling her feather the lunula of her fingernails along my splendorous body. Her touch allowing me to trust that my sincere efforts have not been in vain. Loving me like I am her most prized possession. And nearly putting me to sleep as she sings to me a melody that allows my soul to set sail across the clouds of a starry night.

Feeling her move to grab her phone and glance at the time I watch her regrettably realize that it is getting late. Reaching to caress her face and neck she prepares to inform me that she should go as she thinks about her brother and sister returning home. Following her jawline with my fingers I press myself to remember that this time it is different.

Sitting up to kiss her I feel the reaction of her swathing body as she clings to me. So close to her naked warmth I am happy to see her peart and pleasantly content. Gathering from her reflective eyes her feeling as curious as a child who is in awe of everything that she sees. Her liberated love and paralyzing páthos being my Gula. The dark antelope swirls in her sizzling eyes telling me the story of the world as it was from the beginning. Knowing that she is now home as her lips become my lips. She celebrating with me the greatest love.

"You are thinking about Malik and Madge? Your mom and dad?"

"I am just thinking about how much time that I have left to see them."

"Do you think that your parents will ever forgive you?"

"I do not know. . . . I think that my mom will forgive me. I hope that my dad will someday. My parents are both good parents. I just wish that they could respect what I want without making me push them away."

"Maybe they will come around."

"Maybe," she says, uncertain and unconvinced, wrapping her arms tighter around me. "I already told my sister that Sunday will be the last day that I can see her. She is sad. But she is also happy for us," Mahru looks up. "You are all that I ever wanted from the first day that I met you."

"And you are all that I want," I return, with an immovable gaze anchored from my northern-forest eyes.

"Thank you for being you," she then utters with a grin, standing up to share with me this breathtaking love that tells all inside of her kiss, she feeling my hands move down her body before her feet touch back down to the wood

CHAPTER TWENTY-FIVE

floor.

"Now that my brother and my sister are both home I should probably get going. I do not want them calling my dad and saying that I am not home yet," she explains, following her up the stairs as she grabs her clothes to get dressed.

"There will never be enough time in this lifetime for me to have my fill of you."

"Nor will I ever be able to have my fill of you," she kisses, twirling her lip with a biting grin, telling me with those eyes and that smile that she truly does love me.

"C'mon . . . let me walk you out," I tell Mahru, throwing on my charcoal sweater and my grey knit beanie.

Leaving my front door just barely cracked I then reach for her hand before carefully stepping down the one snow-melted step outside.

Walking to her lightly dusted truck she again stops me with her loving kiss in the mild cold. Still wanting to feel me close to her for as long as she thinks that she can.

"I am afraid to let go of you."

"Don't be afraid. I will call you tonight," Mahru promises me.

Shutting her driver side door after Mahru is seated inside I then step back to watch her turn her truck around. Watching her new tires grip the powdery pavement I still feel a sense of unease letting her out of my sight. Watching her smile and wave before turning the wheel all I then see is her red taillights. The last faint glow of dusk long smothered by a dark cloudy night. Still watching her sea-green truck disappear beyond the luminous red and white streaks of traffic that rub against the black sky.

INTO THE TREES

CHAPTER TWENTY-SIX

As a pale muted sun barely peaks up through the tall evergreens I cautiously drive passed her house gate and park my '91 sedan beside her old Land Rover truck.

Parked on the circular cobblestone driveway in front of her family's French riad style home I stand up outside of my car to see Mahru dressed all warm and eager to feel from me my loving embrace. Gazing into that lustrous gold light shifting in her coffee brown eyes I then feel her shapely body ecstasize in my loving arms. Affectionately reaching for her delicious kiss and subtle squeeze I then carefully follow Mahru inside of her home for the first time quietly awestruck.

Inside of her spacious residence the architectural interior is just as breathtaking as I imagined it would be. Layered with white and cool neutral colors the keyhole arches and backlit indentation stand beneath each elaborately carved skylight. Through each arched doorway lies a sophisticated mix of Islamic style and Andalusian essence, every inch of the house combining the best of Morocco's craft traditions with supreme European style. The wide foyer has in its intricately carved flowerpots French pink bougainvillea and jasmine reaching for the hand painted ceiling tile. Moroccan and Mediterranean accents adorn each seating nook while still drawing inspiration from the simplicity of light Scandinavian design. The smell of citrus permeates the air moseying passed a wide potted orange tree. Turning the corner passed the

CHAPTER TWENTY-SIX

ornate metalwork along the wall I then notice a large gallery print displaying the beautiful White Desert of Egypt. Noticing a small photograph of Khalil in his army fatigues I then all of the sudden feel uncomfortable revisiting in my mind Damien's irascible hostility.

Continuing through the modest grand entrance hall to an imperial wrought iron staircase everything within view is undeniably beautiful. But watching Mahru look back at me I still see in her eyes that this is a place that imprisons her heart from loving who she truly loves.

Following Mahru up the twisty left staircase I feel her small hand curling into mine as she turns her head and catches my familiar smile. Ready to help her bring all of her things downstairs a certain emotion fills me finally laying eyes on the bedroom that she has called or texted me from so many times. Held in sentimental memory in view of her stonewashed linens and lovely French windows I almost blush to the thought of her wanting to run away with me to my humble guesthouse. Her unique lighting and cozy fabrics giving a boho atmosphere to the sumptuous relaxation of her eclectic bedroom. Following the exotic trim to the small second-story balcony I stop to admire the Moorish decorative lanterns beneath the richly colored tapestries.

Peeking into one box and observing what is in her laundry basket I fondly recognize each item of clothing. Picking up a heavier box of photographs with miscellaneous things thrown in Mahru grabs her packed jewelry box and winter coat to follow me outside.

Loading her clothes and belongings into both vehicles Mahru tells me that she has already packed her passport and important documents in with her books and her two favorite blankets. With everything loaded up I try not to burden my mind about what her parents might do when they come home in three days and see that Mahru is gone. Still grasping how much that she does love me to leave her family when I know that she loves them so much. Studying Mahru closely I still find that she is more thrilled to see me than she is sad about leaving without really saying goodbye. Still reservedly sad in wishing that she didn't have to leave like this. Lost in the golden glimmer of her muddy moonradish eyes her kiss soothes my heart feeling myself melt into her love. Brushing my fingertips against her dark eyebrows and pressing my lips to her forehead I then see her perfect smile tasting again her marvelous lips.

Following Mahru back inside the house to the tall black doorway of her parents' bedroom I wait as she places her letter to her parents at the foot of their bed. She leaving only a letter for her mom and dad describing in detail *why* she is doing this. Asking her parents to forgive her and letting them both know that she is happy and for them not to worry. Informing her mom and dad that she is leaving because she is madly in love. Expressing her sincere apology for not properly saying goodbye. Sending all of her love from a letter that may not be received so well. But still saying goodbye with sincere respects. Having firmly decided that she does not want to be with a man who she does not love. Expressing in her letter that she loves her mom and dad very much. And Madge and Malik. And that she will miss them.

Carrying the last bit of her belongings outside I notice that her nervous stare has vanished as I see in her rich brown eyes her knowing that she is ready. Approaching me with her thin fingers repositioning a long black curl from the front of her face I grasp from her warm facial expression her satisfaction in taking on this new life with me. Tasting her delicious lips in her stretchy sweater and bootcut jeans I still wonder how she can leave everything that she knows just to be with me. Her grief and her love content. Her self-confidence blooming with the thought and revitalization of a new beginning. Feeling her fingers touch my skin she feels her ball and chain turn to dust. Beautifully empowered and positively wild she locks her brown tourmaline eyes in with mine. She knowing deep down that she is mine for me to look after now.

"Look at you and me running away together," Mahru smiles, pulling my high buttoned turtleneck snug beneath my chin.

"Are you ready to say goodbye?"

"I mean I never wanted to have to say goodbye like this. But I know that there is no other way. Madge and Malik know how much that I love them. I just wish that my family could be as understanding as yours," she quietly lets out, with a faint sniffle.

"Me too," I tell Mahru, praying that her heart will not stay broken.

Watching her eyes trust me as she stares I notice her feeling what heaven is like in my arms with her body firmly pressed to me. Gently locking eyes with Mahru I look at her in such a way as if to say that I could never break her heart or her spirit. Only ever existing with an undying appreciation. Only existing to uplift and care for her always until I draw my last breath. Even to come find her in death if at all possible. If god wills it. And if the right door is opened to me.

"You ready to follow me?"

"I am," Mahru nods and smiles.

Starting my car I watch her climb up into her thawed truck from the icy

CHAPTER TWENTY-SIX

view of my passenger window. Pulling out of her parents' driveway I still wonder if her leaving like this will involve the police. Still thinking to myself that the U.S. border is only a thirty-five-minute drive if you follow the 99.

Watching Mahru follow close in my rearview my mind wanders imagining the worst potential confrontation. Still trusting that VPD will side with the two of us since Mahru is legally an adult. Hating in my heart that it has to be like this. But still having no regrets. No more resigned to her parents telling her that it is time to be married or even who she must marry.

Quickly turning from Oak Street onto Forty-first Avenue I feel the stiff chaos of it all already receding from my attention.

Parking on the snow-melted driveway behind Louis's house I first unlock my front door before grabbing a box from the backseat. Hearing a frozen wet crunch grind beneath my canvas shoes Mahru comes carrying her stuff from her truck revealing that winsome gaze that I covet most.

Walking with me inside and up the stairs to place her belongings I watch Mahru make herself right at home like she never left the guesthouse. Watching her move about upstairs knowing where everything is a spark of something so rare and beautiful catches fire in my heart. A simple joy that I have not yet felt watching her move her things to where they go. Three days ago having made more space in the bedroom by adding in the stacked shelving to expand the closet and emptying another. Between placing her books on the shelf and hanging her tops up in the closet I grasp how thrilled she is just to be here with me where I am. It showing all over her face when she looks at me and in the way that she moves when she knows that I am watching. Shifting and dancing, swaying her hips and singing in beautiful Arabic tongue. Our eyes constantly shifting back and forth from each other. My lovely Mahru expressly pleased to be a part of this new world that now belongs to only us.

Grabbing her bathroom bag Mahru stops in continued awe of the finished painting that has been mastered in flawless reflection of her warmth and numbing beauty. Carefully approaching her from behind she gently curls her fingers into mine with her bedazzled eyes still so heavily focused. Touching my head against hers she continues to gaze with astonishment. Feeling her smile brim she turns to me with an unending and unveiling fascination as I once more feel her warmth swimming through the waters of my soul to seize my perfect lips.

Following her into the bathroom with her large tote bag I watch her imagine herself taking a bath as she feels with her hands the neatly folded towels that sit at the edge of the tub. Helping her empty her bag of soaps and toiletries she then walks back towards me almost passing me at the doorway. Leaning into her smile she gently tugs me by the string of my pants for me to follow her back downstairs.

Grabbing her last box from the truck Mahru follows me back into the guesthouse after shutting her side-opening tailgate where her spare wheel is mounted. Setting her box down right inside the door and gently clutching her exposed waist I all over again fall in love with her ensorcelling lips. Entranced by her touching spell and eager kiss as I relish in the peculiarity of her rare happiness.

Following me up the wide wooden stairs I admire the sweet nearness of her as she takes each careful step closer towards me. Gathering her warm-blooded hips between the tight space in her jeans I am drawn by her perfect beauty that isolates me from all else as I reach for her.

Loosening the warm threads from our bodies the mysterious art of making love is again born out of what we both crave. Helping undo her Sieve Demi Bra and French Cut Briefs a thural wood patchouli scent spices the air as I am rendered nearly unconscious by the salient visual of her glorious figure. Lying on our bed she turns herself along our thick comforter with her eyes soft on me as if I am all that she now lives for. Loosening my Modus Vivendis and joining her I find her cherry blossom lips reaching for the places on my neck and stomach that make my body weak.

Behind the oak doors of this magical place that we have named we again become as one single flesh. My luminous moon and I becoming an indomitable spirit and strength. Casting her seductive spell with fire and water as I again experience all of what heaven is inside of her clutches. Through the dragon's breath and through the spiritual waters of human bliss she purifies me. Grounded by our love that seems to become more between each passing moment. Making love each time like the first time. Each time knowing a tremendous unutterable ecstasy.

Sleeping into the late afternoon the faint wet drips from the silky cedar branches outside pierce my ears through a cracked window. Waking from the loveliest dream I quickly look to see for myself that she was here and is now as she sleeps quietly next to me in our bed. Watching her sleep so peacefully with her nose under my arm my wish is that she will stay asleep just as she is. Listening to the tiny crackle coming from the musk candle on the window ledge

CHAPTER TWENTY-SIX

I lie watching her dream. Watching her and knowing that I am in love with her and that I have always loved her despite the tiny meaningless differences that the afraid world tries to persuade.

Noticing her to be sound asleep I carefully step down from the warm bed to glance outside. Quietly admiring a coastal fog falling over a wet winter landscape I decide to grab a pair of warm socks from our shared dresser. Wanting to step outside for a moment I slide on my aran sweater and my tan houndstooth pants while still watching her rest. Again rehearsing in my mind how we can run if her dad ever finds out where we are.

Quietly tiptoeing downstairs to the backdoor where my boots lay tilted over I mentally try to ready myself for what might come Monday. Sliding my feet into my boots and sliding on my grey wool jacket I step outside to feel the chill in the air from my small wooden deck. Touching the cracked leather chair outside my backdoor I glance passed the weeping white spruce that clings to the house noticing the light traffic moving up ahead on our street. Feeling an evening mist fall onto my face as I turn to walk further back behind the guesthouse.

Strolling the shady wooded property along a winding walkway passed the water features that moderately neighbor the plant life nearby I still wonder if I can convince her mom and dad of my worth. Still seriously doubting the probability of me ever seeing them face to face as I pass the twisty red bark that belongs to the winter flame maples. Thinking about her dad as I stroll with my hands inside of my pockets and looking into the distance where the trees are the most dense.

Passing the old barn-style shed with a slushy crunch beneath my feet I walk further back along the dirt path beneath a dripping forest. Edging the back of the property I admire the gentle stream that circles the massive alder trees that reach into the sky. Nearing the edge of a wide soft brook that deepens as it flows south I try to imagine what she must be feeling leaving her family. Prepared to make sure that she still stays in touch with her parents and siblings. The two of us seeing what we both want and understanding the obstacles as we dare to face this adventure and to live. Believing that what is the point of all this if not to fight for who we love. Still floating high off the deepest feelings that I have for her as I stand completely captured by the abundant beauty of my surroundings. Passing the tree swing that sways at the edge of the stream as I watch the busy squirrels, painted turtles, and the tiny birds that flutter beneath the dripping wet giants.

INTO THE TREES

Taking a seat on a sitting rock that has been warmed by the sun I watch a grumbling storm pour forth its mist felt by my face and hands. A warm luminance from the soft clouded atmosphere above shines down from the tops of the trees as if I were perched at the bottom of heaven looking upward. Staring up into a bright golden fog I thank god for her love and for the love inside of me that speaks to her. Thanking my higher power for reuniting the two of us and for filling me with such a peaceful knowing. So powerfully possessed by her. Lost to a noogenesis of unimaginable feelings with all of the colors through a different light spurring every lovely emotion. Ready to dream with her and to build with her. Our love measured by the remnants of powerful constellations and heavenly bodies aligning us. And from our beautiful beginning understanding this universal language that we speak.

A dampening sound suddenly reveals a presence quietly crossing the small wooden bridge behind me that channels the water trickling beneath it. Turning to look over my shoulder Mahru walks closer towards me quietly emerging from out of an evening mist. Watching her wearing my glacier grey sweater with my matching beanie I catch her biting her lip with that distinct smile. Tugging at my seedy whiskers my soft gaze follows the shallow frigid stream to where the large sea-mist alders border the giant hemlocks. Feeling her perfect fingers touch my neck I taste her sweet mouth once more. Fully aware of something unbelievably magical about her that has stirred my soul from the first time that I laid eyes on her. Tasting her newfound freedom from her wisp pink lips. My brave Mahru being all that I thirst for. All of my fear and haste dispelled by the sweetened taste of her lips.

"I saw you coming this way as you were walking outside. Just admiring the view?" she curiously asks, almost about ready to try the wooden swing that hangs just a few feet from where we are sitting.

"I just had to see this," I point, still marveling the burning neon sky above the trees that reflects into the slow moving water.

Closing her eyes to the back of my shoulders she then slides her arms under my natural white sweater around my chest. Turning around to kiss her she slides her hands down the muscles of my back. Feeling her touch me I again become spellbound brushing my nose and lips across the bridge of her shoulder towards her neck.

"The sun going down like this is the most beautiful," I tell Mahru, approaching her as she now barely pushes the swing.

"It is," she says, discovering the beauty of this place that seems almost

CHAPTER TWENTY-SIX

impossible to exist, she watching me step closer towards her, my eyes and my smile moving with her.

Slowing the wooden swing down from behind to climb onto it with her Mahru maneuvers to warm herself in my arms. She again finding my lips on this dim dusk that changes color under the celeste streaks that ripple through the warm pink sky.

"Sooo . . . I'm thinking Sunday morning after I have breakfast with Madge and Malik."

"I will be waiting right outside to pick you up first thing," I reassure Mahru with a kiss, still torn about her returning home with her mom and dad so close to coming back.

"Thank you for always being so perfect and for always being so sweet to me."

"Hold me and feel inside that all of mine belongs to you. What kind of man will die if beside he not with you?" I about whisper, remembering how awful it felt the last time that I let her go.

"I am right here," she is fast to remind me. "And I am not going anywhere."

"And I promise that you will never lose touch with your family. And they will always be your family. But you can still be free," I remind her, feeling my nervousness begin to subside.

"I have never in all my life felt so free. It is like breathing for the first time or after holding your breath for so long. I never even believed that I could be this happy. And I was so stupid to let myself be convinced that I should just throw all of it away what we have. I never wanted you to doubt how great that my love is for you. And I hope that I never make you doubt me again," Mahru voices softly, soul-gazing into the only eyes that she has ever thirsted for.

"I am yours forever my Lucius. Betrothed to that magic spell that you cast over me. Forever my beautiful man. So thankful to know you and to know you even more. Whom I will always adore. So perfect in every way. Still loving you like we just met when the color in our hair begins to fade," she continues softly, milking a verbal honey from the ether as she twirls my golden hair.

"A forever love that lives and still with you when I long have died. Flesh will never separate the bond between you and I."

"Always your glowing moon forever," she solemnly utters, tasting my lips as she journeys heaven in my arms. Her khus cedarwood scent grounding me to her hot body and earth. Her exotic face and burning-sand lips like scaling the majestic mountains of Sinai. Reminding me with her sweet soft voice that everything is going to be okay now.

"It is starting to get dark. Madge and Malik I think are almost home now. And I promised Madge that I would make my vegan lasagna one last time," she smiles, catching my kiss with her arms and hands wrapped all around me and in my hair.

"I will have to try your lasagna someday."

"You will love it," she smiles.

"When I get home I should also call my mom and dad to make sure that they are still coming home Monday."

"Good idea. . . . I will miss you."

"I will miss you—like you have no idea," she smiles, and unable to stop smiling.

"But you will call me tonight."

"I will," Mahru promises me.

As the swing stops swaying I caressingly tease Mahru with my lush lips before helping her up from the quiet swing by the stream.

Walking back to her wet sea-green truck Mahru keeps her hand in my pocket holding mine. Beneath the massive snow-melted trees and along the wet dirt path as darkness sets in, that beautiful smile that I adore most watches me with tender eyes. Holding her smooth hands and fingers warm she says my name without saying a single word. Speaking to me with those soft soul-stirring eyes that ask for nothing more except for my love.

Opening her driver side door for her to climb in and kissing Mahru once more I then watch her drive away.

THE SUN WHO KISSED THE MOON

CHAPTER TWENTY-SEVEN

Waking up to a light drizzle misting my window and to her much-sought-after scent clinging to our bed linens I still lie half asleep thinking of her. Remembering how good the body feels feeling her body so close to me. Feeling her magical touch that knows no bounds chasing this wild love. Feeling and sensing her mysterious ways that take me flying high just by looking at her. Something in that beautiful smile of hers that will strike me bewitched for a thousand lifetimes over. Her soothing love and the mere sight of my Mahru always new to these frosty forest eyes that delight in her. And now only twenty-four more hours until she is ready to settle in with me. She being no more just a dream to me.

Climbing out of our bed and throwing on my soccer pants and my thick Forest Marl sweater I prepare myself to check out the only antique jewelry shop in Greektown. Feeling her scarab ring sway against my chest I think and hope to find her something that might complement and adorn such rare majesty. Never having been fortunate enough to come into any precious heirlooms that were passed down to me.

Taking the ring off from around my neck I place it onto my finger for the jeweler to later inspect. Hoping that the jeweler can liken it to something that is just as well crafted and exquisite. Something timeless for my beautiful Egyptian love.

Grabbing my car keys I step outside of my front door to a calm wet morning that carries with it the pitter-pattering sound of an endless drip. The moisture in the air touches my hands and face as a low grumbling thunder bellows beneath a dark Vulcanian sky. Visually enchanted by the thin morning light turning the wet air green as the towering trees like shadows almost turn black. A calm shifting scene that almost cautions warning to what the weather might bring. Entertaining only my eagerness to please her as I intend to find her a small treasure from this charming coastal city.

Turning west out of the driveway entrance I begin to head north towards the bigger city near the bay.

Driving down Granville and about to turn onto West Broadway, I quickly find myself at the edge of Kitsilano right next door to the tea salon.

Pulling into the last on-street parking spot outside of a white brick storefront I park my classic beemer in front of the antique shop. Seeing it all lit up with its hedge green awning and black window framing I glance over to see the owner of the shop unlocking her thin barred glass door. Mindful of the chill in the air I pull my wool beanie tight around my head before stepping out to manually lock my old car.

Moseying inside of the café next door a subtle excitement fills my nerves contemplating everything that is about to happen. Smelling and hearing the fresh espresso grinding behind the counter I feel a little nervous thinking about it. But undeniably still feeling the most peace and joy as if the gracious gods above have mislaid their select drug of choice. So precious and forbidden this love of ours. Always high up riding the pleasant waves of my love for her. Always on top of the mountain. And hoping to hold on to this feeling forever. This thing we have that after today can remain no more a secret.

Quickly grabbing my coffee and stepping back outside onto the sidewalk I then with my hand find one of my old poems in my pants pocket. Right away I recognize it to be something that I wrote her after she painfully left and after what I sadly thought would be her final goodbye. A crinkled handwritten poem that I forgot about and still one that she has not yet read.

Standing outside of the tea salon I refresh my memory by reading it again to myself before placing it back into my pocket.

Now letting my eyes wander further down the sidewalk I for a moment stare off into the traffic moving through the city like a bright combustible river of moving metal all gathering at the light. Sensing the strangest feeling I thereupon become aware of the quiet storm looming overhead and it beginning to blanket the sky with its dark angry presence. Finding myself only briefly distracted from walking into the antique shop behind me my eyes dreamily follow a blackened street lined with dripping bloodgood maples.

Even though it is dark I know that somewhere there is sunshine. And that not far from now it will be my turn to feel its warmth and with it its new beginning. Embrace the dark and its eery quietness with love knowing that you share the warmth of the sun with loving spirits in far away lands. Smile for them in your dreams as they play in the water under the trees that feed from the food of the sun. And play and dance and sing come morning when it becomes your turn again. This and only this is the true joy to living. For it is both light and dark that teach us to love.

Having decided to return home early and without any forewarning Ianna and Khalil suddenly call Mahru kindly asking that she leave the house gate open since Khalil's vehicle remote has had trouble opening the gate.

"Marhaba habibti," Ianna says to Mahru as she answers her phone.

"Hey," she says, slightly delayed and surprised. "Are you enjoying your retreat on Lake Washington?" Mahru struggles to guide the conversation, paying careful attention to her mom who sounds like she is riding in the car.

"We are actually on our way home right now. Your dad and I both have a lot to do before we fly out for the wedding in thirteen days. . . . Mahru? How come I can't hear you? Hello?"

"I hear you Mama. I am right here," Mahru promptly pacifies, having stopped dead in her tracks in the hall near the laundry room. She now quietly walks towards the front of the house so as not to disturb her brother Malik who is making food in the kitchen.

"Okay I can hear you now. Can you please leave the gate open for your dad and I? We will be home in maybe twenty minutes."

Suddenly feeling her stomach knot up with the fear of being confronted and having all of her stuff moved and missing from her bedroom and the punishment that will surely ensue Mahru can only hear her mom telling her that they will be home in about twenty minutes. Almost forgetting where she is and feeling her heart plummet she nearly retrogresses to that previous fear frame of mind. Gathering herself to remember that she has committed herself to me and that she has made the decision to leave and to not be morally seduced by her mom and dad her mom continues to further explain.

"We decided not to stay until tomorrow because your dad and I have too much to do with my store before we leave. And then of course we have your wedding to plan from more than seven and a half thousand miles away. Tomorrow we can both FaceTime your aunt Nura about your wedding dress. Have you already thought about what you will need to pack? Remember too that we can send you the rest of your things after you both get settled."

"I—I have. Everything is already packed," she slips and says.

"Wow—that was fast," Ianna restrainedly tries to assess, reading and detecting Mahru to be a little in a hurry as she answers back surprised about her being so ready to fly out. Ianna then hears nothing. "Is everything okay there at home?"

"Everything is fine. I am just making an early lunch for Malik and Madge," she tells her mother a lie as she tries to sound busy. "I will have the gate open for you when you get here," she then quickly confirms, almost voicing her being so in a hurry to hang up.

"Thank you my love."

"I love you so much Mama."

"Awe. I love you too my sweet girl," Ianna tells Mahru, their vehicle speed and the light rain hitting the windshield making it difficult for her to detect the startled departure in her daughter's voice.

"Bye," Mahru then hangs up, frozen for a second and absolutely shit scared as she feels her heart sink down into her chest.

Getting a feeling after Mahru hangs up Ianna all of the sudden begins to worry, undeviating from the thought of something that she may quietly suspect. And she is afraid of something that she is unable to say or voice as she sits silently looking out of her passenger side window. A recent memory flashing back into her mind seeing Mahru's keys without the cluttered keychains attached. Feeling the strangest feeling like she knows something. Remembering the handwritten letters that she found in her sock drawer and her heirloom ring that is missing. Even now knowing that she could never tell Khalil. Feeling a nervous tingling sensation spurring the memory of her telling Mahru when she was little the story of how her grandmother married for love. Feeling that she heard something in her voice as she thinks to piece it together. Like knowing but too afraid to share it and hoping that she is wrong. But then just as she is about to put it from her mind a stolid Kahlil grows more curious about her strange silence. Even more curious as a tear begins to crawl down

CHAPTER TWENTY-SEVEN

her cheek leading him to ask.

"What? Tell me what is it?" Khalil asks Ianna, his deep smooth voice and agelast face expressionless beneath his dark brow. His rigid bearded glance noticing it to be concern and not sentiment as he now carefully eyes his wife. Even now priming his tongue to uncover an act or wrong that he can only feel satisfied to upbraid.

"I'm just. . . . She is just already packed. I am missing her already—that's all," Ianna tells Khalil, taking a moment to avoid his overbearing disapproval as she weighs arguing with his inevitable hysterics and unapproachable strife.

"I will miss her too. But we knew that this day would come," Khalil tells Ianna.

She then watches Khalil take a breath as he feels some of what she too is feeling.

"If you even thought just a little that Mahru was not happy would you consider asking her what it is that she wants?"

"Is she not happy?" Khalil glares from underneath his furrowed brow.

Completely unsurprised Ianna looks away from a brewing storm of incriminating accusations and even condemnation shifting under his displeased eyes.

"We have been over this before. It is time. She is getting too old. I have bent over so much already. People are starting to ask questions at mosque. The Abadi name will not be shamed anymore by her idle time and progressive ideas," Khalil impatiently forewarns.

"I just know that she will miss us terribly living so far away. Sometimes I see it when I look into her eyes."

"This is why she has you and me to decide for her. Mahru and Madge are both getting too old. She is twenty-one. It is time that she fulfill her duties as a woman. I will not have our name smeared and stained here at home and abroad because our daughter does not want to get married. I am done speaking about it," Khalil begins to get upset, his nerves almost bordering aggression and unable to believe that Ianna could question the will of Allah and his already made decision in choosing a husband for their daughter.

Hanging up the phone with her mom Mahru immediately calls me slightly panicking. Before I can even turn around to walk into the antique shop I see her name ringing on my phone.

"Lucius! Can you hear me?"

"Yeah—I can hear you."

"Listen. My mom and dad left early without telling me and now they will be back home in less than twenty minutes. I am going to start walking to your house right now. Just pick me up if you see me walking. I am wearing my black North Face jacket and my school backpack if you see me."

"Alright. Just keep walking and I'll come get you. I am fifteen minutes away—I am heading your way right now," I reassure her, asking Mahru to stay on the phone with me so that I can better know where to find her.

Throwing my coffee into the waste bin on the sidewalk I unlock my car before hastily peeling away from the curb to run and pick her up. Driving west a bit further to stay off the main road I take the back way towards the university knowing that it should be quicker. Still trying my best to stay cool even though none of this is going according to plan. Telling myself that I am so fucking stupid for not thinking that this would happen. Unavoidable and merciless this nerve-numbing terror that pulses through me as the hair on the back of my neck stands on end. Telling Mahru over the phone that none of this will even matter anymore as soon as I find her.

"Have you left your parent's house yet?"

"I am walking downstairs with my backpack right now and about to put on my jacket. My keys I am leaving here," she tells herself, setting them on the entry table by the front door. "Just don't rush. I will be fine. I am leaving right now," she informs me, unable to lock the front door with her house keys inside.

"I am now walking outside the gate."

"Okay—just stay on the phone with me."

Keeping Mahru talking I listen carefully, following and filtering her voice up against the incessant tapping from the rain. Still rehashing in my head this fallacious psychological pressure that she is facing at home. Feeling ready to voice this clear violation of her human rights to whatever authority. Weighing all of her legal weaponry from moral distress to conscientious objection. It being tremendously unsettling that anyone should force a girl or a woman to be with any man. Feeling this raging rush to reach her aggravated by the many months of her never feeling safe enough to leave. Ready to pick her up and to take her home with me. Still watching my speed and watching the swelling rain as it is really starting to come down.

Listening to Mahru on the car speaker and asking her if she has gotten far enough away from the house I then surprisingly miss my turn. Unable to turn around I know that I can try again further south as I hear her tell me that the

CHAPTER TWENTY-SEVEN

rain is not that heavy just four miles east. Still trying to hear her speak to me word for word over what sounds like the hum of a jet engine spinning. Verbally mapping my every turn over the phone with her as the rain continues to violently pour.

"Tell me what you are not telling me," Khalil demands, bristling with his displeased eyes dissonant and short-fused. Ianna looks at Khalil already suspecting that she has angered the Rhadamanthus within. But come what may she is still unhesitatingly insistent about making her argument as a mother.

"I just feel like she is pulling away. I just have this strange feeling. I do not know how to explain it. Maybe she is not happy. When we get home just look at her Khalil. Have you ever wondered if what we are doing for Mahru is what is best for her?" Ianna bravely questions at the end, almost disagreeing with her husband who would rather dictate from the invidious vacuity of the diehard orthodoxy. Genuinely in his heart wanting what is best for Mahru. But weighing what will make her happy versus what is best for her Khalil then suddenly feels threatened. First doubting himself and then her husband-to-be. Feeling the pressure of him being second to the sheik at mosque and as a teacher of Islamic studies and again feeling threatened by this very moment and by that which he can offer no alternative. Khalil perhaps afraid of being condemned to a place that is more terrifying than this life. Or perhaps afraid of what everyone else will think.

"I will not have her dishonoring our family—and she will not defy me! She is already becoming too westernized wearing those form-fitting clothes and getting an education that she will do nothing with! Thinking that she can just marry who ever she wants because of those stories about your mother. Already I have seen her on campus not wearing her hijab. I will not have her engaging in sex before marriage and getting raped! She will not betray Islam and our traditions!" Khalil angrily shouts, as the rain begins to come down even harder onto the windshield. Parlously brooding on the assumption that Ianna is not telling him something and thinking about when he gets home if he will have to sternly remind Mahru of her duty and responsibility to Hassan.

Driving and feeling the discomfort surrounding Mahru potentially shaming and dishonoring her family straight away gives rise to more heated debate. Ianna expressing genuine concern as Khalil's rigid face becomes knotted with utter disbelief. Every argument a one-sided attempt leading to an intense and fractious back and forth. Sententiously justifying the amandation of his daughter with his temperament and unleashing a sevidical scathefire. Bolstering his disposition and say-so as if the disagreement itself were some type of betrayal. His harsh orotund verbiage and tongue-lashing building momentum as he hardly notices the car beginning to pick up speed. His incorruptible hostility and war of words creating a verbal onslaught as the rain begins to come down even harder.

"She is your daughter!" Ianna angrily shouts with tears streaming down her face.

"She will serve Allah and fulfill her duty as a mother and a wife! This is what must be done!" Khalil's raging voice rattles the front-seat space. The roaring rain as loud as his shouting and almost as deafening inside of their luxury vehicle.

Heading southeast down Marine Drive the raging rain pounds my car like the hard showering clatter of tiny hailstones. Witnessing a salty ocean rain so powerful and heavy like a tropical rainstorm. Unable to see ten feet in front of me as a dark slate grey sky traps my car under a blinding sea of rain. Temporarily frustrated as I fail to hear Mahru on my phone that is also connected to the Bluetooth speakers. Still watching and listening as the rain pounds my car and with my windshield wipers on full blast.

Barely able to hear my moon over the phone I ask her to hold on a second, struggling to see the road in front of me just before the rain begins to calm. Turning my windshield wipers down a notch the rain then mostly lets up.

Along a mossy wooded backroad I slow down just a little seeing how much water has collected into my lane. Passing the flooded part of the road I then carefully allow my car to pick up speed again. More determined than ever to reach her in this weather that has about stopped where she is just a few miles east.

"I can hear you better now," Mahru expresses through a faint sigh of relief.

"I can hear you now too. The rain was just pounding for a second." I make vivid, the rain just becoming light enough for me to turn my windshield wipers to the lowest setting.

"Are you okay?"

"Yeah," I communicate, still listening as Mahru walks quickly in the rain and telling me that she is now heading down Granville Street.

Suddenly refocusing on a buck that is standing too close to the road and watching it look straight at me it then strangely stops raining altogether. The

CHAPTER TWENTY-SEVEN

spine-chilling impression of knowing something awful without warning engulfs my senses seeing the rain immediately disappear. The strangest silence flashing with my heartbeat like I missed something. In that same second I see the stop sign that is bent far enough to surely skew its post to any intersecting driver. Having the right-of-way through a construction intersection where the containers stacked along the road make me completely miss what is coming. In that same split second a terrifying hair-raising premonition pervades my senses right before slamming into the unexpected flash of a two-ton weight going sixty-five miles an hour.

Whhooomm! Crash!

A sudden impact with a crushing force of pressure causes every cell in my body to clench as a hurling ton of steel and carbon fiber tosses and flips me like a half empty coke can spraying the pavement all over with glass and debris. Tumbling and grinding screeching white lights turn to black with only the deafening sound of a gut-wrenching metal and fiberglass furiously tossing and scraping. My one-and-a-half-ton sedan suddenly flipping so fast with me pushing on the frame of the car. The frightening impact throwing me into a body-piercing stack of steel tie rods. Spinning and clenching inside of a hellish nightmare until everything finally stops. My very last thought being only that I was the sun who kissed the moon.

Feeling like I ran into a wall and not seeing who just hit me I do not realize that I have crashed into her mom and dad on their way home. Both Khalil and Ianna not watching the road while arguing and running a busted stop sign. Blindsided at an empty intersection and never seeing the other headlights shining in the rain. The crash causing Khalil to bang his head several times against the window and the roof of the car before blacking out. Both of them tossing around inside and flipping so many times before landing on a grassy drain on the side of the road.

Hearing the most frightening sounds just before losing her cell connection Mahru stops and suspects that something terrible has happened. There being no place for doubt in her mind that it was a car accident. Scared to death and nearly panicking she immediately turns back to grab her truck keys. Fearing the worst and something terribly dreadful she frantically tries to reach me again as she begins to run back home. Emphatically desperate to find me she expunges all of the excess noise in her head specifically ignoring the toss-up that her parents may return home at any moment.

Running through the front gate and back into the house to grab her keys

Mahru then climbs back into her truck to come and find me. She still shouting for me to pick up the phone each time that she tries to call.

Quickly turning out of the neighborhood she then drives west towards the ocean.

Feeling the light rain finding its way in through the missing windshield Ianna climbs over the center console to check on Khalil who has a severe concussion. Shouting for her husband to please wake up Khalil does not respond. Double-checking his faint pulse she cannot believe what has happened as she keeps crying and repeating herself saying that she is sorry. Desperately crying that she fucked up she again shouts Khalil's name without touching him. Afraid and weeping seeing that he is unconscious she feels with her hand that he is still breathing. Pulling a blanket from the backseat she then covers Khalil to try and keep him warm.

Frazzled but still moving to call for help Ianna sees Khalil's phone on the backseat floorboard before stumbling out of the crashed Range Rover. With a hissing steam rising out from under the hood she staggers out of the passenger side door. Opening the rear door through the broken glass to grab his phone and her coat she then steps away from the trenched car. Desperate to pull her wet feet from the marshy runoff she shouts Khalil's name once more before climbing out of the shallow swale.

Walking out into the road Ianna quickly discovers that no one is around to offer them any help. Seeing my crumpled car across the street she then remembers what she hit. Struggling to dial 911 she then immediately tells the emergency dispatcher that there has been two wrecks before telling them exactly where she is. Being told that dispatch is sending a medical unit her phone battery then dies.

Visibly distressed and trembling seeing her touchscreen turn black Ianna still tells herself that dispatch acknowledged her location.

Sensing some small amount of relief establishing that the emergency medics are on their way Ianna then for several seconds experiences a strange sort of clarity standing beneath the darkest sky. Standing wet in the middle of the road her life and her choices flash before her eyes after unraveling her wet pashmina scarf from her long black hair. With blood smeared across her chin she feels a weight release condemning with regret the paths chosen and the paths dictated. Everything from Mahru not wanting to be married to even asking herself if she is truly happy. Feeling so sorry for having raised the

CHAPTER TWENTY-SEVEN

argument concerning their daughter's happiness. Afraid for both Khalil and Mahru her silent gaze stays fixed in view of a dark murky sky. She standing lost to sea in a spiritual fog that makes everything unclear or perhaps perfectly.

Standing near the middle of the intersection feeling and hearing only the faintest raindrops that same white-tailed buck then walks right in front of Ianna near the edge of the road. Startled for a second by how close he is the buck looks right at her as she stares right back at him. Feeling lost to some beautiful unfamiliar place that does not even feel like home she stands watching the deer as it quietly withdraws into a wild field.

Turning to look over her shoulder only to rediscover her shocking state of disbelief Ianna again feels her heart crawling up into her throat. Still curiously drawn to the tragic scene of my crushed car she quietly steps closer, the tiny speckles of blood on her face almost all washing away with the rain. Afraid that she has killed somebody she then sees my head move as a light condensation blows from her tense exhale. Silently biting back her feeling my discomfort and feeling powerless to do anything her eyes then meet mine as she watches me struggle to stay calm.

Pinned to a tilted front seat with steel rebar jutting out at my abdominal side she then notices my nasty injury peeking over the flung-opened door. Ianna on the spot begins to pray that I will not die and that her husband will wake up as she now thinks to check on him.

Watching her step closer in the rain as I hold my nasty wound she reexamines again the trauma to my large bowel. Terribly horrified she kneels down closer having never seen me before. Beautiful and cold she refocuses her attention on me. Offering her hand to put pressure on my wound I shake my head and with my other hand tell her that I can hold it. Not knowing what to do or even what to say to me her rich Kona-brown eyes still offer me a certain comfort. It being in her heart to convey any last message that I may have before I take in and push out my last breath.

Feeling swallowed by the dark as the rain touches one side of my face I then feel her kind hand reach out to hold mine. Fragmenting inside her heart and consumed by this disturbing sense of grief she then thinks of her daughters who are about my age. Watching her familiar face express sadness I then see in that moment my Mahru. Feeling like I know her and exerting effort to look harder beneath her smudged eyeliner I then see that it is Ianna. Recognizing her face from behind the stadium and having seen her hair down in the pictures that Mahru showed me I then wonder what were the chances of them taking that same backroad.

Watching her tears blend into the rain as she convinces herself that she can never be forgiven I still feel my moon here with me. Wishing to part with one simple message to tell Ianna I am still having trouble shaping my verbal staggering. Bearing this awful sadness that is tearing me up inside I just lie still trying to accept that I may die. Listening to Ianna try to offer me hope that the emergency medics are on their way she then tells me to hang on. Feeling like I am wasting away she sees the uncertainty all over my face as I fight this searing pain in my torso. Too lightheaded to move my mouth I ask myself if all of this secrecy was destined to be drug out into the open. Only never did I foresee us becoming so destructive. Feeling like I am hurting everyone and that just as beauty follows me that so does the same in suffering.

Suddenly as she notices her daughter's ring on my finger Ianna then thinks about Mahru not wearing hers and the story of it being lost. Hearing me call her by name and with there being no mistaking who the ring belongs to she then reaches to gently slip it from my finger. Turning my head to where the rain washes my face Ianna then remembers again my letters to Mahru. She then remembers seeing me standing still in a sea of people watching her daughter. Remembering my golden curls and my face and how beautiful I was. And then remembering me walking away after making eye contact with her at the school soccer game.

Unable to express words in her state of disrepair she realizes who I am and how important that I must be to her daughter who she loves so much. Piecing it all together from that time that she saw me more than five weeks ago she now leans forward as I look at her to tell her something.

"Tell her . . . . that I will always love her," I beg Ianna, silently asking please as I shakily place my bloodied letter from my pocket into her hand.

Realizing that I am the one that her daughter loves her tear-stained face becomes wet again with words that the heart cannot utter. Feeling in her heart the sheer weight of this tragedy she again prays silently. Seeing clearly her entrenched world view by which she has judged others and feeling exhausted she regrets not approaching her daughter and preventing this. Afraid that she cannot save love as she looks passed whether or not that it is appropriate. Watching me as I try and lie still she senses my anger and my feeling afraid in my heart for not getting to her in time. Taking my hand that is closest to her Ianna then slips her mother's ring back onto my blood-soaked finger.

"I will tell her for you," Ianna quickly promises me, her wide eyes tearing

CHAPTER TWENTY-SEVEN

up again as her lips turn sideways with grief.

Not ready to close my eyes I sit focusing on the eeriest silence. Slowing my breathing and unaware of my trembling I then turn to look at Ianna. Afraid that Khalil is hurt pretty bad I then shift to fearing for his daughter who is probably worried wondering where I am right now. Terrified that our love should stay forbidden I feel every muscle in my body clenching. Losing blood as death inches closer to me every moment that I ever spent with her begins to flash in my mind like a moving picture. Flashing moments of us curled up on the sofa and me holding her in my bed. Every blanket pulled from the coffee chest as her fingers keep moving through my hair. Her unmatched beauty bearing no equal feeling her breathing chest moving up and down. Her wet hands touching my closed eyes behind the most powerful force on earth. Feeling her naked body as her delicious scent clings to me. Her kind spirit and her perfect love still dancing with me the way the burning moon dances eternal with the sun.

Feeling Ianna hold my hand I try making an effort to wait before following the pale rabbit over to the other side. Desperate I think to myself that I will surely lose her this time. Watching the rain seem to slow down I fight in my heart not to let her slip away from me again. Biting my teeth my tears and blood gather between my shivering lips. Thinking who better than to kill me with a little bit of dark humor. Seeing it in Ianna's eyes her apology that I verbally am struggling to forgive. Still scratching and clawing in my heart to dig my way out of this fresh grave that calls my name.

Feeling my right hand covered in blood the rain becomes heavier. Keeping my other hand Ianna waits silently unsettled feeling too emotionally frail to walk away just yet. Believing that the act itself would surely lay a curse over her and her family. Witnessing in my eyes a sadness so deeply pitted against my turning stomach. Wanting to check on Khalil she finally gathers that I am clearly not going to make it.

Pulling up to the scene of the wreck in the pouring rain Mahru recognizes her mom kneeling down beside my totaled car. Fearing the worst seeing her parents' Range Rover across the street she quickly runs closer towards her mom who is helping me to apply pressure.

Slowing her step so as not to see who is inside Mahru prays that the car is not mine. Approaching her mom as sirens sound in the distance Ianna prepares to hold Mahru back who seems to be teetering on becoming emotionally unpredictable. Filled with the heaviest most unspeakable fear she recognizes me unresponsive and pinned by the steel reinforcement bars shooting out away from the crunched passenger seat. Assessing the vinaceous color spreading and absorbing into my thick sweater her entire world becomes shattered by a debilitating dread.

"Ana asfe. I am so sorry babe. Samihini," Ianna begs Mahru.

"Lucius!" Mahru screams over her despairing mother.

Recognizing her voice I turn my head just enough to make out her brown chestnut eyes watering beside those wet rivulose curls. Doubting her actual presence I then catch her frantic screams mixing in with the sirens. Hearing her distressing cry sobbing my name I fight to wait before closing my eyes. Terrified that my name may never again escape her perfect lips. Afraid for her that an even greater wall will become built up around her heart. Imagining my letters to her all thrown away for fear of them being too painful to remember. And even more afraid that her capacity to love will be put out like a fire that can never again feel as beautiful.

Holding my ailing heart in my hands the fear that I have of losing her again is killing me. Touching her soft fingertips to mine Ianna holds Mahru to the ground. Making every effort to see those eyes I feel my breaking heart torn from my flesh as I scramble to emerge unbroken. This love of ours incapable of being washed away in the rain as black birds give my moon room to grieve.

"Lucius!" her harrowing scream lets out as she again shrieks my name. Unable to keep holding pressure to my wound my hand slips still feeling the pressure being held in place.

Hearing Mahru screaming I lie wishing that I could comfort her. Past being nauseous my entire body feels like a cloud being slowly pulled apart into the air. Gravitating towards sleep I again am truly sorry that it is now my turn to break her heart. Torn between the material and ethereal my heart bleeds being unable to utter any comforting words. Still hearing her screams killing me or making me fight I know not which. Feeling the lion inside of me fighting to the death to stay alive as my soul peers into the underworld. Feeling trapped beneath the ice and enduring the most unbearable pain as I begin to slip away from my moon.

Emotionally flooded with heartache an eery silence then gathers me in its dark hands and shuts my eyes. Feeling my tears falling from the sky I am left only with her screams and an aching sadness that crawls underneath my skin. Into the soft powdery light there is no soothing utterance to persuade my forgiving this end or beginning that is mine. My dying heart like the wild poppy

CHAPTER TWENTY-SEVEN

in the chill of night that has become bent and huddled. My untimely death being no kind feat that is pleasant or even welcoming.

Feeling my Mahru holding dear to her heart this dangerous love I become aware that I am beginning to disappear. Gently slipping away in front of the scattered red and white lights of the surrounding emergency vehicles I fight to no avail like sinking to some aphotic depth and with no breath to swim. Under the shadow of the arching elm where sandhill cranes trail the muddy waters along the shoal an above blur wraps me and covers me in the pouring rain as I feel my love torn beneath the dark cloud.

"Please—don't leave me!" I then hear her scream one last time. Hearing her grating lament drawing breath from her heartbreaking demand I struggle to remain present as she again shrieks a terrifying cry. With her mom still holding on to her Mahru falls to despair beside my shattered car. Traveling the alone path I grasp both the highest of heavens and the chthonic world of the dead as I dance away from the light and into the dark. The last sound nudging my ears beneath the dull blue clouds I hear only her fading cry echoing my name. The moving water carrying my blood to the sea as I breathe my soul to the wind.

"Lucius," the moon whispers to the sun. Feeling her hand in mine I open my eyes.

Made in the USA
Middletown, DE
31 August 2023